!Click Song

BY JOHN A. WILLIAMS

!Click Song

The Junior Bachelor Society

Mothersill and the Foxes

Captain Blackman

Flashbacks

The King God Didn't Save

The Most Native of Sons

Sons of Darkness, Sons of Light

The Man Who Cried I Am

This Is My Country Too

Sissie

Africa, Her History Lands and People

Night Song

The Angry Ones / One for New York

!CLICK SONG

JOHN A. WILLIAMS

HOUGHTON MIFFLIN COMPANY   BOSTON
1982

Copyright © 1982 by John A. Williams

All rights reserved. No part of this work may be reproduced
or transmitted in any form or by any means, electronic or
mechanical, including photocopying and recording, or by
any information storage or retrieval system, except as
may be expressly permitted by the 1976 Copyright Act or
in writing from the publisher. Requests for permission
should be addressed in writing to Houghton Mifflin Company,
2 Park Street, Boston, Massachusetts 02108.

Library of Congress Cataloging in Publication Data

Williams, John Alfred, date
   !Click song.

   I. Title.
PS3573.I4495C5   813'.54   81-13166
ISBN 0-395-31841-6   AACR2

Printed in the United States of America

V 10 9 8 7 6 5 4 3 2 1

My thanks to the National Endowment for the Arts for its 1977 Grant.

To Lori
and to Adam,
to Dennis and Millicent and to Margo Carolyn,
to Gregory and Lucia and to John Gregory

These clicks . . . are amongst the oldest sounds in language . . .

— Gerald Massey
A Book of the Beginnings, Vol. II

In my native village . . . there is a song we always sing . . . it's called The Click Song by the English because they cannot say !CLICK !CLOCK !CWLUNG

— Miriam Makeba

THE CUSP

Yat, yat yot.

Her words were pinched through a throat decomposing to fat, cooled by sips from a spritzer.

She's nervous, I think. Why?

Mafia East Side restaurant, stiff white tablecloths, waiters like black cats touched with white prowling the aisles with ash trays, wine, hot plates, menus, food, glancing at us.

Is that nigger doing it to Ms. Gullian? Just who is that nigger?

Yot, yot, yat, continues Maureen Gullian. She is my editor. We are lunching to discuss my novel *Unmarked Graves,* the fifth her company is to publish.

She is still talking, rapidly and nervously, but her words are like a Mexican bark painting, filled with colors and foliage too casual not to be ordered; words like the soundless sounds of birds in those paintings, whose heads are tilted upward in song or perhaps warning, for those paintings contain in meshing colors the hard horrors of the soul.

Yat, yot, yat.

All I can say, my stomach dropping, is No! I didn't hear!

Yes! This morning!

Up! The glasses and plates shake, tilt, fall over. The brightly colored nymphs who adorn the walls seem to lose their shyness; they stare at me. Real heads swing around. The soldiers in their penguin suits freeze warily, look to Ms. Gullian for a sign. Ms. Gullian — strange — looks relieved as I walk quickly past the soldiers. What am I doing? This is like rushing out of myself. I am out in the sun under which I once loved to walk, along Fifth Avenue, light in the head and heavy in the joint from drinking martinis.

My haste (perhaps it is the napkin that has fallen and tugs at my ankles) sends signals before me. People are staring. What kind of expression is on my face to make them look at me so? Am I a perpetrator of a crime, a murder, a mugging, a bombing here in midtown? Their eyes seem to ask *Why is that nigger walking so fast?*

I do not really know. I beat the traffic sprawled in the roadway like a hacked-up serpent. But it has noise, rumbles, bawls, sweat, pants; it has the soul of incipient rust and knows it.

I lurch under the canopy into two doormen dressed in blue. The building is the Triomphe. It was where Sandra Queensbury lived until she died five years ago, she of the quick hands and quicker tongue; she of the old days, the dispenser of secrets and ugly little wisdoms.

The doormen converge on me.

Who do you wish to see?

Cummings. Paul Cummings. Kaminsky. His wife, I mean. She's here?

Cummings. No Kaminsky. He's — well. His wife is up there. Your name?

One in strategic retreat, backing to the callbox. The other stands his guard, legs spread, hoping I will not razor-shorten him by eight inches.

Once again? Your name?

Cato Caldwell Douglass. It means nothing to them. He calls it up empty of its rhythms. He is surprised at the response. The blocker slides aside, murmuring, First elevator on your right, twelfth floor.

Up the wood-paneled, brass-trimmed lift and out along the carpets, which are the color of day-old blood. The bell. The door opens. We stare. It's been a long time. She has that delightful, secretly wicked look middle-aged New York women possess.

Cate, Cate, oh, Cate.

Embraces, kisses.

I didn't think you'd —

We go in and sit down. The sun is bright upon the white walls.

Kids okay? We never even saw the kids.

She nods.

Why?

4

She shrugs. Allis okay?

Yes. Can I call her? Allis is home today finishing up a proposal for work.

She points toward where the phone must be. I walk through the rooms. He had reverted to the old Paul between relationships, the Paul of goose-neck lamps bent down over typewriters.

Allis is shocked. Oh, she says. Oh dear. Oh, honey.

Be home soon. Wait. Betsy.

She has come up behind me and takes the phone. A helluva time to say hello — again — Allis.

They talk. Betsy's voice is soft. I stroll through the rooms and ask again, Why?

"Hell, I'd never do that," Paul said.

It was one of those afternoons in the classroom. Professor Bark had seemed troubled and sad. "It's something to think about. You're writers or would-be writers. Consider then: your first work. It's a big novel. Techni-cally it's advanced. It becomes a tremendous literary *and* financial success. Metro-Goldwyn-Mayer wants to buy the book for a *lot* of money. Would you then commit suicide like Ross Lockridge?"

He was pacing quickly and lightly, whirling himself about and pacing again. None of us, I was sure, saw the shadows; all would be smooth. Bark stopped in front of me and looked at me. He appeared to be surprised to see me in his class. *What is that nigger doing here?*

"Read *Raintree County* and think about what happened to the author. Think about yourselves. Imagine — success!"

Over beer Paul said, "There must have been something wrong with Lockridge, don't you think?"

"Like what?"

"How the hell do I know? But Christ. To do what he did when he did it. Hemingway would never do a thing like that. Hell, *I'd* never do a thing like that."

Betsy is off the phone, picking her way back through the apartment she once lived in with Paul. I remember when they moved there.

Was he sick, cancer or something?

Her look for a moment is bleaker than it should be. Don't know. Maybe we shouldn't have left him.

What the hell, I say.

5

Her eyes, dark gray, widen. I must say I'm a little surprised to see you here, though.

I turn. I don't know why, either, I say. But I think we were real friends for a very long time. Maybe, in spite of everything, I'm the only one he had.

She sighs. Yes, that's true. He thought of you a lot and often wanted to close the gap, but something always stopped him. Well, it was between you and him.

What?

Everything.

Naw. I just knew him a long time and he didn't always love me for my luck, and I can't say that I loved him for his because it wasn't that and he knew it and knew I knew it too.

That upset him.

It should have.

"Say, what made you send your poems to WCW and not to someone like Langston Hughes?" The smile / sneer.

We sit in silence, Betsy and I, remembering different things.

I say, You don't have to worry about money or anything.

No. He was making lots.

I thought he was.

She frowns. You know I couldn't do it, and I couldn't let him do that with the kids. You understand.

No. I don't understand at all. After not seeing him or you for years, he called two days ago. I was in Denver doing a reading. Allis told him how pleased she was to hear from him. He said he'd call back, but we looked him up —

Unlisted, Betsy says —

— I got back yesterday, lunched with my editor, or started to, today, just now. She told me. So, Betsy, I don't know anything.

He became very Orthodox. Wanted us to convert.

Maybe just a reaction.

Overreaction.

When he stopped being a WASP, I say, he became a good writer, and wrote out of his own skin.

A couple of times, she says without looking at me.

6

He was sure you'd convert, I say.

I never told him I would.

I think, He was so sure that she would . . .

We're silent until she says, You want anything, a book, a pen?

No, there's nothing, Betsy.

Please look around. You ever thought of suicide?

Sure. You?

Before the kids. Before Paul, sometimes.

Why?

It seemed too much to bear, is about the only way I can put it.

But you didn't.

Read Hamlet's soliloquy too often. Made sense. Why didn't you?

They don't approve of suicide over there. I smile at the look she gives me. She follows me through the apartment. I got things to do, Betsy. And I don't want to make it easy for the opposition.

Stopping, I say, I don't think there's anything I want, Betsy.

He'd want you to have something of his.

Thirty years of knowing ain't bad.

I guess not. I keep forgetting that it was so long. Will you come to the service tomorrow?

Yes, we'll come. Where?

Gutterman's, Sixty-sixth and Broadway. Nine-thirty. His father'll do the service.

The good Rabbi Kaminsky.

Yes.

You never met him?

No.

I say to the walls, the discarded corduroy pants and Brooks Brothers shirts, to the rows of mangled McCreedy & Schreiber desert boots, the shelves of books, his all in a row, mine all in a row, the photos of Betsy and the kids, the framed citations, including the National Book Award, the stained coffee mugs, and say to his ex-wife: We were exactly the same age.

She nods, says nothing.

There is no paper in his typewriter. I say, Maybe he shouldn't have loved Hemingway so much, the Compleat American Thing so much.

Well, she says, one wants to belong, if one can. Ironic. Hemingway didn't seem to like Jews.

No. Well, I've got to go, Betsy. You're okay?

I'm all right. See you tomorrow. Love to Allis, Glenn and Mack.

7

Glenn's traveling, I say. We're at the door.

You must be very flattered to have a son who's also a writer.

Yeah. See you, then.

G'bye, Cate. Thanks.

I am walking or at least moving toward home. It's not Paul's death that steers me along this dogshit-covered trail through the Park. I just wish to be alone to think of this business of dying, of being here one moment and gone the next, like swirls of mist, almost as nothing but a passing dampness dried by a flash of sunlight. Nothing more. Nothing else, really. Things live and things die every minute and who knows of them? But I knew Paul; I thought I knew him very well.

Tonight's television news, obits in the morning papers, the lingering reminiscences in the monthly publications, black-boxed in the *Authors Guild Bulletin,* noted in the *PEN Newsletter,* and it would be over, except for his books and what he said in them, the accumulation of his fifty-five years. And there would be those theses turned into biographies, perhaps after a decent interval, of which there were in publishing, these days, fewer and fewer.

Shalom, friend; *ẹkurole,* Paul, son, father, brother; *ẹkurole* and *shalom,* bigot, liberal, hero, coward. Writer. Liar.

BEGINNINGS

1

HIS BLUE EYES twinkled slightly, and he extended his hand. "Paul Cummings."

"Cato Douglass." (Cato *Caldwell* Douglass. At home and in the marines they called me C.C.)

He was tall, tending toward gaunt, in his rumpled Eisenhower jacket, and his face was sharp with angles. He studied me; for a fraction of a second he seemed anxious and the next vaguely arrogant. I had met people like him before, the other, white marines, who chatted with you (seemingly secure in the knowledge that, even though you were a marine too, you were not *quite* like them) when their northbound ships stopped at our atoll, and then went away, leaving us to man our antiaircraft guns against Zeros that no longer came that far south. We had had our combat and had been written up in the magazines back home; we'd disgrace no one.

He rocked slightly and ran his hand through light brown hair that was longer than most men were wearing it.

He did not remember me, but I'd seen him in my Survey of Western Literature class. The hall teemed with people. Students answered the roll for friends who were cutting, and the instructor peering out over the mob, composed mainly of veterans, accepted any voice as proof of presence. I couldn't cut; I was the only black person in the class.

We talked of the branches we'd served in, our wives, the university —
tentative touchings to see which kind of a relationship, if any, would
work.

"This Professor Bark's supposed to be a pretty good writer."

"Oh, yeah?" I said. "Poetry?"

"Short stories. Mostly for *A.M.*"

"Ummm," I said. I didn't know what *A.M.* was.

He sensed that and said, *"Atlantic Monthly,"* without making me feel
like a fool. "Are you a poet?"

"I write some but —"

"I do a lot of it myself," he said, treading confidently over my words.
"But I think I'm ready for fiction."

A coed with honey-colored hair, and skin the complexion of unfrothed
cream, walked briskly by, her buns rolling and swelling in fetching movements.

Paul's eyes followed her with a nonchalant lust. "We dreamed of women
like that, right? I never saw anything like that in two years in Europe."

I wondered what his wife looked like and I wondered about him. I'd
never known a white man who even implicitly was willing to share with
a black man both women and career.

After that first class — in which Bark spattered the awkward silence
with the question "Why do you want to be writers?" an asking that made
us turn to the windows and look past each other until he, eyes filmed
over with amusement, his tone barely hopeful, then asked, "Would Some
One Care To Read?" while Paul, to my surprise, looked straight past
him in those large, almost unbearable silences, and then, as if pushing
upward against wet snow (pushing, I now know, against the historicity
of the situation), I raised my hand and read — Paul and I began our
afterclass beer routine.

I read the long poem about Gittens of our regiment, who, under those
lean, breeze-blown palm trees and glaring white sand beaches lapped by
blue-green tongues of the sea, went madder in that incongruous paradise,
under which three thousand Japanese bodies were buried, earlier and more
quietly than the rest of us. Not wanting him to be sectioned-eight in a
fleet hospital back on Guadalcanal, we did not turn him in. He was not
violent. About once a week he said plaintively, "I'm going home," and
loped to the beach and dove into the sea to begin his ten-thousand-mile
swim to Philadelphia. We would coax him out. Once he did not say anything, so we did not see him go, and never saw him again.

"Good story in that poem," Paul said. A sneer, I thought, lurked on
the edges of his smile. "Probably a better story than a poem."

But I was still bathed by Bark's glance (Heyyyy, who's this nigger?) and nod, still elated that after I'd read, broken the ice, the class had come clamoring after, hands raised like the spears of a medieval mob.

Paul did not volunteer to read, though he had material.

My wife, Catherine, did not really share my elation. Her smiles were filled with pride, and she embraced me as if performing a ritual. Great, I thought. Paul's jealous and Cat yet doesn't know what it's all about.

When she met Paul and Janice (who looked like the coed who had passed us in the hall the day of Bark's first class) she expressed reservations about them. And that is what she called them, Them, or Those People. She seemed to think that they were leading me somewhere or interfering with our life.

It was very late in the semester when Paul read, and I was impressed by his vocabulary and by the very force so filled with assurance with which he read. He had talked a lot about this story. But I was made uncomfortable by it. It was a tale of a tough soldier and a tender whore. Hemingway lurked behind every adjectiveless sentence. I winced when the class, one by one, implacable as a giant amoeba, began to devour him whole. Paul had held forth throughout the semester, offering extensive and exuberant criticism of everyone's work (some of it quite good), buttressed by the statements or works of a multitude of writers whose names hovered always at the ready on his lips. Now he was forced to defend every image, metaphor, period and comma — even concept — like a trapped dog. When the class was at last finished with him, and Paul, slumped low in his chair, rapping his teeth with a pencil, his ears a bright red, gave a loud sigh, Bark offered his comments, sewed Paul back up and wiped away the blood.

I had been promised by Paul's attitude that he was always, at all times, producing nothing short of literary dynamite. It had been, in fact, a small, damp firecracker. Over our beer several times I caught his eye just as it had finished some secret peremptory glance at me. What had I perceived about him, his work, was what the glance asked.

I *had* discovered something; *re*discovered something; and as we sat there, he rather subdued and I patient and, yes, patronizing, I thought back to my boyhood in my home town, specifically of *mornings, springing from Tim Hannon's milk wagon into the daybreaking cool, a metal six-bottle carrier gripped in my hand, the smell of fresh milk, Tim's fat-man sweat and warming horseflesh in my nostrils, when I entered buildings with contempt that once I had held in awe because of their sturdy brick façades and cream-colored trim; they were in the white section of town. For years passing them along a proscribed trail I had a souring resentment* *of the residents. That had passed when I first went inside. The carpets were dirty and spotted and they stank; the walls needed plastering where they were not already stained beyond repainting back to a respectable color, and there was always a strangely lackluster commingling of cooking smells and the odors of fat old dogs and cats. Invariably I set the bottles upon swollen roaches and beads of ratshit, holding my breath until I got back outside, where, at least, the buildings* looked *good.*

Even so, the year I met Paul the world cracked open for me, revealing endless possibilities to be achieved with words. Something began to click within me. I could write! I choked on words, drowned in them, constructed them into ideas; I wallowed in their shapes and sounds, their power to stroke or stun, sing or sorrow, accuse or acclaim. Living meant suddenly more than having a college education and being a husband and father. My life, then close to mounting twenty-two years, seemed presented to me once again. I exulted in the gift in quiet ways that I hoped would attract no one's attention.

I had not had much of a life until the war, to which I'd fled with dreams of screaming down on the dirty Japs or dirty Huns in my silver, bullet-spewing fighter plane, or leading a charge against them on the ground, knee-deep in their bodies. Fled from rat's-ass-end jobs that generations of my family, bitter resignation etched upon their faces, had settled in. The war got me away. It whetted my appetites; its horrors expanded my mind; and what men did to other men in it, underlining the whimsy of the species, brought me at last before Words as the keys to understanding.

We, Paul and I, shared a love of words and writing, and we understood, in that way people often have with each other, that he was the tutor and I the pupil. It was a role he enjoyed; he found it natural. We moved that year and the next, as seniors, from poetry to fiction and back to poetry, the Queen, once more, meeting her demands of precision and grace with the energy of the young, if not the skill of masters-to-be. We spent hours over beer gone stale talking of writing; missed dinners or were late for work talking of writing and writers; shouted writing above the din of small-time bop-playing student bands. But Paul hated bop anyway.

He preferred Dixieland and folk songs and the ballads that came out of the Spanish Civil War, and there were times when I visited Janice and Paul in New York and went to the Stuyvesant Casino to listen to Dixieland over pitchers of beer, and to be near the writers talking of J. D. Salinger and e. e. cummings. And how many nights back on campus did we end the evening with great, mournful choruses of *Irene Good Night?*

A hundred, a thousand, and Catherine liked not one of them. She looked at those times the way a smooth, brown doe would look if does could show anger or disgust.

Looking at her then I would think, It's going.

And I would be afraid.

We had had a thing of long standing, through the gray last days of the Depression, through mutual embarrassments endured in homes where the lights had been turned off because our parents hadn't been able to pay the bill; we shared the youthful shame of being seen in clothes worn too often to school and to parties, of lunch periods in high school during which we ate no lunches because we didn't have them — while we pretended that we simply weren't hungry. After I fled to the marines when they finally allowed us in, she was my girl back home, her letters, tenderly scented, recalling spring proms, following me across the Pacific. She was waiting when I returned. We married and I took her away to school with me.

Won't you come along with me . . .

Catherine was not enrolled. We had not the money for her to do so, even part time. But we had planned, yes, planned. We would do my assignments together; she would use my textbooks. What I learned, she would learn. She, too, would be studying Bacon and Johnson and Burton and Brown and Herrick, Cleveland, Lovelace, Marvell, Donne, Suckling and Crashaw; she would come to read Anglo-Saxon. Catherine would know an incline from a syncline, a fold, a fault, geological time from pre-Cambrian to Neolithic, the shapes of oceans millions of years ago. She would study the palatals, sibilants and glottals; she would get to know it all. She wouldn't have the diploma, but that was all bullshit anyway.

We went on one or two field trips and hoarded our money to see road company productions of Broadway hits, often with Paul and Janice. The months passed. I would return from my copyman job in an advertising agency (sometimes, for small things, they let me write copy) to find the books untouched, the assignments undone, and when. I started to talk about the lessons, a look of fright raced across her face, to be replaced by a grin, a grin with curling bottom lip. "Honey, I don't want to be bothered with that stuff."

To not want to know. There was, of course, nothing special about wanting to know *that* stuff, but all knowing is like climbing steps: one bit of knowledge lifts you to the next step, or should.

So I would look at Catherine and think, *It's going.*

She talked of the days when, finished with school, we would find ourselves respected citizens of a community where I taught literature. Teaching she understood. The writing was frightening her. First, she told me I was working too hard, staying up half the night writing those poems and stories which were, she said when she glanced at them too quickly to have read them, "nice." Then she called me crazy, after which, months later, she tangled the ribbon of the typewriter, that tough little L. C. Smith-Corona portable, so much that it took me a day and a half to straighten it. She stopped giving it up; I had to take it; and after a while I stopped taking it.

We lay in bed listening to each other's breathing, I waiting for her touch, she waiting for mine. Too much drinking at parties gave us our release; the mornings found us distant but polite as ever. It was still going. I didn't want it to go. I felt I owed it more than I'd given it, our marriage, and what of the kids we'd wanted to have? Who else did I know well enough, had known long enough, to want to have kids with?

On one of those nights when we lay in bed I said, "Catherine, I know it's not going okay with us. I don't really know why. I want it to be okay."

I felt her turning toward me. She sighed. "I guess it isn't going so hot."

"Then let's have a baby," I said. "We'll be able to manage through graduate school."

"Cate, do you *really* want to? Really?"

I thought I would hesitate, but I didn't. I said, "Yes, yes, I want to."

We giggled and embraced and fondled each other until I whispered, "We might as well begin right now."

She kissed me and got up and went to the bathroom. She slid back into the bed, murmuring, "All clear."

Paul and I finished college high as soldiers made ready for combat. We did not attend our graduation, and in the quiet summer hiatus, when Catherine went home to visit her father with the news that she was pregnant, I labored in the agency full time or worked at home, taking only a couple of weekends to visit Paul and Janice and to make the pilgrimage to Birdland.

In the fall, Catherine's belly swelling, I joined Paul in Bark's advanced writing course. Last year his look had been like a sad, slow sigh: *Quo vadis, Africanus?* The nigger in his look was gone. It would take me a long time to understand his new one.

Paul and I regularly submitted our work, mostly poems, to the "little" magazines. Once, to what I suspect was Paul's chagrin, Karl Shapiro of

Poetry returned a poem with a note penciled in about the lines he liked.

Recklessly confident, I took to sending my poems to Elder Poets for their comments. William Carlos Williams had sent them back with an angry note — didn't I know that when I wrote to Elder Poets I should enclose a stamped, self-addressed envelope? He did not say marvelous things about my poems. I told Paul.

"Say," he said, "what made you send your poems to WCW and not to someone like Langston Hughes?"

I said, "I went to see Hughes the last time I was in New York."

He sat upright in the booth where we were drinking beer. A distance seemed to grow in his eyes. "What'd he say?"

I told him what Mr. Hughes had told me about my work — exaggerating ever so slightly. (I didn't tell him what else Mr. Hughes said because I didn't want to believe it and I wouldn't forget it either: I would have to be ten times the writer a white man was and then it would be hell, which was not exactly an unusual experience. Agents would return manuscripts with rust marks from paper clips because they hadn't bothered to read the material. Agents and editors would tell you to forget race — but they rarely published anything by a Negro that wasn't about race. Still, they didn't want you to be too serious about anything, even if you were able. But if I just *had* to be a writer, all this and more wouldn't stop me, and that was good. And I certainly had to read Llewellyn Dodge Johnson's works if I hadn't already.)

Paul leaned back in a posture of muted arrogance, his eyes sparkling with a paternal kindness served up with a smile. "Hughes is good for what he does," he said. "I never liked his collection *Fine Clothes to the Jew.*"

I didn't know it. I said, "What do you mean he's good for what he does?" I was rising to Hughes's defense.

"Well! He's not a William Carlos Williams, is he now?"

WCW was assigned; Hughes was not. And Mr. Hughes was not one of those writers who came every Thursday afternoon to read or to regale us with tales of writers and writing — Edel, Bowen, Auden, Ciardi.

And Paul's credentials got in my way. That liberal background in a liberal New York City neighborhood. That union father who fought through the labor wars and was now with Harry Bridges on the Coast. Paul's position in the Students for Democratic Action, which paralleled mine as president of the university chapter of the NAACP. But even with these things between me and my reality, I was beginning to sense machinations, like tiptoeing actors moving behind a set. I suppose that was why, in spite of our drinking days and nights, I had withheld confidences he on the other hand shared with me, perhaps, I sometimes thought, too openly, too eagerly. (I do not know why so many white men seem to do that, as if too heavily burdened.)

However, like entering boot camp or even changing schools, this writing, and its attendant fevers, was new to me and I must have carried my naïveté like a badge. That I had killed three men for sure (I think of them), and perhaps another two, during the war was not preparation for this or what lay ahead. Like most combat veterans, I felt that nothing in civilian life could ever match those encounters with that kind of death.

I did not know that there was another, more cancerous and far less glorious dying; it attacked in tandem, head and soul.

Six months into her pregnancy Catherine accused me of not trying to save the marriage. I was doing the same old things, spending most of my spare time writing or talking with Paul about writing. I laughed and tried to comfort her. If I was spending too much time writing, it was because I was trying to build a future for us; if I spent too much time talking with Paul, it was only so that I could learn from him. The rest of the time, I reminded her, I had to work at the agency to help stretch out the GI Bill and, naturally, I had to go to my classes.

The explanations did no good. She turned inward, and when the baby was born on a bitter March day, the old sense of impending loss and fear assailed me once again. I felt it twice over now.

At the end of the first year Cat and Glenn — for so we named him — went home to visit her father. I think she enjoyed being away from me. I had suggested that we all go, but she insisted that all of us couldn't afford the trip. She was right; there would have been sacrificing later, which I was willing to do. That summer, however, I didn't visit Paul and Janice. I worked and painted the house and thought from time to time of the war in Korea. I was glad I had dependents and relieved that Glenn was a baby. No more war for us, I thought.

Catherine's return did not give our marriage the boost that it needed. Instead, as the year progressed, she and I became one of those habits, limping along, our lives leaking apart. When I was alone with Glenn, I would talk to him. He took his pacifier from his drooling mouth as if trying to respond. He made this sound: !Click !Click, and then, surprised, he would begin to cry until I went !Click !Click. Then he smiled, as if understanding.

At the same time, a certain wan quality came upon Paul, and, strangely, a sheen of gaiety to Janice. Winter came, blustering down from the Laurentians, piling foot upon foot of snow upon the campus. Milk froze. Icicles formed. Cold seemed to have penetrated not only the world but souls as well.

On such a morning, leaving for a class in Anglo-Saxon, I stuck my hand in the mailbox and came up with a letter of acceptance of a story by *Neurotica*. I reopened the door and told Catherine. "Is that good?" she said. I closed the door and hiked down to the bus stop, itching to tell Paul. I felt sharply triumphant when I told him that afternoon over beer. I had read the letter 151 times, knew it by heart. It was my first acceptance.

Shock burst in his eyes like puffs of ack-ack. He tried to smile, then laugh. He hadn't sold anything, and there was again distance in his eyes. Finally, he laughed. "*Neurotica?* What's that, a disease?"

"It's published in New Orleans. Editor's G. Legman."

"A Jew," he said, curling his bottom lip.

Sometimes Paul puzzled me: Was he for or against Jews? There was much news about the death camps in Europe.

"Does it make a difference, and anyway, how do you know?"

"The name."

"C'mon," I said. I was remembering something Richard Wright said: something like a Jew-hater being but three letters removed from being a Negro-hater. And that was something else about white men: they tended to think that they could share the garbage of their psyches with black people, who would lap it up and rise on tiptoes, singing brotherhood. "I don't give a fuck what he is, man," I said. "He's got good taste, better than yours. You didn't like the story — "

"Which one was it?"

" 'The Age of Bop.' I read it last year. Did some more work on it."

"Bach?"

"Bop, man, bop. B-O-P. Bird. Monk. Diz. Max. Fats. Miles — "

"Oh! *Be*-bop!"

"Yeah," I said. "Some Jewish guys play it, too."

He ignored that. He wanted to talk about the story.

"I'd like to look at it," he said.

"Why? It's being published. I don't need any criticism — "

"No, no — "

I lied. "I don't have a copy." I was learning. Paul never passed his work around, but freely criticized whatever work of others that came into his hand. "You wouldn't be jealous?"

His smile was genuine, disarming. "No. I mean, who ever heard of *Neurotica?*"

"You're holding out for *A.M.* or *Harper's* or *Esquire,* right?"

Still smiling, in a parody of the filmic tough guy, he turned up a corner of his mouth. At that moment he reminded me of a marine hero who, after Guadalcanàl and Henderson Field, was sent back home to go on tour. His second hitch took him to Iwo. At home he must have begun to believe the stories of his invincibility; through the corps, island to island, the story went that he leaped atop a rock on Iwo, shouting that the Japs couldn't kill him, he was Johnny Barone. The Japanese did not understand English; they buried Barone on Iwo.

But *I* understood English, or was beginning to. Nevertheless, it was later that I would come to understand. Paul had been so sure of himself, of what he *was* because it had been there all the time, under a veneer of acceptable, right things; there all the time the way it must have been for boxers before Jack Johnson and baseball players before Jackie Robinson.

Sitting there, both of us raking feelings we'd not dared to touch before, I thought of the past summer and my visit to the city while Catherine and Glenn were away again. Paul and Janice loved Leadbelly and Blind Willie Lemon and Pops Foster. I could say that they patronized their pained music. They were warm to the old, black, white-haired fugitives from the Deep South. Yet when I managed to get them to the Royal Roost or Birdland, Paul and Janice were stiff and strange, even antagonistic, toward the music of Fats Navarro and Bird. They didn't understand it.

Paul ordered another round, lit a cigarette and said, "Yeah, I guess I am jealous, and yeah, I suppose I still have some of the white chauvinist in me." (That term was big on campus. The lefty students were all using it, and it crept into general usage. White chauvinist.)

I said, "Yeah."

Our studies eased to their appointed ends, both of us publishing a lot of poetry in third- or fourth-rank publications.

In the spring, walking slowly back home through the panty-raids and clots of weary athletes trudging to their dorms after hours of practice, Catherine said, "When we go home this summer, we're not coming back." She didn't stop, didn't break stride. Neither did I. But I summoned words to give me time to think: "What do you mean?"

"You know what I mean, Cato."

I sighed. We kept moving, our feet making soft sounds in the roadway. "Leave Glenn," I said.

She turned to me, still not breaking stride, and arched her brows. Women do not think men capable of caring for children; neither do the courts. I thought I could. I also knew that Catherine would refuse, because Glenn was the trophy of our marriage. He made her a woman, a wife and a mother, titles the Western woman and perhaps even the world woman cherish.

Catherine said, "Shit," and kept on walking.

"What happened to it?" I asked.

She kept walking and shrugged her shoulders.

"Was it all me?"

"I want to say yes, but it wasn't all you, Cato."

"Look, we can — "

Laughter echoed down the block from a fraternity party. I wondered if she felt as much an alien in that place at that moment as I did.

Her hand, long and slim, fell gently upon my wrist. "Let's let it go," she said almost pleadingly. I could not meet her gaze. I saw, I thought, an endless string of commitments broken, underlining my life. She read me.

"Don't feel guilty, Cato. It's just something we were never trained up to handle."

"*What* something?"

"What you want to be and do."

We walked through a stretch of gravel.

"But Glenn — " I finally said.

"You can see him any time you want to, and of course one day he'll be big enough to travel by himself."

We were back on pavement now. "Why are we so much nicer now?"

She smiled in the dusk. "Because it's over, and we're both relieved. Never thought it would be this easy, did you?"

"I didn't want it."

"I think you did."

I wondered what my father would have said. He had stumbled through his time, filled, I felt, with remorse for having deserted us. Once while on leave from Camp Lejeune I met him in Washington between his convoys in the merchant marine. The last one had seen half the convoy destroyed by German submarines. He did not look too well — nervous, more gray than black of skin. He was doing it, he said, to make some money so I could get a start after the war; he'd never done anything for me before.

"When you get married, son, make it work. It's a lot of trouble, but it ain't no good the other way." We had a couple of drinks and he took me to meet his woman. I returned to camp and he returned to the convoys.

My mother died while I was overseas and they wouldn't let me go home. My father's ship was torpedoed and he froze to death six hundred miles from Murmansk and sank in the Barents Sea. I was not surprised to find that he had left nothing for me after all. But now I wondered if he had felt, when he went away, the same low-moaning emptiness I was already beginning to feel.

As soon as the baby sitter left, we undressed slowly, got into bed and made love half the night.

And when summer came, they went. It hurt.

Paul and Janice returned to New York, where he thought he might take some more writing courses. I worked at the agency and at home. I learned during that time that loners are people to be feared. They make good commandos and shit like that; also good wide receivers. They are small, often warped planets around whom the universe revolves. We admire them, but secretly we fear them. In a scheme where things are paired, night and day, man and woman, boy and girl, the two sides of the DNA ladder, where Yin and Yang and the double placing of the acupuncturist's needles exist, who wants to be a loner? Until God made Eve, Adam in his incredible loneliness must have fornicated with anything and everything he could get a grip on, creating for later generations the heritage of bestiality.

August was my deadline. To get out. To move to New York. To carry my recommendations, crisply enveloped, to the job markets of the Big Apple. Paul and Janice said nothing about the end of my marriage, but then we were the new breed; we did not waste words over such happenings. I had told them before they returned to New York.

Two weeks before I was to leave, a note from Paul informed me that they were looking forward to my staying with them, even though things were a little rocky. My presence might help. I wondered what was going on.

2

I WAS STRUGGLING up the stairs of the brownstone to their flat on the top floor, more out of breath with the excitement of being finally and for good in New York than with the climb, when I heard quick, heavy and, I sensed, angry footsteps sounding above me. I looked up and moved aside just in time to avoid being body-blocked by a large man rushing past. He wore a yarmulka that threatened to fly off on its own, and as he glared at me he hissed something filled with *ssss*'s and *zzzz*'s. I would not know for years that the man was Paul's father.

Paul, moving slowly, as if through water, embraced me. His sadness was thick. "Ah," he said. "You've come. Good. Beer?"

He paused by the window, looked down, and looked again when he returned from the kitchen. The place seemed devoid of something, a vibrancy that had always been there. His clothes were strewn carelessly about; dirty socks were crumpled in scuffed desert boots.

"Where," I asked slowly, "is Janice?"

He speared his own can and sat down heavily opposite me. "Janice. Well, Cate, it would seem that we, you and I, have something else in common. She's gone. Flew the coop, such as it was. Said she didn't want to be married to me anymore. There was no one else, thank God."

I didn't ask how come he was so sure. Any moderately intelligent woman, knowing that ego is more dangerous to control than love, would never admit to there being anyone else unless she was mad herself. His gaze moved to the window. He got up and stood looking out of it. Silhouetted there in the late afternoon light, he seemed to shake momentarily; his head sank slowly down on his chest. I thought I heard, though I wasn't sure, a sound like a sob screaming to emerge, and I thought to myself: He's crying. The sonofabitch is crying!

He spoke, his voice overly strong. "Let's go get us some paint. Let's paint Janice right out of this goddamn place."

"Brown paint," he said to the clerk in the hardware store.

"You should use white for these apartments," I offered. "For more light."

"Brown. It's the new thing. Flat, colored paint. It's my place."

"It surely is."

We bought some more beer, bread, salami, cheeses and fruits, and returned. I had heard or read about binges — marathon fucking, killing, eating, walking, playing records. I had never heard of a painting binge; more important, I had never been in one. We slapped on the paint, ate, drank, sang. The temperature was around 90 degrees. How we sang — all the radical, revolutionary ditties that somehow don't sound good any longer, not even in the throat of Pete Seeger.

When we were not singing, Paul rattled on about his life.

"My folks had great disdain for the American system of education; they didn't believe it helped to produce the necessary revolutionaries. Where we lived, in the co-ops, you found nothing but socialists — no one would admit to being anything else; it was too dangerous. For blocks and blocks you found nothing but socialists: Jewish socialists, Italian socialists, Anglo-Saxon socialists, Irish socialists. It was incredible; one felt buoyed on a high sea, support everywhere, love, humanity, charity in its finest sense.

"When the Depression began to wane there came a change. Education was important, even if it was deep within the capitalist framework. You went to City College, and yes, Harvard and Yale and Princeton, if they let you in — "

"Wait a minute, wait a minute," I said. "What do you mean, 'if they let you in'?"

He seemed to catch at himself, rerun something he'd said in his mind.

"Uh — oh, you know, if you had the right connections."

We moved from room to room, singing no more now, but painting from baseboard to ceiling. We were caught in the middle of a bowel movement. We quit at four in the morning. I did not sleep well. Back when we were most high, Paul, his face splattered, looking like an old man in whom the liver spots / melanin, stronger now, surges back in splotches, embraced me again, the way I would embrace a brother if I had one, and said, "Nigger, it sure is good to see you."

He'd never used the word before, and I certainly hadn't. It shocked me softly, but I considered the fact that we were special friends, special enough to allow him to address me that way. And I supposed that would have been the end of it, except that he was studying me for some kind of reaction with much the same pensive stare of a boy who's turned a turtle on its back.

I woke up needing Paul.

Like a plague sensed, the city closed in on me, surrounding me with cold, damp mists of apprehension. Where I had come from, nothing remained. The future was as slippery as, and the size of, an Indian nut. I could not know whether the interview I had for that day would become a job, despite my ad agency boss having already cut ground with the Philip Morris company. But I counted on it. The possibility that I would not be hired on, however, burrowed inside like a jungle worm, minutely destroying the tissues of my psyche. There was that.

I heard Paul in his room coughing up and swallowing beery phlegm; the sound seemed fitting in all that brown. I tried not to think, resting there, fighting back a horrendous beer hangover, of all the writers I'd heard about who had stalked the city, determined to devour it, but who had instead been eaten, silently, in shabby apartments and bars, in editorial offices, and whose names no one remembered, even though they had published. And there was that.

So. This brown, small space, still drying, like a womb just emptied out, was the only home I had. I thought one of those moans, deep through private darknesses, and remembered when it had been better, not so long ago, with Catherine.

Why is that nigger thinking like that? I asked myself. This is discovered country, the post-Catherine resurrection. I swung, heavy-headed, off the couch and for a bittersweet small block of time willed the sound of her voice, of Glenn's voice, into the room. They came in and went with the whisking sounds of the cars going by down in the street.

I got the job and came home — *home?* — happy, booze instead of beer in my arms, prancing up the stairs, hearing bop in my head.

Paul reluctantly broke away from his typewriter, where he was trying to finish up some work before he began classes at the New School, and before he began a new job editing a legal magazine.

"Well," he said as we toasted. "I was prepared to have you here for a couple of years at least."

"Aw, no," I said happily. For my first order of business now was to find an apartment of my own. We had not talked yesterday of how long I would stay; the invitation had been open-ended — perhaps without any end, with Janice gone. But I feared becoming dependent on him, maybe because I perceived that Paul wanted, even needed, to have me in that position.

That night, my treat, I dragged him to the Royal Roost; he much preferred, I knew, Stuyvesant Casino, but I told him that George Shearing was on the bill with Bud Powell. He didn't know Powell, but nearly everyone knew Shearing. So he came. At the bar we switched to beer, which in places like that was not too much cheaper, and, listening to Bud tearing up the piano, the beginning of a poem came to me:

> *Assonance and dissonance converge*
> *An oblique tone; strange waves carry sheer*

I was into it — the music, the voices of the patrons — free, because of the job. I felt close to a secret that I could not describe in any of its suggested details; I simply knew that it was a secret, a mystery, and I allowed myself to move with its motion:

> *Assonance and dissonance converge*
> *An oblique tone; strange waves carry sheer*

Bud finished to scattered applause. Paul said, as if he had been bored, "And now Shearing."

"Yeah," I said. I supposed he would have also liked Tony Scott and Lennie Tristano.

Bud came to the bar, dark and disgruntled. The mostly white audience gave Shearing a big hand after every number. Bud, standing not far from us, glared down into his drink and shook his head.

When Shearing finished, he was led to the bar, where, sightless, he stood waiting for a drink. There was the sudden sound of bodies moving quickly, of glasses being broken or knocked over, of voices pitched high in surprise and fright. I turned just in time to see Powell punching Shearing in the mouth. Shearing grabbed his face. People were tugging and pulling and shouting. Bud was screaming ten octaves above the tumult, "How come you get more applause than me? How come?" He was led away and a protective, sympathetic crowd closed around Shearing.

Paul shook his head in disgust and frowned after Powell.

That night in the brown womb parts of my first novel came to me.

I moved from Paul's a week after I took the job with Philip Morris. The job was not in copywriting. A Madison Avenue agency did that, utilizing Johnny — "Call for Philip Mor—riss." P.M. was wrapped in brown and beige, and the cigarettes were not yet penis-sized. My territory, for that is what they called it, was Harlem and the Bedford-Stuyvesant section of Brooklyn. I journeyed to and from the local gathering places, usually community centers, demonstrating the P.M. inhaling test, designed to prove how smooth P.M.s were. First, you inhaled your own cigarette through your mouth; then you did the same with a P.M., which was smoother, because the first inhalation had already taken the edge off.

When I had finished, I made my way back through town to my two-room apartment near Columbia, secured through a fluke: a drunken super-intendent lost the rules in a bottle of Carstairs, and by the time the lease was signed it was too late to apply any kind of "gentlemen's agreement." The place had high ceilings, was dim except for about two hours during the day when the sun shone the brightest, and must have had at least a hundred coats of leaded paint on the walls. It was home.

When I was there, dovening back and forth before my machine, ideas funneling, I realized that I had never been alone before. I had been home, then in the marines, then with Catherine, with Paul, and now, approaching thirty, I was alone.

Paul had said, "Save your money. You can stay here a while longer."

Clearly, he did not want to be alone. None of us do. We fear it more than cancer. Perhaps it is because in loneliness we fear the resurgences of former lives or the coming of ghosts. We find in them childhoods not yet outgrown.

The summer was passing amid the echoes of Dodgers, Giants, and Yankees wins and losses, and the parade of Big Fights. Paul was chafing, almost prepared for the class at the New School in which he would blow them all away and in the process be discovered by the teacher, who was also an editor of some repute. Paul and I met often, and when we did, he would have a friend, sometimes a woman, but more often a man, with him. When I had a date, he studied her as much as I studied his. Strange that we should have been still seeking clues to each other. When Paul had things going well with him, he could befriend almost anyone who looked or sounded intelligent. That was the way we had met. I think.

These friends, together with some of his old ones who'd gone to Europe at the end of the war and were now drifting back because it was becoming too expensive, enlarged my circle of literary people. Some had heard of *Neurotica*. A smaller number had even read my story, and one of these was Jeremy Poode.

He was called Poode, but he did not look the way anyone named Poode should look. Tall and lean, blond and well-tailored, he was a slightly stifling presence at our gatherings, which usually took place in the Village, where we believed our history was still being made. His smile even then was more a baring of yellow, longish teeth than anything else. He stifled because we didn't know what to make of him; he was — his own words — "a junior editor on *The American Notebook*" — a publication that seemed to side with the Dixiecrats and Big Money. Furthermore, his woman, Selena, was black. Even without her, though, he would have given us pause, and sometimes did.

She was as tall as he, quiet — close to being severe in manner — the way a court reporter is present but paid no attention to. She wore clothes of whisperingly expensive material; style would catch up to her in twenty years. In her presence, her lids concealing the flash of her eyes, I felt like one entering a darkened storefront where my future might be read. That there was complete physical woman within those yards of material she wore, I had no doubt; she suggested it with every move. Yet I knew that none of those gestures were for me.

Poode and Selena had been captured along Eighth Street by Paul one night, as he swept along toward me for an evening of talk and beer-drinking.

Bob Kass read poetry to jazz music. Bearded, and even when ravingly drunk, which he was quite regularly, he made me think of Santa Claus having a tantrum with the elves at the North Pole. Kass was against everything everyone else was for. "I feel safer that way," he'd said one night, his eyes finally dulled, his beard soggy with beer. He had been too young to fight in the Lincoln or Washington Brigade in Spain, but he'd been the right age to fight for Israel in 1948. "I did my stint in the Negev," he said more than once, especially when drunk, "fighting mirages that looked like great big Arabs." This, while his elbows were gliding through spilled beer.

But beer stains were nothing to him. Kass was as shabby in his surplus army clothes as Poode was Brooks Brothers clean. "What's that all about?" Kass would mutter, seeing Poode enter a joint dapper in one of the plumb-blue suits he liked so much, following Selena, bullshittingly demure in her yards of fabric. "Oh!" Kass would say. "It's them." He was working when I first met him because the woman he had been living with left him. He was in the process of finding another who had a good job so he could continue to free-lance without worrying about the basics.

Food and drink he invariably found in Mark Medowitz's ratty apartment in the Village. We all stopped there on the way to or from somewhere else. Mark drank nothing but wine. Twice the size of Kass, he held his cigarettes between his thumb and forefinger, affecting a European air. Although Mark had been schooled at Harvard, he was not as obvious a Harvard man as Poode was a Yalie. Kass was more gentle with Medowitz for the same reason the rest of us were: Mark was the number two editor of — (I forget the name now, *Snatch* or *Gash,* something like that) — well, a magazine that had, we understood, nationwide distribution. Mark had already published stories by James T. Farrell and Nelson Algren. Knowing then no other editor who, mothlike, had flown near the brilliance of such giants, we loved Mark for the possibilities he represented. And he knew it. Mark, too, had lived in the co-ops.

The fact that Mark's magazine published no poetry left Leonard Blue-Sky somewhat bitter, I suppose. He had published in every little magazine there was, and he was, I thought, a poet. Really. He was, like me in those days, colored or Negro, but he preferred to emphasize the Indian portion of his genealogy, which was Mohawk. The sub-branch to which he laid claim never learned to climb the beams for skyscraper construction.

Leonard and I didn't talk, really talk, to each other because he considered himself better than I, an outsider, one of those who joined the group and, failing at setting down the word in the mysterious sequence necessary for success, got washed down the sewers like dogshit in a heavy rain. Nor did he talk with Selena.

Leonard's wife, Dorothea, a war bride from Alsace, tried to bridge the gap between the three of us. I believe this was so because — big-boned and quite plain, with her English not improving at all — she too was one of the outsiders Leonard secretly dismissed. I wish it had been different. But each time I suggested to him, out of the range of the others, that it would be great just talking to him, he said, "Yeah. Well, let's do it sometime."

And now, long years later, I could cry for not making him know himself and me better. I should have. There was a reality we ignored. I should have shaken him with his weapon, words:

"Nigger, what makes you think you're a poet?" I hoped he would answer:

"The same thing that makes you think you're a novelist, nigger."

29

Maybe we would have bounded to a new plane. But I didn't and he didn't. I grind my teeth when the scenes of our charade freeze in my head. Yes, he was good, carrying with him the threat of greatness, the way Delmore Schwartz must have been between madnesses in which he ran his wife through the chicken yards of New Jersey. Leonard suspected his greatness, but passing through his years in deafening silence, he caved into delusions that fed the homilies passed on for truth. He started drinking firewater in excesses greater than usual. He crashed himself on the wagon (the local AA hadn't wanted him; everyone knew that niggers — and that's mainly what he looked like — could hold their liquor), then smashed himself off it (Bellevue, St. Luke's, name it) time after time, the way he would start pedestrian poems, end them and begin still others.

I have read Hayden. He is great, and / but the choice of one or both conjunctions depends on what is read in history. Leonard Blue-Sky was greater, and gods do not believe they could ever be victims of anyone or anything.

During that year Paul went regularly to his class and belittled the other writers. He brought to our gatherings, which were growing less frequent (because, I suppose, each of us was fearful that the other would publish his novel or collection of poems or stories first, if we spent more time drinking and talking than writing), a strikingly beautiful dancer named Claire. It seemed to be serious between them.

Mark accepted a story of Paul's and gave him a cover blurb. In the succeeding issue, he published a story of mine that was, I am still convinced, far superior to Paul's. I may be mistaken, but I don't think so.

Poor Mark. For his ready acceptance of our need of him had resulted in a deluge of manuscripts zooming in over his office transom. They were also left at the door to his apartment or pushed at him in bars and restaurants. The speed of the word in the Village moved faster than the speed of light. Mark Medowitz was a *contact*.

Struggling for his survival, Mark suggested to everyone that instead of dealing directly with him we take on an agent. Yes, he knew a young, tough one; one who fought every sentence in every contract to secure the advantage for his clients. Alex Samuels. Then Mark moved without leaving a forwarding address or a listed phone number. He was always out of town when the secretary gave him your name, or had just left for same when one happened to drop by the office.

In his next issues he published James Purdy, Norman Mailer and

30

Truman Capote. Of course, we talked about Mark when we did gather. Poode in his brittle way voiced our thoughts: "Mark drinks with another crowd. And there'll be another and another, and that's the way it goes."

I called Alex Samuels. Yes, he said, he would take a look at my work. I told Paul, who said, "I think the teacher likes my work better than anyone else's. I think, then, that I'll go directly through him and not bother with an agent. Let me know what happens, though."

Alex Samuels was a tall, very thin man who exuded a Hell's Kitchen toughness. He made a point of letting you know that he had come not from the Lower East Side, but Eleventh Avenue. He had had, he said, Bruce Jay Friedman and Joseph Heller as clients. They would become well known, he said, if they followed his advice. They'd left him because he suggested too many changes in their work.

"Who," I asked, "are they?"

"Couple of guys starting out. One's doing a novel — I forget which one — called *Catch-Eighteen,* or something like that. Rotten title, but he didn't want to change it."

Alex Samuels had a curious way of looking at me. Perhaps he thought I was a houngan, capable of pulling basketballs out of my asshole, or a dancer capable of outjangling Bojangles. In short, his look read: *What can I do for this nigger?*

"I'll look at the fiction," he said. He gave me back the poetry without reading it. "Poetry never made anybody rich. As for the fiction," he said, measuring his words so that they came out succinctly spaced, "I will see what I can do."

"I've got a friend, a good writer, a friend of Mark's too. Would you be interested in handling him as well?"

Samuels' smile seemed to say *handling as well?* "What's his name?"

"Paul Cummings."

"What sort of things does he write about?"

"Well. I — "

"The race problem?"

"Oh, no."

"I see. Well, when he's ready, I'll talk to him."

It took me a few years and several experiences to realize that Alex had been trying to find out if Paul was black or white. Later, much later, that would be somewhat funny.

Having deposited my stories and sections of my novel with this stranger who wore thick glasses, I left him, cocky in my ignorance, determined to finish the book as quickly as I could.

Paul questioned me as thoroughly as Samuels had:

"Do you think he's good?"

"Did he mention where he would send your stuff?"

"He did say he might take me on, right?"

"How long did he say it would be before you heard anything?"

He was, I know, envious of my willingness to get my stuff out there, as when I had sent my poetry around to the Elder Poets. That he was reluctant to undergo criticism was obvious but, at the moment, muted, happily, because of Claire.

They were now living together, and, as though demanding witness to their love, they invited me to dinner often or to join them at the ballet. Their public displays of affection were embarrassing. They would cuddle nose to nose, cooing, speaking to each other in tender falsettos while clutching each other as if about to slide on ice.

As the months gathered around their affair, the sheer newness of it at first concealed the seeds of discontent. Claire wanted to go out every night to see this dancer or that one perform — d'Amboise, Tallchief, Graham. There were the parties at which contacts were renewed, and the auditions. Paul rushed home from his magazine, flushing free his mind of cases and court decisions he had translated from legalese into English, ready to work deep into the night. Too often he found that he could not, for Claire had made other plans. The first thing to go that year was his class at the New School. He did not say so, but I suspected that his teacher, after all, had preferred other writing to his.

In the meantime, Alex Samuels was not doing much for me and he sent me the letters of rejection to prove it. I responded by sending him parts of my novel as I finished them. I was, in addition, growing restless in my job. I skipped appointments and filed late reports. And, growing reckless, there were times when I suggested, not to a group, but to an individual, that he inhale Philip Morris first, and then his own brand. His own was always smoother then.

I needed the job to support and entertain myself and my dates, and to send money to Catherine and Glenn. The raises I got helped me to save a little, though I wasn't sure for what. Intuitively I knew that I needed to be forced by circumstances to make changes in the routines in my life. The need for some kind of deep change in my life worried me. I dreamed, and it was the same dream: some faceless soldier trying to force his way into my foxhole. I saw his bulk silhouetted against the

Southern Cross sliding down the night sky. Why? Why did I need the change? Why did I want it?

The months continued to ambush my time, dates and days bounding full-blown with meaning from my hasty scrawls on the calendar, and then one day I had finished the novel, almost without knowing it.

There simply was nothing more I wanted to write. I placed a period at the end of the last sentence. No lightning struck the building; there was not even a storm. Nor were there hallelujahs from Morningside Heights. There was only silence, except within myself. I was thankful. To whom? To what? I stared at that last, nigger-black period and felt a great upsurge, warm, good, thick. I never felt that way again when I finished a book.

I don't think you are supposed to feel that way anymore when you have finished your *Dissonances,* your number one, the ace. *Dissonances* was about people like Bud Powell (though I never admitted it when asked) and other musicians who played jazz and were black; about their hustles and hurts, loves and losses.

I did not tell Paul that I'd finished and delivered the final chapters of the novel to Alex until he asked, several weeks later, how it was going. He'd asked not out of any real concern, but merely to keep abreast of events, to assess how far and fast I was going. Every week thereafter, on the phone or in person, he inquired as to the novel's progress around the publishing houses. He seemed distressed if it had not come back after being at a house for a length of time. For then the possibilities of its acceptance loomed larger.

I had plunged immediately into another novel; the poetry now seemed locked away in unyielding meter in my mind. My stories were everywhere being rejected, mainly, I gathered from the carefully worded letters from editors, because most of the characters were Negro and their situations based on that. One or two, rottenly honest, conceded that the stories would turn away Southern readers. Naturally, I told myself that the problem was one of individual editors, weak links in the solid chain, rotten apples in the barrel.

It was autumn, another year winding down, and I was already buying Glenn's Christmas presents, although they may have been a bit old for him — a Jackie Robinson baseball glove and a Lionel train set. And I hoped I'd have a date for New Year's Eve when I returned from my visit with him. Paul and Claire were beginning to have words about time and how valuable it was; Leonard had broken up and reconciled with Dorothea while having severe bouts with the bottle; Selena had left Poode for a Negro man named Robert; Kass had found a woman with a good job. She complained, however, that he still did not write; he made model planes and battleships all day. Mark Medowitz moved to *Esquire*.

So it was the following spring when Alex Samuels called. "I've got a sale for your novel, Cate."

"What?"

"I've sold your novel." (Later it would come to me that agents always sounded like cats lapping cream when they had a sale for you.)

It sank in. "You did? Who to?"

"Smythe and Simkin. Okay?"

"Yeah, sure, sure, fine."

"The advance is three grand. All right, Cate?" He purred.

"Uh — sure. That's okay."

"Can we have lunch tomorrow? I'll explain the contract and you can sign it if everything's okay. Say twelve-thirty?"

I hung up, picked up again and called Paul. "Alex SOLD IT!" I shouted. The salesmen in the outer office peered around the corner at me. Paul was making a gurgling sound. "Great, man!" he finally said. "Who to?"

"Smythe and Simkin."

"Not bad, not bad. Lotta dough?"

"Three grand."

"Uh-huh, uh-huh. We gotta celebrate."

By the time I met Paul and Claire at the Sea-Fare, Kass and Miriam, his new woman, Leonard and Dorothea, Poode and a girl named Mavis, and Mark and someone named Joan, were already pretty high.

"I guess you'll be drinking with another crowd now," Poode said.

"Congratulations," Leonard said, rather briskly, I thought.

"Boy, what I couldn't do with three grand," Kass said.

"The money'll get better, you'll see," Mark said.

"If I had it, I'd take off from the fuckin' magazine," Paul said.

"You may wind up being the best Negro writer in America, Cate, better than Huysmans and Whittington combined," Kass said. He giggled. "That should be worth a lot more dough."

"Good show, Cate," Paul said, lifting his glass in what must have been his fifth toast of the evening. I had the uneasy sense there and at Paul's, where we gathered later, that the readings were off, as when one uses feet instead of meters or Fahrenheit instead of centigrade. A duty had been performed, not a celebration. My envy, I was sure, would have been quite as keen as theirs, had our positions been reversed. Keener.

I met my editor a couple of days later. Rupert Hemmings' red hair

34

was extravagantly combed. He might have been a Hollywood type except that he was an understated man, simple and to the point, like his favorite restaurant, which was plain and bright. Patrons ate with little smiles on their faces, as if they had discovered caches of gold.

"I'm looking forward to working with you."

I didn't know quite what to say.

"I've never worked with a Negro writer before, but I've known some of the great ones. They were always with someone else — Wright, Llewellyn Dodge Johnson. Know him?"

"No."

"He's really one of the great ones, black or white — " He broke off to stare across the room. "That's Amos Bookbinder."

Amos Bookbinder was the first black editor in publishing. His photograph had been splashed inside *Publishers Weekly.*

"Know him, Cate?"

"No."

"I hear he's a nice guy. But look. You're working on another novel?"

"Yes."

"Good, good. Married?"

"Divorced."

"Kids?"

"One."

"You're not a native of New York?"

"No."

"Like it here?"

"Yes, but — "

"But what, Cate?"

"I feel that I need a change."

He leaned back and smiled. "Yes, New York can do that to people. What kind of change?"

"I don't know, but it'll come to me."

"Maybe I can get you some money on the next one — but I don't want to see it until it's finished."

"I don't need it. At least I don't think so."

Looking back, I now realize that that was the statement that made it work, our relationship. I wasn't then a real writer. I was honest. Most real writers refuse nothing with dollar signs on it; they can't afford to.

"Well, if you make a move and decide you do need it, let me know."

We talked of publishing plans for the novel and probed and studied until lunch was over. I arose thinking, Next year this time, spring, the novel would be out. We left, Rupert going back to his office. I didn't want to return to mine. I strolled around the corner to a bistro to have another leisurely drink and to think about Rupert.

I had just ordered my second when Amos Bookbinder came in and stood beside me. "You Cato Caldwell Douglass?"

"Yeah, and you're Amos Bookbinder."

"What're you drinking? Hey, bartender. Let me have what he's drinking and set up another round while you're at it." He smiled at me as we shook hands. "Word gets around fast, so I heard about you, and seeing you with Hemmings, how could I be wrong?"

"How's it going with you?"

"Great," he said. He glanced furtively around in mock fear. "So far."

Understanding, I laughed.

He was well turned-out. One could almost see the tailors still finishing up the suit he wore. The initials AB were stitched on his shirt pocket, and his shoes gave off the modest glow that comes with the polishing of expensive Italian leather.

Amos upended his drink luxuriously. "I'm glad to see you getting published," he said, "but I sure wish I were going to be your editor. Hemmings is okay."

That made me feel good. "Yeah, I liked him."

"You're not married, are you?" he asked.

I said, "No," and waited.

"Maybe we can do some hanging out. I hear your book's about jazz — do a show. Miles is at the Vanguard next week."

"Okay. Sure."

"Listen, man, I've got to get back. I've been at lunch since" — he flicked up a starched cuff and glanced at a huge disc of gold — "noon. It's now four o'clock."

"That ain't half bad," I said.

Amos Bookbinder winked at me. "Call me tomorrow, can you?"

"Phaeton, right?"

"You got it."

He had a long stride, and it was somewhat imperious — the minister walking down an aisle of his church, the undertaker overseeing the ten o'clock ceremonies with an eye toward the next at eleven — and then he was out of sight.

Amos was married to a woman named Jolene. They had a couple of small children. Nevertheless, he and I hung out until all hours of the morning listening to music in the Village bars. Fifty-second Street was all but dead; everything was downtown. We listened to the music and talked and talked until I came to know that he was young and that behind the façade of unflappable assurance he was the kind of innocent I had never been. And that surprised me after I'd read the books he'd suggested to me — Maran, Roumain, Damas, Césaire, Attaway and a host of others, foreign and domestic — all of which suggested a neat synthesis of the kind of history one never found in the ordinary books.

The way we spoke — indeed, the way we thought when we were together — made all things more pressing than the moods that passed between Paul and me. Yet I didn't find it strange; I found it gratifying and, even when Dizzy was doing a solo, and Mingus and Roach and Bud were shaking rafters behind him, Amos and I would be screaming at each other, trying to make points through this or that Negro author.

He did not believe, really, in love or in flag and country, though he had served with distinction for the latter in Korea. He did not believe in hard work, though I suspected that he did more of it than he admitted to. He believed in his indestructibility. He was vulnerable to nothing, over the long run.

"I," he announced when drunk, "am going to change the face of publishing. I will do things no other editor has ever done. You'll see."

He had dreams of triumph, while, more and more, that faceless soldier tried to fight his way into the hole where I crouched fearfully in darkness, totally, sickeningly aware of my vulnerability. One night in the dream, as the Southern Cross exploded soundlessly into light, I saw the face and it was Paul's. The next night, just as somehow I knew it would, the constellation exploded again, and the face belonged to Amos.

In the days following, I neatly stacked the pages of my novel. I set my suitcase into full view, where I could see it every minute I was in the apartment, and one day I brought home the list of sailings for the Italian Line.

The only language I knew very well was English. My Spanish could get me by; my French was just this side of disaster and my German was still incontrovertibly graded F. Who is to say why the Spanish came better than the others — Fate? Later, when I had learned more, which is to say when I no longer trusted all I had been taught, I thought it possible that in some other life, an earlier incarnation, I had been a Moor and had crossed from North Africa to Gebal-Tarik — Gibraltar. I've met people who looked Italian and wound up living in Rome, and people who looked Mexican and went to live in Mexico.

I had few doubts about going. Glenn would need me more later, for the man talk, for the money, if I had it. (Emptiness struck me, though, when I thought of the distance that would be between us. Had my father ever felt it?) Did I need more money? I would make do. Rupert's offer was for an emergency. The clincher was the fact that I wasn't getting any younger. The time was now. I had got assignments to interview Sidney Bechet in Paris for *Down Beat* and Llewellyn Dodge Johnson for *Ebony.* I booked passage on the *Vulcania,* and then took a train out to see Glenn and leave Catherine some money.

He was quiet and courteous and I knew he didn't understand how far away I was going, how I felt. His mother didn't even look at the check. Once she murmured, "It's what you want to do, so . . ." The trip was frustrating; nothing had come across the way I hoped it would.

On that early fall day when they all came down to the ship to see me off, I felt as I had with Glenn, that slow, long pain you feel when doing something by instinct while your head tells you calmly, with the persistence of a phonograph needle stuck in the groove of a record, that you didn't have to do it.

Mark Medowitz brought a bottle of champagne; Paul and Claire, Glenlivet; Kass, who was going to Hollywood to look for work, a list of pensions and a bottle of sauterne. Poode brought me cigarettes; Amos, books and more booze. Rupert sent a telegram and a box of cigars. Paul said, "Maybe we'll come over. What do you think?" I said, "Sure, why not?" They all wished, for I could see it in their eyes, that they were going, too. Their eyes swept over the small, D Deck cabin, swallowed whole the entire ship as they tried to imagine it cresting and knifing the restless high waves of the Atlantic; eyes that looked at me, wondering, *How did that nigger do it?* I'd made the sacrifices they were unwilling to make. They didn't have to make any. And I needed space, surcease from the intimidating American rhythms, the ceaseless self-glorification, sometimes subliminal, sometimes not. So I went like my father to the sea and left behind my son — all I had besides a sold typescript to show that I'd been here.

3

FROM ALGECIRAS I made my way northward along the coast through bone-dry lands, past little memorials set in front of homes commemorating the dead of the Civil War, until, finally, I came to Sitges, about thirty miles south of Barcelona. Oddly, though I had never been there, I was in a strange way familiar with its daily vibrations, the look of it, when I located at the opposite end of town away from the landscaped gardens of the British residents. I was at last alone in a large, cheaply rented house in a sweet quiet stroked by the sound of the waves and sometimes the wind careening against the mountains. I had never known such threat-less quiet in my life.

I sat down almost at once and wrote long letters to nearly everyone I knew in New York, and this was simply because I wished to receive answers. Getting mail is a necessity for most writers; it reaches in from faraway places bringing the smells, colors, sounds — memories — lends vistas beyond the cold, mute typewriter. The Mail tells you that you are not yet dead, even though you may have lived a life that has encompassed both the three- and fifteen-cent stamps.

I initiated a correspondence with Paul based on the image of the Negro in American literature. We had never talked of these things before, feeling under some constraint because of our friendship, I supposed. Much of the imagery, I said, was light, formless and basically filled with a racial prejudice through just about every white writer's traditional, romantic view of Negroes. There were a few exceptions, but usually Negroes were just plain niggers, or they were niggers with music. Faulkner sometimes brought depth to black people. Most American writers who were white, I wrote, still were not freed from prejudice.

Perhaps, Paul wrote, the beat writers would represent a change; he had been hearing much about some of their works that soon would be published. There was also talk about a piece Mailer was working on that drew an existential connection between the beats / hipsters and Negro life.

It was true, I replied, that there might be an existential connection between jazz music and Negroes, maybe just as there was a connection between the German people and Wagner's music. I was sure, however, that the connection did not extend to the beats, simply because they did not *have* to be what they chose to be. The range of choices for Negroes was in most cases nonexistent.

In addition, I noted, since I was becoming acutely aware of it in my Spanish solitude, that Negroes rarely were allowed to be experts about themselves; others always knew more, wrote or said more, or at least what they said or wrote got around more and certainly was given more credence.

In this vein, purified by distance, I like to think that our dimensions expanded. I did not dream the old dream. Time was measured only by the grumbling of my stomach or the call of the mailman. I worked long but easily, like a distance runner who has found his stride, whose breathing and soft thumps of his feet against the ground are his only rhythms. When I felt need of a pause, a change, being as full as a gourmand, and as satisfied, I went to Paris.

Sidney Bechet reminded me of Blind Willie Lemon at the Stuyvesant Casino, but even so his life was better in France than it had been at home. John Coltrane had not yet come along, but one day if someone does a study on the soprano sax and the changes its use made in popular music, they will have to study Sidney Bechet, too.

"Professor" Bechet, student of Bunk Johnson, Big Eye Nelson and Storyville, former resident of New Orleans, Chicago and New York; ex-member of the Noble Sissle and Zutty Singleton bands, among half a hundred more; leader of the New Orleans Feetwarmers and the Barefoot Dixieland Philharmonic — there he was in Montmartre, somewhat less fat, his widow's peak more severe, his high cheekbones less padded with the flesh of younger good times. I heard him play in his club, Le Chat Noir, and with him walked the winter-slicked streets — the Rue le Pic, the Rue Durand, the Place St. Pierre, their shop windows clouded with steam — Sacré-Coeur visible between buildings, and smelled cooking foods whose scents leaked out into the streets. I absorbed his reminiscences there as though I were a well designed to hold an infinite amount of water. As we strolled, secure in our blackness (for brown people, sometimes Algerians, sometimes African-Americans, often South Americans, were abused daily by swooping squads of gendarmes who fought the Algerian uprisings in Paris and who ignored the *plastiques,* which were going off with tiresome regularity over in the Latin Quarter), I drank it all in, digested it.

And I wondered, as all writers must do, if, when I reached his age, there would be younger writers seeking to talk with me, to somehow find their measurements against those I held for myself, or to perceive for themselves the pitfalls I never discovered. This sense was more intense when I found Llewellyn Dodge Johnson.

He, when very young, had come out of the Harlem Renaissance. Through Jean Toomer he'd been turned on to Gurdjieff, who was then at Fontainebleau. Unlike Toomer, Johnson had remained in Europe, even during the war.

He lived in the Rue de Turenne, a short street overlooked by the Eglise St. Denis. It was filled with shops and traffic growling out to the Boulevard Voltaire and the Boulevard Beaumarchais. The street had little character, was almost in transition, as, in truth, all of Paris was. The war had been over for a dozen years.

In his flat, Johnson sat in a soft, deep chair and was dressed in an old suit of good, dark material. The white shirt and precisely tucked gray tie made me think that he had dressed for me. Johnson was a small man and carried about his person an aura of limitless life. He leaned on a dark, carved walking stick, *un jonc,* and remained almost motionless, hunched over, talking about the Renaissance and what had happened to it and its people.

"It was strange," he said. "So many of us were filled with self-hatred. Except Langston. So many of us saw ourselves not through our own eyes, but through Van Vechten's, as he was seeing then, or Johnny Farrar's. The downtown crowd loved us. We had shows on Broadway. Wally Thurman even worked quietly in Hollywood. Then, as always, we were cruel, even murderous to each other, like cocks set into a pit."

In the light I could see a ring of vibrant blue around the pupils of Mr. Johnson's eyes. He fixed them on me. "You young writers should be very careful of that. We don't remember. Each 'renaissance' is the original.

"Toomer," he said. "Jean digested essences, things that escape description by word. Somehow, though, he managed; he had that eerie ability. He was one of us who needed to work beyond the usual definition of the senses. Dreiser tried, but Dreiser failed; Gurdjieff couldn't help him with his writing. Nor could he help me."

He turned his round, smooth face to me and smiled. "People like to think of Josephine Baker around those times too, you know. But there must have been a hundred, for all I know, a thousand poor, cunning, good-looking black girls who walked away with the hearts, not to mention some of the wealth, of the downtown set. Department store owners, city and state officials, editors, publishers. Those girls made Josephine look like an amateur."

He mused. "A long time ago. The edges have become smoothed and softened. Paul Laurence Dunbar wasn't the first nor the last Negro writer to be forced into the bottle; there were lots of us. I was in it myself for a long time, practically until I came to Europe. The tragedies: Bud Fisher going so young; Wally Thurman; the desertions, with Nancy Cunard laying golden bread crumbs for two or three to pick up and follow."

He was silent for a time and, still bent over, he seemed to be looking into an invisible glass ball, watching the past. He sighed. "America is a strange place for a black man to write in. We always found it so, but I suppose only Countee put it so succinctly — " He swung toward me, almost glaring. "You know the poem I mean?"

I quoted the last two lines:

> "Yet do I marvel at this curious thing:
> To make a poet black and bid him sing!"

Mr. Johnson's smile was warm and approving. "Ah, yes, Mr. Douglass, precisely. In America, even if you are writing about a thing as simple as feeling good on a bright, clear morning filled with fresh air — feeling as perhaps millions of others are, they will find it difficult, yes, white Americans will find that difficult to understand because the writer is black and they are white. A few whites will.

"On the other hand, should you write about their direct relationship to you, the only one they know, the correct, objective historical relationship, the one that needs improving on, they will understand. That is all they've been taught to understand, the inherent, basically unchanged state of hostility. That's why in so many words and deeds they deny that history in which we have both suffered and are suffering still. What they did is

42

our mutual holocaust, together our passing through the Red Sea, the epicenter from which or to which the universality of the experience expands or contracts. It seems that we will always move at a fixed distance in relation to each other, but only from one place in space to another place in space.

"I have been in *tabacs* here where I have asked in my French, which is very good French, for a package of cigarettes. The clerks do not understand me. I repeat and repeat, while the expressions on their faces move from shallow politeness to exasperation and finally to disgust — Flaubert was correct to despise clerks — and I am finally put to the humiliation of pointing: 'Those! *Celles-la!* Do you see? Do you see?' My blackness blocks their ability to understand their own language!"

He gazed into the invisible ball again. As if reading a litany he said, "Yet we must continue to do what our natures bid us to do and eventually it is to be hoped that they will be moved upward."

"Is time the answer, Mr. Johnson?"

"Mr. Douglass, time is not the answer; time is only a pawn. The will, will, is the only answer."

"Yes, sir."

"Any more questions, Mr. Douglass?"

"Uh, one more if — "

"Yes, yes, of course."

"Well, why did you stop writing?"

He tilted his head, and through another tolerant, although distant, impishly cold smile, aimed his eyes, thin of light, right at me. "I did not stop writing, Mr. Douglass. I still write. A writer writes. That is self-evident to those of us who are — writers." He seemed to slide a long, smooth time on the end of that word. "I am published in East Germany, Yugoslavia, Japan and India. Next year I will be published in China, and I have reason to believe that all my works will be published in Russia within the next three months. No, I never stopped writing. In America and, predictably, Western Europe, they simply stopped publishing me, publishing *us;* our exoticism wore off. I suppose it would be natural therefore for an American to believe that I stopped writing."

I said, "I see."

And he said, "Mr. Douglass, I hope you will."

Back in Sitges, fortified by *café con leches* and endless cognacs, while the village thinned out before the approaching cold, which had already fitted collars of frost and snow on the mountains between here and Barcelona, I sat and finished up the interviews. Every day now a car in first gear whined away from the beach toward the hard road and Barcelona, the back loaded, the top loaded and tied down; Spain was becoming Spanish again.

Glenn stared at me from a corner of my writing table. He stared at me from my night stand. Sometimes in the middle of a passage, I'd take the paper out of the machine and write him a letter, describing things — the ocean, the mountains, Spanish kids, the weather, the house — anything I'd not told him about before. And of course I told him that I missed him, more perhaps to define the missing concretely, on paper, and thus release a little guilt, than to move him in any way.

In all his pictures there was a curious little curve around the eyes ("you bastard") that unnerved me whenever I looked at them too closely.

I flooded the mails with gifts: a *pic* and a matador's sword in miniature; a small matador's hat, post cards of Parque Guell, designed by Gaudi, a Spanish scarf (indistinguishable from an American scarf), a soccer ball (soccer had not yet become popular in the U.S.), and yet the emptiness persisted, along with the sense that my sacrifice in going away from him was not as great as his.

I would make it up to him, goddamn, I'd really make it up to him and nothing would ever come between us. I took strength in the reiteration of the promise, but it always seemed to fade, retreat somewhere to the rear of things. Then, seeing it there, I called it back again.

I had to, I told myself, exert total control over the events in my life, and Glenn was, after all, a rather special one. Got you, kid, I whispered to the pictures when I came in high. Got you.

Paul wrote that he and Claire had married; I had thought they were on the verge of breaking up. There was less mail; everyone was used to my absence by now. Yet I found myself pacing as I waited for the mailman, who would ride by without stopping. I took to frequenting the cafés the workers went to, hoping that I was less of a curiosity to them than I had proved to be to most of the Spanish people I'd met. In the evenings after my dinner, I went out to drink and meet still more people; I even got into discussions with the beach patrols of the Guardia Civil, which no one else did, or dared to. That was a measure of how lonely I found myself becoming.

Now I went into Barcelona two or three times a week, by bus or hiking. Truck drivers were good about stopping for me. Taking the last bus back from Plaza Universidad, my arms filled with books or groceries or catalogues from museums, I entered my cold and quiet house, flicked a light on over my typewriter, read the words on the paper held in its rubber-metallic grip, and wondered — and these were the first times — if they were worth what I was beginning to feel.

44

4

ONE MORNING I awoke and felt filled to choking with wanting to be with, wanting to be deeply inside of and warmed by, a woman. The village was a proper place, as far as I knew; *las putas* were always in the next village. I saw no signs that the Spanish women of Sitges, or any of the few other European women who'd remained behind, were as eager as I for an eternity of balling.

I simply and painfully missed the hell out of New York; there I knew the rules of the game.

Close to noon the next day, I rode into Barcelona; siesta was coming on fast — the Big Sleep, or whatever they do during that time. I walked up and down the Ramblas and from one Gaudi structure to another; I ate and drank, tried to conceal the heat in my eyes; traffic returned to the streets and the pace of the city picked up as darkness came; and still I drifted from place to place, trying to find a woman.

On my third pass near Paseo de Gracia and Plaza de Cataluña — it was nearly ten and I was growing weary, dejected and more than a little sorry for myself — I heard Afro-Cuban music: *cha chink cha cha !click ba ba ah, yah ba ba ah, yah ba !click chink cha !click . . .*

When I paid the entrance fee, I knew that whatever cool I had, or pretended to have had, was gone. I was going to have to pay for some pussy. Incredible! Unthinkable, but there it was. I stood looking around the hall; the musicians were on a stage. The Johns were young and wore suits — the type of young men you saw in the offices of struggling businesses in Barcelona. They had a little French, a little English, a little German; and they were Catalans and wore gold-rimmed glasses.

The women looked a helluva lot better than they did along the Ramblas and the harbor; they could have been housewives, teachers, secretaries; I looked back at the musicians, who were, all five of them, grinning at me as if they had just measured the size and hardness of my member. They ranged from purest black to mustard yellow. One of them waved for me to come closer to the stage where, loose-limbed and tall, he was shaking his maracas and singing: *"ba ba yah* Hello, Yanqui! *Ba ba !Click!* New York, yeah?"

"We from Oriente Province," the bassist said. "Oh, man, that Fidel, he kicks ass, so we haul ass — "

"Ba ba yah — "

" *— cha chink cha !click cha —* where you livin'?" The maraca man leaned toward me. I liked his face. "Sitges," and I started moving to the music, my coolness undone by a dozen cognacs, some brothers speaking with accents and pussy on the hoof, or was it cash on the maidenhead?

Piano, bass, drums, timbal and maracas, they moved to the finale, all singing, tossing dialogues at each other in the breathing spaces.

The maraca man came down and shook my hand. "We stand up there and play," he said. "We know why we're here. Fidel Castro! No more Batista and the good times. Now, Spain and Franco. But then we see you come and we say: *What's that nigger doin' here?"* He laughed, slapping his thighs, and I laughed, looking past him to the women sitting along the edge of the dance floor.

"Yeah, Luis know. We all know. But now you look." He put an arm around my shoulder and I followed the movement of his head around the room.

"You see, Yanqui? You see her?"

She sat almost alone. There were spaces on either side of her. She was pretty and young — and black.

"Is she Spanish?"

"Carlos," Luis said, nodding toward the bassist, "saw her when she came in tonight. This is her first time, no?" A chorus of *si*'s came from the musicians.

"She is a proud one," Carlos said. "Fafff! It is a fuckin' poor country, and people can't fill their bellies with pride. The Spanish, that's all they left wherever they went — pride. Sheet for this pride."

"Is she Spanish?" I asked once again.

"She has some Catalan, I would bet," Luis said. "Her mother's side." He winked. "The Spanish women, they like Moros, Negros — " he guffawed. "Niggeros, yah, cha, chink, chink, chink," and he was cha-cha-cha-ing, winking, grinning.

I wondered how come he was so sure. No matter, I slid around people waiting for the next set to begin and edged up the rows of chairs where she sat. She wasn't so pretty close up. I stopped and smoked a cigarette, hoping the band would get back to work.

I said good evening to her. She returned my greeting. I asked if she would dance with me when the band started to play again, and she nodded.

"May I sit down?" I asked.

She shrugged. "It's a public place, isn't it?"

The band saved me; we danced.

She was awkward for a few steps, but then, as she came to anticipate me, she improved. When the number was over she smiled for the first time and said, "You dance well."

"And so do you," I said. On the stand, between numbers, Luis went into his little dance again, grinning at me.

"Do you come here all the time?"

"No," I said. "First time."

"My first time, too," she said. Her eyes begged me to believe her.

"Nice place," I said. I glanced at the women — the housewives, teachers and secretaries. They all sat waiting patiently for one of the men to ask them to dance; they possessed none of that jive feminine aggressiveness that one associates with whores. They sat waiting for the beginning of the ritual, a kind of benediction for the "sin" that would follow. She said in what I thought was a bored voice: "We are all very poor and very hungry, and that is why we are here."

We were dancing again by now. I tried not to look at the seated women. Of course I'd heard of the poor in Spain. The government swept the beggars off the streets. Some people lived in caves. The workers labored for a pittance; farming was almost like slavery. Some of this I'd seen — and closed my eyes against it. I'd never been in a situation like it before. The woodman bringing his wood in his bare feet while I wore two pairs of heavy socks and shoes against the cold of the tile floors of my house; people in the market buying *ounces* of meat.

"Married?" I asked.

"No, but some are, I suppose. I have a child, a son." We were standing now, waiting for the next number.

"Are you from Barcelona?"

"Would you buy me something to eat first?" she asked. Her forehead pressed against my shoulder, and she felt suddenly very slight in the arm I pressed against her back.

"Yes," I said hurriedly.

Outside she pressed her fingers against her lips and took a deep breath. "Come on," I said. I'd passed this café at least three times earlier. "I know of a place not far away."

"Just food, just food — "

When she finished the soup she said, "Yes, I am from Barcelona."

She sipped her wine, looked at the glass. She seemed relaxed now, more vulnerable, even with the soft Catalan conversations going on at the bar.

"I lived with my parents until I had the baby. Then, I had to leave. They made me leave."

"Where do you live now?"

She glanced toward the kitchen; the next course would be coming in a moment. She shrugged. "Sometimes here, sometimes there. It is very difficult in Spain if you are poor."

"Where is your baby?"

"With friends. He is not so much a baby anymore. He walks and almost talks." The waiter came with the chicken and rice, the shallow dish of vegetables that were extra. The girl stopped talking and began eating. There were so many things I wanted to ask her. When she came up for breath and another sip of wine, smiling now with a real luster in her eyes, she asked, "Are you rich?"

I shook my head. I wondered that there were people in the world who might believe me to be rich. How very poor they must be!

"American, not Cuban like the musicians, yes?"

I nodded.

"Americans are rich."

"No," I said. She began to eat again, with the slow deliberation of one determined to finish the entire task before him. "A very few are rich, but most are not. Like Spain, like France, like anywhere. All Americans want to be rich, though. That's a part of the culture."

"Rich is good," she said, looking up at me as a few grains of rice sprayed from her fork to the table.

"I have not seen any black Spanish people," I said.

"Because there aren't many. My father is an African, from Sierra Leone. He was a seaman who came here before the war. He met and married my mother. Now he teaches English to the students who think they'll need it to get ahead in the world. I've disgraced them and so — "

48

"Don't you work?"

"There are no jobs for women. Very few. In this country, it is the man first, always the man," she said, snappishly. "I was a waitress until two weeks ago. Business was bad, and nobody wanted a waitress, not even a black one who would be an attraction here, you understand." She dipped back into the serving pan, cleaned it out with a whisk of the fork. "How did you learn Spanish?" she asked.

"In school. Why?"

"The way you speak it, it's cute."

Dessert and coffee came almost as soon as she'd finished. "Well, I guess I'm ready." She finished the wine in her glass, then swirled her coffee and looked at the table.

"Would you like to go to Sitges?"

She frowned. "Sitges? A hotel is closer. Sitges is so far."

"I mean," I said, "to live with me. You and your son."

First she stared and then she laughed, quietly, cautiously. "Sitges," she said again. "But what would I do there?"

"Be with me. I'll take care of you as long as I'm in Spain."

Her eyes flicked quickly back and forth across my face, seeking answers to the questions she was asking herself. She saw what she wanted to see, perhaps what I couldn't conceal. She dropped her head. "We don't even know each other's names."

"Cato Douglass, and I come from New York."

"Ah, New York." There was something like awe and envy in her tone. "Are you married?"

"Divorced."

"Children?"

"A son."

A little smile played on her smooth, brown face. I ordered more wine. "What do you do here in Spain?" she asked.

"I think a lot about my life and the world, I guess, and I write things — books, articles, poetry."

The lashes of her eyes were long and curled. "I see." She put her elbows on the table. I poured from the second bottle. "Do you know," she said, "I have never been with a black man."

"And I have never been with a black Spanish woman."

"*Any* Spanish woman?"

If I'd been able, I think I would have blushed. "No."

"How long have you been here?"

"Since fall."

"How long will you stay?"

"I don't know. Until something tells me it's time to go." I could see her thinking, almost. "There are buses into Barcelona and back every day," I said.

She sipped from her wine again, a long, delicate sip. "I'll go tonight and see." She shrugged as if to say, What do I have to lose? "And if I like it, tomorrow I'll go get my son and come back."

The cab driver was a Basque. Not even the Catalans rested easily with Basques. When he had driven us to my house and I'd paid him, the girl and I stood in the cold, quiet night before the gate leading to it. Then she walked slowly behind me, and I turned to look at her, sensing her thoughts.

There I was, a stranger in her country, living in, it must have seemed to her, a very fine house, while she, a Spaniard in spite of her color (as I was an American in spite of mine), did not know from one night to the next where she would sleep. There was nothing I could say to make her know I understood; my Spanish wasn't good enough. Few languages can adequately explain anything like that. And Uncle Sam must have been smiling out of his star-spangled heaven, furthermore, because, like all other tourists (though black people are special cases), I was proof that Democracy Works! Never mind Mack Parker and Emmett Till and Little Rock; if all was so bad, how had I managed to get away? I was, standing there, my key in the lock, incontrovertible proof that America was indeed the land of the free; the masses no longer huddled, except on flights to Europe during summer vacations.

"Fire?" I sat her down near the fireplace and mashed some paper and pine twigs together and began a fire.

At first I did not hear her. Her words sank in just as I was about to ask what it was she'd said.

"And when you leave?"

Perhaps all things commence from mutual need. What we had ferreted out, one from the other, was our mutual loneliness. (Later, much later, on a couple of midnight-to-dawn phone-in talk shows over radio, I would come to understand how insidious, how pernicious, loneliness could be, understand it through those voices trying not to show it while those same voices, attached to empty souls, wandered over the wires to talk about *anything* so long as another voice responded. These would be frightening experiences, the wee small hour darkness fused with the latest technology — which emphasized the loneliness of the strangers groping through the night.) Besides the loneliness, and the obvious need for someone to respect her real person, I was to her a have. Plainly, she was a have-not. She would let me use her presence, her laughter (I knew it was there), her son, in exchange for living in my house. Clicking in my mind was this further thought: perhaps she hoped she would get from me what no white Spaniard had ever given her. (I had heard them on the Ramblas and *calles* as I passed — *Ssssssst! Mira! Mira! Un Moro! Moro!*) In order to be rid of the Moors they had to laugh at those related to them.

The Spanish make very remarkable floor tiles, and I was studying them because I didn't know how to answer her. When I did look up, she hunched her shoulders, stood, took off her thin, hip-length jacket and said in English as we walked down the hall toward the bedrooms, "Let's see what else goes with the house."

She made breakfast quietly and efficiently and we sat down in a gray dawn. "And now it is morning," she said. "Do you still want to do it?"

"Yes."

She nodded, and I think she was relieved. Monica Jones — that was her name — would go to get her son, Federico García Lorca Jones, and return in the afternoon. Better to have what you know you can get for a little while than to have nothing and not know where anything else was coming from. I could see her reasoning, but the sheer banality of the way things worked made me pensive.

"Is it true," I asked, "that they just stood Lorca up and shot him?"

She nodded. She talked a lot with her body; nodded and made a pistol with her finger and jerked it several times.

"Isn't it dangerous to name a child after him?"

"Oh, they think it is a joke because I am black, you see, and he is black, and when I shout for him in a park — FEDERICO GARCÍA LORCA JONES! — people become frightened until they see who Federico García Lorca Jones is."

> (What a fine little road
> from Cadíz to Gibraltar.
> The sea recognizes
> my step by its sighs.)

I laughed because I felt good, and while she was gone I grew to like her more and I felt this tingling in my body, as though goose pimples were changing places.

We wintered nicely, the three of us. We were triple curiosities in the village: a family, which took much of the danger out of my single, wandering person, a family in blackface, yes, but a family still, and the Spanish have a thing about families.

Then one day while Monica was shopping and I was keeping Federico, the mailman brought a single letter from an S. Merritt. I ripped it open.

Dear Cate:

So you've escaped. I envy you. And I also envy you the acceptance of your novel, but it is all friendly envy. Is there such a thing? Not really, I suppose.

Cate, my marriage — yes, I did marry Robert — is high on the rocks. And I am pregnant. Would you, could you, imagine that he left me for a white woman, one of those long, blue-eyed, blond creatures, classically American, as they say.

I would suppose, dear Cate, that that is precisely the reason why you left, so you too could wallow unmolested in a country far from America, where black women must be almost nonexistent! How alike all Negro men are!

Negro women must put up with this kind of behavior; what else can they do but bear it, grinning only when it is advantageous to do so or when they finally have their revenge?

Will you bring back a European lady? I for one would not be surprised, but I would be civil, should we ever meet again, even friendly, as we were before.

By then I expect to have my first collection of poems ready for a publisher. You didn't know I wrote poetry, did you? Well, you always were pretty wrapped up in yourself.

As ever,
Selena

At first I simply could not understand the letter. We had never been friendly, really. She tolerated me, though I was much attracted to her. And, also, at first I didn't know what there was about her letter, her sitting down to write it, that made me think momentarily of Gittens. But I came back to that thought: Selena had gone a little mad.

I thought of trying to explain it all to Monica, but one had to be an American to understand, so I did not. When she asked why I seemed to be brooding, I said that I was thinking, and she hugged me from behind and kissed my neck and teased me about the limitations of the brain. Federico, sitting on my rug, smiled at us and clicked and drooled.

Rupert cabled that he was on his way to see me with the galleys. The schedule had been altered, and my publisher now wanted to bring the book out early in the summer, after the spring crush. He was traveling to Aix-en-Provence with his family, then would fly down to Barcelona.

Like many, he had never been to Spain because of Franco; he had supported the Republicans. He was coming because of me. Excitedly, I explained to Monica what galleys were, and as I did, little shadows chased across her eyes. What we had not talked about since that first night, my leaving, now loomed large every time the postman came bicycling down the rutted road.

Rupert was surprised at my family. Sitting before the fire one of the three nights he spent with us, he said, "And here I thought you were suffering alone and in silence, drunk on cheap wine, working away. But here's a whole fine family. Pretty much like your own, I guess. You're not alone. That's bullshit, being alone, you know. It's terrible."

Long, long after that night, Monica quietly serving coffee after dinner, then discreetly going off to bed, and long after that, when Rupert died under a thousand tons of snow while skiing in Switzerland, I remembered what he said. Perhaps I remembered so well because it was a thing I already knew.

"It's better, yes," I said. "And I've been working my ass off, too."

"How did those interviews go?"

"Okay."

"Johnson," he mused. "God, he was so much better than so many others back then."

I looked at him. "For example?"

"Hemingway, for starters." He sighed. "How's the new book? Shall I wait to look at it?"

"I wish you would."

I think he preferred that, too. His grunt sounded like approval. "You are planning to come back around pub date?"

"Sure." I thought then that pub date was a momentous event in a writer's life.

"Good. That's wise. Don't cut loose, like Dick Wright. Did you see him while you were in Paris?"

"No. I don't know him. I saw only Bechet and Johnson."

He smoothed his red hair, flaming even in low-wattage Spanish light. "Back home is where the action is. History has ordained it." He laughed.

"But what do you think of Spain, now that you've been here a couple of days?"

"Bad feel, Cate. Very bad feel, even though I haven't seen much. A lot of cops and soldiers around, and the people don't look — well, as though they have options. Ah, well. Tomorrow, France." He peered around and said, "Will you bring them back with you?"

"No, I don't think so."

"I see."

"What do you see?"

"To tell you the truth, Cate, I don't know completely. But I do see something, or I am beginning to. Money okay?"

"Yes, but let me know when you see everything clearly, will you?"

He laughed again, softly. "Forgive me. I do these things with the writers I work with." He gripped my shoulder and rose from his chair. It was time for bed. Our hours of walking along the beach, of strolling from one restaurant or café to others, were over. By the same time tomorrow, he would be gone, and it would not be many months later when I, too, would be leaving. The galleys he had brought were giving me an itch to smell, feel and walk through New York.

And Monica realized it, peering through those long silences to pinion me right after Rupert left. I hugged her and held her hand, but couldn't say what I suspected she wished me to say . . . and I knew that she was, in her lithe, dark way, far too proud to say it herself.

At dusk one day, while she prepared dinner in the small, tiled kitchen, I said, "I'm at a place in my work where I can stop. And the money for those interviews I told you about has come."

She sipped from her glass of sherry, looked over its rim at me, her eyes still mildly accusing.

"So let's take a trip," I said.

That was wrong. Her eyes flashed, golden lightning sharp with possibility, and she seemed to be holding her breath.

"Around Spain," I said. "I'd like to see more of the country, wouldn't you?"

She recovered neatly. "And why not? How? Where would we go?"

"Maybe Yanez would rent us his car. He's not doing much taxi business." Yanez lived with his wife down the block in a hotel that was closed for the winter. During the summer he managed the hotel and dressed every day in suit and tie, but now he wore a beret, a canvas jacket and baggy old pants. He spent most of his time these days sitting in his Seat in the *plaza* waiting for fares. He never got more than two or three a day, all for short trips. His fares were all Spanish and did not tip as well as the foreigners. It was a good thing he and his wife had no children. "I think we could go for a week," I said. "Maybe a little more."

"We'd stay at hotels?"

"Sure, where else?" I put my arms around her. "Would you like that, Monica?"

"And Federico?"

"He'd go with us, of course."

She smiled and hugged me back. "All right, Cate. Let's do it. I would like it."

Yanez tried to hire himself on as the driver, but I told him that I couldn't afford his meals and hotels, and he didn't want to pay for his own.

His wife, padding around in those Spanish flannel slippers, rubber-soled by Pirelli, in their room off the half-darkened kitchen, barked at him in Catalan. He scowled at her, and she barked again. She was, like most Catalan women of her generation, short and extremely sturdy without being fat. I met women like her in the markets; they destroyed you, if you were not quick and strong.

We made a deal and he cleaned out the car. His wife put up a bag of candies for Federico, and we left the next morning, heading south. At Tarragona, we turned inland to Teruel, where I stopped and climbed the mountains while Monica fed Federico. We arrived in Valencia long after dark and found a hotel. We slept late and then at breakfast savored the attention paid to us. We enjoyed the expressions on the faces of the waiters when we snapped at them in Spanish — Monica especially, with her Catalan accent. Then, the car streaming blue fumes, we left the coast and went back inland, to Albacete and from there to Jaén and on down to Málaga, bumping over the roads, looking silently at the hard, sad land, its bare brown mountains, and those small memorials in the driveways of the homes set back from godforsaken dirt roads:

JUAN ALFREDO GUILLERMOS
MURIÓ 5TH DICIEMBRE, 1937

Guardia Civil haunted the entrances and exits to the small villages. They wore heavy, brown leather jackets and rode big motorcycles, or were green shadows in patent leather hats in the stillnesses between stone houses, those streets stamped theirs by the Falangist five red arrows. We came down through the Sierra Nevadas to Granada, bereft now of its Moors, and mingled with their descendants. Federico toddled down walks his namesake must have known, and behind him I strolled with his mother and she told me of Lorca and *Canciones, Romancero gitano, Yerma* and *La Casa de Bernardo Alba.* We held hands. Then I carried Federico through the Court of the Lions and told him about the people who'd built this place. He laughed and played on my face.

At Málaga, before turning north, we walked to the deserted beach, and through air filled with flying sand I pointed toward Africa. "Africa," I said. "Where your father came from. And me. And you, and Federico and millions of people who no longer show it."

Then we drove on through Sevilla and Córdoba, Toledo and Madrid. At Guadalajara, I stopped once again and walked. This time when I returned, Monica said, "Battlefield." She gave me a long oblique glance, a chilling wind suddenly rising and gaining speed over a wide, flat place. "My father told me about the war. Barcelona was in the Red Zone. The soldiers and people going to France came through Barcelona. I know."

"Yes," I said. "In nineteen thirty-six, in Geneva, a little black man warned the world what could happen if the world did nothing to remove the aggressors from his country. Selassie. No one listened and then your war started and then the big one. But even here, even here, if the Republicans had won, the world would be different. Right here that was possible."

"Shhh!" she said to Federico. He was getting fretful. The movement of the car soothed him; motionlessness disturbed him.

"Were you a soldier during the war?" Monica asked.

"Yes." And I knew she was going to ask it.

"Did you kill people?"

Federico looked at me. It was a small person's clear look, taking on the concentric circles of porridge when stirred.

"Yes. I had to."

She sighed. For a second it sounded like the wind outside. She crossed herself.

The final night of our trip back we spent in a converted monastery. Five waiters, all in tuxedos, served us. Monica was gracious in her Paseo de Gracia dress and jewelry, her dark face beaming amusement and tolerance for the provincial folk who had never seen black people and who were peering out of the kitchen and from behind every available door to marvel at the trio of Moros.

We made love long that night, hard and tenderly, and once I thought I felt something wet on her face but I didn't ask about it, for the wine had long since reached its crest and substituted sleep for passion.

After our return to Sitges, the weeks seemed to race in on us. The winds chopping through the mountains were no longer very cold at all. The first Europeans — Swedes, Danes and Germans — began to appear. Merchants became cheerful. Landlords were visible on weekends, puttering about the houses they soon would rent, and mine was already talking about the usual summer increase.

Monica, who had filled out during the winter so that I no longer felt her ribs pushing against her skin when we made love, became more quiet but less accusatory. I lingered longer with Federico García Lorca Jones, building sand castles on the beach and buying him ice cream while the Spanish women smiled their dark approvals. I would start to worry about his life after I'd gone, and then, angrily, stop.

One day I went into Barcelona to arrange with the landlord for Monica and Federico to stay in the house through the summer. It was the same day I bought my plane ticket. Sailing would take too long. I wanted to be overwhelmed quickly by things I knew back in New York and not have to spend days thinking about them or her. I got a stack of pesetas to leave behind, and then I returned home, cradling the bottle of brandy I would drink while telling her that I had to leave, that I had a book being published and that all my life I think I wanted to be a writer and now I was.

The front door was closed. Normally, it would have been open and the screen door closed; normally, there would be wash on the line, some little thing of Monica's or Federico's or mine; normally, they would be in the garden or in the dirt road that ran straight down to the beach; normally, she smiled and waved, and Federico came charging up like a baby bull.

I didn't see them outside. I unlocked the door and walked into the chilly house. I called, and my voice bounced off the tile floors and plaster walls. I called again and started down the hall. Federico's room, across from ours, looked strange. I walked in. His clothes were gone, his toys, bottles. In our room her dresser drawers were empty and there was a note on the bed. The room smelled faintly of Joy; I'd gotten it from one of the black-market operators. I sat down on the bed with its bad springs. With the doors closed, the old Spanish smell of sweet decay, which always made me think of Melville and Benito Cereno's *San Dominick,* tapped at my brain, hung in my nostrils.

I opened the brandy and, drinking from the bottle, read the note. I drank again and then went to see Yanez and his wife. They did not know she'd gone, and his wife said, slapping her own infertile belly, "She is two months pregnant. She said so in the market."

Her note had not said that. I went back to the place where I'd met her and asked the musicians if they'd seen her; they had not. I walked or rode to the places where she might have been, but she was not in any of them. And I had to leave. It was time.

5

IT'S THE RETURNING to familiar places that after a time takes its toll. I didn't know that then. I was ignorant. How could I have known that even the sun had grown tired of its fiery, familiar journey and so on occasion had reversed itself? I didn't know that the moon, too, had wearied of rolling through predetermined cycles and had forsaken for a time its task of tinting the dark with its silver. Such drastic alteration means cataclysm. I had not then met anyone, save Selena, who in protest against the embrace of the familiar had wrought upon himself interior disasters.

It took time for me to discover the old rhythms, to enjoy what I'd enjoyed before. Every impulse within me screamed for me to leave again as soon as I could, to shuck off the noise and dirt and the attitudes of New York, to forsake this whore with the steel and concrete vagina and tongue like glass shards. How could I rest easily after having strolled graceful Ramblas, *plazas, avenidas* and beaches and mountains, all of which, like enciphered stone, still bore the marks of the Phoenicians, Romans and Moors?

"But America is only an extension of Europe," Rupert was saying. We sat blissfully in a midtown air-conditioned restaurant whose walls were covered with sketches of Montmartre. The table was "his," reserved for him whenever he came in. "America is like a Greek colony belonging to Rome. It happens all the time, and then the daughter, for one reason or another, blurs her relationship with her mother."

I would settle back in soon, he was sure, and the memories of Spain would become less sharp. I would even forget about Monica, he suggested, with a smile. I had not told him she was pregnant. In any case, he reminded me, it was in America that I had to make my reputation.

And that reputation was just about ready for launching. He was solicitous and professional during our frequent talks and lunches, and I loved calling for him at his office and being recognized by the secretaries and editors. My dust jacket was already in the lobby showcase, my name in large enough type below the title of the book.

"Ah, yes, Mr. Douglass." Smile. And, almost as if on cue, one editor after another would pass through the lobby, smiling, hand outstretched, floating like soap bubbles little literary chitchat.

Often, the publicity people lunched with us, framing their questions with smiles, dropping the names of reviewers like benevolent spring rain. Chief among these was Maxine Culp, the publicity director. Smiling and touching, stroking and murmuring, she endowed the four syllables in publicity with magical and sexual qualities having nothing to do with her, but much to do with the process of building the reputation of a new author. (Later I would know that there was indeed a sexual connotation to all of this, and that it could be defined simply as an arrangement mutually agreed upon, or otherwise, between the fucker and the fuckee.)

There had not been, Maxine told me, while Rupert's fingers made rapidly closing trenches through his hair, any "negative" advance reviews, only "selling" and "positive" reviews. I did not understand, but it sounded good, as though some specially endowed, faceless legion of supporters was set to wave magic typewriters and produce, *voilà!* a new American writer, piping hot and done to a rich, dark brown turn.

Rupert tended to be reserved at these luncheons, and pulled the reins gently: "Well, it *is* a first novel, and good, yes. But I look for more in his next — " Whether it was with the publicity people or the book crowd, Rupert looked ahead.

I had been living in the Hotel Albert on Tenth Street during these days, and looking for an apartment, which was not very easy if you wanted to live downtown. I felt a strange lack of urgency to renew old ties, except for my son, Glenn. I sensed that old friendships would renew themselves in due course, the way an unconnected but plugged-in electric cord always edges toward metal and spontaneous combustion. I did think of Paul. I even looked glancingly for him along the streets and in restaurants. I had not, though, in truth, called or written to Catherine about Glenn.

I was lucky with the apartment. An old Italian man, who wore a threadbare suit, a spotted tie and a white shirt with a frayed collar, rented me the top floor of a brownstone he had just renovated. He wore a medal on his suit and walked with a cane. He asked if I'd been a soldier during the war, and when I said yes, he rented me the place and told me that he had been a soldier during World War I, serving in the Alps, fighting the Austrians.

"The rats," he said. "Oh, the rats; they were as big as dogs, eating what they ate. Some days they did a lot of eating. It was terrible." He fingered the medal. "When I sleep, I still dream of it. I dream the rats are eating me, that I lie unburied, half-covered with snow, and they are eating me."

Then, for the first time in a long while, I thought of my own dream, of the man trying to get into my foxhole, his motions framed by the stars of the Southern Cross, but I did not want to lose my grip and so said nothing.

"I don't sleep nights," Mr. Storto said. "Then they can't get me. I sleep only during the day. In the daytime they don't come."

I was settling into the new apartment. I had not straightened it out, and was between a dazzling drinking lunch at the Italian Pavillion with Rupert, and a dinner that night with Alex Samuels at the Argenteuil. I was on a Door Store couch, sweating, wondering if the writing life would always be so laced with alcohol, and worrying that I'd never last if it was. I heard on the gray, wooden stairs, which Mr. Storto had not yet covered with asphalt tiles, footsteps, light, clever, and then a voice.

"Hey, Cate! Cate!"

I opened the door to Amos Bookbinder. The sharp angles of his face had vanished; twin pouches of fat on either side had taken their place. I didn't know that the change had been, and still was being, caused by booze and credit-card lunches and dinners in three-star French restaurants.

"How'd you find me?" Spoken, the words revealed to me that I had been hiding. I did not yet know from what.

But Amos was smiling. He strode through the place trailing a sharp cologne. He sat down upon an unpacked crate and through vibrant waves of Beefeater gin asked, "Why didn't you let me know you were back? You're not drinking with another crowd already, are you?" He laughed and slapped his thigh. "Ain't that what that — what Poode always says?"

I shrugged. Habit, glimmerings of Monica. "I wanted to get a few things straightened out before I hit the streets."

"You need more than a month, man?" He studied me with that severe yet approving glance older brothers and grandfathers have. "Y' look good. I been readin' the advance reviews. They're good." He nodded. Between thumb and forefinger on each hand he pinched the creases of his pants and hiked them high enough to reveal the neat ribbing of his Supp-Hose.

"But listen," he said. "When you get tired of your publisher — or even for your next book — talk to me. I'll give you a good contract."

My response, mild surprise, came too slowly.

"What's the matter, whatsa matta," he exploded in a fragmenting iron-gray fury, "you don't think a Negro editor's good enough for you?"

"I — "

He spun on his heel and stopped, his back to me. "Fuck it. Let's go get a drink to celebrate your book."

"I have to get dressed." I was not accustomed to the fury.

"That's all right," Amos said, his voice soft and somehow curled at the ends. "I'll wait. Where's the booze?"

Moving down the street with Amos was like cruising beside a deluxe model of a Cadillac car, yet I moved with him, connected in ways obvious and not, and thought of Selena, whom I would ask after when we stopped. But he got to his questions first.

"How was the pussy over there?"

"Okay," I said. "What little of it I had."

He did not believe me, but, then, black people seldom have believed each other for reasons that are as complex as fine-woven Sardinian weave, and so symptomatic of what we have been and what we have become that psychiatrists will not even begin to sense the boundaries of that existence for another millennium.

Had I seen Richard Wright?

No.

What had he, Amos, been doing?

He'd just signed two first novels, and he wished I'd sign with him. I told him that I would consider that when I finished the next book.

"Seen your friend Paul?"

"No, not yet." Amos was one of those people who spoke more forcefully with his eyes than with his voice, as if in some long-forgotten past he had learned that in silence lay the path to survival.

"I read a couple of his stories in some of those pussy magazines. You really think he can write, huh?"

I said, "I guess he's as good at what he does as I am at what I do."

We were in the bar now, and it was dark and cool and fittingly Spanish. We toasted the book. Amos said expansively, "Things are looking good for me right now, Cate. I can cut it in this white folks' book business. Say, you know Selena Merritt? Used to hang with that white boy, Poode?"

"Yeah. I heard from her. Has she flipped?"

"Just about, but she's doing better." He glanced at his watch. "She writes some pretty good poetry, you know." He stood up from the stool.

"After your dinner let's meet at the Showplace and see Charlie Mingus and Yusef Lateef."

"I'll be tired," I said. "Not to mention drunk."

"Hell, you can sleep late. You don't have to report for work."

"Yes, I do."

"You know what I mean. My wife, when she meets a writer, she wants to know where does he work, what does he *do.*"

I wondered if Catherine had thought that. I must, I told myself, call, now that I was settled.

"Okay," I said to Amos, "I'll meet you later." We had a second drink and he laid atop the bar some bills as crisp and crackling as he was dressed. Dusk, diffused by silver, indicated a gathering of moisture in the air; I cabbed uptown to meet Alex. He greeted me expansively, and the maître d' displayed what I assumed was the proper deference to one about to lay out fifty or sixty bucks for drinks and dinner.

Neat, perfectly formed beads eased down the sides of the martini glasses. We lifted them in toast to the novel. "So you saw Rupert today. He's a good man. Best goddamn editor in town. He'll be editor-in-chief before long and that certainly won't hurt your career, Cate."

We talked about the new book, *Clarissa,* now close to the end, and about the publicity and advertising for the one ready to come out.

"Don't count on a lot of ads now. But you're going to be the best Negro writer in history. Dick Wright's out of the country; the glow will fade from Whittington; Huysmans, while not quite a flash in the pan, always says the same thing. Himes has vanished . . . what's the matter?"

"You got to do better than that, Alex." He had already designed the ball park I was to play in.

"What?"

Did he really not know? Was it all so automatic that no one thought about it? "Nothing," I said. I was afraid to tell him he was a bigot. Ruin my career. Find another agent? Sure, but things were just beginning to *click* for me. Besides, how bad could it be, to be the best Negro writer in history? But the possibility of being — my *wanting* to be — far more kept me silent. At that moment, everything seemed gray and, in a sense

I could not perceive, threatening — a chorus of cellos being bowed in the lower registers.

(Now, how often do I think of what he said? His words were symptomatic of the disease that afflicts my life and the lives of all to whom I belong. The words are no longer spoken, they being in obvious bad taste, the user too targetable, but the disease, in silence, has deepened and is now all the more malignant because of the absence of the words.)

Alex said, "Some change of mood. Seen Paul?"

"No," I said. "Next week."

"His book's coming along, and he's had a couple of near misses with *Esquire* and *The Saturday Evening Post.*"

"Uh-huh."

"Yeah." He nudged me. "How's the lamb? Okay?"

"All right." I felt out of place. I hated the way being there made me feel.

"When do I get to see the new book? I mean, we ought to start thinking of more money than the last time out. Right? The advance reviews have been great."

"Amos Bookbinder said if the money isn't going to be great, he'd make an offer."

At the mention of Amos' name, Alex turned quickly toward me. He opened his mouth, shut it quickly. Then his words, carefully formed, I thought, came out. "You don't want to go over there, Cato."

"Why not?" I said sharply.

He finished chewing and laid down his fork. He touched my forearm for emphasis. "Trust me. You pay me." In a sudden low rage, he said, "Why not trust me? That's not the house for you. Phaeton is not the house for you. Amos is new to the business. He doesn't have a reputation. And the way he's going, he won't acquire one. Rupert is a fine editor and a fine person. He'll do right by you." He was chewing with the viciousness that made me think of Mr. Storto watching rats chew up the bodies of dead soldiers. He sighed over his sweetbreads. "Let's have lunch next week and then we can compare notes on the reviews that should be out this week. Only five days until pub date, Cato."

I was thinking. Amos bellowing at me; Alex disparaging even the discussion of a publishing liaison with Amos. The shape, the monstrous size and shape of this disease. And yet I lowered my eyelids and blinked it away.

By the time we had finished dinner, we had also finished one aspect of our relationship, which would be, for as long as it lasted, different. I refused his offer of a lift, and I walked to the Village, moving slowly, seeing the neighborhoods change. I expected the walk to still the something like panic that was tapping at its eggshell, trying to get out and, in the emergence, becoming quite something else.

In the Showplace, it seemed to me that there was as much madness in Mingus as there was cool in Lateef. Maybe it had to do with the instruments they played. Amos had his feet up on a chair. He flicked glances flecked in red at me and tried to order me a martini.

"Just beer," I said. "That's all I want."

"C'mon, man. Get you a drink."

"Beer, Amos, nothing else."

He dismissed the argument with a wave of his hand.

"Anyway," I said, "when did you start drinking so much? Jolene doesn't like it, I bet."

"You think it's a lot? You think it's a lot?" He spoke fast, his voice pitching itself higher and higher — for the second time that day.

"Shit." I was staring at the three empty martini glasses on the table. "You've been drinking those bombs since this afternoon."

"I can handle 'em, I can handle 'em."

"You all shut up down there," Mingus said. He scowled and shifted his bulk alongside his bass viol.

We shut up. It was strange, my anger seeming to home in on Amos, and his on me, and Mingus' on both of us, and ours on him. Lateef blew his oboe, oblivious of everyone in the house, then switched to the argol, which called up visions of distant desert lands, Tauregs and Mehari camels.

(And now, like so many others, Mingus is gone, a fugitive from "classical music," which did not believe he deserved a place with it, being as he was, and he turned to jazz music to preserve a semblance of sanity; to jazz music to avoid being consumed by bitterness converted to blasting rage. Amos and I had shut up because we recognized Mingus' Abednego to our Shadrach and Meshach.)

One set was enough for me. I liked the music, but things were growing in my head, sour things, and I needed to let that night slip uncelebrated into eternity.

I did not sleep well. I slipped in and out of it like one going through a revolving door. I woke sluggish and evil. I moved about the apartment without purpose. I really looked at things. I touched them. I drank my coffee, which scoured my throat like hot bitumen. My head collected from somewhere and held the wan Billie Holiday tune, *Good Morning*

64

Heartache. But I had soulache. I stared at one of the walls; they were pristine, white with new paint, unhung yet with shelves or pictures, and I thought of running at it full speed, head down, as if to gut Nagurski, Grange and Harmon in one, and split my dolichocephalic head in all its Negroid length right in its center, to leave trails and splatters of red blood and yellow-gray brains and pink bone and black skin and hair thereupon, a Pollock or a Middleton.

I sat at my machine and ripped out a page and replaced it with a fresh sheet and wrote to Catherine, asking if I could have our son for a couple of weeks. I did not write that I needed him, because I did not understand yet that keys were being tested in the lock of my sanity and that in the process of being his father there was palpable, selfless purpose, and, quite possibly, in nothing else. Instinct told me that I needed to begin readying him.

Then, like Mr. Storto, I went to bed, and this time I was released to sleep by the letter I'd written. The day noises of the city ceased, and a silence descended, and I felt that I was slipping into a death shaped like a long, quiet, secret corridor in the Great Pyramid. Set was pursuing me. My son, Horus, was pursuing him, and Isis pursued us all, pausing only to lift the covers of the Canopic jars in which she hoped to find my parts. We rushed on, three mobile collections of the motes of the universe, past sarcophagi and more Canopic jars, until a bright, cold light appeared at the end of the corridor. I rushed faster, the things growing on my feet whispering as I went, and then the shaft was no more and there was nothing under foot save space and a bigger, swelling brightness. Beating my arms like wings, I was swept upward toward the sun, whose heat was already beginning to sear me, and with the eyes of Horus, I beheld far, far below, a man all in white, who cried up at me without a change of expression, "Take care! Take care!"

I THINK I reached for the telephone on its last ring. It seemed to be very heavy, and I was panting when I spoke into it. Rupert was calling to make a lunch date for publication day.

On pub date a congratulatory telegram arrived from my publishing house. There were no reviews in the papers. "Tomorrow, they said at the *Trib*. Before the end of the week, they said at the *Times*," Maxine Culp said at the pub date lunch with Rupert and me.

"And if not," he said, "so what? It's nothing. Happens all the time and not only with first novels."

I was more concerned with my trip to pick up Glenn. Would he know me? Would he like me or the things we would be doing? There had been moments after Catherine said he could indeed visit me, if I came to get him and returned him, when I could not think of Glenn without thinking of Federico, and once I thought of Federico, I wondered whether he and his mother were hungry.

Rupert, for perhaps the fiftieth time since he signed me, raised his glass — not without a certain air of finality — in a toast:

"To *Dissonances*."

"*Dissonances,*" Maxine said.

I said, "Yeah."

Two days later, the afternoon waning, the cab pulled up before my building and deposited me and my son, Glenn, a few feet from Mr. Storto, already moving toward us on the shit-stained sidewalk.

"Mist' Douglass, Mist' Douglass, hello — "

"Hi, Mr. Storto." He glanced at the huge suitcase Catherine had used to pack Glenn's changes in. "Meet my son, Glenn."

"I see, I see," he said, his eyes switching from me to Glenn and back. "Glenn. A nice American name. You didn't tell me. He's a fine boy. Tomorrow, I'll take him for an Italian ice, okay, Glenn?"

I no longer remember the specifics of that visit, the first. Of one thing I am sure, and it is that I tried too hard to be exactly what, I don't know. With his eyes Glenn kept asking: Who *are* you? Why are we like this? Do you *really* like me? Then why aren't we all together? Why don't you like Mom? Why doesn't Mom like you? What's your picture doing on that book? Just who *are* you, anyway? Where do you work? Do you like being by yourself?

We did play catch in Central Park and row a boat; we went to two or three movies. I touched him often.

There were those lunches and dinners with friends who wished to be kind and wanted to see Cato the father, instead of the writer.

I studied my son's face, the shape of his head, the length and breadth of his body while he slept, exhausted with the variety of cartoons he could watch on New York television. It was the same way I used to study Federico while he napped.

Sometimes, mysteriously bidden, I turned and caught him just shifting his eyes away from his study of me. Well. We had to begin somewhere, and that was the time, that summer, when *Dissonances* was published.

The time of Sandra Queensbury, she of the quick hands and quicker tongue.

"Do you suppose we might have lunch? I'd really love to talk to you about a project I have in mind."

The voice was cool, sure of itself and sexually urgent in an uncommon way. Of course I could have lunch.

Sandra Queensbury, I was told, was discussed wherever and whenever writers gathered, drunk or sober. Her stable of writers read like *Who's Who* in American letters. She had grown up with books and publishing in her father's office, and had taken time out only to go to the best schools, foreign and domestic. When her father broke with Milton and Meade and began his own company, Ilium, Sandra fitted in nicely.

For a legend, she was surprisingly young, in her mid-fifties, and so neatly turned out that, for the first few seconds I saw her, I was back in childhood, believing that pretty teachers did not defecate.

I'd arrived before she did, so I watched the maître d' hustle toward me when I was seated at "her" table. I rose, naturally, and we exchanged greetings. As she was sitting and asking after Rupert in the same breath, her martini arrived without her having ordered it, as far as I could tell.

"Your novel — well, I must tell you — do you know anything about dowsing?"

"No." We were both having the smoked salmon.

"Usually people do it with maps, divining rods — " She laughed. "Do you think I'm crazy?"

"Uh — no."

She patted me on the shoulder with fingers that seemed to measure. "With a manuscript or a book," she said, "I begin reading. Then, perhaps I read a certain passage. Something makes me trace a finger over the lines of that passage, and if I feel heat, yes, a definite warmth, I know the writer is special. Your writing gives off such warmth, and flashes too."

I said, "Really?"

"What I had in mind," she said, briskly now, "was an anthology, which you would edit, an anthology whose theme would be race. Something like Locke's *The New Negro*."

Right away I wanted to do it. The money would come in handy, too.

"It's time for an update." She smiled so prettily that I didn't notice her right shoulder had slumped. I didn't believe it was her hand beneath the table tracing quickly and surely over the upper part of my thigh, and then, more sure of itself, stopping in my crotch. With gentle squeezes and strokes, she seemed to be measuring my member, not so much with any kind of subdued or secret passion, but with the dispassionate cool of a surveyor setting numbers for future construction. I was too startled and embarrassed to move; I looked at her the way a bird looks at the snake that is hypnotizing it. "That is what I call more than adequate," she said, laughing softly, removing her hand gradually.

"You think so, really?" I was flustered.

"Ah, yes, yes."

Another round of martinis was placed gently on the table.

"What do you think of the anthology idea?"

"It sounds good."

"I understand that Alex Samuels is your agent, so I must talk with him. If you like, I can get you a better agent. People like Alex, well — "

"What?"

"It's nothing. That's the way things are now. Oh! I must talk to Rupert and explain that I'm not trying to steal you. He's very jealous about his authors. But if you ever — "

"I'm happy."

"Of course you are. And Rupert's a dear. Are you separated or divorced?"

She had done homework. "Divorced."

"I've had four, and I may be working on my fifth. But back to business: How soon can you get started on the anthology?"

"Next month."

"Why don't we have dinner at my apartment and discuss this further? There are some things from the twenties and thirties that I'd like to show you. My father was very active in the Harlem Renaissance."

"Uh — "

"Say this Friday. Seven-thirty."

"Uh — "

We parted in front of the restaurant. I glanced up at the sign: Le Moustier. Wasn't that a section of France where caves had been found in which there were artifacts going back twenty-five thousand years?

The anthology hastened the reunion with Paul.

"You know that story of yours, about the interracial couple?"

"Why you sonofabitch," he said. But there was pleasure in his voice. "Where have you been? I knew you were back. Why'd you wait so long to get in touch? They wouldn't give me your number at your publisher's."

"I was in the Albert until I found a place not too long ago. Then Glenn came — "

"Who's Glenn?"

After a pause I said, "My kid."

"Oh! Yeah, yeah!"

"Then I had to get this place straightened out, and the book — "

"I see they didn't review you in the *Times*. Will they? If not, that's bad, man, very bad." He didn't sound disturbed. "But you did all right everywhere else. Thanks for the copy. Sign it for me, and we'll have to talk about it."

Like hell we would, I thought, then said, "How's Claire? I was a little surprised that you got married."

"She's okay. Still with the dancing. Europe okay?"

"Didn't get around much. Mostly Spain. Thought you were coming."

"We got married instead." He laughed. "Cheaper."

"The gang's okay? I heard from Selena. You give her my address?"

Paul whistled. "Yeah. She's flippin' like crazy. Poode's okay. He'll survive. Kass seems to be doin' all right in Hollywood. Can you believe it? What about the story?"

"Leonard?" I asked, ignoring the question.

"Hasn't changed except for the worse. The story?"

"I'm doing an anthology for Ilium. I'd like to use it."

"Can we gather for a drink, man?"

"Tomorrow. Why don't you and Claire come here? Be good to see you."

"When did you change publishers?"

"It's just a one-shot deal. I'm on a streak, that's all."

"The new book?"

"Almost finished. Yours?"

"Just about, just about. Okay, we'll see you tomorrow. When?"

Rupert had of course grumbled when I told him about Sandra Queensbury's offer. "They don't sell the way novels do," he said. "Not even Martha Foley's collections. Maybe Sandra's got something up her sleeve, and Cate, I sure hope it's not you."

I hoped my laugh was strong enough to be convincing. "I need the money, Rupert, and besides, I'll be finished with *Clarissa* soon."

"Well, I certainly feel better. You know, I can get you some money — "

"I'm okay, now."

He understood. But what he did not understand, nor I, was that I wasn't happy about how having money made me feel. It was strange, because I didn't mean a lot of money, just money where before there had been none. Having it made my spirits lift, and a certain serenity mixed with some cockiness pervaded my being. Perspective, while not lost, became a little blurred. It had been a long, long time since a skill in growing food or finding it, or fishing or hunting, was the only way to avoid sliding down into the abyss; now it was money; the skills had become hobbies or anachronisms.

My profit margin could be increased only at the expense of the contributors, by getting permission to reprint stories, poems and articles cheaply. The less money I paid out, the more I kept for myself. That often meant lying and cheating. Properly priced material required a diligent search; works that were not always good, but had been written by well-known authors, were what most editors wanted in their anthologies. Of course, these always cost more.

I offered Paul a hundred dollars for a seven-thousand-word story. He threw up his hands in mock distress and said, "I'll take it, I'll take it. I don't have a name yet, even though I made the cover of a national magazine."

Satisfied, I bounced against the back of my canvas sling chair. Sling chairs were stylish and inexpensive.

Claire looked very well. "Paul has finished his book four times, Cate," she said, playing with her hair and looking at the ceiling with the air of one close to boredom.

"Naw," Paul said. His glance at her was slow lightning. "I'm just not pleased with the ending."

"Oh, shit," she said, whipping her legs over an angle of the chair, momentarily displaying powerful thighs, a view Paul shared with me through his embarrassment. "You don't really want it *out* there where people can criticize it — "

"What crud!" Paul shouted.

I thought there was more pleading than anger in his voice. He extended his hands, palms up. "It's just not finished . . ."

"Why don't you let Cate read it and — "

I said quickly, "I think we've outgrown that, Claire. But what does Alex say?"

"He's a fucking agent!" she screamed. "What does he know? He sells."

"I'm sure that simply going through the process of reading so many scripts, he's developed some taste through osmosis," I said. Her judgment made me think hard about things I had not wished to think about at all.

"I don't work like Cate," Paul said. "Never did. Different styles, honey."

"I can see that, Paul," she said. Her tone was patronizing. "That's why I thought it was a good idea."

I said, "Listen. Do you want me to get Rupert to look at your book?"

I could feel Claire holding her breath. I heard Mr. Storto downstairs talking loudly to someone.

"All I can say, honey, is that it works or it doesn't," Claire said. Her voice was soft but firm. Perhaps she was beginning to understand that Paul could not accept "no" in his life when it came to writing.

He said, "I'll let Alex be the judge."

I shrugged.

Claire brushed back her hair. She knew.

"When do I get my dough?" Paul asked.

I handed him permissions forms. "Sign both, keep one."

"It's really good seeing you again, Cate," Claire said. "Have you got used to being back?"

"No, not yet."

"When you do me in contributor notes, put down that I spent some time in England and France, okay? Jazz it up a little."

"When was this?" Claire asked. She was puzzled.

Paul glanced at me sheepishly.

"In the army," I said. "I don't mind, man. Paris, Left Bank?"

"But of course," he said, grinning.

"Oh, for Christ's sake," Claire muttered.

"You don't understand," he said sharply.

"The hell I don't."

"How's your father?" My timing was good. The heat went out of them. I sensed that Claire was more interested in his response than I was.

Paul hunched his shoulders. "Don't know. Last I heard, he was all right."

Claire added, "We never hear from him."

Paul said nothing. He looked very tired and pale, and while Claire was in the bathroom, he said softly, quickly, "I think I goofed. I don't think I should've married her."

The evening bent under its own weight and finally, reluctantly, it seemed to me, they said goodbye. After I closed my door, I could hear them talking sharply on the way down.

7

ROUTE 129 flows black, asphalt softening, the power lines beside it singing in midsummer, through the center of Middlebury College's Bread Loaf campus on the western slope of the Green Mountains. The buildings were white trimmed in green, and set gently back into the landscape, as though not to disturb it. I had not told Paul about my coming here.

A year had passed and I had buried myself in work, completing Sandra's anthology and compiling notes for another novel. There had been of course the visits with Glenn, the dinners with Paul and Claire and two or three less than satisfactory affairs, all ended by mutual agreement. Mostly, I had worked and had been satisfied. It was time to take a break now.

All through our time in college Paul and I had been advised by writers' magazines and bulletin-board notices that here at Bread Loaf, summer after summer, the crème de la crème of the literary world gathered to exchange ideas, relax and enjoy the scenery, all this overseen by Mr. Robert Frost in nearby Ripton. Wait, I thought. Wait until I get back and drop *this* on ole Paul.

I shared a room in the cottage with Ike Plunkett. I supposed this discreet arrangement had been made because we were black. Ike was tall and lean. He had cool, almost innocent eyes, but he also possessed a pattern of speech that held a wide range of insinuation.

If for a moment I had been jarred by our segregation, even though it may have been intended to put us at ease, I was ultimately glad. The others in the cottage were petty, often dull and self-centered. Roye Yearing was an exception.

He was a hulking, gray-skinned man who seemed to be both haunted and driven by ghosts the rest of us couldn't see, let alone understand. Roye was quiet, almost reticent, until he had had a few drinks. It was his car we used nearly every morning to drive into Vergennes, arriving at precisely the time the state liquor store opened.

The women fellows and scholars lived in cottages across the road. Among them was Selena Merritt. She kissed me on the cheek when we met, but from that moment on said little either to Ike or to me, even during those periods in the afternoon when we worked our way toward one hangover after the other, having discovered within the first few days that not much of substance was to be expected from the staff of lecturers or the workshop leaders.

Instead of attending the sessions, we played tennis, went swimming, sunbathed, went into Vergennes for more booze.

Invariably, while the schoolteachers and literary groupies rushed to breakfast over grass still thick with dew, we slept late, staggered up for lunch and the games or the trip into town; at three, the sessions ending, the herding instinct brought us together, where, once again, we began the day's drinking until five.

At that hour the staff, scholars and fellows gathered in the staff cottage for drinks and literary gossip. It was traditional that a scholar or fellow serve drinks to the staff. A tradition, I supposed, that was designed to keep people in their places.

Tonight it was Ike's turn to serve, but he remained seated, licking his lips exaggeratedly over a huge drink he'd made for himself. The staff turned its collective gaze on him — and on me and Selena as well — though it seemed gentler when it fell on her. They shuffled about, hands in their pockets or tightly gripping their pocketbooks, trying not to stare at Ike.

One of the staff, clearing his throat, said, "Plunkett, I believe you're doing the honors this afternoon, hummmmm?"

"No, Plunkett ain't," Ike said. The "ain't" was loud. "Marse Lincum done freed us slaves."

For a second Selena went from black (or somewhat so) to ashen white. Someone chuckled. Someone else jogged in breathing heavily, looking for a Coke. Roye Yearing, already deep into the wind, thrust his head forward and shifted his glance from the staff member to Ike and back again, trying to understand what was happening.

The director sighed and led the way to the bar to fix his own drink. *God,* he seemed to be thinking, *why did we let these niggers come?*

"Tradition, my ass," Ike muttered to me as, one by one, the staff helped themselves to the booze. The people of our cottage surreptitiously slapped Ike's back, but an unspoken threat was framed by the staff's glances at Ike.

Curiously, no one had minded the tradition of servitude until Ike mutinied, and later that night, as though to celebrate that mutiny, we gathered in a field not far from the cottage and built a fire. As we lay in the cooling grass under the spectacular sky, I wondered why the heavens seemed to be so much more dazzling in Vermont than anywhere else.

Roye Yearing, now quite drunk, was proclaiming yet again that he was the best fucking writer in the world, the very fucking best. Fuck everybody. Hic!

Ike, making that affricative, clicked sound so many black people make when exasperated, said, "Roye, goddamn it, I'm tired of hearing how good you are — "

"Right, Ike. The fucking best."

There was always a lingering, desperate quality in Roye's voice when he talked that way; we heard it within ourselves and came to like Yearing for daring to voice what we could not.

Ike snarled in disgust and we laughed softly. Sounds were coming from the cottages, through whose windows shone wan lights, small picture screens across which figures moved, giving off disembodied laughter and drunken yelps. Our group began to break up.

"Night, Selena!" Ike called. She was easing off with a fellow who was in the cottage next to ours.

"This afternoon," Ike said when we were alone, moving closer to the dying fire, "I ran into Selena. She was very friendly. We talked and walked, and she looked that way. We peeled off on a trail and found a spot where we could, you know, sit and be alone. You know how a woman will be with you, smiling and carrying on, obviously waiting for you to say the right words or to do the right thing?"

"Yeah, I know."

"We talked about writing, family problems and so on. We held hands. We kissed. I started to ease up her dress and lay her down and, man, she went suddenly stiff. Begged me to stop. You know, you get to that point and your dick's as hard as times in 'twenty-nine, and here the woman's closin' the door and screechin' for you to stop knockin' on it. Well! Is *that* a come-on? Is that what gives her her kicks, like pretending rape or somethin'? You don't know. You just keep on.

"Her eyes went outa focus. Rolled up, and she starts foamin' at the mouth. So she ain't foolin'. I fixed her clothes and sat her up. Joint's limp as wet macaroni anyway. I held her until she seemed to be okay."

I said, "I thought she had problems but I didn't know they were that bad."

Ike took a long pull from the bottle of gin and passed it to me. "And that silly Roye," he said. "Why does he have to get so drunk every day? We're the ones who ought to be falling-down drunk behind this jive literary scene."

I passed back the bottle; it was almost empty. I thought of what Mr. Johnson had said about writers being in the bottle.

"Shit," I said, "I'm not going to let them do that to me. I'm not going to pickle my liver, dick or brains."

"It's the soul you really got to watch," Ike said. He turned up the bottle and finished it.

We got up and started for the cottage. Bread Loaf had so far been a bust for me, more illusion than substance. I was not sure I wanted to stay until the end of the period. I wondered how Paul would have liked it. He would not have felt an outsider, as I did, as Ike did. The things that were said during the lectures might have had appeal for him; I didn't know.

Around ten the next morning, my thoughts turned to leaving, I walked slowly through the woods. I had come because for Paul and me Bread Loaf had been such a special symbol during our college days. Maybe it had changed. Maybe I had changed.

Ike was definitely going to stay. "New York isn't going anywhere," he had said. He had had a conference with one of the staff, who told him that he should always put into his work something about how much Negroes hated whites.

"Oh," Ike responded. "Why should I?"

"It's the truth and it sells."

"Okay," Ike said. "Would your magazine buy this story?"

The staff person said, "No. We don't handle race-related material."

"You're fulla shit," Ike told him. He had not returned for additional conferences.

Now I was following a footpath, walking slowly, watching blades of grass spring upright, released from the weight of the dew. It was pleasant, moving through the mottled shadows cast by the climbing, warming sun.

76

I smelled wild mint as I paused by a brook to look for trout. I moved closer to the water, peering in, listening to the sounds it made when it flowed between crannies, sucking and foaming.

I remained motionless, hearing the water, the bird cries and, in the distance, the voices of the people over near the cottages.

She must have seen me before I saw her.

I had noticed her before, walking through the campus alone, always carrying a yellow folder. It lay beside her now, warped and twisted. It was easy to see that this woman was angry.

"Hullo," I said.

"Hi." She tried to smile, but it went as quickly as it had come. She flicked at her eyes with her fingers.

"Anything wrong?" I asked.

"No. Everything."

The folder looked as though she'd tried to tear it.

I hunkered down near her. "Cigarette?"

She took one and I lighted it for her. I had one too. "How's it going?"

"Terrible."

"Oh." I tried to recall what someone had said about her, but couldn't. "You're in the poetry seminar?"

"Wrong. I was. But I'm going home today. I think."

"Uh-huh. Have they helped you? Hey, look at that trout." I pointed.

"Yes, I see it."

"Have they?"

"Oh, why do you ask?"

"Because they can't help everybody. Some of us are not capable of helping anybody." I picked up the folder and tried to straighten it out. "May I look?"

"No!" She snatched it out of my hand, and I was rising, going, fuck it. "That bastard!" she shouted, but the woods gave her nothing back. She said less loudly, "To tell someone that they had wasted time and money coming here, that I'd never be a poet!" I stopped.

"They think they have to say something," I said. "They get paid."

"I wouldn't want to be a poet and have to associate with such heartless, crude, backbiting people — "

"Yeah, it's a strain. I've been thinking about going home, too."

"But you've published. You're a novelist."

It warmed me that she knew something about me.

"What can they teach you?" she asked.

"Nothing. I don't know that I came to be taught, but maybe there was something. What did you think they could teach you — the words, the feeling, the form? Those are individual things, you know. Uh, what's your name?"

"Allis."

"Allis. You know, they can talk about them or show you how other poets use those things, but you teach yourself, really, the way a housewife teaches herself to cook and bake without the recipes. Anyway, maybe you shouldn't leave until old Frost puts in an appearance."

"In only one lousy hour," she said, "I've come to hate and despise his lovely, dark and deep woods."

We finished the cigarettes.

"Well, you shouldn't let them run you out," I said.

"Why are you going?"

I watched the water splay out over a flat rock. "Because I keep discovering that I have to teach myself. If I hadn't come, though, I'd always think I missed a lot. Something I know, yet don't want to know, was reinforced for me. I was out here thinking about it." I asked, "Want to walk?"

She nodded and got up.

"You forgot your folder."

"I didn't forget it. Could you tear it up for me? I don't want someone to find and return it to me."

"How many poems in there?"

"Eighteen."

"You have copies?"

"No. I don't want copies."

"You sure about this?"

"Yes, yes, I'm sure."

I picked it up. "Tell you what. I'll start it for you, but you finish it."

She studied my face for a long time, then said, "Oh, all right."

When it was finished, we walked without talking until we came to a small waterfall. We climbed up beside it to a ledge and sat down and smoked again.

"Nice spot," I said.

With a heavy sigh she lay down in a patch of sunlight. "Yes."

"You shouldn't quit, Allis."

"He may be right," she said quietly. "Allis Greenberg may indeed be a flop as a poet. It was just the way, the awful way, he told me."

"Ah, well — "

"You live in New York, don't you?"

"Yeah. You?"

"Yes. May I call you Cato? Cato — "

I said, "America, especially the American South, was very big on things and names Greek and Roman. Cato was a high-toned name they gave to some slaves. In Rome, there was a Dionysius Cato; nobody knows anything about him. There was a Valerius Cato, no relation to our Catos, who was a poet — used hexameter. Of the real Catos there was the Elder who was also the Censor. He fought against Hannibal, Third Punic War. His son, Marcus, was a soldier and a consul, and then *his* son, Marcus, Cato the Younger." I paused to smile at her. She smiled back. "He was a Stoic. Fought against Spartacus. Being fair was his undoing, but that was said to be an old family trait. This Cato sided with Pompey against Caesar and when Caesar won the battle of Thapsus, Cato committed suicide out of a sense of fairness for having deserted Caesar in the first place. His death was considered courageous and noble. He was the last Republican to stand against the dictators. That's about all I can tell you about Cato, which you may call me."

She laughed, flashing gray-green eyes at me. "Jesus, you sound like an encyclopedia."

I laughed too.

We sat there several moments without saying anything, until she, stirring, her body telegraphing that she was going to ask something, said, "What makes one a writer?"

I tossed a twig over the ledge into the waterfall. "I don't know and I don't think I ever will."

"Ummm," she said.

"Allis. I'd like to invite you to a picnic this afternoon, right here, with wine and cold cheeseburgers."

"I think," she said, "we can get tuna fish sandwiches instead of cold cheeseburgers."

OH, GOD, Allis says, when we enter the funeral parlor.

She does not like to be near death or close to where it is being lamented. She remembers her father and sometimes, even now, thinks that she hastened his death by her marriage to me. I never listen to such rationalizations. He was going to die when he was supposed to die, and our marriage altered the schedule of that event not one bit. But it causes her to watch Mack very carefully so that she can anticipate any leaning toward his becoming religious. Her father was a practicing Jew.

Many of our friends, themselves atheists, have been confronted by their children, who have wished to join or attend churches and synagogues, as if to vault the religious void created by their parents, who believed that working intellect was quite enough.

Yes, Allis tries to anticipate. She has closed her mind to the probability that our son, if he chooses to become a Jew, will be the kind of tolerated Jew, if he is lucky, that Sammy Davis, Jr., was. Mack is not now, nor will he ever be, if I read him correctly after these twelve years of his life, a song-and-dance man. Although she realizes it very well, Allis does not wish to believe that Jews know how to say nigger.

I protect my sons. I kick ass when it comes to my sons, for I do not want them to be so hurt that that hurt can be converted into self-destruction. I won't tolerate it.

I apply the principle of vaccination — giving a little of what you may get in larger doses, fatal doses — in order to build up immunity. I told this son, Mack, when he was younger and asked about things:

You are and will be, to many different kinds of people, just a nigger. What you think of, and what you do for, yourself is the important thing. Got it?

Got it, but —

What?

Why do all the black kids call each other ah, er — that name?

Huh? I was thinking of a ditty I'd heard him sing to himself in his room:

> A fight! A fight!
> A nigger and white!
> If the nigger don't win,
> We'll all jump in!

He said, Why do they?

I guess they don't have much respect down deep for themselves or each other. Maybe they haven't been talked to by their parents.

They called me that.

Ah, I say, well.

Aren't you gonna *say* anything?

They call me that, too, when they think.

You?

Yes.

Shit!

Mack! Mack. But I got it together here, you know, respect. How could I be Mack Douglass' father and not respect myself?

Glenn, of course, long ago passed through the crucible that fires the soul and sears the brain far darker than the color of his skin. And Alejo, pobrecito Alejo! *There, growing up, he had not even the rind-bitter solace that many others were being called Moros, too. Like grains of sand, from one end of the world to the other, these hurts grow together in a mighty, universal desiccation of all that composes life. I cry that I could not hold Alejo's hand while talking gold into his blackness.*

Mack seemed to be occupied with some heavy thought. His eyes searched my face as though all his previous examinations, the hundreds of thousands of them, had failed to reveal what he now sought.

What? I respond to Allis, her sudden stopping on the carpeted floor. She inclines her head toward a placard.

PAUL KAMINSKY (CUMMINGS) PARLOR 3

We head down the softly lighted hall to Parlor 3. This makes me . . . She breaks off.

I know. Death feels very close to her now. Me. Close to me, because we were the same age, Paul and I. I say, C'mon. I don't think that, and you're almost my age.

That's the furthest item in her mind. Allis, although I may not be there, is determined to see her grandchildren, Mack's kids. I have no doubt that she will live until then, however long it takes. And she should.

The box is all.

Unadorned, it sits alone on a foot-high stage. We walk softly into the parlor, glance about, then slide into an aisle. Rabbi Kaminsky sits apart from Betsy and the kids. Well, he does not know them.

Rushing down the stairs so long ago, Paul's father seemed like a huge man — taller, broader, more ferocious-looking. Now, he seems to have been melted down by a long, searing process. This, then, is the man who, in Paul's fiction, his early fiction, was the socialist, Harry Bridges' confidant.

He looks like Paul, Allis whispers.

Yes, I say.

I wonder about my own father, his golden smile, his stinking cigars. I didn't love him and I didn't hate him; I did not really know him. His advice to me when I reached my fourteenth birthday was that I should get me some rubbers. He was three years too late.

I wonder how it felt to freeze to death while drowning. I hope he was snocked, unable to feel anything. When I think of him, I think of Malaparte's descriptions of soldiers frozen to death in Lake Ladoga, staring sightlessly up at him while he stood on the surface of the iced-over water. It must have been like peering down at specimens from a horrible epidemic. I know that in the first second of plunging into freezing water, the sensation that flashes through the legs is one of instant, gratifying warmth. What a marvelous machine the body is. But then the machine quits and the materials of which it is composed go the way of all matter in that situation.

What? Allis asks in a whisper.

Nothing, I answer. I had sighed.

Paul's father stands; the parlor stills. He moves slowly to the coffin. He straightens, and his eyes, a weary shade of blue behind his bifocals, look out disconsolately at the rows of people, then slide down to the coffin. He leans upon it, his fingertips like small rays emerging from the blackness of the cuff of his jacket. The fingertips begin to tremble, and *I am Paul feeling my father's ancient fingers trembling upon my pine box. How out of joint . . .*

It is strange how in his grief Paul's father reminds me of Graenum; I can almost measure the accumulations of weariness because of deeds half or undone, realizations met far too late to do anything about them.

"Hah!" he said when I entered his apartment in the ILGWU Houses. "Medowitz tells me that you want to marry a Jewish girl. So!"

We shook hands. He was all in black, save for a white shirt opened at the neck and a gray sweater with a hole in it under his jacket. His yarmulka was cocked crazily on both the back and side of his head. He looked up at me, for he was a small man, studying, his hands resting easily in his pockets. "Are you a revolutionary?"

The question gave me pause; then I said, "Some people think so."

"And you?"

"I think so, yes."

"Come, let's have a drink." He led me by the elbow across the room and poured thick, silvery slivovitz into two small glasses. He knocked his back. I did the same. He filled the glasses again and we sat down.

"Mr. Douglass, let me ask you — the girl's father?"

"He won't see me."

"Her mother?"

"Dead."

He cocked his head and squinted one eye. "Why should you want to do this? What will the father do for you? A revolutionary should move on his own terms. You think if you convert he'll like you?"

"Rabbi Gordon, I don't know. I wanted to help Allis maintain her ties with her family."

"She asked you to do this?"

"No."

"You didn't ask her to convert — what're you, Christian or Muslim?"

"Nothing."

He wagged a finger at me. "Where did you start?"

"I guess you'd call it Christian."

"And now, you any kind of a religious man?"

"No, not in a religious sense."

"Why not?"

"It's all shit."

"Ahhah," he said, running an index finger back and forth across his lips. "Ahhah. Ahhah. Judaism too?" With a smile.

"Yes."

"Would she want you to do this? It's not like you were going to temple every Saturday when you met?"

"Rabbi — "

"Call me Graenum. What's your first name?"

"Cato."

"Cato? What kind of a name is that?"

"Roman."

"Roman. I see, I see." He looked puzzled. Where would I get a Roman name? He said, "But you were saying, about this Allis — "

"I think she would be pleased, not for her, but for her father. She happens to like her father. She always got along well with him. She has no other family except cousins and aunts and uncles, things like that."

"But you don't really want to do it, do you?"

"No."

His laugh was soft. "There is a little — arrogance? — about it, eh? Well, comes the revolution," he said in such a way as to make me think that not since he'd left Europe had he had any real faith in revolutions. "You're a good fellow, I can tell."

"How?"

"I'm a rabbi." He laughed again and moved closer to me, tapped me on my knee. "C'mon, son, c'mon. You think if you convert, never mind your obvious lack of faith, he's gonna love you? You can be the most famous writer in the world — Medowitz told me you're a writer — the most famous, and you know something? Her father's not gonna love you, ever." Like an actor he held the level of his voice up, so that I waited for the next line. "And I don't have to tell you why."

He poured again, sipped and set his glass down, then tented his fingers. "If you want, I can give you a piece of paper that says you're circumcised, take a drop of blood and all that — "

"I am circumcised."

Graenum laughed loud and merrily. "Who isn't these days? So tell your prospective father-in-law. My advice is this: Fuck it. Go to City Hall. Get married. Stay healthy, have children and prosper." A weariness had entered his voice, edged with a rage that had worn out a long, long time ago. "I could give you nonsense, but this is a realistic world, my friend. If her father doesn't like you now, all the Jewish papers in this universe will not help you. After all, we're just like everyone else, no better, no worse. We are chosen just like all others. Go to City Hall."

His teeth click. Paul's father's teeth click as he begins the service and I glance around in time to see Mark Medowitz slide into a seat.

O Lord, what is man that thou shouldst notice him?

The sight of Mark, whom I have not seen in at least a decade, shocks me. His beard and hair are white, though both are stylishly cut. I wonder if he is glad to be back in New York, away from television and back with print. Do I look as old? Probably not; we age well, we are always told.

There is choked anger in Rabbi Kaminsky's voice. Allis, whispering the words along with him, looks quickly at him: *What is mortal man that thou shouldst consider him?* A tiny sob escapes him; we know what he is thinking. He pauses, his fingers now trembling upon the box the way fingers seek the frets on a guitar. They steady.

Man is like a breath;
His days are like a passing shadow.

Three rows in front of us an immense lady turns and smiles at me. I smile back. It is not until she turns away that I realize that she is Dorothea Blue-Sky, Leonard's widow. I feel a slight warming in my member. Perhaps the reaction is very ancient, dating from the time that fat women were the most desirable; Venus of Willendorf, Ati of Punt.

The young man beside her glances back at me. He resembles both Leonard and Dylan Thomas. Leonard adored Thomas. Another glance. I imagine his mother's whisper: "That's Cato Caldwell Douglass."

He flourishes in the morning . . .

It was Leonard who called to tell me that Paul had placed his novel, and when Paul himself reached me, two hours later, I was still angry: Why hadn't Paul himself called first? Why had I been made to feel that it was Paul, Leonard, et al., against me? That had been very implicit in Leonard's voice.

"So. I hear you had a good trip to Europe," Leonard said. "And the novel and Bread Loaf and the anthology — we have a lot of catching up to do."

"Are we in a race, Leonard?"

He laughed.

I asked, "How's your stuff going?"

"It goes, like — it's going."

"Yeah. Poetry's rough."

"I'll make it."

A conversation like that is filled with holes — even the words don't mean that much — and finally we quit; we would see each other at Paul's that evening.

"How come I had to get the word from Leonard?" I said, when Paul called.

"He called?" The surprise in his voice was not genuine. "Aw, I meant to get to you sooner. Something came up."

"Yeah," I said. "Coopersmith, huh? What's the advance?"

"Same as yours; three," he said. His voice seemed to curve. "You're coming over for the celebration tonight, aren't you? You gotta."

"Oh, I'm coming, I wouldn't miss that, Paul. Can I bring a couple of people?"

"The more the merrier — if they bring booze."

I called Allis. Would she be home later, much later? Yes. What time had I in mind? After midnight. Then I would be sleeping over? Yes, I said. That would be a good idea. Also, it would give her time to finish up some paperwork for her job at Cumer, Slate and Finch. Fund-raisers.

I called Ike Plunkett and Amos Bookbinder, who were talking contract, and arranged to meet them at a bar uptown and from there go to the party.

I started walking; it was autumn, my time of year. The bar was one I knew would be hospitable to us, for the Upper West Side was not an altogether friendly neighborhood then. Amos brought gin and vermouth, Ike had Scotch, and I had gin.

"Coopersmith's doesn't pay three grand for a first novel," Amos said, midway through his first martini. "Paul lied to you. I can get the exact figure if you want."

"No. What'll you pay Ike?"

"Shall I tell him, Ike?"

Ike said, "Why not? It's only money."

"Twenty-five hundred and his is a small novel, sixty-five thousand words." Mine had been a hundred thousand. The new one, as far as I could tell, would be longer.

"You know why your boy lied to you, doncha?" Ike said.

"Sure," I said. "Shit, yes." I turned away. I hated being put on the defensive, hated their smirks, because Paul was white and my friend. "It's all so childish."

Amos laughed. "But very, very old. You all's concern should be whether or not they're gonna let you go by John Whittington."

How to describe those days when we all, occupied with the physical and psychological demands of running the race, as though we were charioteers in a Roman circus, mounted our machines, eyes fixed on the acclaim raining down from the Literary Establishment upon John Greenleaf Whittington? Or we could have been poised on our marks like Eulace Peacocks, Jesse Owenses, Ralph Metcalfes, Archie Williamses or Cornelius Johnsons, deep in the bowels of the Berlin Stadium, "American Auxiliaries," awaiting the gun. Leonard had been right; there was a race and a race and a race, though we had not known, just as our counterparts a quarter-century before had not known until our race, the Chitlinswitch Special, was over, forgotten, done with; ours was only a heat. Whittington and two or three others were in the finals.

We sensed before we allowed ourselves to know that they had been sent to guard the approaches to the Pyramids from the other Africans who were always disembarking along the nearby Nile.

Perhaps it was Richard Wright's sudden death in Paris that had created the race. Then had come the steady flow of rumor and disjointed pieces of information, and more than once I remembered what Sandra Queensbury would tell me. But not then. Not in the bar that night.

Then I felt as Ike did — he'd winked at me as though to suggest that Amos had just landed from another planet and obviously did not understand the situation, which was simply this: WHOever guarded the approaches was going to have to give way before us.

The party was already going, folk singers in one corner, dart throwers in the bathroom, the drinkers with their bottles in the kitchen. Paul embraced me and raised a gleeful shout when we deposited our booze with him. "Hey, man. Glad you got here. Did you catch Leonard? Fantastic. What, no women? You picking up here? Let's talk when we can. See Claire? Wow, what a fuckin' mob, but great, huh? God, it's good to see you."

He was high, feeling good, magnanimous and explosive with laughter. I liked him that way.

Dorothea Blue-Sky was pregnant, delivery imminent, or so it seemed, and looking at her through the crush of loud, well-fed people when we turned from Paul, who was already engaged in three different conversations,

I thought of Monica in her Spanish silence and poverty; I wondered about Federico and my own child.

"And why, pray tell, are you looking so sad?"

It was Selena Merritt, wriggling uncomfortably in the arm Amos had thrown around her. She was smiling down at me because I had flopped on the floor; moving about was useless. I moved over. She sat down and kissed me on the cheek.

"Hello, Selena."

"Why?"

"Looking so sad?"

"Yes."

"I was thinking of something sad."

"I'ma get a drink," Amos said, and vanished.

"You're gonna talk to me now, huh?" I said to Selena.

"Cato, darling, I always talk to you." Her laugh was like the clinking of ice cubes.

Poode appeared, carrying two drinks. He gave one to Selena and crouched down beside us. We shook hands.

"How've you been, Cate? Been a long time."

"Yeah. I hear you're with *Reviews*."

"Right. Waiting for the old hands to die. Say, I liked your book."

Pouting, Selena said, "Yes, but why didn't you review it?"

She was awfully sexy when she pouted like that. I had seen her like this only with Poode.

"Sweetheart," he said, after kissing her, sucking on her lips, and she on his, "I'm only a rung on a very tall ladder. I tried to get it in."

She giggled.

"What?" Poode said.

"I tried to get it in," she said, laughing. He laughed too.

Where, I wondered, was his Mavis? They kissed again and I crept away, the sound of Leonard's voice now striking my ears in familiar metered tones. Drunk, now, weaving in a corner, his eyes fixed on a vision the rest of us could not see, he recited into the stilling rooms, the words falling and rising,

Good men . . .
> *Wild men . . .*
>> *Grave men, near death, who see with blinding sight . . .*

It was Dylan Thomas and not, Leonard Blue-Sky and not, a strange synthesis, and the writers, actors, dancers, the dart throwers and drinkers, the people, glanced from Dorothea's huge belly (to be Dylan Blue-Sky) to the sweating, shining face of her husband. Finishing the last line, which bounds upward for two words and then slants down, Leonard, even as people lifted their hands to clap, assumed a humbled, bent posture, though still weaving; a look of cunning anticipation replaced the severe/serene expression he'd worn while reciting Thomas and his voice was pitched higher as he spoke:

Air a-gittin cool and coolah
Frost a-comin in de night

and he did the whole Dunbar poem, winking at me, at Amos, at Ike and at Selena, did it in dialect as Dunbar wrote it. I felt a deep shame as his voice creaked out, a perfect imitation of an old man talking to or thinking about the strutting turkey who is unable to read the signs of the times, and the shame was that I had never thought of Leonard and Paul Laurence Dunbar together; Dylan Thomas and the others, yes, but Dunbar, never. Then why would he never talk to me, never *get down?*

Ah, he had been so very, very far ahead, had already reached the peak (his posthumously published volumes, three of them, including what is now known as "Native American" verse, thundered briefly through the universe, like rocks metamorphosed, and then were buried under till), and stood weaving at what proved to be not a peak after all, but an abyss, and then really got down to the serious business of drinking himself to death in a thousand bars, some better than Dylan Thomas' White Horse on Hudson Street, but many, many of them a hundred times worse, then he fell in.

"Sign him," I said to Amos. "Sign him."

A man who made love to words like that and let them make love to him . . . "Sign him."

"I don't fuck with poetry, man. It doesn't sell," he said.

We, Leonard and I, never had a talk, the talk I think we should have had. He did not want to admit to race, nor to having the fears it imposes, nor to perceiving the certainty of victimization because of it; Leonard wished to be the pure artist, a man of all men and a scribe for all of their seasons. When he saw, before the rest of us, that he had been born far too soon, he hastened out of his life, perhaps so that he could return to another. He still had time left then, as I eased away from the party; it was growing late and the people raucous. Ike had found the ear of Poode's embittered girl, Mavis, who had long since stopped launching withering glances at Poode and Selena, and Amos had already gone. I went down the stairs and hearing noises coming from a closet built under them, disregarded my first instinct, which was to ignore them, and opened the door and quickly closed it, having seen Claire going down on a guy from the New York City Ballet. I went out into the street, carrying with me her hot eyes rolled toward me, fear and hatred colliding with her desire.

I hurried to Allis.

PAUL'S NOVEL, *Western Directions,* was published the next spring. It was about a beatnik cowboy who is involved in a range war on the side of the good guys. Selena's first book of poetry was due out soon, and its publication would coincide with the opening of a long one-act play of hers, *Ann Zinga of the Congo.* A joint party was planned at the Limelight down in the Village. But I did not go, for the evening before, a Friday, Sandra Queensbury picked me up for a trip to West Hampton, where we would spend the weekend.

Her house (and her husband's) was an overlarge Cape Cod with weathered gray shakes. It was set among the dunes, and its front faced the sea, whose waves desultorily boomed against the beach. She seemed happy there, calmed, and watching her move from place to place, humming, I wondered if when I reached my fifties I would exude as much sex in a male way as she did in a female way. I hoped so. We ate, drank and made love, and ate, drank and made love again. We talked of our anthology, which had had good library and school sales. Saturday we left the bed only to shower and eat; we brought drinks back to bed and read until, once again, we felt like making love. In between, propped up in bed, she read manuscripts.

While I slept Sunday morning, Sandra drove into the village and brought back the papers, the *Times,* the *Tribune* and *Reviews.* Poode had written a review of three children's books. I mentioned it.

"I didn't realize you knew Jeremy," she said.

"Oh," I said. "Do you?"

"Of course. Knew his folks and most of his relatives. What do you think of him?" She removed her glasses, set aside a manuscript.

"He's all right, I guess."

Sandra reached over to the tray, picked up some toast and leisurely spread strawberry jam on it. "Know anything about him?"

The way she said "about" made me lower the paper to study her.

"Yale. A little conservative. Single."

"That all?" She smiled.

I thought, then said, "Yes. *Is* there anything else?"

"Ah, yes." She said it rather heavily, I thought. I went back to the paper, wondering what it was.

"Interested, Cate?"

"No." But I was.

"You fraud," she said, kissing me. She smelled of the strawberry jam. "Of course you are. You should be."

"Well, tell me."

Her eyes twinkled. "I really shouldn't."

"Then why'd you bring it up?"

"You brought up his name," she said. "Then I was tempted to tell."

I wished I were with Allis. Suddenly I couldn't explain to myself why I was here.

Sandra placed her feet in my crotch and wiggled her toes. "What'll you give me if I tell?"

The sun was streaming into the bedroom, turning gold everything it touched. I wondered what Mr. Queensbury (though that wasn't his name; I'd never heard his name; Queensbury was Sandra's maiden name) was like in this room.

Sandra brushed back her hair, straining her chin forward as she did so. "I annoy you now, don't I?" Gently, she forced the paper down and then turned directly toward me, her legs crossed. She took my hands and placed them upon her upper thighs.

She said, "Cate, you must've guessed that I like young men and that you certainly are not the first to have come here or to have bedded me in my own apartment in Manhattan. Yes?" She smiled. "Yet I'm not altogether a dirty old woman."

I said nothing; just watched her measuring her words. "I'm going to tell you about Jeremy, not because you're good in bed, but because you are, I think, just good in a lot of special ways." She chucked me under the chin. "It shows, darling, and it's lovable, but there is a world out there, outside this bedroom and all that sun and sea, that's a kind of nightmare and certain things happen all the time. I know about most of those things; people like me, we know them."

"And people like me?"

"People like you always suspect what we know to be fact and, of course, we always deny the facts. Jeremy. He's a nice enough young man; he'll go very far, I believe; further than most Negroes will go in this business."

And now she lighted a cigarette and took a sip of coffee that had long since grown cold. People like me, I thought.

"Oh," I said.

"Quite right," she said. "Had you suspected at all?"

"No."

"It really is too bad," she said, "that you're so dark — though I love it; there remains a kind of purity in that that exists nowhere else. All this Scotch-Irish, French-Italian, Polish-German foolishness — you know Woodrow Wilson didn't trust that. During the First World War he insisted that no hyphenated Americans guard Washington. The nation's capital was guarded by Negroes. Ironic . . ."

My attention had strayed. She saw it.

"Cate, if you were the color of Jeremy, in this book world not even the sky would limit the distance you could travel. You would be one of the select, a priest, a monk shuffling through the corridors of a musty castle, privy to special knowledge.

"Don't you love books, words? You do. I know you do. Something about them. Remember Bradbury's story? The German book-burnings? Then there are those quaint American school boards and other apple pie groups that decide which books shall be available to the public. A banned book is a burned book."

She pulled the sheet up to her chin and peered at me. I had never seen her face so expressionless. "The power of books and the words they contain, my dearest Cate, is recognized, and a number of them come out every year subsidized, you know, by the most inartistic sources, but often are written by the most literary of your colleagues, knowingly and unknowingly both."

Now she looked at the hem of the sheet, plucked at it.

"Praise and damnation are often planned, though we will never admit to such goings-on. And by now you must know that a number, a considerable number, of book reviews reflect not artistic but certain political considerations.

"Jeremy likes to say of writers, when they are successful, that they are now drinking with another crowd. Isn't that right?"

"Yeah. That's right."

"Well, so's he now. And that's some crowd."

"Sandra, why are you telling me these things, not that I believe them. Should I?"

"Dear Cato Caldwell. I have given you a short cut to understanding where you are and where you may not be going. You can believe or not, as you damn well please. But you will remember."

Clarissa was coming out, and over lunch Ike Plunkett was telling me that he was leaving Amos to go to Ilium because his novel, as I had observed, had not done well. "Man," he said, "they didn't do anything for me in publicity or advertising."

I thought that *Crows in Flight* had been an exceptional novel, one of about a half-dozen that were published as if in secret that year.

"Who's your editor at Ilium?" I think I already knew the answer.

"Sandra Queensbury. She's good. You had her for that anthology."

"Yeah, she is good," I said, and though we were both looking across the room, we were considering, I think, the same person. I had not seen Sandra since West Hampton last spring. It was now November, early, that time of the year when the cold made me think of Spain.

"Yeah," I said again. "She's a nice lady."

"Uh-huh," Ike said. I knew he too had had the view of Central Park, the view of sun and sea, from Sandra's bedrooms.

"She sure sounds like Hitler's momma sometimes," he said.

Puzzled, I frowned at him.

"Jews," he said, lowering his voice. "Jews in publishing. Taking it over and shit like that."

Then I remembered what she had not said about my agent.

Ike went on. "A whole lot of Negro writers would still be waiting to get published if it weren't for the Jews — "

"And a lot of WASP writers WASP publishers didn't care about," I said.

We stared across the room, for a moment said nothing. I finished my coffee and tossed the napkin on the table. Who, I wondered, would come after Ike?

"Listen," he said outside the restaurant. "Have a good Thanksgiving, man."

94

"What're you gonna do?"

"Oh," he said, pretending a certain vagueness. "I may go out to the Island."

Paul had been mean in small ways, and restless, since his novel had been published. It had received lukewarm reviews, where it was reviewed at all. In a kind of surly, I'll-show-those-sons-a-bitches mood, he began his second, still holding down his job. He had been unabashedly sure of prominent reviews, so sure; and not wishing him to be hurt, I'd wanted that for him, too. At the same time, however, I was fearful and envious that those reviews just might happen, and when they did not, I was relieved. As a result, we hadn't seen very much of each other, so his phone call was something of a surprise.

"How goes it?" I asked.

"Shit."

"What?"

"Fuck it, Cate. Look, man, do you suppose you could put me up for a couple of weeks or so?"

I knew he was waiting for my question. I was instead thinking of my privacy, which would evaporate with his presence. I would not be able to enjoy that leisurely intimacy I enjoyed with Allis. "Sure," I said. "Allis and I are going away for a few days anyway for Thanksgiving — "

I thought I heard him say "Oh!" with something lingering and painful in the sound.

" — so you can have it all to yourself for a few days. Unless you want to come with us."

"Well . . . no. I mean, I wouldn't go with you . . . Sure it's no bother, me being there?"

"You kidding? Of course not."

"Can I come over tomorrow night?"

"Sure. Let's have dinner then."

"You're on. See you about seven."

"And so," he said at dinner, stretching back in his chair and smiling that tough smile I remembered, "I'm at loose ends again."

"Oh?" I would play Mr. Bones to his Dr. Interlocutor. The other end man / person was not present.

"I've had it. We've had it, Claire and I."

He seemed to be waiting for a response.

"Oh," I said again.

"You don't seem surprised."

"I don't?"

"You suspected."

"Me?"

"Bastard." He bent to his food.

He fades and withers in the evening.
O teach us how to number our days,
That we may attain a heart of wisdom.

Allis moves very close to me. I feel the contours of her hip, its warmth, the very strength of its presence. I think of how often, how very often and how very long, I have stroked this hip and the other; how many countless times I have lain across them, moved between them, behind them. How much I admire the solid swelling, broadening of her hips, never mind her vanity, which recalls smaller, more svelte shapings. Feeling my pressure, perhaps more unseemly than the situation calls for, she looks at me and we exchange smiles beneath Paul's father's breaking voice. Death does have its dominion, perhaps in theory like the medieval flatness of the earth; but life has one, too.

Mark the innocent, look upon the upright;
For there is a future for the man of peace.

The first time I closed with those hips, those swellings of her body, was when Allis and I left Bread Loaf two days after our meeting in the woods. We drove southward slowly, seeking a place off the main roads where we could stop for the night. We did not talk much about this stopping, the making love; some things do not have to be discussed to death. You just know when they should happen.

I simply said, "Let's find a place to eat and stop over." (For, at that point, nothing had been said about it.)

"Okay," she said. "I keep hearing about this great New England fish chowder and delightful colonial bedrooms. Let's find them."

We drove then, slowly, looking for a place.

We found an inn wedged between a stream, grassland and mountains. It was small, friendly in soft afternoon sunlight. Nevertheless, we entered it with the natural apprehensions of the time, given who we were. There was, however, no crusty old Vermonter to be startled, no descendant of that clan who had closed doors in the faces of Ethan Allen and his Green Mountain Boys on their way to Fort Ticonderoga. Instead, the inn was owned and managed by an ex-jazz musician whose single, immense claim to posterity was that Charlie Parker had let him sit in during a set in Framingham. Daniel, too, had played alto sax. It was hung above the bar where all this was discussed, the car still unloaded, for I had liked Bird, also. Daniel gave us the "suite," which was a small room with a grand view and a working fireplace. We stayed two days and nights, and when we were leaving, Daniel invited us back to spend Thanksgiving. That was the beginning of the ritual and this, now, would be our second, and driving up we were aware of it. Where did we go from ritual? The question filled the car. At Daniel's inn it bobbed up between us during our early morning walks in the snow; it haunted the comfortable spaces when we sat in the suite before the warming fireplace. The question begged the answer, for one does not do the same things repeatedly, even the maddest of us, without pausing at some deeply interior moment to wonder why. I liked being in that sturdy building, the wind at night fondling, rather than buffeting, it, while Daniel played Charlie Parker records. I liked being there with *her*.

"Hey," I said. It was late and Daniel and his woman were downstairs with another couple. Allis and I were mellow with drink and food. I had been studying the flintlock with its pitted barrel and chipped stock that hung above the mantel, together with a darkly rusted huge-bladed knife with a bone handle, a blockwood plane and an aged two-headed ax. These were the tools of the ghosts of men who, in their greed and fear, sensed through the generations of their genes that here in these mountains and valleys of a newer Europe lay the last desperate hope of their kind. The hands that had held those tools and weapons shaped this land, and not enough of them had been Israel Potters.

I knew what they would have thought of us.

Allis, breaking from her own reverie, knowing what was coming, said, "Hmmmm?" Her eyes darkening with sleep, she smiled. She placed her face on my neck. "Hmmmm?"

"Where do we go with this thing?"

She sat up and stared at the fire. "You fancy something different, Cate?"

"Don't you?"

She nodded. "Yes."

"But?" I asked.

"No real buts. When."

"There's got to be a when."

"I know. I know." She turned and studied me. "Are *you* as certain as you sound?"

"Me? Yeah."

She rested her head on my shoulder. We stared at the fire lashing and humming in the fireplace as though an ultimatum had been seared in the firebricks behind it.

From downstairs came the determined, wavering, Charlie Parker–like sound of Daniel playing, note for note, riff for riff, Bird's solo from "All the Things You Are" off the *Jazz at Massey Hall* album. He was indeed, as he had said, a helluva lot better than Jimmy Dorsey.

We returned to New York that Sunday night, rested, my head cleared, my lungs still tingling, I believed, with the frosty fresh Vermont air.

"How you feel, Mr. Douglass?" Mr. Storto. He was just coming out of his apartment. He glanced at the darkening street behind me. He was up now for the evening; he would putter around the halls, picking up paper, plastering over little holes, and then he would go inside and watch television or take a stroll around the block.

"Okay. How're you, Mr. Storto?"

"Ehh, you know, you get old what can you do? That friend of yours, he's all right?" He pointed to his head.

"Yeah, what happened?" The old apprehensions rushed back.

"All the way down here, I hear him holler on the phone, and then he punch the walls. I guess it's all right, though. He drink?"

"He doesn't get like that. He just broke up with his wife."

"So that was it." He thought a long second, shrugged, mooched up his lips. "Who goes crazy over that? Another woman will fix him fine." He turned to go, stopped and called after me, "Your lady, you know, the regular lady — " He smiled. "She's nice. I like her. The others, Mr. Douglass — " And he walked away with a brief laugh.

Paul's clothes were all over the apartment — corduroy pants, Brooks Brothers' shirts, McCreedy & Schreiber desert boots, underwear. Everything was in disarray. Cursing, I set my bag down in the only clear space left. My work on the typing table had been shoved and bent to one corner. My machine held one of his pages. I read the top lines:

When a man is cold and hungry, food and clothing are the only goals, but a man can only eat so much food or wear so much clothing, and after that there has to be something else.

Bullshit, I thought. I felt no urgency to continue. Wearily, feeling that Paul's mess was a gesture of contempt for me, I began to clean it up. I wondered if he'd found a place or had a solid lead. It was true that I had lived with him, but this was the first time he'd lived with me, and I was unhappy, though committed. Well, I'd just have to spend more time at Allis', because I doubted this fucking arrangement would work very well.

I arrived back in the apartment midmorning the next day. I had spent the night with Allis, leaving her place after she'd gone to work. We had agreed on a plan that might hasten Paul's departure, and would put it into effect that night.

I found a note from Paul: "Sorry about the mess. See you after work."

I had finished putting food into the refrigerator and the cupboards when the phone rang.

"Hi, babes."

Maxine Culp. "Hi," I said.

"You *are* scheduled for the *Times* this round," she said, "and reviews are in from Chicago. They're fantastic!"

I warmed to the conversation; lunches were being scheduled, interviews and the like. "Finally," she said, "two things. First, I'm leaving Smythe and Simkin to start my own literary agency." She cleared her throat. "Everyone gets tired of Alex Samuels, you know. And second, your friend Ike Plunkett? Did you hear about it?"

"No, what?" I could not imagine anything untoward happening to Ike; anybody else, but not Ike.

"He was arrested Friday night for possession."

"Possession? Possession of what?"

"Heroin."

After a moment I said, "You're crazy."

She laughed. "Oh, no, I'm not. Check around. I'll see you for lunch tomorrow and — oh, yes! Take a look at Brentano's window!"

"Really?"

"A small stack, but a stack. See you."

I disconnected quickly and called Amos. I was lucky; he was in.

"Oh, I know why you're calling. Yeah, it's true, the dumb sonofabitch."

If true, then, I supposed that Ike had seen the last of Ilium and Sandra Queensbury.

"Dumb, man, *dumb*," Amos was saying. "He thinks that because he's a writer he can get away with shit like that. White folks can, but not niggers, especially not one named Ike. Shit. Mailer almost did in his ole lady and got nothing but a slap on the wrist, and here Ike is, doin' it to him*self* and — "

"You mean he pops?"

"When he's got bread, sure he pops. Pops like a motherfucker, but he's running out of money, Cate. He signed for a book before he went over to Ilium, got most of the bread up front and has turned in zip. White writers do it all the time, but shit, that nigger was making me look bad. I had to tell him no. Walk. That's how come he's over there, I don't care what he told you."

"Is he out on bail or what?"

"Don't know, can't care, Cato."

"Well — "

"You know anything about junkies don't have no bread?"

I confessed that I didn't.

"Leave it; he'll work it out."

"But, Amos, look. He's a writer, man, a Negro writer."

"Yeah, and a junkie, too. I got to go to lunch, man. Hope *Clarissa* sails."

Clarissa got up and somewhat off the ground, but it did not sail. It did better than *Dissonances,* though, gathering reviews, if somewhat cutting or bland in most New York papers, and as a result got more notices in the rest of the country. The novel was about an old black lady who owned an old white dog; both are headed for the grave. Clarissa has outlived three husbands and five children. The novel is a long flashback, told while the old dog peers lovingly and sadly up at her as she slowly locks up the house for yet another night, which they may not survive.

I didn't understand the drill then. But over the years it percolated down into my perception the way water trickles through sod and stone unseen into cold, dark, still subterranean pools. Much later, asking myself why, like a speleologist asking himself in the darkness of his damp travels, where, I came on the pools, calm and still and cold — answers as ancient as the formations that held them.

There were other, more pressing things to discover that winter.

10

ALLIS' PRESENCE in the apartment did not after all help to turn Paul out. He lingered on, typing desperately through the night, breaching our passion with the sound of his clattering machine and long, heavy sighs, which were interspersed with his loud suckings on his cigarettes. He lunged at the ring of the phone, and if it was Claire, he lowered his voice. He allowed as how they were trying to reconcile their differences, so for a few weekends he packed up on Friday night to move back, but always on Sunday night, slamming through the door and pounding his bag down into a corner, returned, embarrassed. Finally, one Friday he left and did not return.

Allis and I, half-naked over Sunday breakfasts when we read the pounds of papers, wondered if all was now well. It was not; Paul had simply moved somewhere else.

Ike Plunkett, I heard, had made bail — and promptly vanished. The writers who'd put up the money were, strangely, I thought, not terribly upset. Ike's act, I reasoned, confirmed for them something they'd secretly believed anyway and they seemed not unhappy to have paid for it.

That winter, too, between Christmas and the New Year, Allis met Glenn. She did not force herself on him the way some women had done, assuring him that I did indeed love him very much, that I was a rather special kind of father, etc., etc., while, as nine-year-olds will do in those shadowed, instinctive corners of their minds, he wondered how often I was making love with her.

It was well that Allis didn't attempt to capture his attention. Glenn knew, the way kids know things adults forgot long ago, that she was a special person in my life and perhaps would be in his. He sulked but remained, on the whole, well-mannered, if bitchily tolerant. We didn't discuss Allis when we were alone. I waited in vain for questions. Maybe I should have put them to him; I didn't. I did know, though, that he was happier when we were alone, trudging through the city or going to museums.

We did not return to the Museum of Natural History until he was seventeen. On that nine-year-old visit, in midday, we hiked up the stairs through a gently falling snow, past Teddy Roosevelt astride his horse, a black man on one side, a red man on the other. For years I've longed to add to that semicircle wherein are engraved his titles — statesman, soldier, etc. — one more: bigot. We passed his statue and entered. Upstairs where the dinosaurs are, I left him for a moment to get a drink, and as I was bending over the fountain I heard his voice. I charged into the room where he stood, screaming as hard as he could, his legs apart, his body trembling, a dwarf pitted on the blade of his fear of the million-year-old bones of the dinosaurs. I snatched him up and felt his body trying to flow into mine.

"What's the matter, what's the matter?"

"Take me *away* from here, I want to leave here," and his body, sixty or seventy pounds, strained for the exit. "I'm scared."

I started walking. "Of what?"

His eyes rolled over his shoulders to the twenty-foot skeleton of tyrannosaurus, and then I remembered how frightened I had been of Orson Welles's voice when he said over the radio on Sunday: *Who knows what evil lurks in the hearts of men? The Shadow knows* . . . I was Glenn's age at the time, and the Shadow scared the shit out of me.

He wanted to be the hell away from that place. I carried him all the way out, feeling his heart pounding through our coats. It took eight years for him to return, and when he did, he stood peering through the rib cages of the dinosaurs, smiling wanly. He glanced at me and I smiled and then we both laughed and went home to get a beer.

That year when I took Glenn back home, Catherine and I, alone while I waited for a late plane to New York, sat and talked. Glenn slept. I don't know what happened, really, but one moment we were at the kitchen table, and the next we were in her bed. It meant nothing, because I asked her if it should. "Nothing," she said. "But it was nice." Yet on the way home, I wondered what it would be like together again in New York. I called her when I got home.

"I've been thinking," I said.

"I wonder what."

"Really, Cat."

"Do you think I haven't thought about it? Oh, I have and reached the point where you brought it up, like tonight, but I could never see myself saying yes. I'm all right now, and there's a guy, and I'm going to be all right."

"It wasn't just for you."

"Glenn adores you, Cato. He always talks about you, and whenever he's been to visit you, for weeks he walks and moves and tries to talk like you. He's all right."

"That's because of you, Catherine."

"And you. A lot of fathers just keep on walking."

"So . . . ?" I said.

"You've got your career now, and I'm glad and, well, it's all right, Cato, the way it is."

"Okay. Just thought I'd ask."

"Glad you did."

"We've got West German, Italian, Dutch, French and Spanish sales," Rupert announced at lunch. We were in his favorite restaurant at his table.

"Spanish?" I said. I had figured *Clarissa* would be one of the many books the Spanish authorities might ban.

"That's right. So you can see that we're doing all right by you."

I nodded agreement. The paperback sale had gone well, but nothing like the deals that would be made later in the decade and into the 1970s. I had no real complaints about money. Now, Rupert was pushing another contract on Alex and me, since *Clarissa* had fulfilled the option clause in the initial one. What he was offering seemed to me to be less than what I thought I was worth. How does a writer measure his worth?

The time invested, for one consideration, I suppose. Not only the time it takes to write a book, but the time, in all its evasive essences, that it took, the experiences, the deprivations (if such there were), that readied one to announce through his sheaves of papers that he was a writer.

These were intangibles, having almost no weight on a publisher's scale. This was before the computers.

"How much do you need to live?" Rupert was asking. It was not all that unusual a question, but it was filled with traps. If, for example, one of Rupert's big literary names could command an advance against royalties of a hundred thousand dollars, and it took that writer (as it has in more cases than will be admitted) twenty years to complete a book, then the writer has been living on five thousand dollars a year, excluding any subsidiary rights that may be obtained on completion of the work. A writer who takes a five-thousand-dollar advance for a book that took three years to write is obviously in love with his career — a fact editors are keenly aware of.

I knew that Rupert had already calculated my needs, not my wants, over the years I'd been with him, but there would always be that discrepancy between what I needed and what I wanted. "I'm planning to get married," I told him.

He stopped eating and seemed to press a mental button that quickly recalculated my needs. "Oh, yes?"

"Ummm," I said.

"Anyone I know?"

"No."

"Nice?"

"Yes."

"Well," he grumbled, wiping his mouth with his napkin. "We're talking about art, not a piece of dry goods."

"Some writers manage to live well on their art, Rupert."

"I know, I know."

I wondered suddenly if Rupert had these kinds of conversations with white writers. "I'll talk to Alex," I said.

I liked Rupert, but a chill had crept between us. It was money, upon which your career was built, fuck the writing, and I was beginning to sense now the way it all worked, and I silently cursed myself for not perceiving it worked the same way whatever the endeavor. "I'll talk to Alex," I repeated.

"Sure, but remember that you're only two books out, Cato. We're for the distance, not the sprint."

Rupert did not count my anthology. We didn't talk about the new contract anymore. Instead, our conversation moved to Europe, where Llewelyn Dodge Johnson had just died in Paris. "He must have some memoirs," Rupert said. "I'd love to publish them."

The lunch was the worst we'd ever had, and it was our last. Not because

Rupert and Alex obviously had agreed that what Rupert offered was adequate; not because I was pissed at both of them, sure that the old conspiracy that attends the creation of cheap labor was in force; and not because I was considering a change of agent and publisher. It was because Rupert got killed.

The sun had been bright and unusually warm on his favorite backslope near Verbier; he liked it because he had it pretty much to himself. Who expected an avalanche in February? It was small, as avalanches go. It merely detached itself from the slope with a kind of a sigh and hissed down upon Rupert, covering him and passing on. They would not find him until May.

Like everyone else, I made the duty calls to his widow when she returned and then, again like everyone else, angled away.

Another Smythe and Simkin editor, a colleague of Rupert's, called and we lunched. I didn't mention the meeting to Alex. Meanwhile, Amos called every day, offering lunch or dinner, the wine-and-dine treatment at which Amos put every other editor in New York to shame. I realized that the situation in publishing wasn't any different from other American conditions, given the factor of race. How much clout did Amos really have? (One always tried, the advice went, to get a senior editor, one with muscle enough to beat down opposition and provide you with an obscenely huge advance.) Was it possible that Amos was more than Phaeton's token Negro?

If I signed with him, would that lift him into truly senior editorial ranks?

Would the deal be mutually advantageous, the kind of relationship that would grow in size and strength, and would it, *could* it (bite your tongue, Cato!) prove to be the kind of togetherness we Negroes needed so badly, and would we then be counted as formidable as others in the ethnic editorial-publishing-literary battles already raging in the quiet, sleekly carpeted offices and reviewing factories?

"Come to Phaeton, man."

There was a purring quality in his voice. I had used it to woo women, had used it to emotionalize issues when rationality did not work. I had heard preachers use that tone, and politicians and editors and students. We have learned, and very well, to bend the language any way the bending will benefit us; but the way we speak it, the tonal qualities inherent in any speech, reveal more than the words couched in them. Voice-print technology carries us back to beginnings, puts into machines what our generations already had programmed for us.

I said, "Amos, look at this situation like a bus. We don't all want to crowd together in the front, back or middle. Let's spread out, because as soon as we gather in one place, as we used to in the South during slavery, then, man, we're vulnerable. I gotta think about it."

"Yeah," he said, not quite concealing the sneer in his voice, which said, *You think you're pretty goddamn special, Cate, but you ain't shit, really.* I heard him.

And then I began to wonder, not in long, but in brief flashes that pierced the dark of whatever I was then, whether it was true that if you peeled away all the layers, painstakingly and with enormous patience, you would find that editors really envied their writers and perhaps even hated them.

11

SPRING. Sunlight slanted into the apartment at a different, brighter angle once again. There was a loosening of movement in the streets, like water in a stream freed at last from ice.

"I got a Goog! I got a Goog!" Paul was shouting into the phone. I had not seen nor talked to him in a couple of weeks. He was shouting in much the same way I had shouted to him when Alex sold *Dissonances*. I too had applied for a Guggenheim, but had been rejected. Paul had not told me of his application and I had not told him of mine. I assumed that I would be a shoo-in for it and had not wanted to upset him. I guessed that he had not mentioned his application in case he was rejected.

"Good," I said, as heartily as I could.

"You can use me as a reference when you apply," he said. His tone jarred and upset me, brought with it all those overtones, those little stitchings that become whole literary goods.

I waited a moment, then said, "I did."

Now he paused. "You applied? And they turned *you* down?"

"Yeah."

"Oh," he said. "Shit."

"Well — "

"Next time."

"Oh, yeah, I ran into Leonard the other night coming from the Five Spot." It was time to change the subject.

"God, Cate. What's he up to?"

"Same thing, except worse. Walking up the middle of Third Avenue cursing, staggering. I got him to a shelter."

He had been as light as a feather, pugnacious, yes, but his punches were like the flounderings of a baby. "Hey, man, let me get you home," I said.

He smelled like fresh shit and looked even worse, and his face was marked with those scars and swellings drunks often have, as if they had tried to walk through walls. "Cato Douglass, man," I kept saying to him over the music spraying off the stamped-tin ceiling of the nearby club.

"I don't hang out with no niggers," he said, the words dipping and diving like the flight of a swallow.

"Yeah, yeah." I wondered if Allis had reached Dorothea.

"Writer. No. POet, moth'fuckin' POet. Who you?"

"Cate. Cato Douglass."

He tried to shake away. "Doan know no fuck–in CAto. Niggers got some strange names nowadays. CAto." He giggled and I almost laughed myself.

"No answer," Allis had said, circling us warily.

"Listen, honey, take a cab and go home — "

"You going to take him to your place?"

"No. But maybe I can get him into a shelter a couple of blocks down."

"Take a cab," she suggested, then said, "Oh."

No cab would stop for Leonard and me, and if I'd been a cab driver, I wouldn't have let Leonard within fifty feet of my car.

"Who you?" Leonard asked again.

"Shut the fuck up," I said. We had had some plans for that evening, Allis and I. "CAto," I shouted, "CAto. Go home, Allis."

"I'll be at your place," she said.

I started walking with an arm around Leonard. God, did he stink; stank from every pore, every hair, every single part of his body; and I wondered, in my anger and misery, limping down the street with him, if the stink had begun in his mind.

"The tiger in the tiger pit," he whispered, *"Is not more irritable than I."*

"Hey, Leonard," I said, stopping.

"Make black, bid sing," he whispered, and he lifted his head, opened

his mouth and tried to sound a note, a high note, which, dragged protest-ingly up from his being by the gallons of the cheap wine he'd been drinking, started, cracking to be sure, from his mouth only to turn into a tsunami of vomit whose wave I almost completely escaped by letting Leonard fall to the street and jumping away.

I dragged him to the shelter, knocked on the door and made my way home, smelling shit and puke every step of the way.

That was the last time I saw Leonard Blue-Sky.

"What can we do, Cate?"

"Dunno. Discovered they had moved, so it was a good thing I didn't try to take him home."

"Maybe Dorothea has given up," Paul said.

"Looks like it." I was wondering about that long, tight friendship Paul and Leonard had had.

"Want drinks and dinner tonight?"

"Tomorrow?" I countered.

"A deal."

"See you."

I hung up slowly, thinking about Paul's Goog.

"So," Allis said. "Paul got himself a Guggenheim. With one lousy book." She sat curled on the couch, shoes off, her feet tucked beneath a cushion.

I sat down heavily beside her. "Yep."

"But what you submitted, that novel you're working on, *The Hyksos Journals*" — she sat up brightly — "number three! It's better than the others. Your best, I think."

I said, "I wonder if it would help Leonard if he got a Goog. He's been turned down by everyone — Saxton, Whitney, Guggenheim — "

"It must help," she said. She had a way of looking very carefully at me without seeming to. "But you didn't need it, really need it."

I agreed. It was but the trappings of recognition that you were be-ing stitched into the proper literary framework, an imprimatur that you were okay for further processing. Some people just needed the money, too.

Allis jabbed me with her toes. I grabbed her foot and held it without looking at her. She slipped it out of my grasp and hugged me, and whispered between her kisses, "You don't need it. You don't need it at all, baby. Sometimes you become like them or try to, and you *know* you can't. You can't be like them at all; they won't let you." She said teasingly, "These little hungers of yours, that adolescent ego peeking through. That's not really you. I should say, that's not mostly you."

"Are you going to charge me for this hour?"

She kissed me tenderly; I kissed her back with more heat than tenderness. "Ah, you, ah, want to pay out in trade, is that it?"

And later, in bed, listening to music, thinking about her leaving in the morning to go raise funds for Cumer, Slate and Finch, I said, "We really ought to make a decision, Allis."

In the silence I heard Mr. Storto calling out to someone in the street.

"Yes," she said. "We should."

"That's what I said."

"Cate, you know I'm not brave, I'm not tough."

"You think that's what it's gonna take?"

"Won't it? And will Glenn like it?"

"He'd have to, wouldn't he?"

I knew she was thinking of her father and those relatives — cousins, uncles, aunts — whom she visited on the holidays or weekends after they complained about how seldom they saw her. I envied her that; in a world where everyone seemed to have family, save Glenn I had none. Yet as Glenn would have to get used to the idea of Allis as a stepmother, so too would her relatives have to get used to me as a son, cousin or nephew-in-law. Whether they did or not was of no consequence to me, but would be to Allis.

She lay face down beside me, her arm across my chest, her head turned away as if to deflect from my sensibilities the thoughts I knew she was having.

"I can't," she said, and then was silent.

"Okay."

"I don't mean that."

"What do you mean?"

"I mean okay, but, holy shit!" She started to giggle. "I just had this image of all my Jewish family throwing up their hands in horror, rending their garments, howls, tears, curses, banishment — "

"So tell them I'm a Falasha, a black Jew!"

"Falasha! You think they want to know from Falashas?" She turned toward me and buried her face against my chest. Once again, before she fell asleep, she said, "Holy shit. I'm gonna do it."

"Hey." I nudged her back into wakefulness.

"Ummm?"

"Sorry about Bread Loaf?"

"Not for me. You?"

"Only sometimes. Not now."

"G'night."

"Night."

"I've had it with New York," Paul was saying. His fork screeched against the plate as he rolled his spaghetti around it. "I need a change, like you went to Europe."

"Where would you go?"

"The Coast. San Francisco, and maybe even Chicago."

"Man, you can't do without New York. You're a New York writer."

"The hell you say."

He chewed slowly, broke apart some bread and set it aside in favor of a sip of the wine. "Besides, the writing's not going well."

He looked right at me and smiled. He'd never admitted to having problems with his writing.

Paul said, "It's not the job. It's not even the writing. It's the content. I mean, it doesn't seem to matter, when I read it back, and I want it to because I think writing should matter."

Now he ate the bread. "Even — especially the one I'm almost finished with, that got the Goog, work in progress; it's shit."

Most writers don't mean it when they say that, and Paul certainly had never said it before, not to me. I knew what it was costing and tried to turn it aside.

"If you get to the Coast you'll be able to see your father," I said.

"Uh — yes, yes, of course," he said, with a curious lack of warmth. "There is that." He pushed back, holding his glass of wine, and studied me, as he had many times before. But this time he seemed to be deciding something; whatever it was crested to his eyes and then the moment was past.

"When?"

"Don't know exactly. I guess when I finish the book."

"I never thought of New York without you, Paul."

"Listen, Cate. To be honest, I can't tough it out. The competition, including you, is too much." He laughed softly. "I need the distance."

I drank my own wine and chewed on the bread. "You had a black-white thing before, Paul," I said. "How's it now?"

He rested his elbows on the table and bowed his head between his arms. "Not so hot." His voice was muffled.

"The Goog helped, didn't it?" I was fighting hard to keep the rage out of my voice.

"It should have, yes."

"If it makes you feel better," I said, "it did make me feel the way you're supposed to feel when you don't get one and a friend does. For a couple of hours."

"Yeah, I imagined that." He raised up. "You should have got one. You really should have."

"Allis said I didn't need it."

Paul laughed again, that careful, circumspect, ill-at-ease laugh. "Neither did I."

I poured some more wine.

"I'm sorry," he said quickly.

"For what?" I asked just as quickly.

"You kids gonna get married?"

"Yeah, I think so."

"When?"

"Dunno. Gotta make some plans. She's gotta tell her father. I gotta tell Glenn."

"Who's — oh! Your kid, right."

I leaned back against the booth and scanned the room. The usual Village crowd plagued by the flower lady who visited several restaurants, trying to catch unprepared young men out with romantic young women who considered gardenias and roses part of the perfect evening.

"I'm seeing Mark tomorrow," I said.

I enjoyed the way I sliced him open and poured in the salt. "He wants to talk about some television stuff."

"Oh, yeah?" Paul rocked forward on his elbows again. This time his head was up, like a retriever sniffing the wind.

"What's he got in mind?"

"I'm writing a series about Negroes, here and in Africa. You know, with the civil rights movement and all going on."

"Travel, too, huh?" he said.

"Yeah. Afraid so. Around the country. Maybe Africa."

"Great for you, Cate. I hope it works out."

Shit, it had to work out. I was the only nigger writer Mark knew. But I said, "Yeah, me too."

Paul's voice was stern. "Look, what're we gonna do about Leonard?"

He's your friend, I thought. You can feel for him as long as he stays in his shit-smelling shadow. God, don't let him become famous.

12

OF COURSE we had all wondered why Mark left *Esquire* and moved into television. We'd expected him to end up at one of the major publishing houses instead, where he one day would publish all of us with fanfare and flourishes. We waited for him to surface; we waited quite some time before he did, at Public Service Television, which was the only channel we all claimed to watch, except for an occasional Sid Caesar special or Jonathan Winters or Ernie Kovacs.

People who work in film often have an air of self-importance; they ride different vibrations from the rest of us, and, mostly, they are not modest. Mark had become like that.

"You can do so much more with *pictures,*" he proclaimed at lunch. "Television now is like Hollywood in the twenties — still growing, still overflowing with possibilities. Put together with good writing, nothing beats it. It's a natural. From going *out* to the movies, we now go *into* the room where the set is."

"Yeah, yeah," I said. I was almost drunk enough to agree even with Beelzebub.

"This project can be the most exciting thing on television. Commercial TV would never touch it. We can. A little Murrow, a little of the Mike Wallace interview, with lots of action between."

He slammed his palm on the table and the breadsticks bounced. "How godlike pictures in motion can make us, man! We can die in one film and return full-blown to life in the next. Little Caesars in one and crusading editors of Big Town in another. I want to use it to catch what's going on out there, all its ugliness, all its bravery and beauty . . ."

So the lunch proceeded. I'd arrived at one of those plateaus for a time. I would be in film! I would create the images that would appear. (The creation of images, visual images, not the kind each of us conjures up in the mind while reading a book, seemed then to be a kind of summit. For certainly people like me had had so little to do with that creation — perhaps because of the dangers inherent in it — that this opportunity smacked of an undreamed immensity.)

Barely sober, I danced home over spit-and-gum-stained sidewalks, happier with the *chance* than with the name and phone number of a sympathetic rabbi who would marry Allis and me. I waltzed and boogalooed homeward. I was gracious and did not jaywalk; I nodded encouragement to sweating, evil-eyed cops; I smiled at the whores and mumbled daring words of endearment to them that made them smile and gaze wonderingly at me.

Film! It was the shaper of our opinion. If it had twisted history out of shape, I would help to untwist it; ole C.C. would get it together.

I heard Mark's voice, pitched high on Negronis: "We've got to do it now, Cate! The world's watching this country. Negroes have taken their grievances to the streets! Martin Luther King is as famous as Jack Kennedy! Will civil rights work, or is this the setup for the Big Pogrom? We've got to get started in a month and I've got to have some kind of script in a couple of weeks. Okay, Cate?"

I danced on home to find in Mr. Storto's small lobby an attractive woman, lightly painted and seductively dressed in murmuring chiffon.

She smiled. "You Cato Douglass?"

"Yes," I said. Eagerly. "Yes, I am."

"I'm Amy Polner." She held out a hand, and I took it, wondering if I had met her somewhere before. "Can we talk in your place?"

Could we talk in my place? Was she kidding? "Sure we can."

She started up the stairs, swaying like a willow in a summer's breeze, hot and filled with exciting green smells.

Who was she? Perhaps she'd seen my photo somewhere, in a newspaper or a magazine, on a dust jacket? I was starting to have what they called A Name, so Alex Samuels took great pains to tell me. Was she a writers' freak, a groupie? Did it, after all, matter? She was attractive, with all the proper possessions startlingly in the right places. Yes, I considered one more, final infidelity. This would be my bachelor party, my stag party, with the real thing, no movies. My penis began to swell and ease its way out of its appointed place, and I figured this certainly would be a most gracious way to spend what was left of the afternoon.

Still swaying upward, she said, "I'm Allis' cousin." She turned and smiled, as if sensors in the back of her head had communicated my shriveling disappointment.

"Oh" was all I could say. By the time we had reached my door I was both angry and sober. Inside, she stood inspecting the apartment. For Allis, I wondered? Did she imagine her prancing about, clothed only in streetlight, or sitting at my table, relaxed with sleep and loving, over a cup of coffee? Did she see her folded softly upon my bed or couch?

"Drink, Amy?"

"No, no thanks. You go ahead and have one."

I sat down across from her instead. "You bring congratulations, right?"

She laughed. "Mine, yes. From her father, no."

She pointed a cigarette at me and I lighted it. She said, "Why do you have to get married?" and blew out a cloud of smoke.

It was a rhetorical question. I waited.

"Can't you just live together?"

"Umm. Then her father could truthfully say that his daughter didn't marry that shvartzer."

"I guess so. Yes. Look, he didn't ask me to come, but I do know my uncle. Why do you need another marriage? And you have a kid . . ."

"I'm not ever going to ask your uncle — Allis' father — for anything, not even the time of day; he doesn't have to worry about that. Besides, the marriage is a kind of commitment we've decided to make. Everything that goes with it. You seem to be saying that her father would prefer her to live in shame than in the honesty of a marriage, yes?"

"In a nutshell." She laughed softly, with some pretty embarrassment, and crossed her legs with a fine, soft sound. "Do you think Allis can take it?"

"Yeah."

"And," she said, "you?"

There was a knowing behind that pretty smile, pretty in the way that hunting arrows, with their precise barbs, can be pretty, and I remembered a photo story I'd seen years ago, in one of those pocket magazines that were all the rage, about a black man. A series of photos showed him surrounded by cops, backed up to the edge of the water on a beach. It was in California, where everyone is backed up to the edge of the Pacific Ocean. The guy had gone crazy, the copy read, under the pressure of being married to a white woman.

"Me?" I said. "I guess I can handle it. Pressure's my middle name."

Amy mashed out her cigarette. She folded her fingers through each other and looked down at the floor. "Allis knew I'd be coming," she said.

"She didn't mention it to me."

"She said it would be a waste of time."

"Then why did you come?"

"He did ask me to come, Cate. I didn't want to, but — "

"Well, you see, you have wasted your time. And you've pissed me off — "

"Wait. Fifty thousand dollars. He'll give it to you if you — "

She stopped and hunched her shoulders, waited.

Fifty thousand dollars. I got up, moved across the room and sat down again. Amy was averting her flushed face. What an awful lot of fear the money represented, or hate. Fifty thousand bucks in one lump sum. "Fifty thousand dollars?" I asked. There was a tremor in my voice.

Her voice was hopeful. "Fifty thousand."

"Oh, Jesus."

"Aren't you tempted just a little, Cato?" More sure of herself now, her smile mocked me, mocked everything I was or ever would be; it perceived my vulnerability, my suspected price. In another time, another culture, Mr. Greenberg simply would have said no, and had I persisted, had me done in. Had he been bold enough, he could still have me done in.

"Listen, does Allis know this?"

"No, of course not."

"What do you mean, 'of course not'?"

"She wouldn't think much of her father then, and that would hurt him."

"But, shit, I'm going to tell her."

"Do you think she'll believe it?"

"You're implying something you'd better not say, Amy. If I tell her, she'll believe it. Why in the hell wouldn't she?"

"I meant — "

"I *know* what you meant." I moved to another seat again. "What I should do is take his money *and* marry his daughter. But you consider me to be a man of more honor than that, don't you? The Christian in

116

the pit will not fight off the starving lion, just climb right on into its mouth, right?"

"Then you won't — "

"No, I won't. I want to tell you something; then you leave. I feel as though I've been walking through a dark place in which I've imagined all kinds of dangerous and disgusting things, Amy. But you've come to lead me out into the light, where everything is so much uglier, and frightening."

She was still now and I sensed her sudden fear; I wanted her to feel it; I wished she were Mr. Greenberg.

"Look," I said. "I've killed men I didn't even know, men with whom I never exchanged the time of day, and I don't remember how I felt before or after. But I know this: if your uncle walked into this room now, I would kill him and feel very, very good about it.

"You don't understand the extent of the insult, do you? This is not a movie, girl, and it probably is a good thing that you are a girl, or I'd kick your ass, too."

Stop, I said to myself. Stop now. I went quickly to the bathroom and closed and locked the door. I sat on the stool and started to count to myself. At fifty I heard the door to the apartment open and close. I counted on to one hundred and went out.

Amy Polner was gone.

I sat down on the couch, my heart pounding with the rolls and snaps of adrenalin. I could hear it in my ears, feel the echo in my eyes. I wanted to destroy, utterly, beyond recognition, and with all the sound I could summon — a billion volcanoes erupting simultaneously with a billion earthquakes. I wanted blood to flow, "even unto the horse bridles, by the space of a thousand and six hundred furlongs." I could, at that moment, smell blood freshly let, and it seemed that I could also taste it.

I was overwhelmed by wrath.

And then I pulled my feet up, exhausted, the pounding subsiding, as though easing me off to death, and I slept.

Fair old men with kindly faces beckon me out of my hole. After moments of wondering, my suspicions obvious, I think, they extend their hands to help me out. There is a radiance about them and they do not fear my carbine, do not shy away from my fear-stink. Next, we are sitting in a circle. There is a collective wisdom about them; it makes me feel good.

"If we say this people exists and prospers through the man and this people is overwhelmed by still another people, nothing can remain of them, for perhaps they, too, are male-descended.

"But if we say this people exists and prospers through the woman and then this people is overwhelmed by still another people, everything remains of them, even if this second people is a male-descended people."

They seem to be chiding me. I say to them, "I am an honorable man; what do such intricacies mean to me?"

They become Japanese soldiers. They pass me a Raleigh cigarette. I do not care for Raleighs. They taste and smell like dried cowshit. I prefer to spend the nickel for a pack of decent cigarettes; never mind the Red Cross freebees.

As I light up, they pounce on me; I roll free and dive for my hole, forgetting to fire the carbine.

Suddenly, it is night, and I hear them laughing at me as they crawl toward my hole along the cardinal points of the compass. I am surrounded. The Southern Cross blazes overhead. I scream for help.

I awoke to the quick-dying echoes of someone screaming. I sat up and peered down into the streetlights. It was night. I saw Mr. Storto leaning against a lamppost. There seemed to be nothing untoward going on. I touched my throat; I could not figure out why it ached so much, as though I'd been chain-smoking.

It could not have been myself I heard — could it? I stumbled toward the shower, wondering.

After the shower, with warm coffee on the stove, I cleared my writing area. Then I sat down to begin Mark's script.

I worked into the day and through it and back into the night again before I stopped to eat a sandwich. The phone had rung several times. I had not answered it. The apartment reeked with the smell of stale cigarette smoke. On the third day I broke through the form, that curious combination of word-directed pictures, and I felt moving; I talked to the words and my fingers and my machine. Yeah! Do! Oooohooo! It was doing what I wished it to do. Yet I was becoming conscious of an abyss between what I was saying with the script and what I knew to be Mark's inability to understand it. I had to sit back, not to think of the pictures, the words and their structure, not to think of pacing, but of Mark's reaction to all these as each, mortared together, made plain my individual philosophy.

And I resented it. My fingers sought out the keys again. To hell with it. Mr. Johnson said that we should move them *upward*. Okay. Up we go.

On the fourth day, having slept a few hours during the night, I called Allis at work.

"Where in the hell have you been?" she asked. Her voice was cold.

"Working."

"Working," she echoed. "Working where?" she almost screamed.

"Here."

"Where's here? What's this shit?"

"Home. I'm doing that script for Mark."

There was a silence before she spoke. Her voice had changed. "Cate, what's wrong?"

"You haven't spoken to Amy?"

"C'mon. Is that what's got you pissed? I haven't seen her since I told her not to bother."

"Okay, listen. Your father wants to give me fifty thousand not to marry you."

There was silence at her end.

"Did you hear me? Fifty grand. I didn't know your old man was so rich." Still the silence. "I told Amy to forget it."

"Can we talk about it, Cate? I didn't know. I'm sorry. I'm ashamed. I'm pissed. I'm trying to understand, though, why you didn't answer the phone or why you haven't called me until today."

I grunted.

"It doesn't have *any*thing to do with us, Cate; not with *us*. Do you want it to? Will you let it?"

"It refused to bounce off me, Allis."

"I can understand that. Shall we talk about it tonight?"

"Okay. Okay."

"And try to understand?"

"I don't have to try; I understand, but I am tired of people asking me to understand. Shit, Allis, *I* want some understanding."

"Sorry. That was badly put."

"Sure was."

"Are you all right? I mean — "

"I've just been working. I'm all right. You?"

"Better now."

In her kitchen that night we talked as the ghosts of our histories, and those peculiar loyalties that come with them, lurked behind every word, gesture and glance.

She was sitting primly across from me, her knees together, her hands folded tightly in her lap.

"I apologize for my father. Deeply and sincerely."

I waved it off. "I didn't think this was going to be a cakewalk. But I didn't expect this, either."

"Neither did I. What is it you want me to do?"

"Do? Nothing."

She raised her brows. "Nothing?"

"Not now. When I come back, maybe."

She looked down at her knees, then studied my shoes. "Oh, dear," she said. "Is that what you want?"

"Allis, I need a little time; it's gotta bounce."

"Yes," she said. "Of course. I see. Maybe we can both use the time. Makes sense."

"Yeah." My conviction rested only in my anger.

"How's the script going?"

"I'll have the first draft finished day after tomorrow."

"And," she asked, rubbing her face, her eyes not quite focused, "when will you leave?"

"In two weeks."

"Uh-huh."

"You'll be busy, finishing up, I guess. Meetings, rewrites — "

"I think so."

"You'll call, won't you?"

"Yes, I'll call."

13

He fades and withers in the evening.
O teach us how to number our days,
That we may attain a heart of wisdom.

Why? keeps running through my thoughts. Why? Have I not touched on every reason? Did I not know this man — or the others?

I look at Dorothea Blue-Sky's bulk, at Mark Medowitz's bent, white head, which is resting against his splayed fingers as though it contains too much to be supported by his neck alone, and I wonder why. With Leonard, I think I knew why.

His voice gave out that winter night (I was later told), slicked on fortified wine, while he stumbled and skidded along Lower Broadway, flopping into snowbanks, his trousers stiff with urine gone to ice. But Leonard had no Hoyt Fuller to play to his Conrad Kent Rivers, no Frank Piskor to play to his Delmore Schwartz, and the last snowbank that clutched at him held him fast in a dirty white embrace. It loved him to his death, and the khaki-clad sanitation men, who daily find parts of bodies and other débris of our time on their jaundiced rounds, found him as the sun broke through a cloudy sky over Wall Street and blackened Trinity Church, and chopped him loose.

I look at Mark again and wonder, Why not him? Why not *me? Why,* Jolene?

Why had she not simply packed up the children and left Amos to his authors, his publishing company, his parties, his rages? No. She would show him!

While Amos was partying in New York, covering his wounds with martinis, scraping away the accumulation of that week's dumpings from colleagues, bosses, agents and even writers, she, Jolene Bookbinder, on that weekend's visit to relatives in East Orange, New Jersey, took their kids into the garage, closed the door, placed them in the car with her and gave them candy; and then she started the engine and carried them off with her, leaving behind a note of only three words:

FUCK YOU, AMOS.

Jolene Bookbinder never cursed.

I was moving through a world of the created insane, I think, and I was afraid.

The yarmulka on my head reminds me of bishops, cardinals and popes, of the doomed (sans electrodes) whose caps are made of metal.

I gaze at Betsy and I muse about her life with Paul. I am looking at her and hearing as she hears, the sound of heavy, quick-striding footsteps. Betsy turns. Her profile seems a close-up, her age very nearly revealed in the small valleys of pain and disappointments on her face, which reflects at that moment, however, nothing more than interest. (Who *is* that coming down the aisle with such a flutter?) The moving woman's presence strikes on her senses, and Betsy's eyes flash smoking anger as they key incredulously on the woman, and I, like a camera, truck with her glance until I see who it is Betsy has already noticed, and in alarm I cut back to Betsy at the moment her lips compress and release. Did she say "Bitch"?

We have seen Selena Merritt.

The years show on Selena's body, which is heavier now, its height, once so majestic, leavened by the bulk that moves under the draped clothing. Yet her face is strangely gaunt, as if worn fleshless by too many false smiles. Selena is, one still reads, a Personage, the Great Twofer, black and woman, that these gray last days so vigorously demand. She slides prettily, though funereally, into a pew.

Bitch! Betsy says, almost loud enough this time for everyone but Rabbi Kaminsky to hear. We all look down or up or straight ahead. Selena sits quite at ease.

Allis and I exchange glances. Well, well! she whispers. I look at Mark, whose wink is long enough to tell me that what I had heard as rumor he had known as fact.

Now Allis glares at her. For Selena over the years has blithely pronounced, in article after article, that white women are stealing black men. That black men have no wills of their own; that they, not so deep down, either, despise and are disgusted by black women. There is no lack of platform for such pronouncements by Selena and two or three others who are like her but younger, thus indicating a continuity of the attack. The magazine and book publishers never seem to tire of these statements. They run as regularly as trains used to.

I understand it: supply the weapons for the attack, but remain distant from it; let them destroy each other. Confuse the issue, for the women will not be the shock troops; they will not throw the hand grenades, aim the M-16s — except for a few.

There are fewer black women than black men, they cry; this white female theft must stop, they say, not understanding that it is we who are expendable, not they; that as long as they can perform coitus, we remain a people. (I seem to remember this from a dream.)

Allis glares as one who insists on remaining knowledgeable in the face of ignorance; she glares because Selena is far less honest than people presume; she glares because Selena begs to be used and because, given her relationships, her words are consummate bullshit.

Mark the innocent, Rabbi Kaminsky says. (Who among this group, I ask myself, is innocent?) *Look upon the upright.*
For there is a future for the man of peace.
Surely God will free me from the grave,
He will receive me indeed.
My flesh and heart fail,
Yet God is my strength forever.
The dust returns to the earth as it was,
But the spirit returns to God who gave it.
The Lord is my shepherd; I am not in want . . .

It is over. We will not go to the cemetery. We drift to the hallway, where Mark is waiting. We smile. He opens his arms and I open mine. We embrace. We have moved closer to Paul, through his life to the other side. We both study the detritus of the war littered over our faces and bodies — the eyes that will not stay met, the smiles that are not really smiles, and the clothes and the cut of them, of course. It is all there to be seen and digested, clucked over or wondered at later, in solitude.

Cay-toe!

It is Selena, of course, brushing through people, all teeth and withered dimples, pushing before her the scent of musk.

Christ, Allis mutters and manages to melt into the crowd of mourners, leaving me in Selena's clutch, her generous embrace complete with kiss and breasts mashed against my chest.

Her eyes, framing out Mark, say: *Don't be a nigger in front of these folks — kiss me back.*

Her eyes also say: *I guess I ripped this little party pretty good, didn't I, Cate?*

She says, How have you been?

She basks in the recognition, the turned heads, the sweeping glances. That's Selena Merritt, the playwright and poet!

Ah! Selena Merritt! What's she doing here?

Didn't I see your wife? she says. Such women who do know Allis' name discard it. She becomes Your Wife, as if somehow nameless. Such women, if they have occasion to call and Allis answers, dispense with the costless little courtesies, brusquely ask for me, hoping to wound my woman. And, for a time, they did. Now she says, This is Mrs. Cato Douglass and may I know who is calling him or take the message?

If the answer is no, her response is, Fuck you, Selena (or whoever it may be); I suggest you write a letter. Bango!

Selena is now all concern, turning her head this way and that, as if genuinely looking for Allis. Her concern is fleeting.

I have to go, she says, but let's do have lunch or a drink, please Cato. It's been far too long. Poor, *poor* Paul. To Mark as she is already moving away, Hello, Mark. Good to see you. She leaves, smiling regally as she threads through the crowd. Mark and I watch.

Did she have a thing with Paul? I ask.

Around the time he won the National Book Award, he says.

We have stepped into a small alcove, out of the crush of people. We are both thinking, I imagine, of that time when we began to question the things Paul had told us.

14

THAT HAD BEEN on the trip, halfway through the American leg, actually, in San Francisco.

We had crossed the George Washington Bridge and somewhat nervously entered America. We sat in the VW bus according to our status: Mark, the director and overall location boss in the jump seat. The driver was Ted, a huge guy who would help with the equipment. I sat behind with the cameraman, Dolph, the soundman, Vernon. Like Ted, Vernon was also big, and he was black. Dolph still spoke with a German accent. I was sure that the producer, back at 10 Columbus Circle, and Mark had selected Ted and Vernon as much for their size as for their skills.

I had been right about the script; changes had been made or suggested, and some froth had replaced substance.

At our meetings before departure, we had agreed by implication that we were not like those inhabitants west of the Hudson River. We were New Yorkers — several obvious cuts above your average American. We in the Apple told other Americans how they were, recording, or causing to be recorded, the events of their lives that might be of interest to others.

We had not yet burned churches or bombed the homes of ministers; we had not had to call in the U.S. Army or U.S. marshals to secure the peaceful entrance into school or college for one or two Negro youngsters.

Our people spoke out against such atrocities; our people went out from New York to march or bus themselves through hostile territories. Our leaders constantly addressed themselves to the racial inequities distant from New York. Our unions were integrated — why this very team was integrated. (See?) Martin Luther King, Jr., came to our town to relax. The national headquarters of the NAACP, the Urban League, CORE and half a hundred other organizations were in New York. New York supported the Movement. Starting with the activities of one John Kasper, the New York media covered the racial war, if not on the first page or segment, then soon after it. They increased their staffs in the South and hired intrepid stringers. And New Yorkers would be filing into the Village Vanguard to pay Le Roi Jones to excoriate them for being white.

Etc., etc., etc.

But the city *was* our warren, our burrow.

And now — somewhat nervous? Shit, we were afraid. *Out there* they bloodied and crippled those who recorded their riotous actions; *out there* they made cameramen eat their Arriflexes and Bolexes; *out there* they took the Uher tape recorders and sound blimps and beat the sound men with them. It seemed to us that some parts of the nation were littered with rolls of exposed film and sound tape, ripped cue cards, shattered camera lenses and tripods and hastily abandoned spiral notebooks and broken-headed correspondents.

Cautiously we worked our way through the cities and towns of Middle America — Newark, Paterson, Rochester, Buffalo, Cleveland, Chicago, Kansas City, Denver, Cheyenne, Salt Lake City, Boise, Seattle, Portland. In each there was the scramble to make contact with the local civil rights leader and his counterpart on the other side; in each the days were filled with unloading and hooking up the equipment, making last-minute script changes, writing up the cue cards; in each Mark paced while snapping at Dolph to hurry or to "do this one quick and dirty, baby," but Dolph, always elegantly casual in dress and manner, was taking his time, checking the blimp with Vernon, fixing a focus, framing the background against which I would stand, running off at the mouth, while I tried to look as if I knew what I was talking about. Strangers, drawn like iron fragments to the magnet of film, of television, put on suits, shirts and ties, best dresses, and best performances, to sit or stand with me before Dolph's camera.

Negroes, scattered like a broken string of beads in the mountain states, voiced precisely the sentiments of those to the east who were huddled into their assigned enclosures.

Whites were uneasy, but agreed that what was right, was right, though they were not always sure that the method for achieving it was the correct one at this time. On the whole, America then, on that leg of our trip, was an amiable enough place. But there was an endless void between the white people I talked to and history. This was all right with Mark, was what he wanted, the surface of things — slick, but sounding solid, appearing like the real thing.

Dolph and I, I came to learn, worked for something else: the nuances, the uncertainties, the sprays, like spittle, of anger, bigotry and unconcern. His close-ups (I was to see later, back in New York, when the dailies were run for us) revealed shallowness, false anger, plain bullshit on the faces of some of the people I was interviewing. Dolph had a way of curling his lip at many of Mark's directions, like a small boy who, face averted, silently snorts at advice. Mark did not know what Dolph knew, nor did I until later. Dolph was remembering a Germany of shattered glass and night visitors, of populations that later claimed not to know what went on in those camps outside their towns; of train searches to snare those slipping back into the country after fighting with the Thälmann Brigade of the International Brigades during the Spanish Civil War. Dolph had been one of those survivors. He went to France and, trapped there during the debacle and fall of the country in the summer of 1940, he joined the French Foreign Legion. Dolph never went further than that. He viewed our work as something he had seen before, unfolding before, but this time, perhaps, he could do something about it.

We shipped the Northwestern dailies to New York from Portland and took the Pacific Coast Highway down. We wanted to give ourselves a chance to rest, to think and mold the script to fit new angles. We'd do San Francisco and Los Angeles, then head southwest and, of course, south — with a set of California plates instead of the New York ones.

By the time we'd reached Eureka we'd rid ourselves of the little angers and exhaustions that had been compounding along the way. As we curled through the redwoods, I suggested that we look up Paul's father, Joe Cummings, at the headquarters of the International Longshoremen's and Warehousemen's Union headquarters; the second in command to Harry Bridges would not be hard to find. And a man close to Bridges who had outlasted Martin Dies, Edward Holt, John Wood, J. Parnell Thomas, Harold Velde, Francis Walters, Edwin Willis *and* their committees, along with J. Edgar Hoover, surely would have something to add to our story. (The Black Panthers hadn't come along yet and Berkeley students did not yet know what they were discontented about.)

Mark thought Paul's father would make a great insert.

Driving in the shadows of the great trees, I said, "The co-ops seems to have been a very special place, Mark. Paul says it was what made him."

"It was a special place then," Mark said. He seemed to be looking at something on my nose. "But I don't think Paul ever lived there."

I laughed. "Sure he did."

Mark shrugged. "We're the same age. Maybe I'm a couple of years younger than Paul, but I knew everybody five, ten years older than I was, and maybe five years younger. Man, I would've known Paul; everybody knew everybody else, or *heard* of everybody else, and I'm telling you, Paul Cummings did not live there."

"How come you never said that when you talked about the place with him; you remember those times when we met in the Village and got drunk, when you worked at that *Gash* magazine — "

"Shit, he said he lived there, which meant that he wanted to have lived there, and it was a special place, so if he wanted to say he lived there, okay by me. I didn't give a fuck."

Weakly, wondering, I said, "He wouldn't have said it if he hadn't lived there."

But Mark was bending to his clipboard, checking schedules and expenses.

"Joe who?"

"Cummings, Cumm*ings*," I said. He was the seventh person I'd asked. I was beginning to wonder if the union people were all dummies. But something nagged at me. Something didn't feel right.

"Joe Cummings works with Harry Bridges, the president. He's Bridges' right-hand man."

"No, Joe Cummings, no. Look, buddy, there ain't no such animal. No Joe Cummings *ever* worked with Harry, and I been with Harry since he stepped off the boat from Australia — "

"He's got a son, Paul — "

"No. Listen, I'm busier'n a bedsheet in a whorehouse. Television, ya said? Is there anything *I* can do for ya? No, well, ya better run along then, bud. Somebody sent you for a left-handed monkey wrench."

I walked out of his office and through the hall, thinking of Wobblies, radicalism and Joe Cummings, all shrinking fast into the perspective point of my mind. How could the Third Vice-President (for that's what the desk plate had read) *not* know Joe Cummings?

128

Where *was* Joe Cummings?

He existed, of that I was almost sure, until, walking back to the hotel, I recalled my conversation with Mark about Paul and the co-ops. One. Two. Then I was not so sure, which led me to ponder two obvious questions:

One. If Paul had not lived in the co-ops, why had he said so?

Two. If Paul's father was not Harry Bridges' right-hand man, why had he said so?

Before telling Mark, I called every J, Joe and Joseph Cummings in the phone book. Compared to the inches and inches of Browns, Joneses and Williamses in the directory, this was a snap.

"Hello, Joseph Cummings, Joe Cummings, with Harry Bridges and the IL and WU?

"Joe? Joe Cummings of the IL and WU?

"Your son, Paul, Mr. Cummings —

"Hello?

"Hello."

I called Paul. His telephone had been disconnected. And then I called Allis.

I would be calling her often, it turned out, but this time I wanted her to go by Paul's apartment and get the information on his father and call me back.

Paul had moved. There was no forwarding address.

"Fuck 'im," Mark said. "We'll go without it. You know something about this place, don't you?"

(I did remember, in a disjointed way, something about the Fillmore District. I'd been mad about a chorus girl who worked in a two-line chorus when I was at Shoemaker, waiting to be shipped over with the outfit. Catherine was back there, in the East, and I was on the edge of the vast Pacific, immersed in its nightly foggy sweatings over the Bay Area. The chorus girl and I slid back and forth on the A train, making love in every shadow along the streets; we had every drink conceived of by every misanthropic bartender: sky-blue P-38s, B-17s that were bomb-blast red and 50 Calibers that were gold and shot through with cherries.)

I said, "Why don't we tie Northern and Southern California together?"

Mark was going over the California segment of the script. I knew that he was uneasy about the history of bigotry against the Chinese, the Spanish-Americans and the Japanese-Americans; he didn't have to tell me that he wanted to have as little as possible to do with Tule Lake and Owens Valley, though he certainly saw the relationship between the way those people had been and often were still being treated, and what had happened and was still happening to Negroes.

Dolph sat a little distance away, checking the charge on a battery, I thought, and occasionally he'd look at me, his eyes blank, as if waiting for something to impinge upon them. I could hear Ted and Vernon talking down the hall.

I knew what was going on. Mark had invited me to play the game. He needed me and surmised that he could control me. Now I was playing too rough, linking truths that he knew very well, was in fact to some extent closer to them than I. He was puzzling over my inability to dance on that tightrope strung between truth and entertainment — albeit high-class, educational entertainment.

He said, "Well, okay, Cate, but I really don't think we ought to back too far into history. The Chinese railroad workers and the Japanese camps — you know, we ought to keep hammering, hammering, on the Negro thing."

Dolph cleared his throat, got up and left the room. Even as we were looking at the door through which he left, he returned and, leaning in, said directly to Mark, "The first person to die in a gas chamber was a Chinese man named Gee Jon. Denver Dickinson was the presiding official. In Carson City, Nevada, nineteen twenty-four." Then he was gone.

For 119 years the Legion (composed of only two regiments) was where men went to forget their pasts. The old romance clung as Ted wheeled us down the highway past wind-seared cypress trees, endless vistas of the sun-struck Pacific and through dozens of towns. There was something missing from Dolph's story. Vernon had replaced Ted at the wheel and Ted was now sleeping and dusk was coming on.

"You're Jewish," I said.

Dolph smiled his little smile. "Yes," he said. "I am a Chew. And I was a Thälmann." He shrugged. "They really wanted my head. Lousy Cherms." He closed his eyes. I wondered why Mark had not taken him down to Hollywood to hang out with the movie types. And then, close to dozing myself, I understood that Dolph would have his own bunch and that it would have nothing to do with Mark's. That made me feel better, for some reason, and I went to sleep.

Los Angeles then was raw and huge and still growing; its grids of streets formed at the base of mountains north, south and east of it and ran, often, as on rhumb lines, westward straight to the sea. Many corners were sprinkled with black men and women waiting for buses that were always late, crowded and still far from their homes. They had that look on their faces. There is a look that clamps on the faces of black people which is sometimes incompletely described as sullen; it is that and more. The expression is like the one on the face of the La Venta–Tabasco head — imperious, wrathful, calculating and filled with cold suspicion of past, present and future.

In Los Angeles, if you have to ride the buses, you are nowhere else but at rock bottom; and these people, strung out from Hollywood and Beverly Hills, Encino and Sherman Oaks, San Marino and San Gabriel, were still struggling to acquire that first used car, the one they probably would see on the weekend commercials when the clunker was king, the clunker that could take them from Watts to a job and back without falling apart.

We shot on Central Avenue, at the Golden State Mutual Life Insurance Company, where, with costly lighting, Dolph panned slowly over the murals done by Charles Alston and Hale Woodruff — *The Contribution of the Negro to the Growth of California* — which had everything, everybody, in them. Black executives and film people fell under Dolph's relentless camera, and soon we were all edgy; the real meat of the trip was coming up: Southwest, across the South and back to New York.

Mark seemed unusually pensive after his nightly call to the producer. "I don't understand why I *feel* this way," he said, when he had assembled us in his room the night before we left. "I mean, we live here in this country, right? We're Americans, right? Then, why do I feel this way — scared shitless."

Vernon laughed.

"Rick said to be very, very careful," Mark said, after glancing at Vernon. "If it looks sticky, Dolph, one take; if it looks very sticky — "

" — no take," Dolph finished.

"Right." He sighed. "Ted, you and Vernon, well, Rick says you guys, when it gets rough, get between *them* and the camera. We can always stick in some voice-over."

"Yeah," Ted said.

Vernon said nothing. Mark looked at him again. "Vernon?"

"Yeah?"

"The Nagra's dispensable, if it ever comes to that."

"I know it."

"What?" Mark said.

"I said, I know it's dispensable and, as far as that goes, so is the camera, Mark."

"Depends on the situation. You wanna say something, Cate?"

"No."

"Got the route down, Ted?"

"Bakersfield to Barstow and Route Sixty-six to Albuquerque, first stop."

"I don't believe it," Mark said softly. "I'm really worried."

"*You* don't have to worry," Dolph said. He inclined his head in Vernon's direction and then mine. "They do."

Mark was thinking of the black and white Freedom Riders, I knew, who had been beaten indiscriminately earlier in the year; he was thinking of the old guilt by association.

"What," I said, "me worry?"

We broke up. I was in my room packing when there came a soft knock on my door. I opened it to Vernon, who slipped in fast, carrying a brown bag. "You nervous?" he said with a grin.

"Mark made me nervous. Shit, I was all right before."

"Aw," he said, "ain't nothin' to it, but just in case there is, here. That's eighty bucks."

He handed me a brand-new leather holster in which rested a .32 revolver; he dipped into the bag again and came up with a box of shells. He grinned again. "Just in case."

Reaching for my wallet I asked, "Where did you — "

Vernon waved away the question. "This is Los Angeles, man, a wide-open country town where you can get anything you need, anything."

"What'd you get?"

"A Derringer for my sock and a thirty-two."

"Anybody else?"

"Look, man," Vernon said, pocketing the money. "I got all I can do to look out for number one, dig? But as long as I was buyin', I figured I could just as well see you down, too, know what I mean?"

"Yeah."

"See you."

15

ARMED WITH LISTS of the Ralph McGills, Hodding Carters, Judge
Warings and Martin Luther Kings of the South, we slipped into the warm
underbelly of America, a region that was quivering up out of the quagmire
of its past. The Northern mills that had moved south half a century before
to cheap labor, the dozens of military installations that had sprung up
with the wars, the space centers, the flexing of Southern and Southwestern
economic (political) muscle, made it a land in transition, restless among
its oil fields and soybean and grain and peanut fields; it was quick-tempered,
suspicious, uncertain. Alan Shepard might make his hotshot fifteen-minute
suborbital space flight; there might be disaster at the Bay of Pigs; Kennedy
and Khrushchev might argue in Vienna, but those were sideshows; the
main event was race and it was enlivened by semantic acrobatics, political
sleight-of-hand and brute force.

Oddly, where Ted and Vernon often had seemed to be irritable, snappish,
through the latter part of the Northern trip, now they were calm, watchful
and patient. I had not been so nervous since I was based at Camp Lejeune.
Then, I was vaguely aware that the South was a bad place. No knot
grew in my stomach then as it did now; it rested there, heavy, clinching
and unclinching itself, pulsing, heating up and freezing over by turns. I
had not known such fear before; perhaps I hadn't been old enough before.

Perhaps I'd felt, foolishly, that my uniform provided dispensation. Even overseas, I didn't have that fear of Southerners, for I carried a gun, too; was *there* to carry a gun and to kill with it.

Now, what corpsman would come to rescue me? What general would declare the action over, at an end? What court here would acknowledge my citizenship by rendering justice?

> *They don't come by ones*
> *They don't come by twos*
> *And they come by tens.*

The intervening eighteen years had imposed a hard learning on me, and it was made all the harder by my recognizing that I was feeling now just exactly the way many people *wanted* me to feel. Slashing through East Texas toward the Louisiana border, I felt sacrificed and as vulnerable as an ant crossing a summer sidewalk before a bunch of kids whose only entertainment was to crush it. It did not give me pleasure that the others shared the same feelings, no matter how they tried to conceal them. There were times when we were prowling through upcountry Louisiana and Mississippi that we looked at each other more closely than we ever had before; we seemed to draw together like the members of a squad sent out on an uncertain patrol. We laughed a bit too heartily at jokes; we made too big a point of not wiping off the mouth of whatever bottle of whiskey we were passing around.

We stayed in Negro hotels, money having won out over the managers' fear, and when we could not find them, we slept in the van, aping the impossible postures of the dead, though none of us ever slept soundly. We lived in the fear that gas stations would not fill us up, and underfoot in the van lay a carpet of bread, cracker, cookie, hamburger and hot dog bun crumbs. Even staying in contact with the producer and our friends and families, a matter we'd taken quite for granted, was a problem as we moved through great forests of pines or dry, hard hillsides or endless, poorly tended fields. New York did not have the market on busted and rifled public phone booths, and the places where we stayed, if not without phones altogether, usually had but one, located in the most public of places, which, always grudgingly, we were allowed to use one at a time, and at spaced intervals so that we would not tie up the line.

The police tailed us, sitting on our rear for miles while Ted, grinning nervously, crept well within the speed limit, and then, one night, we hit Montgomery, where we were told we could find a good place to stay in Tuskegee. We bumbled our way out of town on Eighty-five, looking for

Shorters, where we would turn off on Eighty. It was night and we were tired, having loaded and unloaded several times to shoot people and places and do interviews in the Cradle of the Confederacy.

"We got a tail," Vernon said. He was spelling Ted at the wheel.

Ted said, "Want me to take it?"

"No can do now," Vernon said, and he mashed the accelerator.

"Isn't it a cop?" Mark said. He was tensed and turned around, looking out the rear window.

"No. Wouldn't be much better off, anyway," Vernon said. "Here they come!"

He gripped the wheel. We all turned backward and to the left, watching the headlights of the tailing car, high beams on, racing up.

"Hang on!" Vernon cried, and he braked suddenly, kicking it into a lower gear when the van screamed almost to a halt. The other car flashed by; we saw a blur of white faces, heard rebel yells, heard *thunka-thunka-thunka* before the sound of shots.

"They're shooting at us!" Mark yelled. We could already feel the air streaming in from the bullet holes in the side of the van. I sensed movement up in front, where Vernon was, a movement both covert and angry. My gun was in my hand. "Anybody hit?" Ted asked. His voice was shaking. "Dolph?"

"Naw."

"Mark? Cate? You okay, Vernon?"

We were all okay.

"They're gonna be up ahead," Vernon said. "Bet your bottom dollar on it." He picked up speed. "Cate, you ready?"

"Yeah."

I think Mark turned to look at me; if he was surprised, the darkness concealed it.

"You guys got pieces?" Ted asked.

We didn't answer; we stared ahead. Vernon kicked on the high beams. I heard Dolph working at his camera case.

"Aw, shit," Mark said. "Aw, shit."

Now Dolph hung himself over the front seat between Vernon and Ted. I heard Vernon say: "Hey Dolph, what's that — hey! This cat's got him a cannon! A Luger!"

Dolph said nothing. Was there no traffic on this goddamn road, I wondered. Would it make a difference?

"There!" Vernon shouted. He jabbed his hand leftward. "That's them! Off on that dirt road!" He quickly lowered his window and started firing at the car before we were abreast of it. Dolph leaned out behind him and I opened the side window. Vernon was flying and we were firing like hell. Dolph's gun carried real authority: PA-BoOM! PA-BoOM! PA-BoOmbPABoOM! When we flashed by, we saw figures running and ducking. I thought I heard glass breaking. Vernon was so intent on firing backward that he almost ran off the road. Ted grabbed the wheel and veered us back. My hand had stopped jerking; clacka clacka clacka. Empty.

We started laughing. "Hu-boy, man, shot the shit outa those redneck fuckers," Vernon said. I couldn't stop laughing. Even Mark was roaring. Dolph chuckled and looked back through the rear window.

It was five minutes before Ted said, "We'd better forget Tussegee tonight — "

"Tuskegee," I said.

"Whatever. We better keep on truckin' till we get to Atlanta."

"Yeah," Mark said. "Fuck Rick. He's there in New York. No one's shooting at him. We just won't film anymore in Alabama."

"Pull over, Vernon," Ted said. "I'll take it."

"What if we hit one of them?" Mark asked.

"Too bad," Dolph said.

"That's just why we gotta keep goin'," Ted said, scrambling into the driver's seat. With the doors momentarily opened, the smell of the night-time South whipped in. I thought of Toomer's *Kabnis* and the fears that came with the night.

Mark said, "How far is Atlanta?"

"About a hundred and fifty miles," I said. "A hundred fifty miles and a hundred dog-ass towns."

Dolph said, "Reload."

There was a pause. I reached for the box of shells. I heard Vernon reloading, and Dolph, and then the silence became deeper yet. Ted settled, cleared his throat, and we moved quickly through the night, almost catching up with the lighting provided by the headlights. The van ran smoothly. I found myself listening for a tire to blow, the axle to crack — for something bad to happen so that we couldn't get out of that place. The dashed center line, like big tracer shells, rushed up through the darkness to hit us head on without impact.

We were vibrating between the deepest fatigue and the tensions of fear. I thought, quite consciously this time, of my foxhole and the smells and sounds that surrounded it. Why did I consider that to have been at war and this, my present condition, to be something less?

Fool.

Goddamn it, I thought. I still had so much to do: a child to help raise, another to find, another woman to wed (yes, yes, piss on her father) and so much writing to do, all the way out to the edge of the language. There were things I wished to see and do and feel and smell.

But there I was, with the others, fleeing, scared shitless, through the night, as fearful that I might have killed someone as I was about being killed by him. More. What insanity!

"God, I hope you guys didn't hit one of them," Mark said.

The rest of us listened to the tires whisking over the road and listened to the echoes of what he'd really said. He too was more afraid of killing than being killed.

Hours later, just outside Atlanta, in College Park, we found a public phone booth that was intact. Mark wanted to call the producer. As he scrambled out of the van, we heard the sound of jets. Mark paused, stuck his head back inside. "Pack up everything," he said. "I've got an idea."

"What?" I asked.

His smile seemed to float in the shadows. "I'm telling Rick that we're gonna charter a private plane to New York. Now." He turned to the sound of the jets. "That's gotta be the airport, right, Ted?"

Ted was already bent over his maps, steadying a flashlight. "Yeah. Atlanta Airport."

"Pack up, pack up," Mark said and ran to the booth.

"Those cheapskates at Ten Columbus'll never okay it," Ted said.

We heard a siren back on the road and turned, holding our breath; it faded off in another direction. We focused on Mark's silhouette in the booth. Through the open door, the jets sounded strangely sweet. The idea had quickly taken root among us. A plane! We could be out of there in an hour, two at the most, and if they were looking for us on the highways, they'd find nothing but the van. We would be at La Guardia by daybreak, back in New York. We'd be safe.

Mark was shouting; his voice carried nearly to the van, and then he seemed to calm, as though he'd been mollified. Seconds later he held up his hand with his thumb and forefinger pressed together in an O. We hopped out of the van and ran to the booth.

"Who's got some dimes?" Mark asked, thumbing viciously through the phone book. "Ted, get those plates off the van and take all the papers out of the compartment. Here, here's one."

He dialed three companies before he found a pilot willing to take us up right then.

The dawn, lacking thunder, came up behind us on the starboard side.

I felt as one with every escaped slave who had at last crossed into Ohio or a safe place in Pennsylvania. They had been on foot, of course, and I was flying high, comfortable at ten thousand feet and moving at better than two hundred miles an hour. Yet the cause behind their flight and mine was unchanged.

On the plane, half-listening to Mark explain that we'd be met and dropped off in the city and gather at 10 Columbus Circle day after tomorrow to see all the U.S. dailies and make final plans for Africa, I'd been sure that after I collected my mail from Mr. Storto and went to my apartment, I would fall apart with fatigue.

That did not happen. I was eager to stand at my window once again and look down into the street; I watched people, looked at things. I bathed myself in the safety of those ordinary acts. I was in my town, my neighborhood, my building, my apartment. I seemed to ache with the weariness of a year's travel, but we'd been gone only a little over two months. I moved to the mail.

Glenn's cramped, careful writing. "Thanks for the check. Made our junior high school basketball team." Christ, where was it all going? Making teams already.

And the bills.

Maxine Culp, Literary Agent. "Been trying to reach you. I'm set now and have some clients. My invitation still stands, if you tire of Alex." She wrote about Jolene Bookbinder's death and reported that Amos had disappeared for a few weeks. I had never met Jolene and she was not real to me. She was to Amos undoubtedly, now, the far side of reality. I felt relief before I felt sympathy. All combat soldiers do.

More bills.

Paul Cummings was, his letter informed me, "vanishing for a while. Traveling and thinking. 'Woodshedding,' I think you'd call it, Cate. Assessing my work, what direction I should take. And my personal life, too, chum. That's a mess I mean to straighten out. The Goog will help me while I go on this self-shrink bit.

"I may just pop in on my old man in San Francisco when I finally settle out there. I'll be in touch — I can't ever see us really being *out* of touch. [About his father: liar, fuckin' liar!]

"I may not be around when you and Allis do your thing, so here's looking at you, kid. I hope it works like hell. There's one thing, though: Leonard is worse than ever. Keep an eye out when you can, okay? When I get an address, I'll send it on."

138

Royalty statements. As usual, I owed the publisher.

I decided to call Allis later. And then I was hungry. I fixed a big drink and opened a can of corned beef hash. I ate furiously, and the warm food, the ambience of safety, converged on my fatigue. I crawled into the bed and slept. Slept while an insistent part of that machine, my mind, suggested, formed decisions:

¡Ay! ¡Jugemos, hijo mio,	Let us play, my son,
a la reina con el rey!	at being king and queen.

And when I woke, at an hour stilled in time by its darkness, I went to my bookshelf and pulled down the Spanish edition of *Clarissa* and hastily scribbled down the name of the publisher: Amaya, Barcelona. It would be a place from which to start.

I went back to bed with a sense of accomplishment; the darkness had framed my plans. But tomorrow (today) there were still others; I had to call Allis.

We lay once again nude in the aftermath. (For then our bodies were taut and young, unlined and resilient, and we were proud of them.) I had told her of the trip, of Mark, of Dolph and Vernon and Ted, of the escape. And after a while I said to her, "I think I may have a child living in Spain. I want to find it."

"Oh," Allis said. "I see. You didn't tell me." She looked at me and waited.

"I tried to find the mother before I left. Monica."

Allis' expression was unchanged. "Why is it that you never said anything before?"

"I wasn't sure that I wanted to do anything about it. Anyway, what was there to say? It happens. Like weather. I guess I thought a lot about it on the trip."

"Uh-huh."

"I thought I'd stop in Barcelona on the way back from Africa."

"What about Monica?"

"Monica? Nothing."

"Did you love her?"

"No. I was lonely."

"What was she like?"

"Quiet. A little sad. She had a kid already."

"Was she pretty?"

"Sometimes — I mean, yeah, I guess she was."

Allis found a feather, picked it up and watched it drift to the floor. "What'll you do if you find them?"

"Try to help. Money, I guess. Maybe she'd let me bring him here."

Now her face was all question mark. "Here?"

I just looked at her.

She said with a sigh, "Yes, I guess you'd want that — "

"Would you," I said, "*mind?* Can you see a kid with us?"

Her smile was wan. "I don't know, frankly."

"I worry about him. More than Glenn. Monica was so poor, close to starving. I can't let that happen to *my* kid, Allis."

She rubbed her eyes. "Funny, how the past comes dragging in behind you, like my father."

I didn't say anything.

"That's not quite the same though, is it?"

"Not at all, except that that's the way it is."

She said, "I can't talk to him about it, Cate."

"Seen him?"

It took a long time for her to answer. "He doesn't want to see me."

"Monica," I said, "had that problem with her father, too." I held her tight. "Why don't you meet me in Paris," I said.

"Shall I? Would you want me to?"

"Yeah. Let's do a week there and come on back home."

"What if you have the child with you?"

"Then I'll need some help. If I don't, then we'll party."

Now she was smiling. "And after?"

"Mark was asking me when we would use Graenum Gordon — "

"You told him we wouldn't?"

"Yeah. You should have seen his face. Until I told him we'd be using someone else."

People are pushing us out of the alcove. I am looking for Allis. Mark lingers by, obviously not in a hurry, obviously wanting to continue touching the base, and so, once outside, we stand again chatting emptily, until he says, "Let's grab a coffee." We head for the nearest shop. I cannot quite digest all the changes in the neighborhood. The old San Juan Hill is gone; Lincoln Center, Juilliard, etc., etc., are there now, surrounded by the space that is always absorbed by people.

It is not that talking over the old times is an exercise that bores me; rather it is that certain untoward events, such as Paul's funeral, seem always to provide the catalyst for these exercises. We must *happen* on them, then milk them back over the years to lend substance to what we are. We must forgive or pretend to have forgotten the awkward circumstances.

The series had won the Best Educational Documentary the year it appeared on television. Mark, using my material, had finished two others, writing them himself. The first time, I called to complain about his bold theft and he said with a laugh, "Cate, the material was too good *not* to use again." I didn't bother to phone the second time. What was the use? Men more formidable than I had had their skills pilfered. When I think of the traffic lights that surround the world, haughtily stopping traffic or commanding it to go, I think of Garret Morgan, whose invention was neatly boosted by Big Business. The list, in every endeavor, is endless. I knew it then; I know it now. Yes, what was the use; given history, wasn't it foreordained?

So now the three of us are in a booth, inspecting each other with theatrical fondness, remembering the old days.

16

THE SKY was restlessly awesome — a vast inferno of color: here a boiling pale green simmering up to a faience blue; there a swirling curl of gold through which appeared a smear of red that tailed off to tendrils of orange and gold and brown. It was as though history had been distilled into color, as though dynasties had been wafted into the skies above their resting places down on the earth. Great fluffed clouds drifted through it all, now assuming the profile of a long-dead pharaoh, a slender maid carved from calcite, or a range of breathlessly high mountains resting on the base of the rays of the setting sun.

Beneath us, the captain now announced, was the city of Alexandria, of Alexander and Philadelphus and Julius Caesar and lost, burned and stolen knowledge. Its lights, browned by the atmosphere between the plane and the ground, blinked weakly as it slid back under us. We began our descent for Cairo.

We were arriving in Africa without Ted. The producer at 10 Columbus had decided that we should hire local drivers familiar with the roads. (This would be one of the better decisions he would make in all his years in television.) We would also fly. (My script called for shooting in Egypt, Ethiopia and then West Africa.) Therefore, we would not require a driver.

We made the most of our stops in London, Frankfurt, Nicosia and

Athens; now we had to get to work, with the cooperation of the Egyptian Ministry of Tourism, we hoped. That we were coming into Cairo at all was something of a miracle orchestrated by my threat to quit, the suggestion that the producer was a latent bigot ("Egypt after all is still a part of Africa, Rick"), and my implacable insistence that Ethiopia and Haile Selassie were very much a part of where I was going with the series, as I saw it. I exhausted him with arguments, history and his personal vulnerability. ("If the League of Nations had listened to Selassie, there might not have been a Spanish Civil War, perhaps not World War Two, and perhaps no concentration camps, Rick. But who was he? How did they regard him, Rick? He was a short little nigger, running a nigger country that no one gave a good goddamn about. Especially, they denied that any wisdom could be formed in the brain and mouth of this short little nigger, and so they did nothing. White people may have forgotten, Rick, but blacks have not." Ah, yes, I really laid it on him.)

The Comet was cutting back on power, suddenly, so that I felt stuck for a moment in the darkening sky, nudged by the finger of God. The pilot was immediately suspected of having pushed the wrong button, pulled the wrong lever. People turned to each other, whispering furiously, casting indignant glances up toward the cockpit. White Westerners never believe non-Westerners capable of maneuvering such intricate Rolls-Royce- or Boeing-produced equipment. But we stayed in the air, slid into our assigned pattern and landed at Cairo without incident.

I took a very, very deep breath and closed my eyes and tried desperately to strain out the history I'd been taught and to see this land that I was about to touch perhaps for the first time in five hundred years with eyes and soul only mildly wounded by my sojourn across the ocean.

I glanced quickly at Vernon; he seemed to be at peace. Dolph still dozed. Mark fretted.

A representative from Tourism greeted us. Something had happened to our hotel reservations. We would not be staying in Cairo after all, but a little bit — "little bit, little ways" — outside. "Nice place."

A joint called the Mena House (right out of Kipling) he said, and mumbled something about Pyramids, Sphinxes . . . His presence didn't hasten us through customs, and by the time we arrived in Gizeh it was approaching midnight.

I was tired, but I could not control a humming undercurrent of waking sensibilities. A thousand teachers, five hundred thousand repros of Egyptian wall paintings, five hundred books complete with plates, had not prepared me for this Egypt: there were so *many* black people there.

But one does not travel through Africa as much as it travels along the senses, sometimes tenderly, often brutally, always, however, igniting some dormant dream or nightmare, a déjà vu and slowly, very slowly, came the perception of an awesome arena in which had been played out the mightiest dramas conceivable.

From the Pyramids at Gizeh and Meroë, the emperor's battered palace at Addis Ababa, to the old structures at Great Zimbabwe; from Katanga and the havoc the Belgians called independence, to the oil fields at Port Harcourt and the slave ports at Badagry, Cape Coast and Elmina (they never stop taking from Africa); and then, crossing the rivers, the Nile, the Blue Nile, the Niger, the Benue, the Congo and a hundred others, we passed over a dozen countries, all larger than the European nations that had only recently "freed" them. Yes, flew over their orange-brown plains and buff-colored deserts, their rain forests curled and napped like green hair; we sweated and cursed in our hired vans, at our drivers, who handled the cars as if they were Shango riding thunderbolts; we located in city and bush, shooting, interviewing, writing and rewriting. Everywhere Kennedy's Camelot Corps, knights and damsels, poured into the continent as if, with sheer will alone, they would roll back five hundred years. But Africa absorbed them as it always had everyone else, everything else, conqueror or not, and remained Africa, victim, conjuror, a big, sly, patient, ancient black lady who had forgotten or concealed more knowledge than most other lands have yet to know. Its vastness intimidated; its rush away from its own theft-plagued civilizations to the ones that had enslaved it, puzzled, irritated. Cultural domination did not deploy divisions in the field; its troops were phantoms: Peugot. Triumph. Ford. Dunhill. 555. Benson and Hedges. Marlboro. Nestlés. Presley. Barclays. Chase. BOAC. Pan Am. KLM. Gordon's. Johnny Walker. Bovril. BBC. VOA. Lucille Ball. Car 54 Where Are You? Carrier. Philips. Sundowners. Marilyn Monroe. Sidney Poitier. G. Mennen Williams. Averell Harriman.

The West, with its terrible references, was wedged between us, me and the Africans, Vernon and the Africans. We skated on the surfaces of things frozen in our memories. All these people and all this land suborned by the usual coalition: the people with the money and the people with the madness. There had been too generous a nature in this land: *You must not oppress the stranger. You know how a stranger feels, for you once lived in a strange land.* See now how the stranger has abused your generosity!

I had pondered these things at night, sweating, half-drunk beneath my mosquito net, listening to the million sounds of life, and thinking,

All day long and all night through
One thing only must I do:
Quench my pride and cool my blood,
Lest I perish in the flood.

The Negro, that was the title I wanted for the show. *The Negro,* and how I wanted the inevitability of him to flash across millions of sets, leaving a shadow; wanted viewers to ponder what Locke, Spengler and De Tocqueville had predicted. For how could it be otherwise one awful day? To defeat this people utterly?

Out of an aqualithic interior the African had come, a Ta-nuter so awash that rivers carved by their surging paths twenty-five thousand years ago still remained, flowing more slowly, meandering more deliberately. They had survived the pluvials, these people, and they had survived somehow unspeakable cataclysms now collected in a thousand myths. *(Ouagadougou was lost four times and Ouagadougou was found four times.)* And did the continent crack, leaving that awful wound, the Great Rift, and raising the Atlas Mountains? Did it crack while men watched, and did the waters dry up, leaving deserts and the Sudd and salt mines men would kill to control? Perhaps the survivors had already moved to the delta, and perhaps the mass cracked once more, isolating them, leaving them to nurture civilizations that would be assigned to others because these people were a generous people, giving their gods to the Greeks, who sailed them to Rome and to the corners of its empire: Shango, for one, becoming Hercules, Atlas, Thor, perhaps. These Africans even absorbed the mysterious Garamentes, who reappeared as Coromantees, some to remain, others to travel that woeful passage over the sea. Defeat these people? Look, there, shitting over the open sewer; but his folk mastered, indeed, may well have invented, iron and the use of copper, bronze and gold, while — it has been said so often before — Europeans were buggering each other in caves and painting themselves blue; and his land hosted both the pygmy Akka and the giant Wa-Tutsi and all the sizes in between, as if this land were the stage upon which a previous engagement called "civilization" was having a revival.

I wanted this in my film.

Finally, we stood at last on a beach of Côte d'Ivoire. (The citizens could not register at the hotels nearby; they were for whites only.) Dolph was shooting me against the sea, on which, just as Mark had planned, there sailed near the horizon a vessel whose leaks and tattered sails the camera could not see. It was the shape in profile that Mark wanted. The ship sailed, I talked, and when the vessel was out of the frame and I had finished my lines, Mark yelled, "CUT!" and it was done.

17

IT WAS SODDEN and gray in Barcelona. I was sitting in a café in the Rambla de los Estudios having a cognac, pondering the sense of freedom I felt. People flowed up to Plaza de Cataluña and down to Plaza Puerta de la Paz. Here and there in the movement of humanity I saw a Negro, always a man. If Monica was still in the business, it was too early. But I was restless in my hotel room. I had explained the situation earlier to my publisher, a young Catalan who wore French suits. He would check with the staff about a black family named Jones. Such a family, he assured me with a smile, would not be too difficult to detect in Barcelona. Failing that, he said, he would ask a friend, a police functionary.

Because he said nothing about the Guardia Civil, I guessed that it would not be too cool to suggest contacting them. I strolled through the streets until I came to a car rental and then drove out to Sitges.

Yanez was in the *plaza,* sleeping in his taxi, his arms folded over his chest. I hesitated before waking him and studied the car; it was the same old battered Seat.

"Señor, Señor Yanez," I said. "Wake up." I held under his nose a freshly opened pack of Old Gold cigarettes. (No, I had not stayed with Philip Morris.) "Guardia Civil," I snapped and he jerked awake, eyes popping.

"Señor Douglass," he said, rubbing his eyes and grinning sheepishly. He reached for a cigarette and I lighted it for him and got in beside him. We shook hands heartily.

"You've returned."

"Yes, I'm looking for — " and here I pondered what to say. Yanez and his wife had called Monica Señora Douglass, knowing or, at the very least, sensing what the arrangement actually was. "Monica," I said.

"Not since you left have we seen her, my friend. Not once." He shrugged and lowered his eyes. "The child? You've come because of the child?"

I nodded.

Then he nodded. He smiled. We sat in silence, I watching the dreary panorama of women dressed in black traveling to and from the market; women dressed in black on their knees scrubbing sidewalks in front of their shops; the men selling lottery tickets; the men standing talking in front of the *estanco* or slipping briskly into and out of the *bodegas* holding their bottles; the priests walking grandly down the streets, passing kids playing *futbol;* the two-man Guardia Civil patrol walking with measured stride through the *plaza* — nothing had changed.

"Well, what will you do, Señor?"

"Don't know." I gave him a copy of the Spanish edition of *Clarissa.* I wasn't sure that Yanez and his wife read books, but what the hell. While I lived there I claimed to be a writer; now they had proof.

Yanez looked at my picture on the back. He seemed impressed. He looked at me quickly, somewhat shyly, and then said as he stroked the book proudly, "Ah, who would have guessed it. And in Spanish, too."

He now offered me a Bisonte, took one for himself. He tilted his head back. "Business is bad, Señor Douglass. Franco, he makes the promises, you know, but nothing happens."

"How's the hotel?"

"If not for that" — he made an airy sound — "nothing."

"Yeah."

"It's good that spring is coming soon. They say a lot of tourists will come this year. I hope so. Tell me, is it good to come again?"

"It's good to be back, yes."

"Is that your car?" He pointed at my rental.

"Rented."

He slapped the steering wheel and laughed. "Well, this one still runs. Remember?"

I smiled, remembering our trip in it. "Sure, I remember."

He turned toward me and put a hand on my shoulder. "Señor, it isn't very likely that she'd come back to Sitges unless she had" — and here he briskly rubbed his thumb and fingers together — "lots of money, you know."

Yes, I guess I knew that, but I'd also thought that perhaps our time together had been special enough to have triggered in her the desire to be somewhere nearby. My pitiful vanity, my secretly huge ego, my adolescent efflorescenses powdering out. I nodded in agreement. "How's your wife?"

"Still complaining. Today she went to Castelldefels to see her sister. On the bus."

At least, I thought, I wouldn't have to pay the courtesy call and suffer her accusing glances.

"Bad weather," Yanez said, glancing at the overcast sky. "It's all that atomic-testing business."

"Anyone living where I used to live?" I wanted to stop by there, walk down to the beach.

"A fat lady from Switzerland. A painter."

"Ah, too bad."

"You can drive around there, of course."

"Of course. I have to go, Señor Yanez. I must get back to Barcelona."

He said, "Do you think it's a boy? Would you look so hard for a girl?"

I wondered at his question. "It's mine, whatever it is," I said.

"Señor," he said as I was getting out, "come back when you find him."

"Okay. Good luck." I gave him the Old Golds. He waved when I started up and pulled away.

There was a note at the hotel telling me to call my publisher at home immediately.

"We have found for you," he said breathlessly, "a family Jones that lives on the corner of Calle Balmes and Calle de Rosellon, you know where that is?"

I assured him that I could find it and he gave me the address.

"Señor Jones is a black man and his wife is Spanish. That is as you told me, correct?"

"Yes." I wondered if that was the only such Jones family they'd located.

"We don't have any other, I am sorry."

He invited me to dinner at the Petit Soley in the Plaza Villa Madrid. I accepted.

Señor Jones, who looked, I guessed, the way Federico might look when he was grown, answered the door. He seemed at first startled to see standing under the weak light in his foyer another black man. Then he smiled. "You're an American, I can tell that," he said in English that reminded me of the way West Indians spoke. "Come in."

He was dressed as all men of his class in Spain dressed: a white shirt with slightly soiled collar, a tie, a sweater and a suit jacket over it. "Please come in. I don't see many American black people here, although some do come to play music. Coo-tie Williams, Duke the Ellington, do you know them?"

I was sitting where he had waved me. "Sherry?"

I accepted.

"Please bring two glasses of sherry," he said in Spanish, and down along the tiled corridors a woman answered and minutes later she entered, looking very much like Monica, a shawl over her shoulders.

"He's from America, my dear," Señor Jones said in Spanish.

I had stood and now I gave her a little bow and she smiled. I saw that she had brought three glasses of sherry and, taking the last after serving us, she sat down.

I told them my name and what I did for a living and that I had been in Barcelona four years ago. "I met your daughter then," I said. "And I am looking for her now."

Señor Jones said briskly, "We do not know where she is. She has been away from here over four years." He stared into his sherry. I looked at Señora Jones. Was it possible (it always happened in fiction) that somehow mother and daughter got back in touch? She, too, peered at her sherry.

I stifled a shiver. The marble floors gave off a sharp chill and they were not using an electric heater, at least in this room, nor a *butano* stove.

"So you have heard nothing?"

Señor Jones met my gaze directly. "Nothing. May I ask, Mr. Douglass, why is it that you want to find her?"

That question, of course, had to come.

"Where," Señora Jones asked, "did you meet her?"

"In the restaurant of the Majestic Hotel."

Señor Jones almost dropped his sherry. The Majestic was still a pretty grand place. "In the Majestic — "

"Yes, Señor. I liked her very much and we had dinner two or three times more and she showed me around Barcelona."

"She has a child. Did she tell you?" Señora Jones said.

"Ah, yes. Federico. He often came with us." I knew that the señora would like to think of a third party, someone to watch over her daughter.

"But," I said, "you've heard nothing? You've no idea where she might be?" God, I thought, they don't even know about the other child.

"We had some — er — differences," Señor Jones said. "She was an adult, you know, but young people can be so forward — "

Señora Jones was nodding agreement. I could see in both their eyes that I might be their salvation. Respectability. Their savior from their daughter's shame. It seemed like a good place to hand them a copy of *Clarissa.*

"Yours? Yours?" Señor Jones said, whipping out his glasses and sliding them into place. His wife leaned over his shoulder.

"Is it for us?" Señora Jones asked.

"Yes, certainly," I said.

Señor Jones sat back and removed his glasses. His wife took the book from his hand. "Was there something important about wanting to see my daughter?"

He was thinking of marriage.

"She was very kind to me," I said, "and so I thought I'd try to find her again. This is really just a short visit."

"Are you — married, Mr. Douglass?" Señora Jones asked.

"No, I'm not."

They exchanged glances. I checked my watch, then fished out a pad and wrote my name and address on it. "If you see her," I said, "please ask her to write to me."

I walked. I went to the dance hall where I'd met Monica, but it was early. I asked after the Cubans, but they no longer worked there. No one had heard of her. It was hard to know if they were telling the truth. Who was I? A stranger. They owed me nothing.

Plaza de Cataluña, encircled by neon signs from the tops of buildings around it, was almost empty. I moved, eyeing every female figure that vaguely resembled Monica down the Ramblas to Calle Cañuda and the Plaza Villa Madrid.

The publisher was waiting for me and grandly escorted me to a table. We were the attraction; I was the attraction in that Catalan intellectual gathering place, and I rather enjoyed it.

Had he found the right family? I told him that he had, but my friend was not there. He was sorry, very sorry. What would I do now?

Paris and then home.

18

I THINK that we were both relieved when I checked into the Danube to meet Allis without a child in tow. Of course, we walked a lot and found the spots where American writers of another generation had eaten, had hung out, had, ultimately, come to despise and envy each other. We usually spent an hour or two at the Café Tournon, which was where Richard Wright had held court. Mainly, then, I was trying to understand this country that had invited Wright to live in it in the first place, and then turned its back on him when his work encompassed its hypocrisy. Encompassed? Struck at the heart of it.

And what of that woman who held hands with me as we shuffled through Paris, confident that we would not be lynched, but not so sure that we would not be spat upon? She surrounded my thinking, as one pads a precious object, with love, an endless patience with the elements of chance and circumstance that had brought us together. We did not talk of her father, and I had no parents to talk about; we were as the eggs of a creature of time, abandoned, left to our own devices, sucking for nourishment on experiences our forebears, not we, had suffered. Those things remembered, but unknown.

Paris was neutral territory and in it we discovered that we still liked each other enough to talk of love; in it we gathered strength, leveled out our mutual weaknesses, raised our mutual strengths, and then we turned westward, like birds readying for the rising of the wind, and we went home to be married.

It was by then spring in New York, which moved us infinitely more than it had in Paris, and the sap from a thousand notes, written in longhand and stored in the head, began running together, wanting urgently to become a novel.

There was, happily, a ton of mail to wallow in, from Paul, from Amos, from publishers and editors, from Glenn, from distant places and people I'd never met but who had met me through my work. And then we had to find a judge who would marry us in his chambers, and I had to visit Glenn, and we had to move Allis' things to my place, which was, but not much, bigger. Besides, it was in the Village, where we presumed there existed a tolerance for people like us or, if not, at least a check on obvious acts of intolerance. Rick and Mark wanted me present at the screenings of the dailies and for part of the editing, and Alex Samuels had lined up three articles for me to write.

Much of the mail consisted of books publishers wanted me to read and praise so that they could lift quotes and use them in advertising, on book jackets or both. All but one of the books were written by black authors, a fact I noted quickly, but without rancor, accepting with a certain graciousness what appeared to be a growing literary status. That I would be sent the works of more white authors I was certain. Since Amos had sent two of the books, I called him, thanked him for his letter and asked how he was doing. He sounded depressed and distracted and only mildly surprised that I was getting married. Would I be interested in doing a book on Africa? I told him I didn't think so, because I hadn't sorted everything out yet.

"You just don't want to be published with me, do you?"

And God, yes, I did, I did, but we were both "debased" workers; he thought he was a producer. I produced. He was a cog in the long, capitalist chain. We were powerless. Never mind that he had been made to look as one with power; *petits rois* were a part of the landscape. And Amos still consumed more than I did, though it was not his money. That was entrapment, for he had once felt that he had to live personally as well as he lived on the job. Whole cultures had thus been encoded into the system. Had Amos not had to answer to bosses, had he even said, "I have no power. Maybe together we can get some," I would have signed in a minute. But he continued to believe that he was what they never would let him be.

Welcome home.

However, all I told Amos was that there were experiences in my trip that I didn't want to reveal to anyone, much less in print, just yet, until I'd had time to place them in context. He didn't believe me. Nevertheless, resigned, he offered me a lunch within a few days and I accepted.

Paul had been to the Coast, where he'd seen his father, and was now settled in Chicago, near the university. His description of his neighborhood smacked of a test run, a draft; what they call, in feature articles, color; what they call, in novels, description. I think I was supposed to respond with a comment on how much it affected me. Instead, I thought, *He is still lying! Lying!* Why does he go on and on about this fucker who's supposed to be his father when no one's ever heard about him, as though some information would not wash over me, as though I had not yet learned that too many bad guys point to the days when, briefly, they were good and left and concerned with injustice, as though I did not now know that his father had given him his points?

As I pushed aside the mail in a heat, together with soiled clothes, I knew it all had to do with *me*, not him. *I* wanted him to be different, to believe and be a believer in the shit (as we all wanted to, but at someone else's energies), and he felt this pressure increasingly in ways not spoken. I wanted him to confess, renounce, deny by his acts that his heritage could be based only on my disinheritance.

I wrote feverishly, telling him about my visit to the ILWU, about Mark and the co-ops, about the energy he had used up prolonging his liberal fairy tale. I told him that I now understood the deception. Yet, truly, I did not, could not, would not. For I needed to believe that he was real and solid just as much as he needed to believe that I needed men such as he had pretended to be.

(I did not get an answer from Paul until much later and it was not in a letter, but in a copy of his manuscript, *The Burnt Offering.*)

Glenn. Jesus. You lie around with a woman and juices start popping and running and meeting up with other juices and before you know it there's a creature standing before you with a voice gone almost to bass, bigger than you; you can almost hear *his* juices washing around inside him and feel the electricity crackling from exploding hormones. Jesus. I touched him a lot. We studied each other a great deal and we talked about basketball and track, which he was into also. Looking at him, watching him pretend to be Oscar Robertson, Elgin Baylor or Rafer Johnson, I saw his boyhood sliding by. I wondered just how ready he was. He reminded me of the child in Spain.

"Hey," I said to him.

He stopped bouncing the basketball and looked up, surprised, though with a smile. "What?"

"I love you." I knew it would be perhaps the last time I could say it.

"Aw," he snorted and, head down, smiling still, he went back to dribbling the ball in his mother's backyard.

Catherine wished me luck.

Back in New York, I was shocked once again to see myself on film. I marveled at how well I'd absorbed the mannerisms of the television journalists: a nod here for emphasis, a twist there, the straight-at-the-camera look, the slightly pressed lips to underline the cut from me to the action. Scene after scene of *The Negro* rolled smoothly on; the illusion was of one massive telling, slick, superficial and palatable, with, here and there, *my* statement coming through, slipping quickly, like a spitball over the corner of the plate. The show was but half-edited; there would be more. I did not know why I felt both pleased and disappointed.

But the day was coming.

She was contemplating me when I opened my eyes that morning. She smiled. "This is the day. Are you ready?"

I eased my knee between her legs. "Ah," she said softly. I grasped her hips, rounded and warm, and turned her on her back; her legs slid upward and apart. "Oooo."

Two hours later Allis stood, her arm through mine, the light in the judge's chambers reflecting off her dark blond hair, her hip resting against mine. Her lace ecru dress, subtly cut, was swelled with the gentle protuberances of her body. She was studying the judge with amusement. For, his golf bag sitting in a corner, he was marrying us in something just short of a rush. The words said, he kissed Allis and took my hand. His hand opened as if expecting, as if in search, while his eyes clouded for an instant. I quickly gave him the bucks in my other hand. How quickly and brightly then came his smile! How firmly did he shake my hand!

Then Allis and I took a cab back up to the Village. For a luncheon party.

Mr. Storto. Amos with a striking peroxide blonde, Mark, Dolph, Vernon, young people who worked with Allis at Cumer, Slate and Finch.

One of those hovered near us. She thought we were terribly in love, awfully courageous, and the parents of the new world the sixties were creating; we were to her Izanagi and Izanami, Adam and Eve, Qaholom and E Alom, but most of all, she thought we were Kaundinya and Soma of the proto-ancient Khmers: *The men . . . are black . . . but many women are white.* We drank champagne, stuffed ourselves with blini with sour cream and caviar and Polish vodka thick as syrup.

God, you two look well, Mark is saying.

Allis makes a face. Lately she complains of lines in her face, the bigness of her hips, the bulge of her stomach. But I insist that the body knows how to care for itself. Besides, she looks sexy and I love the feel of her, the slopes and mounds, the curves of her.

You look okay, too, Mark, I say. What else is one to say — that you look like death taking a shit?

He makes a depreciatory gesture, smiles.

How're your kids? He'd married then divorced another production assistant on the David Susskind show. Maybe there was another wife. I didn't ask. What does it matter?

Okay. Fine. This Glenn Douglass, that your kid? The *Jumper* book?

Yeah. My son.

Incredible, he murmurs. I smile. It seems that writers who hang around the movies or television or who are journalists all want to write novels. They want to do up the King, believing secretly that they will not *really* be writers until they publish a novel. (I have sometimes wondered if they are not right.) Earning a million bucks doing scripts or articles, nonfiction books, is not enough; by God, they *must* do that novel.

Mark sighs. I'm working on a novel.

I want to tell him about the other writer in my family, Alejo Cato Donoso, but I do not, since he is quiet about his own kids. Did they disappoint him? Do they dislike him?

And you two have a kid. Boy? Girl?

Boy, Allis says.

Did you see Leonard's kid? Mark asks.

Good-looking boy.

Dorothea's eee-normous, he says. In the little silence that follows I wonder if he, too, feels a sting of guilt for not taking the time to speak to her. She is in some demand now; she speaks to literary groups, college groups, about Leonard and his brief lifetime. And she published a book about him some years back.

Well, Mark says briskly, as if getting down to business, why did he do it?

I say, I thought you might know. We were out of touch. You saw him from time to time.

Yeah, I did, but I don't know any more than you do. I mean, after such a slow start and then zooming right on up, marrying Betsy, the kids, the acclaim — shit, I don't know.

Betsy says he wasn't sick or anything.

But maybe she didn't really know. After all, he says, they weren't together.

Mark drums his fingertips softly on the table; Allis sips her coffee.

It's frightening, she says. Even now there are days at a time when we don't exchange more than ten or twenty words, right, darling? And I try to imagine what you're thinking, how the work's going, and I try to make conversation and it always falls flat. She is talking to me, but looking at Mark, as if in some way pleading a case.

And then all that tension melts away — suddenly vanishes. What's frightening about it is being alone. I'd hate being a writer who's physically alone nearly all the time.

I hug her. She will never lay claim to being a poet and never sees herself bent over the kitchen table, writing, while Mack and I slide through the apartment.

I think it was something else, Mark says.

Like what? I feel a growing chill. In my mind I see myself again rushing along Fifth Avenue to his home. What cause had I to run? Why such haste to get to his death? What *is* the prevision of people who take their lives that the rest of us do not see?

Mark answers, Like what? Hell, I don't know. He may have been tormented being a WASP when he was really a Jew. When he declared, he seemed content. Maybe he wasn't.

Mark was gesticulating, his eyes watering, as if in fear of something distantly perceived. Maybe, shit, he just discovered that it was *all* crap, that none of it was really worth the sweat. Paul could be like that, you know. Just pull up stakes and move out.

Allis looks a little frightened. What?

Mark says, I dunno, dunno why he did it.

I think, What *was* it that climbed into Paul's foxhole? What? I notice Allis' profile, her lashes extending from her suddenly downcast eyes, and I realize she is thinking about me, about my nightmares, and wondering (though knowing) why they have returned.

We are all quiet. I am remembering.

There were times when the distinct smell of burned wiring hung inside my nostrils for days. At first I used to examine the apartment, checking the plugs and wires, but then, even outside, I could smell the burning. I reached a cunning conclusion: there was some connection inside *me* that was overheating, preparing to short out. Then it passed, that and the running. The running: there had been times when I awoke at godless hours of the morning sitting straight up in bed, Allis crying and hanging tenaciously to my shoulders or my legs.

"Cate! Cate!"

Of course, her voice would eventually penetrate and still those kaleido-scoping horrors in my head.

"My God! You were screaming and crying and kicking — "

"Uh!"

"Cate!"

"Ohhh."

"I never heard such sounds before. Are you all right?" She clutched me tight and stroked my back as if I were a baby and, exhausted, I rested upon her.

The burn smells and the running stopped for a while, but now they are back.

Mark smiles at us in the silence.

It *is* all crap, you know, Mark says. He shrugs. I knew it back then, when I moved from one side of the desk to the other to be an editor. It was always money. He shrugs again. Money. I knew I'd always get a paycheck while you guys on the other side wondered how come editors didn't love you enough to publish you. Television was even better. He leans forward. I'm writing a novel about all of it.

If it's all crap, Allis says with surprising bitterness, why do you want to write a novel? Besides, you just mentioned it.

Mark smiles. Well, why not? Perhaps he chose not to hear Allis.

Yeah, I say. Why not? Everyone's got one good book in him. The problem's getting it out.

Mark laughs. Hey, man. I'm in TV. That's no problem.

Yes, Allis says, that is a problem.

Ha, ha, Mark says. Weakly.

I make getting-up motions.

Let's stay in touch this time around, Cate, Mark says, passing me his card.

Yeah.

Ready, dear? Allis is standing.

I think of something, but decide not to bring it up. It really is time to go.

Outside, walking arm in arm up Columbus Avenue through the old

Irish neighborhood that contains a brave mix of just about everybody, pleased that people still look at us, look at *her,* their glances lingering on her face and then, of course, her body, Allis smiles and says, I really am tired of people who announce, just announce, that they're writing a novel. Goddamn it, if writing one's all that important . . . She shakes her head of curls dark blond and gray.

We ought to walk more often, she says.

Next thing, it'll be jogging.

I'd like to jog.

S'long.

Wouldn't it be fun jogging with Mack?

You're kidding. No. Not with anyone. Miss him?

She thinks, then says, Ye-ss. I thought the time would never come for him to go anywhere alone, and now he's at camp, I miss him. A little.

After a while I say, He looked like shit, didn't he? Mark.

She laughs. Hard.

On the other hand, I say, I probably looked like shit to him.

No. Never.

Not never. Not yet. I stop. Let's get lunch and a drink.

She stops. Really? Honey, what I said back there —

It's okay. You're right. It's a lousy way to make a living, to live. And teaching. I'm sorry.

It used to be exciting. Or is that my imagination? Maybe we're just getting old.

Naw. Prime of life. Prime time. The time's prime. Listen. Let's go home and make love and drink and eat there.

Wanna?

I wanna.

When you are very young you cannot imagine two people past fifty, a man and a woman, lying around nude in a sun-filled, air-conditioned bedroom during a summer afternoon, alternatingly drinking wine and making love.

But when you are fifty or over, it seems quite right, better even than when you were twenty-five.

19

WE HAVE TO get up and get to doing things. I am pulling together some notes for a new book. And I have to straighten out the house. Company is coming, company of a sort. And Allis has to do some quick shopping for dinner. Nothing special, because the company is not all that special. The company is Maureen Gullian, and I'm not happy with her or Twentieth Century Forum Publishers, so the situation is tit for tat. Even before I addressed the sales meeting, they had expressed a distinct lack of enthusiasm for my work. That atmosphere seemed to have surrounded the work of nearly all black writers, though of course no editor or publisher would admit it. They want to score, bag a book that'll make beaucoup bread. But the times are tough. Even white writers are screaming with the pinch of things.

It is now recognized that the big change in the business has arrived, and it is that art comes after moneymaking, which is to say that art exists only as commodity. We learn from our literature mainly how to entertain, be entertained and to escape the terrible truths that have slyly informed our lives.

Maureen Gullian is too young to understand. Maybe, though, she is young enough to understand it precisely.

Goddamn. As soon's she comes through the door carrying the almost obligatory bottle of wine, the vibrations go bad; something becomes altered in the apartment. If Mack were here, Gullian would be overly attentive. As it is, she is more solicitous of Allis than she has ever been. Gullian is, she says, distraught that she was the bearer of the bad news of Paul's death. She seems unable to look me in the eye.

They don't want it, I think, and I near shit when she takes the manuscript out of her shoulder bag and sets it on a table. No, they don't want it. Most writers reach that point in a relationship. The experience is not novel. The word must've come down to Maureen the day before I went to Denver. The publishing committee meetings. I look at her. She is uneasy. Her legs and thighs are pressed tightly together, as though she needs badly to take a piss. We have done four books together. Maybe it is time to move on. To hell with the problems, like taking another leave from the branch of the university. Shit, there's money enough. And maybe I myself was thinking about making a change, if one could be effected these days. I have become too patronizing about Gullian's lack of knowledge of important things, which, naturally, should find expression in books. Yes, I was looking for another rather hefty advance on *Graves*. I long ago gave up counting on royalties. Nearly everyone thinks that writers live very well on them and that they never stop coming.

The royalties that do come — $3.54 or $17.83 or $31.11 or $6.93 — will not support us; indeed, they will not keep a squirrel in acorns. However, I am glad to get these piddling sums, because I appreciate publishers with style enough to calculate, to add, subtract, divide or multiply and finally send them on to their writers. Other publishers accumulate these minute sums owing to several writers over several years and forget, I suppose, to send them on. In the secret dark of publishers' accounting divisions, and also in bank offices, I am sure that nimble-fingered and quick-brained minions manage to lose $6.93 about every second of the working day, not to mention in overtime.

Anyway, fuck returning to the branch of the university this fall. My last leave was forced. By circumstances.

It follows that dinner is a disaster. We do not talk of business until it's over and Allis begins to clean up.

I watch Maureen light up one of those long, lean little cigars she likes to smoke. Maureen has decided to lay it all on the table. Most times I like that quality in people. This is not one of them.

The new book, she says, as though it had no title. It's been around the house. She grimaces.

I say, Yeah?

She studies her cigar. Her legs are still pressed together. Ten grand advance, she says.

I *really* pissed them off at that sales conference, didn't I?

Maureen is trying hard not to say more. She does have a lingering sense of order and justice. How could one have been taught by nuns and not possess, in however small degree, however religiously perverted, the urgency that wishes the precision of the square, the closing of circles, sunrises followed in due course by sunsets, and satisfied writers?

Ten grand, I say. That certainly will not do.

After four books and almost ten years, I think, watching her puffing on that goddamn 150-millimeter cigar.

They won't give me any more, she says, plaintively. The numbers tell us no.

What numbers?

The computer. BOOK.

That thing in what Jock calls the War Room?

She nods, and a silence of sorts, gray and heavy, billows through the room. They know there is no way I can accept this advance when I have been munching (not gorging) much higher on the hog. Free enterprise moves on. I am, then, a free agent, a Curt Flood, an Oscar Robertson, a John Mackey. Hell. I am now a member in good standing of the Llewellyn Dodge Johnson Club.

I was just thinking, I say to Gullian, of that clause I had inserted into my contract: that should you leave TCFP, I'd leave, too. Ha, ha.

I —

I wave her into silence. Fuck the words. Who needs them? She is making faces. I almost feel sorry for her. She mashes out her cigar and strokes out another and lights it.

Allis is returning to the room.

What's this about a contract? Allis says. She has coffee.

I say, Oh, Maureen's offered me ten grand for *Unmarked Graves*.

Allis is cool. She sets down the tray, looks from me to Maureen. We watch her pour. She hands Maureen her cup and says, Cate said this would happen, Maureen.

Maureen almost chokes on her fresh cigar.

It's not even strange that she offers no apologies, not even a bit more of a defense for herself. She simply sits, smoking and sipping and crossing and recrossing her legs. Finally, in a tight voice she says, Would you want to do a biography of Paul Cummings? I could get —

She sees my look, then says, May I use your bathroom?

Allis points the way. Maureen goes. I look at Allis. She looks at me. It's only money, she says. Her tone is flat and hard because she knows of course that it's only money, but that it is nevertheless the instrument of measurement.

There are, I say, other publishers.

Yes.

But we both knew that this was coming, that things would reach their crest, as they always do in America, and slide over into shadow. I am not a fad; I'm not invisible, a commodity, an invention, and therefore had no right to expect a contemplative old age, a purchased parcel of this place. My delusion was short; the war has no end, and we will be at it until we either disappear into each other or destroy each other.

Oh, fuck Maureen, I say.

Have you?

Christ.

Allis is smiling. C'mon, have you?

I wonder why she is asking now, after all these years of working with women in publishing, knowing that they cover the industry (as they're starting to call it now, like Hollywood) the way grass covers Central Park.

No, hell no.

We hear the toilet flush. Seconds later Maureen is in the room, gathering up her bag. Now she says, I'm sorry, Cate. It's the computer.

For some time there has been talk that TCFP was tracking sales with a computer. Top Secret.

But now it's the computer's fault. No longer the secretary's, the mailroom people, the switchboard operators; no warm bodies to seize on, only the latest techno-gadget (not so new, 1936, approximately), a goddamn updated Turing machine, a Turing-Church machine, artificially intelligent. For example, such machines regularly fuck up subscriptions, grades, the movement of things, including missiles. They are lightning-fast with numbers and words — information — when not malfunctioning; they tell you how people will vote and for whom, how folks "feel" about things. So beloved are these "instrumental reasoning" devices that they are baptized with names: HAL, ELIZA, DOCTOR, NOVA, etc., and people are known to have tried to converse with them.

Yeah, I say. The computer.

Maureen's at the door. I do not kiss her. Allis does not kiss her. The bullshit is over. The fucks stop here.

When she has gone, we walk to the window. I hope she gets mugged, I say.

Double-mugged, Allis says.

20

IN AUGUST of the year we married, free of some article assignments and well paid for them, and also buoyed by a good advance on the novel I called *The Hyksos Journals,* which was now sweeping along almost under its own power, we joined the March on Washington.

There seemed to be a collective indignation in the air, even though people were more trusting then than now of government. They had been, however, outraged by fire hoses and police dogs that had been loosed on the King-Shuttlesworth forces in Birmingham. Even I was hopeful, for that midnight shoot-out had faded somewhat with the passage of the months.

In Washington on that fine, warm day we sat, feet dangling in the Reflecting Pool. The speakers spoke. The enormous brooding statue of Lincoln peered down at the thousands upon thousands of marchers. Everywhere the television cameras, manned by their crews, were aimed at us, waiting for the routinely predicted eruptions of violence that never came.

Later in the afternoon, the speeches over, the mighty cheers for them no longer even an echo, we drifted through the crowds to find our rented car. We passed a group of George Lincoln Rockwell's Nazis standing in formation and we drew aside to study them.

"Why am I afraid to spit on them?" Allis whispered.

Farther on we saw a group carrying placards. Children were with them, marching with embarrassed, fixed smiles on their faces. The placards read: BLACK AND WHITE — WE'RE ALL RIGHT. And they chanted this slogan belligerently. We stopped to watch the mixed group of men and women, black and white and, we supposed, their children.

"Why are they doing that?" Allis was nervous.

"I don't know."

"The kids look so frightened," she said.

The parents reminded me of couples I sometimes saw in the Village bars, screaming at each other or waiting to be insulted. They want sympathy for marrying each other, I thought.

"Let's go," Allis said. "Those poor kids. I can't bear it."

The day's ambience had been sullied. I despised that group for letting the world mess them up like that. Had they thought their marriages were some kind of game, some sort of showpiece? Was it possible that they really loved their salt-and-pepper misery? Whatever, they were not going to be a mirror for us.

In November, Abraham Zapruder was taking pictures with an eight-millimeter camera near a grass-covered mound in Dealy Plaza, Dallas, when John F. Kennedy's head was all but blown off by gunfire. Zapruder's film, and stills from it, laid down the fresh spoor of a blood-and-power conspiracy some 344 years old, the kills commencing not on November 22, 1963, but on April 14, 1865. In the days following November 22, I perceived an ageless Thing rushing gleefully out of history, laying waste to goals and dreams, and damming and diverting our less than inexorable shuffle toward the execution of the possible. The death camp–like ennui, almost as visible as those Pacific island sheets of humidity, which grew moss on shoes, tents and clothes, lay tightly on the nation, despite the quick formation of commissions, despite the pomp of the Death March in Washington with short-striding Selassie and long-striding De Gaulle — the beginning and the end, so to speak. Words packaged as information about the event rained down upon us like the droppings of a flock of pigeons with congenital diarrhea, and smelled just as bad.

During those days Allis and I talked of leaving the country. We talked of the bigotry, the unending parade of mediocre politicians who assumed center stage instead of the statesmen we needed so badly. We talked of the right atmosphere in which to raise our children, free of the American taint. We talked through complete nights, drifting off to sleep only when the sky seemed to shiver and then begin to brighten. Always we arrived at the point where we had to ask, Where would we go to preserve ourselves and our generations? She never mentioned Israel and I never mentioned Africa, or if we did (I do not remember now), it was only in passing. We talked, and that was all we did. When we, with mild regret, concluded that nearly every place on earth was becoming like the United States we turned our concerns to living within the confines allotted to us.

We, Allis and I, seemed to have known each other before, somewhere else, in some other life. Now we were a combination of those occurrences — good friends, lovers, and now, as the times and we ourselves seemed to demand, husband and wife, wife and husband. In ways we never bothered to try to understand, our thoughts, even the words we were about to speak, overlapped, without common reason for why they should have. We acknowledged its strangeness at first, and then came to take it for granted even when foul moods precluded the possibility of that commonality of thought. Then, we could never understand how it was that I or she didn't understand precisely what was being communicated. Perhaps it was better that way; it kept us more human than might otherwise have been possible.

Those were the days not only of the husky martini, but the gimlet and Gibson; we exchanged cocktail and dinner parties and sometimes Allis joined me from her midtown office to have long, wet lunches with editors. At various times we saw Poode, Selena, Amos, Maxine Culp, Sandra Queensbury and Roye Yearing at the parties that were held.

From time to time we journeyed to Harlem for dinner, to a little restaurant on St. Nicholas Avenue, not far from the old Alpha Phi Alpha fraternity house.

On weekends we slept late, and then cleaned and waited for the Village to come awake. When it did, we browsed or visited, usually briefly, as if performing a ritual, after which I rushed back home to work, leaving Allis to shop luxuriously in the Italian markets. Sunday mornings we lingered over breakfast with the *Times* and the *Herald Tribune* reading the book reviews written by or about writers we knew, I watchful of the signs Sandra Queensbury had warned me about. Now and again the reviews of the books by black writers would appear, lumped gracelessly together, as if by theme, but really by race, which meant, of course, that the editor had a problem. Sandra notwithstanding, only a fool could not have seen what was going down. Was up? (The Main Metaphors are always sexual.)

Whittington and Huysmans remained our standard bearers. Their work seemed to have been programmed into the SATs on one level, and devoured whole by the Academy on another, and had thus become standards, like *Back Home in Indiana*. I had not met Huysmans, but had heard that he called himself a Negro, not a black man. I had read his novel and his collection of verse. In his lectures, which were judiciously spaced, and in his articles, of which there were few, Huysmans in beautifully turned-out language suggested that writers who were black too often used race as an excuse not to write as exquisitely as he had. He deplored "sociological" novels, with their unending burden of race. Yet at the heart of his own assemblage of metaphors was jazz music (of his youth) and this, of course! had not been born through ignorance of bigotry nor through a tenderly forged racial experience. How cunning! To utilize precisely what one condemned, believing no one was watching the pea being switched! But of course they knew — and loved it! And some of them even wrote cunningly about it.

Whittington embraced his Negroness, hammered out with breathless, raging emotion what being Negro had always meant in America. He slashed through his readers' consciousness, slitting neurons with a scalpel, and when he was finished he wrote that even so he forgave white America and truly did love his oppressors. ("Love them that hate ye.") And they loved him back and came to believe that he was, when you got to know him, genuinely very sweet. In their collective essence he was to them quite harmless, would titillate, not terminate.

It was all like watching a giant black-and-white film in slow motion that had been directed with a very heavy hand.

When Allis and I finished with the papers, we often strolled out for brunch or to see a movie. Ours was a quiet, gentle, work-filled life. But the world impinged on it, daily, with the ready insults of the eyes and mouths, the careless challenges (all of which then came from whites alone; that would change) of the people who offered them, believing they would be accepted.

Allis used her poetic alliteration to great effect, I thought, when rising to some of the challenges thrown by women: "You silly, slovenly, stupid, bigoted, broken-down bitch," said with a cold precision I'd never before observed. Or to cab drivers who had last words as she left a cab I'd put her into: "You poor, Protestant [it didn't really matter that they might have been Jewish, Catholic or Muslim], prickless piece of puss" — again delivered like hot ice. Of course, they didn't understand — but they were always unprepared for a response.

Coming out of a mobile hospital once to find my outfit already gone north to the next island, I'd had to fret a couple of days in an all-white

Out Going Unit camp. God, how they glared or laughed and nudged each other and pointed at me when I got on the chowline. On the second day, I reached across the serving table, grabbed a guy with each hand and pulled myself up on the table, promising to kick their asses if they didn't stop smiling. The whole chow hall quieted. (It was a small camp.) They stopped smiling. The routine was good. So I used it when Allis and I were out. It worked, except for one night when they didn't come by tens, only threes, and beat the living shit out of me on the corner of Sixteenth Street and the Avenue of the Americas, while guys picked their teeth as they watched from a white saloon on the corner. Nineteen years after, the "bad nigger marine" routine ran out of steam. But I had the answer for that, too.

They all seemed to want to make us feel guilty for being happy, for fucking up the sad and dreary continuums of their desperate histories. They wished to be like us, I think, as foolish as us, or as wise, as willing as we were to toss their ridiculous rules like chaff to the winds; they envied us and yet I could never be sure that they ever saw our faces, really; they saw instead our bodies only from our knees to our waists.

Still, the Village was something of a refuge whose racial mores possessed a kind of liberal continuity. These were bent from time to time and sometimes even briefly snapped, as they had been on Sixteenth Street.

I saw Amos infrequently now, for lunch or a dinner out or in our apartment. From Paul there was nothing. Glenn spent a part of his summers with us and each year his presence seemed to make the apartment smaller because he was bigger. We never felt so crowded as when he was there, even though we tried to spend as little time as possible in the place.

Mr. Storto saw him growing, but nevertheless, for three years running, carried Glenn, who went without the slightest protest, to the circus.

During this time we'd been trying to have a baby, knowing that would force us to find a larger place. We knew we needed one, but kept putting off a search. Our lives were intertwined with Mr. Storto's. We had ices together, coffee together, snacks together; we solved all the problems in the world and even sometimes helped him clean up after a tenant moved out.

I suppose living down there made us feel in some way that we were younger than we were. However, the fact that we had not yet rung any bells sent us to the doctors to check out the equipment we were working with. Maybe it *was* older than we wanted it to be. They said we were all right, that we should continue to plug away. And so we did, relentlessly,

167

often to the point of exhaustion, because we had read somewhere that that was when all the little, teeny things inside were most receptive. Sometimes Allis even took a cab home at noon, thinking we'd change the schedule, change the luck.

In the same week that the publication date of my third novel was set for the spring, Allis missed her period. An examination confirmed the pregnancy. We had done it.

Mr. Storto had only one-bedroom apartments, and anyway we now thought of parks and public playing areas, of which there were not too many in the Village, and none near us. We found a larger place on the Upper West Side as spring moved into summer and the ghettos in half a hundred cities exploded into flames and rioting. People started *not* to look at us. Oh, we'd catch eyes now and again, but more often people quickly looked away, pretending great interest in another kind of scenery.

"Well," Mr. Storto said. "I don't know about up there. In the Village, you always safe, always comfortable — you know what I mean, uh?"

"More space for the baby, Mr. Storto," I said.

"I know, I know. But you gotta come back and see me and bring Glenn, okay? A fine boy. Now maybe another one?"

"You *will* come and see us, won't you?" Allis asked Mr. Storto.

He had provided us with excellent references that in part (together with a push from a city agency) secured our new apartment. The landlord had not done handsprings when we signed the lease.

"Sure, I'll come," Mr. Storto said. "Sure."

"We'd like that," Allis said.

When we were alone, sitting among the packed cartons, thinking of my, our, years in Mr. Storto's building, I said, "It's just too much!"

"What?" Allis was smiling. She smiled a lot now. "What's too much?"

"Look at it. Christ! A baby, a new apartment, and Glenn goes to college this fall."

Her smile widened. "Isn't it great? And another book to be published. Fantastic."

In our new building the nonlook became look again — and sometimes stares. Even the nattily uniformed Negro and Puerto Rican elevator men seemed uneasy with me. (Who *is* this nigger?) There were no other black tenants in the building. But there had been no others in Mr. Storto's, either. Perhaps the difference rested in the transitory nature of much of the Village, which was for the young, mainly, and the brazenly artistic.

In the building we saw few young people. Instead, there was a solid sense of middle-agedness. The men wore suits; the women, dresses. Although Allis and I were not kids, we felt ourselves to be outside the world represented by that brown brick structure of fifteen stories and the people who lived in it.

Mornings there meant a concerted rush for the elevators, which Allis joined resignedly. After, housewives shopped and, standing close to each other, gossiped in the carpeted lobby or carried their books or magazines to the laundry room. The place was middle class and comfortably close enough to the Park to give the tenants an identification with those who did live on, not just off, Central Park West. And there was the canopy, with the address on the front and sides, and the taxi-light signal.

Sitting in the freshly painted, newly furnished apartment, with its spacious living and dining room, its eat-in kitchen, walk-in closets and two baths and bedrooms, its partial view of the Park from a certain angle, we decided that we liked it.

"But," I said, "I feel as though I've moved into another part of my life."

"Is that bad, honey?"

"I just don't know if it's good or bad."

"Now there's room for Glenn. And we do have to think of our child." Then she said, "We don't have that much time, you know." More cheerily: "Besides, man does not live by typewriter alone — "

"Never wanted to."

"Typewriter and sex alone?"

"But why not, gorgeous?"

"Because you really want more."

This she said with finality, and I had to think about it. At question was not only the racial "twoness" that Du Bois wrote of; it was also the twoness of wanting things, relationships, while being fearful that they could be lost; it was the question of being warrior-ready for situations that were historically always threatening (though *that* posture had done no good on Sixteenth Street and Sixth Avenue), but desperately wanting a peace that seemed determined never to arrive; the question of being poised to die, yet eager to live.

"Yeah," I said, "I do." I wanted off the knife edge. Yet I did not wish to be like those Southern tribes, believing that the world was as civilized as I was; I did not wish to be caught admiring my Pyramids and temples, my herds, flocks and fields, when the Northern tribes swept down again, as they always had, to decimate the civilization I'd built within myself.

Our hands met in the middle of the bed; we intertwined our fingers. We slept that way every night.

"Man, I was really gone. I flew."

"I wish I could have been there."

"Me, too," he said quietly.

Glenn and I were sitting in the other bedroom, which he was using this trip. I was holding a preparty drink — we were having our housewarming party, and the apartment was smelling faintly of the Joy Allis had put on after her bath.

(Joy! Alegría! Joie! Gioia! = Monica = my child;
that child = Glenn = child = child unknown = Monica =
Joy = Allis.)

His look was shaded, but it accused. He was seventeen now and would be off to Yellow Springs in September. Where did it go?

"I'm sorry, truly sorry," I said. He would not be running track nor playing basketball at Antioch.

"Really, Dad, you don't mind my not playing, do you?"

"No, of course not. Why should I?"

"Because you played. Mom told me."

"Not in college, my man. Anyway, so what?"

"I thought — "

"Hell, no. They're games. Kids play them. Some people just never grow up. You did, I think. But I am sorry I never saw you in a game or running the eight-eighty. You must've been pretty good, judging from the clips your mother sent."

"Well, I wasn't the worst. Dad?"

"Huh?"

"Did your father ever watch you play?"

"A couple of times. I didn't especially want him to." I slapped his back. "I wasn't as good as you."

"What did you do together?"

Ah, Glenn, I thought. Guilty, guilty, guilty. Are you the court? Then I ask for mercy. I am repentant — but only because you may have been unhappy. I said to him, "Nothing much — "

I followed his eyes to the door into which Allis was leaning. God, I thought, she is really fine!

170

"Okay in here?" she asked.

"Sure, why wouldn't it be?"

"I dunno. Sounded low and serious. Like the room, Glenn?"

He smiled and stretched back on the bed. "It's great, Allis. I like it fine." Allis came over and bent and straightened his tie, then stood back and studied it critically.

"Nice tie. You look so much like your father . . . Are you seeing — anybody?"

Glenn looked at me as if I should decipher what she meant. "You mean, dating?"

"Yeah. They still call it that?"

"That's what we call it. Uh, I was dating a couple of girls — "

"A couple?" Allis teased. "At the same time?"

"Not quite," Glenn said, uneasy.

"We're very proud of you, Glenn," Allis said. "You've done well in school and now you're off to the big leagues — college."

"The what?" I said.

She shrugged, and said, "You know, college, the big leagues after high school, right? That's all I meant. So it isn't the big leagues. Fire me."

"I won't fire you, but I'll make you a malted. Everything ready?"

"As ready as they'll ever be, kid."

"This your first grownie party?" I asked him when she'd left.

"Yeah. We don't have parties at home."

"Oh. Catherine tells me she's thinking of getting married. He a nice guy?"

"He's okay."

"Yeah." We sat listening to Allis move plates and pans around in the kitchen. I really wanted to tell Glenn about his brother or his sister, but I knew I couldn't, not then.

I had of course written to Señor Jones about Monica, a polite, interested letter that never mentioned my marriage. For I knew that I was important only so long as he thought me eligible to become his son-in-law. Yes, he responded, he was most glad to be advised of my change of address in case he heard from his daughter, though he did not expect to. But one never knows, *no es verdad?* So. I couldn't tell Glenn because I could relate only the beginning of things, not the end, and fathers do owe to their sons at least the direction in which the road is going.

Later he would understand.

I said, "Listen, kid. I'm really glad that you and Allis get along so well."

"She's okay, Dad. Can I tell you something, though?"

"Sure," I said, but I was not so sure I wanted to hear it. "What is it?"

"I told Mom how nice she was and she's really glad everything's worked out between us." He wrinkled his nose. "She said she didn't know why it was, though, that every time a black man became famous, he married a white woman."

"Catherine said that? Well, come on. I wasn't famous then, I'm not famous now — "

"She thought so, Dad. Anyway, I told her that was not the way it was."

"Hasn't been easy for you, has it?"

He grinned. "It sure has been interesting, though."

I thought Alex Samuels was handing me a housewarming gift, but before I could say thanks he said, "From Paul. Copy of his manuscript and boy is it first-rate, absolutely first-rate. There's a letter for you with the copy."

He relayed all this with a great smile that made me think of an agent who already had in his pocket excellent contracts for a paperback sale and BOMC. Such enthusiasm never greeted my own work; he always accepted it with the resignation of one about to do the stations of the cross on his knees.

"This is the book he got the Goog for?"

"This?" He pounded a stiff finger against the package. He sneered. "Naw. He dropped that. It was a piece of shit, anyway."

His eyes were skipping around the room, now filled with people from Cumer, Slate and Finch; the others were, in one way or another, associated with books and writing. "Hummm, Amos," he said. "He's given up wooing you, I guess."

"He's still my friend."

"I'll say hello to him."

Alex went before I could give him a drink. I dropped Paul's manuscript in the bedroom and returned. Glenn glanced from the records he was playing for us and smiled. I winked at him and wondered why it was that book-people parties almost never included music. They just stood and talked, talked, talked.

Two people from C S & F involved me in their conversation. Their drinks were in good shape, so there was no immediate chance to escape for refills. The topic was inevitable, coming to rest on Martin Luther King, Jr., Malcolm X, the rebellions of that moment, LBJ's War on Poverty.

And what did I think of Allis' promotion to account executive? She was great, just great. Nice place we had here. My son seemed like a helluva bright kid. Was I working on another book? Was one ready to come out? Interesting. Did we miss living in the Village? Interesting friends we had. Mostly literary people? Allis was one bright girl. Bright.

They had promoted her with great speed after we were married. "Douglass," Allis had said, "is not nearly as Jewish as Greenberg. Darling, we really must confound the hell out of them."

"Yeah. If they only knew that Douglass even with one *s* means dark or black in Gaelic. They can't win, babe, can't win."

MIDDLES

1

The Hyksos Journals came out, surrounded by cautious though favorable reviews. By that time I had read the complete manuscript of Paul's *The Burnt Offering* and was waiting for his arrival back in New York.

"We have much to talk about, man," he'd said in his letter, and "if the book didn't explain enough," he would explain in person.

Hummm, I thought.

Jeremy Poode, who did an interview with me over a long lunch (his first and last with a black writer), had already heard of Paul's book and was eagerly looking forward to reading it. Poode and I had never been very friendly, but our conversations when with other people were bright, punchy. We were considered to be close. Now there was more distance between us than ever. He had married and was living in Short Hills. No one knew his wife. At lunch Poode did not talk of Selena, nor did I. I had received a gracious note from her, admiring *The Hyksos Journals* (except for the section where black men made love to white women). Poode had somehow kept up with my marriage and travels and knew Mark was doing *very well* (his emphasis) in television.

"How," he asked, "would you compare yourself to people like Wright, Whittington, Huysmans?"

"We're all black."

"I mean — "

"There was something else you're getting to?"

His vaguely blue — sort of purple, rather — eyes remained steady. His pen, angled above his pad, was motionless. Now he leaned back, glanced around a moment. "Strange title. Does it mean what I think it means?"

"I dunno. What's it mean to you?"

"The Shepherd Kings. Invasion of Egypt, about two thousand B.C."

"That's one theory, Jeremy. But I prefer the one that holds that the Hyksos were a cult composed of dissident Egyptians — though naturalized — and that there was no physical invasion from regions distant from Egypt. The revolt came from within or from the slums just outside."

"Ah," he said. "Yes, of course." He wrote carefully.

I studied him. Why, this man, I thought, could destroy me with a sentence, a word, even a mark! — ? (   ).

When he looked up I said, "We shouldn't be doing this to each other, Jeremy."

"What are we doing to each other, Cate?"

"Let's put it this way: you're mostly doing it to me."

"What?"

But I had seen it in his eyes, his very demeanor.

"Look, Cate, let's get back to the book, okay? Now, are you saying that when — *if* is a better word — this society falters, starts to unravel, it will be because of forces from inside rather than outside?"

"Yes."

"And that the Negro problem will be at the core of it all?"

"Yes."

He smiled. "Not Huysmans' line at all."

"No."

This was the first of many interviews I would have and they all would be similar.

The interviewers, with their pads, pens and desperately neutral glances, always asked about other black writers, as though they were the only writers you had ever met, read or studied. They ignored the fact that you must have had to study their writers, since works by nonwhite writers rarely, if ever, found their way into textbooks.

(We will for now forget those periods of the pre–Harlem Renaissance, the Renaissance itself, and Renaissance II, which are traceable to trouble on the plantations and later in the streets.)

The interviewers judged all writings without hesitation, suspending, however, literary judgment only in the case of nonwhite writers, because the interviewers (and critics and reviewers — often one and the same) were so innately positive that literary ingredients could not possibly be present.

They patronized, or tried to. They were snide, or tried to be. They were overtly disdainful of nearly every story you related because they were still secretly surprised that you could hang a sentence together at all and compose narrative and dialogue. Like pecking birds, they tapped at the surface of things; beneath that surface, vast gaps were being closed to within percentage points, even according to their rules. So they insisted that the novel be written so that they could understand it, the way they understand rock's emphasized beat, the way they could not understand the subtleties of a Thelonious Monk; they forgot, if they ever knew, that the novel *is* novel and therefore often requires decoding, which they do very well when the writers are white. They wrote for each other. The author under discussion was often secondary. The literary community, though powerful, was really small and quite incestuous. If then they wrote badly or viciously about an author who was black, they knew in advance that that author or his agent or publisher probably would not return to haunt them. For what real contacts did the author have? Whom did he or she *know?* Therefore they turned to nonwhite authors with a distinct sense of relief, for surely we were a people without leverage, familiar with few power brokers in the business who would be willing to go to the wall for us. These interviewers, critics and reviewers, by their acts and attitudes, acknowledged the war. They regarded almost every work by a nonwhite author as a political action. They were almost correct (because a few of those works could not by any unwinding of the imagination be so considered), but failed to understand the politics — or, conversely, understood them perfectly. They did seem to comprehend, along with some like-minded editors, that they were functionaries of the cultural mechanisms of the West, a gemot whose verdicts became, if not the law, the practice. How could they then allow certain other people into their ranks on other than a temporary / token basis? To be sure, they admired Latin writers — but those in Latin, not North, America; they admired black writers, but many of those were from Africa and, in the case of Afro-Americans, dead; from the Caribbean they much adored, obversely, the minority rather than the majority writers, those who deplored, laughed at or debased the island societies of which they were part; they exulted when good works on the Indian experience appeared, though not those written by the Amer-Indian himself, and they preferred Asian female writers to all like John Okada. And because they were a club, they frequently relegated to our ranks a few of their own.

So, no, nothing beyond temporary / token (beyond the meager exceptions), because we just might hang around long enough to review the works of white authors. God! Something startling might be written (and perhaps even published); some new (or possibly old, unchanged) truth might be perceived under black light, as Diop peeped the hole card of several generations of Egyptologists; some carefully arranged literary status might be imperiled (but, surely, only briefly).

They went to very great lengths to maintain the cultural mechanisms in good order. They caucasized Pushkin, who fathered the Russian language through poetry, plays and fiction. Oooo! they skim over his antecedents as rapidly as they do Dumas's or Colette's. They suggested that Chesnutt not use his photograph on his book jackets, and perhaps the same suggestion was made to Frank Yerby. They fucked up their own rules on a regular basis: black literature one decade was that literature written by people who were black; the next decade it also included nonblack authors writing on black themes; it was zit! and then zat! Now you see it, now you don't. *And* even if you *did* see it and call the hand, you were bitter, self-serving, overcome with the effects of racism, without sensibilities.

We all knew this and talked about it among ourselves, compared idiocies and idiots, when we could gather without the hostility such knowledge engenders. Yet none of us dared to say it aloud or to write it because we were each hopeful that we might be the one next in line to pass over the Great Divide into Nigger Heaven, joining Whittington and Huysmans.

And they knew it, too.

Poode's interview, when printed, was bland and circumspectly bigoted in that cozy New York manner, filled with fleeting asides and throwaway lines. It ran beside the review, whose lead read: "Watch out, John Greenleaf Whittington, move over, Elliot Huysmans — here comes Cato Caldwell Douglass!"

It was what they called a "selling" review, and it was enough to give the reviewers on the other side of the Hudson their cue not to be terribly nasty to me. For Poode's publication established the line to be followed, and, indeed, with one or two marshmallowy challenges from competing publications, the line tended to be obeyed. Poode's interview mentioned that my wife was white, as though that were some mitigating or castigating factor that explained or excused, I don't know what.

(When some white personality's wife is black, somehow that escapes attention.)

And afterward, curiously, congratulations began to arrive over the phone and by mail, several of which contained the review / interview. Even the note from Sandra Queensbury, written in aquamarine Super Quink Ink, began: "Congrats, I think, Cato. I hear Ike Plunkett is back in town. Have you heard from him?"

There it was. A tune piped, however dissonantly, in the insular melodies of New York set the lemmings in motion from one end of the cultural apparatus to the next, pulling along the media in a gigue to which most authors respond with palpable relief.

Oh, I danced a few numbers, danced my ass off, but I didn't stay for the whole ball, gripped by the sense that, with two or three exceptions, it was the kind of bullshit I could now do without, though it would have been heady stuff had I been twenty-five.

Poode's interview was followed by a rash of invitations also, to parties and places, most of which we did not accept. (Without discussion we had agreed that we would not serve as a token mixed couple. A fat, ugly, little man, said to be brilliant, had shocked the liberal literary community, of which he was once a member, by writing, among other things, that the sight of mixed couples stirred him to disgusting prurience.

There were requests to read or lecture at colleges; these had a certain appeal. There would be bright students, liberal professors, teachers like Bark; there would be acres of soft-swelling greensward upon which would sit concrete and brick copies of the architecture of the Golden Age of Greece.

Was I to realize *then* how the reading circuit would expand until it would become a firm adjunct to the writing itself, or how it would change essentially private people into atrocious actors and some into drunks quite unable to prevent themselves from puking over podiums, or transform them into cocksmen and cockswomen and hapless victims of logorrhea?

Could I have suspected that some of those writers who would invite me to read at their schools would, in return, expect invitations from my school when I began to teach — the old QPQ? Who would warn me of grand fees, parts of which were expected to be kicked back to the inviter? And who would be so bold as to tell me that I could expect audiences from six hundred to six — more often the latter — until I published another novel and if the reviews did not maim me?

Paul's letter was long, part confession, part apology. It was strange, coming as it did after the typescript of his novel. We had not been in touch for about three years until that arrived. As I had gone to Spain to clear my perspectives, so he had left New York to order his. I recognized that, but I was vaguely troubled that my presence and work had made him uncomfortable enough to leave the city. His discomfort, however, made me aware of an unspecific capacity vested in my just being what I was.

Paul's was the kind of letter I knew he'd made a carbon of (as I would have done), one destined for posterity, when his biographers got to work piecing together his life. The letter was also designed to head off any lengthy discussion of the subject that had caused it to be written. (*That* would not work!) All he said in the letter he had said more eloquently in his book. For then I was but *one* of his audience, not as, with his letter, *the* audience, who brought to the work more knowledge of the book's sources and nuances than would a mass of readers.

I had never supposed that the bigotry in the United States was devastating enough to make a Jew want to pass forever as a Gentile. I had known Jews who changed names to beat the medical and law school quotas, but they'd not changed their religion. One could understand, even envy, that ability to use the great American "asset." For black people there were no assets, no matter how much one related to Indian relatives or to the occasional white sheep who showed up in the family photogravures.

This, though, was different. I, and I suppose others, had been inconvenienced, misled, lied to, so that Paul's story might possess the shape of truth. Now here he was with the real truth, whole and nothing but. Was there a point in continuing a friendship founded on such shifting sand? I could have let it go in Spain, but hadn't; not even on my return, though I took my time renewing it. And he could have when he left the city, but hadn't. We were two disparate elements of the whole, sharing the public experiences, jealously guarding the private. There had been a spill-out; balances had been subtly altered. We were like two kids on a teeter board: if one jumped off, the other plummeted down.

We met, as he had requested over the phone, for dinner in the Village. He seemed relaxed, cool in a guarded way, and slightly bemused as we embraced.

He stepped back, still gripping my shoulders, and studied me, the way an older brother might regard the younger. "It's good to see you, Cate. So solid. So sure of yourself — "

"Rock of ages," I said. "The tree planted by the water."

He laughed.

We sat down and ordered drinks.

"How's Allis?"

I wondered if he was supposing that she was overjoyed at the news that he was really Jewish. "She's good," I said. "Sends love. She's pregnant. November."

"Oh, yeah! Marvelous, just marvelous!"

I smiled in spite of myself.

"You got anything going for you in the way of women, man?"

"A Betsy."

"A what?"

"Woman named Betsy. Looks like this is it."

"Great," I said. "Fantastic. She from here?"

"No. Chicago. And you know, man, strange. After I've gone through all these changes, she's not even Jewish."

I said, "Well . . ."

"You liked the book?"

As I said, "Yes, it's a fine book, Paul," I flashed on Walter Pidgeon saying that to Van Johnson in a film made, I think, from something Fitzgerald wrote. "I mean, it was really good."

"I'm glad. That was important to me. I think Alex'll do well by it."

"I think he will, too."

"I liked *The Hyksos Journals,*" he said. "Apparently, so did everyone else."

"But they didn't understand the fucking thing."

He said gently, "They never do, but does it matter? You know what you did."

"I know, yes, but it would be nice to know that out there, tapping through the darkness, some others knew too."

"Yes, yes, you're right. By the way, man. You know that whole Hyksos business, I mean the historical occurrence, is extremely anti-Semitic."

I remained motionless over my food for a moment, then said, "I've read the pros and cons — Philo, Josephus." I decided to change the subject. Who needed this right away? "Too bad about Leonard."

"Yeah, but I knew it would go something like that."

"He seems to be doing better dead than when he was alive," I said.

"Yeah. That's classic. But I want mine now, don't you?"

"I'm with you, man." We laughed brittle little laughs, and I said, "Listen, Paul. Mark suspected all along. About you, I mean. That business with the co-ops."

Fright tracked quickly across his face and vanished. He ate silently, watching me. "He said he would have remembered you. That shit you put us through with your father — that was pretty fucking unnecessary — "

"You met my father," he said in an unnaturally quiet voice.

"When!" I challenged him. "When the hell did I ever meet your father?"

"The day you moved to New York. The day Janice left. You must have run into my father on the stairs. He stamped out angry because, even though I was rid of the shiksa, I wouldn't claim my heritage. He left one second and you came in the next. He's a rabbi."

I recalled that hot day, painting his apartment, and I sighed. "So, now. What does it all mean, Paul? I mean, what's changed?"

"I guess what's changed is that I'm no longer ashamed of or afraid of being a Jew."

"Uh-huh."

"You know, loud, pushy, money-grubbing — all the stereotypes." He studied me. "And the fear. I belong to a people whose ass has been kicked forever. We let the Germans destroy us, but you know, they were only mopping up for the rest of Europe — "

A reversal, I was thinking. Saul / Paul, at first a persecutor of Christians, then his trip to Damascus, a vision on the road, and then the ministry (with Simeon called Niger and the rest at Antioch) and dropping the name Saul and becoming Paul, who later would vanish somewhere in Spain. I was wondering, too, why it was that Jews suffered so much in temperate zones and not nearly so much in the subtropics.

" — we ate shit for breakfast, lunch and dinner and, listen, Cate, I wanted no part of it. Other kids played ball on Saturdays; not us. I tried to hide my yarmulka; our parents spoke Yiddish and English with an accent. Our lives were twice encircled: Is it good for the Jews and is it bad for the Jews — "

Priests and cardinals and popes wore yarmulkas, I thought, and other people also wondered if events were good or bad for them.

" — in the army I could press the trigger of my M-1 and the people in my sights died — "

"I know the feeling," I said, remembering it, the mixture of elation, of awe, of power, all overriding, dominating, just subjugating a quick sense of grief brought on by the broken commandment.

"I know you do," he said sharply.

As he talked on, now loudly, now intently, voice just above a whisper, I reflected on that ancient and mystical and perhaps even physical bond between the black people and the Jewish people, who were white. Much of that was changing these days, was being obscured, but there persisted among black people in the South an admiration for the Jews that was not based only on spirituals and Bible lessons about the Hebrew children; in other parts of the country, we lashed and lunged at each other like lovers, one of whom is about to depart.

We knew that had we been in Germany or anywhere in Europe, we would have gone to the ovens as we in our millions had already gone to the sea; they seemed to have always overcome; we were, all over the world, still overcoming in the future imperative.

He was still talking.

Maybe, in some very distant time, the people who then lived in Europe perceived the Jews as an ethnocentric group, while they saw themselves as theocentric. ("Africa begins in Spain; Africa begins in Portugal, in Italy, in Greece, in France," and for the British *all* the niggers were lined up at Calais.)

Paul called for cognacs while I thought of Moses, the man called Moses, with his slowness of tongue, strangeness of speech (was it a !click-ing?), which experts claimed was a stutter, and of God changing the color of his hand (aha!) to that as leprous as snow and back again; and the business of Miriam and Zipporah — fables, all fables or, rather, allegories, concealing truths in pieces like puzzles. It all lay shrouded, concealed, and belted like a wondrous woman in simple but fine linen; you know what is beneath: the private mounds and clefts. Micrometers of cloth may separate you, yet you may never know, truly know, what it would be like to be, finally and blissfully, inside that cloth.

"Negroes don't have the problem," Paul was saying. "They know precisely where they stand."

He seemed to be waiting for some kind of response. I was thinking that, wherever I had been, meeting a Jew had always been more comfortable than meeting any other kind of person. How old a thing was that, I wondered. To Paul I said, finally, "I'm not so sure what it all means, Paul, to be a Jew. I mean, I've read things and heard things, the history, the laws, the customs, all right. Good. But you make it sound as if the color of the sky has changed for you, that somehow pussy is different, that things for the rest of us are somehow — not quite as good. Hey, look, you ain't been a Jew but for five minutes, as far as I'm concerned. You wanna be Jewish, okay; but you don't put friends through changes because you have problems with it; you wanna be a goy? That's okay, too, but no changes. So what's it mean?"

His face was draining. He seemed to gather himself. "For one thing, maybe the most important as far as you're concerned, Jews were never involved in slavery or the slave trade — "

He stopped short when he saw my expression. Gently, I told myself, gently. I laughed. "Well, we weren't involved with the ovens. Almost even." I felt the urge to cradle the side of his face in my hand, and I did. "Paul," I said. "This is Cato. I remember your anti-Semitism, remember? And here you are, already assigning virtue to yourself. What shit's this? We had some fun before this religion thing — what's it to be, race or religion, huh? But before you lay all that Jewish righteousness on me, you check out the Jacob Cohen family, the Salinases and the Mordecais of Charleston; you see who owned the family Langston Hughes came from, the family that Chester Himes came from. No gold medals, man. Sorry."

He chuckled softly. "None?"

"Did you want one?"

"Guess I just wanted to be what I really am, Cate."

"Well, welcome to reality. Drink to that?"

"You're on."

Perhaps it had been, after all, his "Jewishness" that had formed the basis of our friendship.

"Listen," he said, "how's about the four of us meeting for dinner next week? I'd like you to meet Betsy."

"Sure. You did say you were going to get married?"

"Yeah."

"And not Jewish? I figured that was important now."

"She'll convert."

"That'll make it okay?"

"Sure."

I sighed. "I don't really understand, but what the hell. I'm glad you're back in town. You'll do well with the book."

We were outside now. "Catch up with you, maybe," he said. He punched my arm softly. "Joking, man." But St. Paul had outpreached the others at Antioch, even Barnabas.

As I left him I said, "Listen, Paul. Even Negroes bought and sold slaves." I walked down the quiet streets to Mr. Storto's. He was leaning against a lamppost. "Ah!" he said. "Mist' Douglass! How are you? How's Miss Douglass? Let's get an ice."

We stood talking, licking the ices. I told him the pregnancy was coming along fine. "You know, Mist' Douglass, that's the way it should be, not some over here, an' some over there, an' this guy, he wants to fight that guy. All bullshit. I'm glad. I bet you glad, too, uh? Say, how's my Glenn, eh? College? Boy! That time, she flies!"

He promised to visit, but somehow I knew that he didn't intend to leave the Village, his turf, yes; something in the way he said it and, more to the point, he hadn't yet come. He was like a lesser Roman emperor who waited by his streetlight in front of his small palace for people to come and pay him court. We shook hands and then I went home.

"Did you," Allis asked, "give Paul his medal?"

I didn't answer; I was still going over the conversation with him.

"Well, then, how is Paul?"

"Okay. He's going to get married."

I thought she muttered, "Again?" but I wasn't sure.

She lowered her book and rested it on her breasts; waited until I was settled in bed. "Anyone we know?"

"Not from the way it sounded. That is, he didn't say so."

"Nice Jewish girl, I presume?"

"No, not Jewish."

She turned on her side toward me. I kissed one of her breasts. I supposed that as soon as our kid was old enough to start walking around, we'd have to wear bedclothes. I'd miss the being nude. Allis propped her head against her hand; her elbow dug into the bed beside me. "Hold it. Wait a minute. She's *not* Jewish? I thought — his first wife wasn't and Claire wasn't, then he went into this big thing and now his third wife won't be."

"He's confident she'll convert — "

"All the nice Jewish girls around here, like Amy, why should he find a shiksa and then convert her — you know something, your friend Paul — "

"Yeah, what?"

"Maybe it's a smart thing to be a Jewish writer these days, darling. Just maybe it is."

"C'mon, Allis."

"I'm sorry, honey, but every day I'm finding things that're not nice about so many people we know. By the way, do we have to go to Amos' this weekend?"

"Yeah, let's do it. Paul wants us to meet Betsy next week, too. Dinner."

"Betsy? Ross?" Allis laughed and ducked under the sheet. "I *want* to meet her."

"Listen, Paul always gets attractive women, you know that."

"Hell, you didn't do so badly yourself, or do you find me unattractive now that I'm pregnant?"

"Looking at you makes me think of that kid in Spain, honey."

She was silent, examining my mood. Then she said, "Cate, darling, I really don't know what we can do now. You've been in touch with Monica's father —"

"I know. Forget it."

"I think you should, too."

"I do try to forget."

Allis sighed.

"Stopped by Mr. Storto's."

She leaped at the chance to change the subject. "When's he coming to see us?"

"I dunno. He always promises."

"A young couple moved into the building today. Already this place seems less a geriatrics ward than before."

"Did you talk to them?"

"No, but they look interesting." Allis put her book on the night stand and turned out her light. "Amy called tonight. My father wants to see me."

I said, "Uh-huh," and turned out my light.

2

AMOS had bought an old house on a mountaintop in the Catskills. I supposed that he drove there to get the demons out of his system, the ones that lurked in his office, the bars and restaurants in midtown Manhattan, the ones that ran across his soul in cleated shoes and the ones that would tie him for the rest of his life to that garage in East Orange, New Jersey. We had visited once before; it was a distinct change from the extended literary loop of Manhattan, the Hamptons and the Cape. No self-respecting writer or editor who wished to be seen would ever isolate himself on that mountaintop, where the nearest neighbor lived a half-mile away.

The trip up was different this time. The angers exploding around the nation were reaching a crescendo. People were being hauled from cars and shot and / or beaten because they were black (and sometimes because they were white). People were being shot in their cars waiting for traffic lights to change. Police were Bogarting people just because they could.

As we were leaving the apartment to go pick up the car, I said to Allis, "Put this in your bag."

She glanced at it once and glanced at me and opened her bag to accommodate the .32 I'd bought from Vernon. We did not discuss it, for there was nothing left to say; it'd all been said for us. Allis, yes, opened her bag and I placed it in and she closed it and we went.

(There must have been several million black people equally prepared, equally ready to react when pushed past some line already drawn and designated as the place to make the last stand. However, not being forced back beyond it, we must live now with relief riding one shoulder and guilt for feeling it upon the other. Perhaps we had drawn the line too far beyond the center of action.)

We arrived at Amos' without incident, and when I got out of the car after the three-hour drive, I breathed deeply. The air, nourished by vast stands of sugar maples, beeches, white birches and red firs (reminding me suddenly of the innkeeper Daniel) was neat, fine.

"God, *smell* that air." She laughed. "I'm glad we came."

Later, after a walk in the woods and some desultory fishing in his lake, we fixed dinner, then sat with drinks on the porch, where we could see all the way down a fifteen-mile-long valley from whose bottom was rising a slow, silvery mist. The night was coming down.

"Ike is in very bad shape," Amos was saying, "but he's working. I'll be damned if I know how he's living, though. Then, you know, man, nobody wants to touch him. Hey! The word's going around on your boy Paul's book. The fix is in; they're gonna make it a big one."

"Well, it is a good book," I said.

"Shit. I read an advance copy. It ain't raisin' no hell, Cate. What do you think, Allis?"

We both knew what Amos was driving at: a Jewish point of view.

"It is a good book," she said. "But I've read far better ones. There's the gimmick in it, I guess: the confession. It's an invitation for people to read what the system made Paul do; deny what he is. And people enjoy being reminded of how powerful the system is."

"Black writers do some of that," Amos said.

"Exactly," Allis said, and went back to her knitting.

Amos said, "It's time to ease John Greenleaf and Elliot Huysmans a bit to the side, man. This shit goin' on out in the street can't last forever."

"I hope at least until it does some good," Allis said.

"It'll *look* like it's done some good," Amos said. "But they got all the systems in place. We can't win, you can't win, I can't win, because the rules haven't been changed." He glanced at Allis. "It's not just black writers; it's all writers. I mean, Jesus, if writers would only try to understand that by virtue of the contracts they sign they actually subsidize the publishing industry in the same damn way a cat on the assembly line subsidizes the auto industry by agreeing to a contract that views his labor only as a cog in the profit system."

190

"Ah, shit," I said. "We all know that art is commodity."

Amos chuckled. "Yeah, baby, but do you have any idea how big that game is? No. Of course not. How the fuck could you?"

"So tell us," Allis said.

"I'm gonna." He fixed himself another drink. He seemed to be slipping into a quiet rage.

"You hand in a partly finished manuscript, Cate, right? The advance is ten, twenty, thirty grand, whatever — "

"More, more," Allis stage-whispered over her knitting.

"They'll give you maybe twenty-five percent when you sign. But they got all of the advance blocked out, and the other seventy-five percent they put in the bank. It draws interest. It's your money. You don't get any share of the interest.

"Then you take that six-month royalty-period shit. It don't take no six months these days for publishers to count sales and deduct for books returned. Booksellers can't afford to hold on to books for longer than three, four weeks; they gotta make room for the others. Man, they could balance the books in a day, because they're all getting computers installed. It's business, you know; it's money. They just use your money during that six-month period to do anything they want to do.

"That clause — it's an option maybe good for taxes — that says you agree to take down no more than twenty-five thou a year if your book hits big? Suppose you break a leg and make a million or two — "

"Break a leg, honey," Allis said.

"Let's just take a mill," Amos said, waving his arms frantically in the air. "If a publisher insisted on the letter of the contract, goddamn it, it would take you forty years to get it. Forty. Man, they could use your money up a storm — "

He broke off and looked at us almost in surprise. "Aw, shit, forget it. I mean, you writers are daydreaming; ain't no fuckin' art; all there is is money. Money! Money!"

We sat embarrassed and I found that I was angry, too. "What else, man?" I asked.

"Don't matter. You writers ain't never gonna get your shit together long enough to change nothin'. Each of you is a fuckin' *king!* A fuckin' *queen!* Goddamn bell-bottomed philanthropists. Man, all you cats is where Noonan's painters were, just what they was: suckahs! Suckahs!

And suddenly he was shouting at the top of his voice out into the night. Allis jerked away. I stood. Tears gushed down Amos' cheeks. He bounced on taut buttocks, his legs held stiffly out before him.

"An ain't nothin' worse than a" — and here he gathered himself —"a niggah suckah — nig-gah suck-ah!"

Just as suddenly he stopped. The echo of his voice, diminishing as it sped, rolled round and came back: NIGGAH SUCKAH—NIG-GAH SUCK-AH! A chorus of peepers slid in together with the sound of trees hissing at the stroking of a cool, night breeze. It was as if, so great was Amos' anguish, the earth and its essences had to respond.

"Go on up, honey," I said to Allis. "I'll sit with Amos a while."

"G'night, Allis." Amos' voice was pleasant and calm in a stiff, theatrical way.

Allis went to him, kissed him and with her forefinger wiped away some of the tears. When she was gone I said, "I didn't know you cared about the writing."

"Shit," he said in a mournful voice, "I *always* cared about the writing. I thought I could play the game and then pick up the ball and start a new one. The game was very expensive, Cate."

I hauled out of the closet some bolts of Nigerian cloth I'd bought on the trip through Africa, and Allis made me a dashiki. Everyone was wearing them by now, of course. Some were made of silk with imitation stones set in them; some had zippered pockets; some had intricate designs woven into them. Afro cuts put many black barbers out of business. Conks went quickly out of fashion. Even whites had their hair frizzed up and cut into Afro style.

I wore my dashiki the night we met Paul and Betsy Rawson for dinner. She was the way apple pie is said to be, very American — tall, slender, blond and very good-looking in an irregular way. That European "human débris anxious for any adventures" never could have imagined that the centuries would produce out of their collective, mean existences anything like Betsy, but there she was, murmuring about her Scotch-Irish, French-German, Italian-Austrian roots. "A mongrel," she said, giggling, "soon to be a Kaminsky."

"Was that it?" I asked Paul.

"That *is* it," he said. "But I'll continue to use Cummings in the writing."

When the meal was about half over, the conversations veered; Paul and Allis talked to each other while Betsy leaned forward to talk to me. (After all, did not bums beat their way through crowds to get to me for their handouts? Didn't strangers in town somehow fix on me to ask for directions?)

"I'm really so pleased to meet you at last. Paul's so often talked about you. I feel that I know you and Allis already!" She looked wistfully at Allis. "How pretty she is."

Paul and Betsy had met in Chicago at a party for Saul Bellow. "It's good to be settling in New York," she said. "Chicago is like Sparta; New York is Athens." Betsy kept gripping my hand, squeezing it in frenzied displays of instant friendship. Paul smiled tolerantly at us; Allis, through her thin smiles, studied her.

"It must be rough for you two," Betsy said.

Allis had overheard. "Why do you say that?"

"Interracial marriages are not very popular these days, isn't that right?"

"Oh," said Allis. "That."

"Well, you and Paul will be something of a mix yourselves," I said.

"Oh, hell, it won't be the same," Betsy said scornfully.

I'd given her the chance to be a martyr. Some of our acquaintances made much of such religious distinctions in their marriages, though very often neither husband nor wife practiced anything. Perhaps they were only trying to move closer to Allis and me, or perhaps we seemed to give to them the shared sense of danger they assumed we felt twenty-four hours a day. I recalled some of the parties or places we'd gone to where the black women had cut Allis dead or had given me endless grimaces designed to reflect their contempt for me. For us. Whites, on the other hand, considered anyone black to be militant, or believed the books we were writing to be nothing more than militant political statements. They wondered how come, then, we were married; how come we were going to have a child?

I said to Betsy, "Actually, we do all right. Pretty much just like everyone else."

"I'm glad," she said, gripping my hands again.

"She's got the hots for your old hands," Allis sang to the tune of "I've Grown Accustomed to Her Face." She was creaming her face in the bathroom. "I'll say this: she is very direct. I think I like her. She's probably too good for Paul."

"No. She may be just what he needs."

A couple of days later I called Alex Samuels. He came on the line with a rush. "Cate, listen. I'm in the middle of something big for Paul. I'll call you this — "

"Don't." I was suddenly so angry that I felt it possible to squeeze the phone into fragments.

"What?"

"You're fired, Alex. Shit. I call you and you can't talk to me because you're busy doing something for my friend, something more than you ever did for me, right?"

"Okay, Cate, if that's the way you want it." He did not seem to be distressed. Rather, he sounded relieved.

I dialed again. "Maxine? You've got yourself another client."

"Really, Cato? Great! But what did you do with Alex?"

"We're finished."

"Wanna have lunch?"

"Sure. Soon." And it was done.

The phone rang as soon as I'd slammed it back into the cradle. Ike Plunkett wanted to talk to me. He was on the way over.

"It's the Big Payback Time, man. The Big Payback."

Ike was high and it was noon. Allis would be keeping a date with her father just about now. Ike and I sat over tuna fish salad and cold cuts and drinks. But he wasn't eating; he was drinking and gazing around the apartment with perpetually startled eyes.

"Yeah, I heard you'd married a chick from Bread Loaf. Yeah, I heard that. Yeah. Big Payback. Them brothers in the street ain't kiddin'." He hummed something tuneless.

"How's the writing going?"

"*It's* going all right. I'm the problem." He hummed again. "Say, Cate, let me hold fifty until next week. I ain't got no food at home, man."

"I can let you have twenty-five, Ike. I ain't got fifty."

"That's cool, man."

"Why don't you eat somethin', man?"

"Eat? Oh. Uh, I don't like tuna fish."

"It's food, you turkey."

But he had started to nod. I gripped his shoulders and shook him. "Ike. Hey, Ike."

He came awake, trying hard to focus on my face.

"How's your kid, man?"

"I got to go," he said. He shivered. He moved on buckling legs to the door.

"The money," I said, holding it to him.

"Money?" He had stopped. "The money."

"You wanted — "

"Yeah, yeah." His nose was starting to run. He took the money, brought it close to his face to look at it and went out.

I closed the door and quickly checked the chair he'd sat in, pulling up the cushions and feeling very carefully in the crevices. Nothing. I felt no shame, simply an emptiness, an exhaustion. There had been no bag of heroin, no needle, no syringe. Cops would not be rushing down the hall at this very moment to batter in my door and carry me away for possession and use.

Ike's desperation was well known. And this led to the quite natural suspicion that he would do anything to make sure he continued to get the dope he needed to satisfy his jones. So I looked under the chair cushions.

Like nearly everyone else those days I was not immune to the idea that because I was a black writer there were forces naturally aligned against me. We all felt that. We all knew that at least one major publication had published an interview with Richard Wright before his death that in fact had never taken place. This was done with the specific aim of discrediting him. We knew that the authorities were harassing the Black Muslims, the Black Panthers and black people generally.

Some writers therefore turned up at readings, conferences and festivals with bodyguards. And I for one certainly felt better with my revolver than without it. We floated on turbulent seas filled with swift currents of rumor: the FBI, the Tactical Police Unit; government agents carrying HEW identification cards; the blacks were going to blow up New York this weekend; the Puerto Ricans would do it next weekend; the Weathermen were going to do it today; everyone complained of strange sounds on their telephones. Those white women giving up leg to black men were really agents, so zipper up yo dick. People wondered just whose list they were on, the Feds', the local's, the state's; no one believed that he or she was not on a list.

Yeah. Big Payback Time, all right.

These thoughts stayed with me through the afternoon. The sounds of schoolchildren down in the street, the elevator clattering up and down at a more rapid rate — these signaled as precisely as my watch that Allis would soon be home and that, whether I'd worked well or not, we'd talk as usual over a drink before she started dinner.

Allis was pensive when she came home. "How'd it go with Ike?"

"Lousy. He's in bad shape. How'd it go with your father?"

"Oh, darling, he looks so old. And at first it was kind of stiff. He kept staring at my big belly."

I handed her a drink. She kicked off her shoes and sat down. She looked sad and distracted.

"He apologized. Said I should make sure to tell you. He wants to meet you, too."

"What'd you say?"

She sighed. "I told him it was a hard thing he'd done — and that you were as hard as he. I think what's going on these days made him give the situation some thought."

"Apology accepted."

"Oh, Cate." She looked tired, dejected.

But I said, "Does he want handsprings? Do you want handsprings?" She waved a tired hand. "I know — don't."

Of course she knew. Mr. Greenberg might finally accept us as family. Or, rather, we might accept him. But nothing would make me stop remembering. It would always be there, even when we smiled at each other and patted each other on the back. It would be there, and that I could not help. "Aw," I said. "Shit."

Allis looked anxiously at me, as one might do to calculate just how much weight I could bear. Her eyes were not so much hooded as shaded. She would accept either a yes or no, I realized, just as she knew that the right to demand the meeting was not hers. Still, it would please her. "It wouldn't be a big thing," she said. "Just to see him now and again. You know I'm not asking you to like him."

"I know. I don't care."

She stirred cautiously. "I told him I'd call and let him know. It doesn't have to be soon, honey."

The elevator was now banging up and down even faster, and once someone got off on our floor, sighing.

"Any time."

"Cate — "

"Umm?"

"Nothing. All right. Thanks."

"For what?"

"I know you don't want to do it."

"C'mon, honey. It's all right. I mean, it's not as if he and I will be slobbering over each other. It's okay."

3

I HAD ARRANGED with Catherine and her husband to take Glenn to college and get him settled. We decided to drive and have him see something of the country. He met me in New York so that I could help him shop for clothes and we could have a couple of days of just hanging out. We walked about the city eating hot dogs, stopping for beer, and once we joined Allis for her crisp walk around the Central Park Reservoir. She had taken a leave from her job, and she was not sure about returning.

I took Glenn back to the Museum of Natural History. He smiled. He looked carefully at the dinosaur skeletons that had frightened him so much, and when we left we stood outside on the stairs that somehow always reminded me of *Potemkin,* and suddenly we were laughing so hard that we couldn't talk, laughing at the years that had dashed so quickly by, laughing in amazement that we had survived them and were still more or less together, laughing at the old fears that now seemed so ludicrous. People looked at us and, chuckling themselves, peered around to see what we were laughing at. Perhaps a pigeon shitting on Teddy Roosevelt's head?

With the New York wardrobe packed (somehow I could not imagine him out of his dashikis and into a suit) and after a lingering goodbye with Allis, who would be spending the time with her father and Amy,

Glenn and I got in the car and drove off. The first stop was Catherine's to collect the rest of his things. Her husband wasn't there; she had taken off part of the day to be home and help Glenn finish packing.

She asked, "How's your wife?"

"All right. How's your husband?"

We laughed and sat down. "Sounds funny, doesn't it?"

"Sure does. Like two other people." But her eyes were following Glenn as he passed back and forth with books, records, brown bags filled with something or other. "He's a nice kid, Cat. You did a good job."

"I'm grateful. Kids're into everything these days. That dope scares me."

"I don't think you have to worry about that."

She was a little plump, but otherwise the same.

"We'll be able to see him often enough," she said. "But I know he'll want to spend a part of his holidays with you."

"We expect him."

"Won't be too crowded, with the baby coming?"

"Aw, no."

"What do you want, a boy or a girl?"

"I'll take a girl this time."

"Glenn always tells me how nice your wife is; he likes her."

"Well, she likes him, you know. That helps. They do fine, Cat."

"How's the writing?"

"It keeps coming. I still don't know anything else I'd rather do."

"I'm glad. You seem to have it made. Saw a rerun of your television show. But I still don't know why you called it 'The Negro.'"

I shrugged. "It seemed right." The rare times we met lacked for me at least some flash of the old times together, some bridge. But the thing was complete; even Glenn now seemed separate and quite apart, an entity we were watching with no small wonder as, long-legged and slender, he passed back and forth before us.

Catherine rubbed her chin with a forefinger and looked just past me. "I guess the sisters in New York are giving you a fit these days."

I grunted. She was not going to join the chorus now, was she? "Yeah. Hot and heavy."

"It's just the times," she said.

Glenn came to a stop in front of us. "I guess I'm ready."

Catherine stood quickly, her eyes casting a quick appeal toward me. "Jesus, where did the time go?" she said. She fussed at his clothes, made a face at his Afro. "I just can't stand all that hair, but that's the style — "
She paused. "Cate, you wore your hair long like this, remember?"

I laughed. There it was, the bridge, the flashing back. "Only because I couldn't afford a haircut, not for any style."

Glenn laughed. Catherine smiled smugly. "No. You wore it like Bayard Rustin. Remember when he came to the university? It was in our freshman year. That was when you started to wear your hair long."

I remembered Rustin but not the hair, but I said, "Oh, yeah. That's right."

She walked us to the car, her arm around Glenn, his around her.

"Drive carefully, Cate." I guess she said it because she had to say something.

"Don't worry. We'll call."

We left her plucking her lips, a bewildered expression on her face.

And because he had to do something, Glenn was scavenging through my camera bag on the seat. He pulled out the gun.

"What's this?"

"What does it look like?"

"That's a real one?"

"Yep."

He put it back.

He directed me to the turnpike and we headed west. I could almost hear him thinking in the silence. I said, "I can't really believe this. You going off to college. Jesus."

"And in another six months I'll have to register for the draft."

Vietnam, the war and Glenn, I thought. I hadn't wanted them to come together, and as far as I was concerned, they wouldn't.

"You'll be okay as long as you're in school. You do plan to stay in, don't you?"

"As far as I know now," he said.

"What does that mean, man? You are going to school and you will stay in school." He had frightened me. After a while I said, "It's a good, quiet place. A learning place."

"Don't worry. I wasn't thinking of joining up the way you did."

"I hope to hell not."

"I had things figured, like, if I get a low draft number and my grades were falling apart and the war got bigger — "

"Like what?"

"I'd claim sickle cell anemia." His look was so challenging that I almost didn't laugh.

"I have a couple of things working. Wanna hear 'em?"

"Sure." He squared around to listen.

"First off, by hook or crook, you are not going. Period. That's it. I don't give a damn what it takes. I'm sorry about the other kids. I'll ship your ass to Canada. Also, I heard that the Israelis were letting people come in, but that if war broke out, you'd be expected to help. Then there's Sweden."

He nodded and in silence watched the countryside flash by.

"Dad, why did you join up? I mean, can you explain that to me?"

I thought about it, then said, "Every war seems to be different. I didn't know anything then. Maybe they're never different. I didn't know they were segregating troops and blood. I really thought it was a different kind of war, where everybody mattered. Didn't take me too long to find out otherwise. And then I didn't have much to look forward to at home. My life would've been shit if I hadn't gone. I gave 'em war service and they gave me school. I'm not sorry. I lived. My going broke the old pattern of our family. After eight generations we get a look-in. I'm sorry your grandfather — well, you weren't even born; Cat and I weren't even married. But I'm sorry he was lost. What can I tell you — for a long time it seemed to have been a different kind of war, one that was right, but I'm no longer sure there's any such animal as a right war."

"Allis lost some people in the camps, didn't she?"

"Yeah. A shithouse full. Maybe it was a right war, because if it hadn't been them, it sure as hell would've been us."

We were silent, pensive, most of the rest of the way to our motel, and long after we arrived at Antioch and called Catherine and got settled, and on the drive back to New York, I thought about that talk. Somehow, the others did not seem to be quite as important.

When I returned from the college, embraced Allis (as well as I could) and had gone over the mail with her — books ("We hope you will like ———— ———— well enough to say something about it"), invitations to give readings or lectures (almost all of which were apologetic about the size of the honoraria, which, compared to the present, were actually quite large), probes to see if I would be interested in teaching, this time from Boston University, the University of California at both Irvine and Santa Barbara, Brooklyn College and Case Western Reserve, and bills, which we stacked to one side — Allis said, "Oh, you must call Maxine tonight. At home. The phone was ringing when I walked in. Said she'd been calling for two days."

"Ah," I said, "developments."

I had had Alex return the chapters of the new novel. Maxine had carried them over to Smythe and Simkin to ask for considerably more money than they'd paid for previous advances. Developments.

I fixed some drinks. "How was the visit?"

Allis said, "All right. Nothing special. How was your trip? Glenn? The school?"

We talked until we were hungry, then decided to walk out for dinner. I quickly changed my shirt, transferred my gun to my belt and pulled on my dashiki. When winter came I would have to carry the weapon in my pocket. It was almost good to be back.

4

SHE STRODE between the tables of La Grenouille like one who secretly expected to determine the fates of the literary types sitting in the restaurant.

Why was I guessing that?

Perhaps it was her alert youthfulness. She did not move, for example, the way Sandra Queensbury moved, lacking in body as she must have the postures demanded by Sandra's multiplicity of experiences. Sandra knew books, people and things, and so moved with the assurance of that tradition, which is to say that surprises were events she no longer expected to experience. Nor did this young woman possess that superior serenity sometimes displayed in public places that had been a distinguishing mark of Rupert Hemmings. Donald Jopoco, who had succeeded him as my editor, himself had a certain absent-minded air in public places; he could be there and yet, like Robert Lowell, a universe away. Jopoco made the waiters smile, for he gave them a second's superiority while he whirled slowly looking for the table they patiently pointed out to him. But what he knew, he knew very well. And there were other editors one recognized in such places, men and women then at middle age, this one having edited J. D. Salinger and that one Delmore Schwartz; another having worked with the early Mailer and still another with Steinbeck. Who could doubt that each had precise portraits of himself tacked in the closet of his mind?

The arrival of new people in publishing (like Maureen Gullian, still approaching, now with a wave and a lengthening of stride) seemed to coincide with the sudden corporate interest in books. And now and again one heard or read of staggering sums of money being paid to writers — two or three, perhaps. So there arose a quiet new concern at this time. How could so much money be paid to two or three writers without other writers having to make do with less for their own advances? One could not expect to give *both* France and, say, Senegal fifty billion dollars each, though French is spoken in the two countries.

Maxine had waved back. "There she is," she said, a smile climbing carefully upon her face. "Now we're gonna deal." This said while she studied the approaching woman. "Fuck Donald."

"Ah — hi — hello," Maureen said. I couldn't tell whether she was really breathless or faking it; perhaps she was learning fast. I half-rose and took her hand.

"I'm so pleased to meet you. I've loved your books, loved them." She sat down, still talking. She said to Maxine, "I can't believe this." She smiled at me.

Maxine said tolerantly, "Maureen, calm down. He's real. He's here to talk to you." She waved to the waiter. "*We're* here to talk to you."

Gullian ordered a Bloody Mary then propped her chin on her hand and just studied me.

(Who *is* this nigger?)

"I'm sorry," Gullian said. "I won't tell you how hard I've tried to get to talk to you. Everyone was so discouraging. Alex said you were happy, *very* happy at Smythe and Simkin — no sense bothering you. So when Maxine called — wow!"

She would fit into, I thought, the enclaves at the Hamptons, Provincetown, the Cape, St. Vincent, Aix-en-Provence, Ibiza; it wouldn't be hard for her to join the switch from the Rive Gauche to the Rive Droite. But, two things: Did she know that *Areopagitica* was not a Latin airplane, and could she get the bucks?

The bucks turned out not to be a problem. They were not staggering in number, but, on the other hand they were not, by ordinary writers' standards, what chickens ate either, and so I trotted into the stable of Maureen Gullian at Twentieth Century Forum Publishers.

By now, demonstrations against the war were occurring throughout the country. They were, somehow, as if by some secret twelfth-century

Albigensian design, occurring at approximately the same time that black people were setting the torch to America. The disruptions were diffused and therefore far less potent than they might have been if combined.

However, together with Paul and some other writers, I journeyed to Washington for the Writers' March to protest the war, sardonically aware that there had not been a writers' march to protest racism. Still, one hoped that these meandering streams would find a common channel and form a mighty river. There was by now every assurance that Paul's novel would be a success. I believed he made this trip mainly to acquaint himself with the rigors of being in the public eye.

It was Friday, early afternoon, when we arrived, our group having purposely planned to skip the activities at the Ambassador the night before and the earlier functions that were scheduled at first one church and then another. We were sure that Mailer would hog it all up, and try to cast Goodman, Macdonald, Coffin and Lowell and whoever else was there into shadow.

Perhaps it is always so when artists gather; maybe that is why we are more effective as individuals. We don't trust each other's motives.

As we approached the Department of Justice Building, our ranks soggy and drooping first this way and then that, joking, calling out to acquaintances, promising to meet for drinks after, a horde of men, in suits, splattered out along the line of march with cameras. They could not have been news photographers, for writers made news only when they have fucked the system, like Clifford Irving, or have won the Nobel Prize. No, these photographs would be in the files by dusk. I hoped fervently that my gun would not fall to the ground.

We sauntered up before the JD Building, bunching up, waiting for the speeches. I saw one other black man there. "Whaddya say, Blood?" he said to me.

People had recognized Paul, and while he was talking with them, I stood a little aside to allow myself to feel as I always did when I came to Washington. Here was the heart of the American paradox right smack dab in the middle of a black population; here was Washington with its acres of marble and grand domes and shafts; here was Jefferson's memorial — how could one detect in its quiet splendor Jefferson romping in the old hay with Sally Hemings and then keeping his own children by her in slavery? He who feared God was just. Here was the brooding Lincoln, all questions of his origin chiseled away in white marble, he who feared to unleash "Ethiopia" upon those gentlemen rebels of the South; and lancing into the sky, Washington's monument, sleeker than

Cleopatra's needle, visible to all descendants of slaves, of whom he had many. Behind us, the House and the Senate, where so many national crimes, masquerading as laws, were routinely devised and passed. Washington.

Up behind the milling small mob of writers, sitting at a window with bars on it, was Robert Lowell, there and not, apart but with, smoking, his great underslung jaw and rimmed glasses thrust toward this still dream-fed group.

People started making speeches, and young men, the masculine pitches of their voices not quite yet settled, blurted out that they were destroying their draft cards, and did indeed rip their cards. Paul, moved, I suppose, by these declarations, went up to the speaker's stand to say that since he had no draft card, he was tearing up his honorable discharge instead as a symbol of protest against the war.

Then we seemed to dissolve, our group moving respectfully behind Mailer's as it ferreted out the nearest saloon. We listened to statements, arguments, questions, but it was plain that nothing had been settled; the old gestures had been made and rejected out of hand, as governments in their massive nonentities will do. Perhaps it occurred to all of us at the very same time. We had produced no heroes that day, but the situation called for a hero, indeed, demanded one. Who would shoot MacNamara or Johnson or Rostow? Can I have a volunteer?

As we settled on the plane back to New York an hour or so later, someone said, "Don't worry. Norman will do something."

Burnt Offering was published to ecstatic reviews. Some WASP reviewers likened Paul to Bellow, Malamud and Phil, not Henry, Roth, but could not find nor recall any firm with four Jewish names in it, so one reviewer simply headed his review "Hart, Schaffner, Marx and Cummings," and let it go at that. (The same man had once written that Whittington and Huysmans certainly were *not* to be mistaken for Amos and Andy.) Others praised his fine sensibilities, his courage in baring his soul. All this often on the front pages of book review publications. Hardly any of them mentioned the quality of the writing, which was splendid; it was composed of some blessed alloy, woven fine; it was resplendent; it nearly blinded.

I suppose that had it not been for the imminent birth of our child, I would have felt a keener jealousy, a deeper bitterness.

5

M ACK ARRIVED on a Thursday night in New York Hospital.

We had gone to the hospital in the morning, before the rush hour, when the streets appeared fresh and strong; at the time when filmmakers took the first clear light of day to shoot sequences of their pictures. The cab pulled over within seconds, although I was prepared for all the heroics — jumping in front of one to stop it, flagging down cops, commandeering a car from a bewildered private citizen at gunpoint.

Allis' pains came and went through most of the day. She was not dilating. Was it because of age? I helped time her breathing, her pushing; I held her hand, wiped her forehead; our fetid breaths mixed. Evil-eyed West Indian nurses passed, regarding us with disdain. In adjoining rooms I heard shrieks from time to time. By now, traffic along the FDR Drive rushed steadily along.

We had been eating a steak, Catherine and I, the first we'd had in a month, when she went into labor. It was frightfully fast. I knocked at Kendall's door across the hall. He was an engineering student. He'd bragged that his jeep had been sent home part by part, crated, from Europe, where he'd fought with the 29th Division. The Kendalls had two kids. He drove us to the hospital around seven on that March evening, along roads crusted with snow and ice. Glenn was born two hours later.

206

The nurses then were Irish and it was St. Patrick's Day; they pinned a bit o' the green on Glenn's swaddlings and called him O'Douglass.

"Push, baby," I urged Allis.

"Aaummph!"

"Again, harder."

"I am, damn it! AAaauuuooouuummpphh! There!"

"Good."

She rested, sweating. "I'm tired," she said.

"I know," the doctor said. "But you must keep pushing."

Twelve hours later he decided that he would have to take the baby. "Now."

Mack was born near midnight. Allis was all right, but exhausted. They'd already sewn up her belly. The doctor and I smoked a cigarette together and I left.

For York Avenue it was already late. The singles bars hadn't yet taken over the East Side. The street was quiet, settled for the night. I hailed a taxi. It kept on going. I hailed another and it did not stop. I had experienced this before, had been to the Hack Bureau many times. This night of all nights I'd wanted to contemplate my son, though I'd hoped for a daughter.

The next cab went by, the driver paying no more attention to me than he would have to a johnny pump. My hand, with the gun in it, was almost out of my pocket before I realized it. I shoved it back and started racing toward the cab, now stopped at a red light a half-block away. I was going to kill that motherfucking driver; he would be completely unrecognizable when I finished with him. I was going to drag him out of his fucking yellow cab and beat the shit out of him until he died right in the middle of the dogshit-littered street. I had not run so fast in years; the street seemed a blur; my body ached with the anticipation of my hands on his neck. Didn't he understand what was going on in the country at that very moment? Didn't he comprehend the extent of his jeopardy? Had he not *ever* read Izzy Stone? I ran, leaning into the night. I was almost there. I could taste my gorge bubbling furiously like a Krakatoa summoning explosive powers that would decimate.

He must have glanced in the mirror and spotted me, the black slender apocalypse streaking like a part of the night itself right at him. The cigarette in his mouth stiffened as if even it were fearful. I grabbed the door handle with my left hand and flung it open, seizing his neck with my right. He was a big man, soft to the touch, and my fingers sank like the talons of a hawk sharply into his neck. His face snapped toward me. He was afraid. He stamped the gas pedal and the car lurched forward, pieces of the flesh of his neck packing under my fingernails. The door handle snapped away from my left hand and I spun and fell down in the street. He gunned his way through the red light.

I walked home because I knew that I would shoot the next cabbie and I didn't want to do that with the new baby, the new life that I had to care for. My left hand was so sprained that I couldn't use it for a month. But my right hand felt very good.

My anger speeds me into my foxhole. I crouch there, smelling my fear. Fear smells like snakes, which are not supposed to have scent. There is silence, an unimaginable silence, as though nothing is moving — wind, waves, palm leaves, bright tiny things in the sky; it is like the moment billions of years ago, before the Big Bang.

I think of pawns, that first row of symbolically short pieces whose numbers are fingered silently forward to permit the gallops of knights, the obliquities of bishops, the linear dashes of rooks and the dalliances of the queens.

I hear a noise. The universe is back in motion.

"Stop," I say to the noise in front of me. It must be a Japanese soldier. Yet I imagine the faces of Keye Luke, Richard Loo and S. I. Hayakawa; didn't Hollywood make all Orientals the same?

"Stop. I don't want to kill you. And I don't want to be killed. In whose book is it written that I must be killed by men as powerless as I because someone luckier, whiter and whose historical turn it is, perhaps, says so?

"You out there. Yes, you. What I want is the fearlessness that comes from having nothing to fear, not the fearlessness of the Gawains, Rolands and El Cids and Colin Kellys. Listen: I will walk with you across the Nihon-Bashi Bridge and you will walk with me across the Brooklyn Bridge and look down and together we will see Walt Whitman on the ferry looking up at us, puzzled. I will admire your gardens of chrysanthemums and you will praise my brave stands of autumnally brilliant sugar maples, all right?"

I came awake slowly, the way one does in a foxhole when the senses provide some assurance of safety with the coming of dawn. You remain motionless, your eyes searching the universe within their range. And then you move. Slowly.

The bed seemed large without Allis. I stretched and turned to fill it, noticed the baby things, and these reminded me of the shards of shit zinged into my head last night. As I looked, my inner eyes seemed to close and then open on another morning strong with the ascent of its young sun. I smelled water whose waves brought with it the scents of tropical places, of oil, of aluminum eaten away by the salt sea, and of rotting corpses filled with sea worms.

Treasure Island, near San Francisco. From there we would be shipped to various separation centers, given our ruptured ducks and slipped back into a society that had already changed beyond our most fevered imaginations. I sauntered up and down the streets of the former amusement park, pleased to be alive, to be still young and strong and, in all visible respects, whole. Marines and sailors slid along the streets, going as I was to the nearest chow hall, where, in the exuberance of victory, we were fed steak any time we wished it. After three years it was strange, but it felt uncommonly good.

And then a hush, lean and without a name yet affixed to it, pressed down along the street. Like everyone else I stopped and began to watch the cause of it; like everyone else I could not prevent myself from taking one or two steps backward.

Down the street, in spotless fatigues, creases razor-sharp, marched a phalanx of three hundred Afrika Korps prisoners of war. Though no one was calling cadence, they marched in unison. There were no bands to arrange their pace, no flags. They were uniformly large men and all were freshly shaven. Their peaked caps reached for the same precise angle. *Brrr ummp, brrr ummp, brr ummp.* Their feet were all hitting the ground and lifting from it with terrifying precision, like history being repeated beyond Santayana's imagination, this while from other streets I could hear navy petty officers and marine corporals and sergeants exhorting their disheveled crews to work details with youngish cries of "Hut, two, hut, two, ya lef, ya lef . . ."

Rommel's men, their lines cast-iron straight, came on, little smiles on their faces, just as they had come on for millennia out of their northern mists in the shadows of Arminius and Siegfried.

Brrr ummp, brrr ummp, brr ump.

This time it was the janitor sweeping the walk outside with his worn broom.

Flowers, I thought, swinging out of bed to make some coffee. I would take flowers to Allis today.

I called Glenn. "You got a brother," I said.

"Does he look like a sprinter or a distance man?"

"More like a fish right now. Did I wake you?"

"Yeah, but it was time to get up."

"Everything okay?"

"Yep."

"Okay. See you."

"Tell Allis nice going — and you, too, fella."

I found Allis' father's number where she'd left it. His voice carried the sound of expectancy mixed with reticence.

"Mr. Greenberg, it's Cato Douglass."

"Who? Who's this?"

"Cato Douglass." I dragged out the pause. "Your son-in-law."

There was a longer pause on his end. I waited. Finally, he said, "Ah — yes. Cato? Hello."

"Hello. I thought you should know that Allis had the baby last night. It's a boy."

"She's all right?"

"Of course." I guessed that he wanted to ask, but didn't dare. "We named him Mackland."

"What?"

"Mackland. That was my father's name."

"Your father, yes. Allis told me he was killed in the war. I'm sorry. Well, it's nice that you name your son after him. Honor thy father." There was another pause. "Cato, we have not talked."

"No."

"When are visiting hours?"

"You're going to the hospital?"

"Naturally."

I told him the visiting hours (though we would never meet there) and then he said, "Listen. I'm sorry about everything. Truly sorry. I know that doesn't make it better, but — well, goodbye. Thanks for calling."

Newborn babies are like first flowers, first warm days, first reds and golds dripped on the foliage in the fall. Maybe it is only that new babies make you momentarily conscious of life's changes, for there you are, the frenzy and passion of the conception long, long past, with this five- or six- or seven- or eight-pound creature in a corner of your apartment reeking with everything Johnson & Johnson ever manufactured in the way of infant emollients and powders.

Tenants stopped by to see; congratulatory notes were slipped under the door. The elevator men smiled when we boarded their cars and then it did not seem troublesome that Mack Douglass was going to be with us, more or less, for seventeen or eighteen years. The approaching Christmas season made it all the more pleasurable. There were two other events that we looked forward to: a big party Paul was throwing in honor of his book (and, he told me, "a fuckin' great paperback sale") and his new bride.

"Betsy?"

"Who else, man? That's what it was all about."

"Did you have a Jewish wedding?" (To which we were not invited?)

"Ah — no. We'll do that later, when she converts. Like you, we did City Hall." (Oh.)

And Glenn was going to spend a part of his vacation with us.

HE ARRIVED in a long leather coat, bell-bottoms the saltiest sailors on the Barbary Coast would have envied and a mountainous Afro. An ankh dangled around his neck on a gold chain and his bag carried a red, black and green I.D. tag.

He embraced me. We laid the shake on each other, with all the cuties: grips, snaps and twirls.

Did he hesitate to kiss Allis or was it my imagination?

He looked long at his brother, but I couldn't read his mind. "Cute," he announced.

School, was it okay?

It was. A few demonstrations.

What for?

"Black Studies," he said.

"Did you get them?"

"Yeah. Sure nuff did."

I could not shake the sense that he was being stiff and barely cordial with Allis and there was more distance, or seemed to be, than I had expected. A tension crept into the apartment.

"He's changed," Allis said.

"Of course. On his own now — "

"That's not what I meant." I knew that hadn't been what she meant. "He seems — well, hostile."

"C'mon. Do you think so?" The word was one I'd thought of and quickly discarded. I couldn't discern any reason for his hostility. But it was there, covert, beneath his often extravagant politeness.

I sighed. I'd been to a few colleges to speak, the English departments feeling some pressure to respond positively to the action in the streets. Black students at the integrated colleges attended readings and lectures in small, sullen bands, challenging visiting black lecturers to be or sound as revolutionary as they thought themselves to be; they appeared to be more interested in displaying what was then called "black militancy" before mainly white audiences than in what was being read or said to them.

What *was* one to say to them? Like everyone else, they had roles to play; we all played roles assigned to us by unknown directors in a play without name before an audience of shifting, unreliable sympathies. The mainly white audiences expected (one could both see and sense it) instant miracles.

Had Glenn suffered and changed because of isolation? My son? I had managed, but I'd had a family with me. There had been the Paul Robesons, the George Gregorys, the Sterling Browns, the Jerome Hollands, the Saunders Reddings — they had managed in those cold white colleges; had they turned hostile toward their parents or was it simply a different time?

I sighed again. Allis said no more.

A couple of mornings later — the day of Paul's party, in fact — I was in the bathroom. Glenn's hair was everywhere. (He picked it for thirty minutes each morning.) I realized that Allis had decided to stop cleaning it up and that he wasn't going to do it either.

"Hey, Glenn. Clean up the hair." I knew he'd never dare leave Catherine's bathroom like that.

I still remember my amazement at the way he turned to me, quickly, his teeth bared. And I also recall my own shock, for there it was, overt, barely held in check, his hostility, the posture of his own private, youthful revolution against Whitey and all the Nee-groes who had dealings with him — or her. No more than a second passed as we stood there reading each other with the greatest intensity. I had had occasion to spank him perhaps four times in his life, and each time I labored over my apology. As I gazed down the tunnel of his contempt, he said, "What hair?"

I half-turned away from him. "Look. Allis has been cleaning up behind you; it's as if you're leaving a mess just so she can. And, hey, I see

you with your feet all up on the bedspread, shining your shoes. Why?"
Smirk.

I saw myself afterward. I'd slapped him, hard, and he'd gone over
backward, eyes bulging not with hostility, but surprise and perhaps a
little fear. I'd leaped forward to catch him, to prevent his head from
hitting the door. He thought I was following up with another blow and
covered up. I caught him and held him. His eyes burned into mine. He
loosened himself, went to the closet and got his coat and stalked out of
the apartment.

"You'd better get a baby sitter for tonight," I told Allis when she came
into the living room, where I was sitting, trying to listen to what my
racing heart was telling me.

"Where's Glenn? What happened? I heard the door."

I told her.

"Aw, no. Where do you suppose he went?"

"I dunno. He'll be back, but I don't think we ought to count on him
to sit with Mack tonight."

"You okay?"

"Yeah, sure."

"Is it the black-white thing, do you think?"

"I guess so." I walked to the window and looked down into the street.

"It'll pass," she said. "Won't it? I mean with him?"

I didn't answer because I didn't know.

"I'll see who I can get," she said.

I went to the bedroom to take another look at Mack; it seemed that I
was always doing that. I'd done it with Glenn, too. When I came out,
Allis was on the phone in the kitchen. "I'm going to the Park," I said.
She nodded.

A cab swerved toward me and slowed when I reached the corner. "Fuck
you," I shouted. The driver shrugged and picked up speed.

I gained the track that runs around the reservoir and started walking
southward, just walking, just thinking, and before long I was on the Fifth
Avenue side, moving northward past the Guggenheim Museum. On my
side of town once more, I moved down to the walks, which were gray
with the cold, although it hadn't snowed. I saw him on a bench between
Ninety-sixth and Ninety-fifth streets, and I moved toward him with a
heavy sense of relief.

"Looking for something?" he said. He had crossed one leg over the
other. I could tell he was cold. His face looked strained.

I sat down beside him. "Yeah, my son."

"Hmmmm," he said. "Little kid?"

"No. He's eighteen."

"He run away or something?"

"I don't know. One moment he was there and the next he was gone."

"You spanked him probably."

"Yeah, I guess I did, in a way. But maybe he had it coming."

"Well, you know kids; they never feel that way. But, you must be pretty bad, mister, jumpin' on an eighteen-year-old."

"He wasn't just any kid and I suppose that's why I lost my head."

"Blew your cool."

"Blew my cool, yes."

I followed his eyes to a spot above the Guggenheim and wondered what he was seeing. I said, "Parents always worry about the bad company their kids may keep — drugs, muggings and shit like that. They worry about influences and what they can do to some silly shit like the values the parents hold jointly with their kids. These days, junk and rip-offs are about the least worries."

He looked at me and just for a second I thought I saw a glistening in his eyes. I went on talking. "Just last week — I didn't get a chance to talk to my kid about this — just last week a young black girl, a sophomore at one of those exclusive places like Radcliffe or Vassar or Sarah Lawrence, killed herself. Seems as though the other black kids on the campus, all as militant as hell, had put it to her: whether she was black enough to kill her mother, who was white. Really put it to her. Militant fuckin' kids who don't know the front end of a gun from the asshole of an eel. And wouldn't want to for fear the shit'd really be gettin' heavy then — "

I stopped because my voice was rising and I didn't want him to hang his head the way he was starting to. "Don't," I said, "run us through that mill, Glenn. It's not that choices will have to be made if you do; there aren't any choices to make. *We have a relationship whether you like it or not,* you and I, Allis and I, all of us. I wouldn't like it if you walked out on it, and I don't think you would; I mean, I'd be unhappy because, well, you know, shit . . ." The top of the Guggenheim gleamed brightly for a second, as if being viewed through water.

"I don't know why colleges are so bad for kids today. You were never so antagonistic toward us before you went away. That's what it was, right?"

He said in a small, quiet voice, "Yeah."

"There are a lot of assholes out there that I wouldn't think twice about when it comes to blowing away time. But Allis isn't one of them and you fuckin' well know it. If you want to talk about it, let's talk — the way they do in college? But not that little kid shit with the hair and the shoes . . ."

A squad car, looking bigger and meaner than usual because it was creeping up the sidewalk instead of the road, eased toward us. The cops looked us over. They seemed to be very young. They kept on going, gained the road and crept away, blue exhaust fumes licking lazily from the rear of the car.

I waited for him to say something. He did not, just kept looking up, then looking down.

"Glenn, there's a lot of that now," I said. "Antagonism. So much of it's directed along the easier channels. You know, toward people who aren't going to do anything about it for one reason or another. Not fair. No good. Chickenshit. Antagonize the cops. Bomb a precinct house. Kick Lindsay's ass. Shoot up the Congress. Not your family. Not your friends."

Glenn studied my face, said nothing.

I said, "But you don't want to die. Nobody does, yet everyone will."

"How close were you to being killed during the war?"

"Why?"

"What does it feel like?" He had read the look on my face. "Well, you were the one who brought it up," he said.

"Do you want to know the truth?"

"Yeah, sure. That's why I — "

"That squad car that just went by. I knew I was scared because of the way I felt when it didn't stop, when I knew it was going to keep on going. How did you feel? The same way? Yeah, no?"

"The same way."

"You know why, don't you?"

"Close?"

"Yeah." My bitterness rang like brass in my own ears. "If they had decided that we were fugitive Black Panthers that would have been it. If they had decided that they'd had a dull day and needed some excitement, like shooting some niggers, that would have been it. To answer your question, champ, I feel very close to being killed whenever I'm within shooting range of a cop."

He bounced his heel on the walk a few times. I looked at him and laughed. "During the war it's better because the other guy knows you got your shit, too. And you do."

"Dad?"

"Yeah?"

"Do you have the gun now?"

216

"Yes."

"Then what were you afraid of?"

"I was afraid *for* you. The mouth is not faster than a bullet, and I know you're not ready to die. Let's go home."

We started walking. He said, "Are you?"

I thought about that one. I said, "No, but I think I'm readier than you."

Allis looked anxiously from his face to mine. "Want some coffee? Must be cold out there."

She poured it while we took off our coats. Glenn was pulling back his chair at the table then stopped.

"Listen," he said to Allis. "I'm sorry. I didn't mean to do those things or behave the way I have." He sat down. "I feel under some compulsion to *hurt*. Dad's right. If I hurt you, you won't hurt back." He picked up his coffee and set it back down; his hands were trembling and he couldn't hold the cup. Allis started to move toward him, her arms upraised to place them on his shoulders. I scowled at her. She stopped and waited.

"It's a tough time to grow up in," she said, finally. She set the creamer softly beside his cup.

"Thanks," he said.

"You won't have to baby-sit tonight, Glenn. I've got a sitter."

For a moment he looked frightened, abandoned. "No, I'll sit, Allis, really."

"We just thought you might not want to be bothered tonight."

"No, no. I'll do it, okay?"

We looked at each other.

"Besides, I have a date coming."

"Ah," Allis said.

"Oh," I said, starting to feel that I had my son back again. "I guess in that case — "

Paul's party was actually a book party and was a surprise. We were, as we entered his apartment, feeling much better about Glenn. But we were still shaken; our innocence had been splintered; we had discovered that we were vulnerable.

We noted quickly the other guests. I took Allis' arm and steered her toward the sound of clinking glasses, the slick rasp of ice cubes. Had Maxine told me she would be there? No matter; she was. And why hadn't Paul mentioned that his party was really a Book Hustle, complete with caterers and photographers who crept about to snap the right people together? We had got halfway to the sounds of glass and ice and pouring, and I was thinking that Paul was now drinking with another crowd, when he spotted us.

"Hey, Cate, over here. Here, Allis." He waved to us out of a clutter of book people. Betsy started toward us at the same moment that Jeremy Poode stopped us, Selena Merritt in tow. We shook, embraced appropriately, chatted, as I kept edging Allis toward the bar. Betsy intercepted us. Roye Yearing called out, "Heard from the Bread Loaf crowd?"

"No. You?"

"No. Talk to you in a while."

With Betsy, then, who I felt had rushed to us to help absorb the impact of the unconscious imperial command from Paul: *Hey, Cate, over here.*

We got our drinks and Betsy guided us toward Paul. We tried to exchange news, gossip, talk of the baby. We were unable to. Paul's eyes kept darting to this reviewer or that, to one established writer or another, while at the same time holding whispered conversations with Alex Samuels.

"Big party," I said to Betsy.

"God, I didn't know it was going to turn into this," she said. "His publisher wanted to do it."

"Betsy," Allis said. "We want to congratulate you on the wedding, your marriage — "

"Yeah, yeah," Betsy said. "We got married. We hope it'll work."

"What an attitude," Allis said.

"You know what I mean."

I left them and went back to the bar. Elliot Huysmans and John Greenleaf Whittington were there.

"Hello, Douglass," Huysmans said briskly, studying me, moving slightly in one direction and then another, as a boxer might move, feinting, looking for an opening. He kept squaring his shoulders the way Jimmy Cagney did in his early films. We had never met before. We shook hands. I turned to Whittington, whom I was also meeting for the first time. "Hello, Cato Douglass. I'm glad to meet you at last. Do you know — " He gestured toward the people near them.

I nodded, said, "Yeah, sure [shake], sure, how's things? [Shake] What's new? [Shake] Sure." And then we stood looking at each other, looking into our glasses, which we all had just filled and could not readily fill again. Like waiters, we looked each other directly in the eye, yet did not see. Where was Allis? Come, love, rescue me, us. Her back was turned and people were crouched over, looking at something in her hand. A photo of Mack.

Into the poisonous silence, walking prettily, came Sandra Queensbury, and greetings exploded about her like wet cherry bombs and they all moved away. "My God," she said, "the whole of Dickie's List plus the retainers. How are you, Cato?"

Now she looked like the commencement of a legend; age was rapidly overtaking her. "I'm okay, Sandra. You?"

"You can see that, dear. Lovely, your wife."

"Yeah, and I like her a lot."

"That's important. How's your work?"

"It's okay."

"When are you going to join us and leave the rabble?"

"I'm all right for now."

"So I hear. Maxine got a good deal for you. Are you sleeping with her?"

"No."

"That's just what she said."

She fixed herself a drink, casually surveying everyone. And then said, "Do you recall that story of Paul's that you published in *our* anthology?" She smiled coyly — no, seductively — and at once I guessed that she was still "dowsing" first novelists from Wyoming or Arkansas.

"Yes, I remember it. Why?"

"Really, Cato, it wasn't much of a story, and you knew it." Mark Medowitz had just come in, and Shelly Popper, who reviewed for the *Voice.*

"Then why didn't you throw it out? You threw out others."

"Because, baby, I knew that you and Paul were old college chums, and in this business we have to help friends out, right? But tonight the fix is on. I like going to Fixings. Your Paul is in." She chucked me in the ribs with her elbow as she moved away. "You look good. Do call me sometime."

"Yes, I will." I started toward Allis. Maxine stopped me. "Allis looks marvelous, Cato."

"Yeah. I hear you discussed some sleeping arrangements with Sandra Queensbury."

"Isn't she just about the nosiest old bitch you ever saw?" Maxine was looking at me with a new slant of her eyes. She started to giggle. "Oh, Gawd!" she said. "When she asked I never thought that — "

She turned to have another look at Sandra.

"That was a very long time ago," I said.

"Really? I hear she's still quite active. Bravo for her."

"Hey, I gotta get to Allis. I'll see you."

I was almost to her. A woman blocked my path. "Mr. Douglass," she said firmly. She was one of the most unattractive women I'd met in some time. "I'm Maude Tozer with *Passages* — "

"Ah, yes. Books editor."

"You know. Good. I want very much to do an interview with you. May I call you?"

"Sure. Whenever you're ready."

"It'll be this week."

"Okay, I'll be waiting for your call."

Maude Tozer had very bad breath. She was dressed from head to foot in swirls of taupe-colored garments out of which stuck her thick legs and large bosom.

"Who is *that*?" Allis whispered when I reached her. I told her.

We moved around the edges as the decibel level increased along with the drinking. "Did you ever sleep with her?" Allis asked, nodding toward Maxine.

"No. You've never asked me that before — why now?"

"Because close to you she moves the way women do when they know you very well."

"She doesn't know me that well."

"I meant before we were married, did you sleep with her?"

"Again — no. Aw, shit, let's go home."

"Because I asked that?"

"No. Because you know I hate rituals."

"Paul's marriage?"

"No. Paul's — success."

"Ah, so that's what the celebration's all about. Not the marriage. I got that feeling from Betsy, too. Yes, of course. And there is something different about him already — "

"What?"

"A certain ease, a lessening of tension; he always seemed tense and depressed to me, but now he's like someone who's landed safely after a very long trip."

"The trip," I snapped, "was short."

"Hey, we're on the same team, remember?"

We started toward the door, but Roye Yearing was veering down on us. "Fuckin' great party," he said. "But what's goin' on? Why are all these literary assholes here? How come you're here, Cate? Hello, Allis, how's things?"

"What're you doin' here? I didn't know you knew Paul."

"Shit, I don't. Heard he was an old friend of yours, though. I just got this engraved fuckin' note and I figured why not." We watched Allis saunter toward the door.

I was trying to swing around him. "Great party, anyway." I thought Roye had dried out.

"Heard anything about Ike?" Roye was moving with me.

"Nothing."

"Aw, shit. He was such a nice guy. I heard all about that drug shit. Is it true?"

"I'm really not sure, Roye."

We were at the door now. Roye lifted his glass. "May the demons go easy on ya, kid." He bottomed his glass, clapped me on the shoulder, pecked at Allis' cheek and started back to the booze.

"Hey! Hey!" It was Paul. "You leaving? Christ, man, we didn't get a chance to really talk. Sorry. Let's just the four of us do it soon, okay?"

He embraced Allis, then me. His release, sort of a gentle guiding, was like the practiced handshake of a politician who doesn't grip too hard, and manages somehow to move you past him so he can take the next hand and the next and the next.

7

GLENN was leaving.

We stood on the corner trying to hail a cab to La Guardia. His leather coattails flapped in the stiff December wind. Glenn seemed very tall and strong, standing there. And he was certainly far older in many ways than I had been at eighteen. For a moment I envied him that.

"Standing here," he said without preface, "just standing here, Dad, you know we might be just a couple of rocks at the bottom of an ocean in someone else's universe." He smiled.

"What?"

"Or we might be some cacti in a desert through which some guy's walking right now, this second."

I studied him carefully. "Oh. Is that Planck with some stretching? Quantum theory, multiple worlds?"

"Yeah. I read about it." He took a deep breath. We were still looking up and down the street for a cab that was unoccupied. "I thought about us," he said. "You and your world — "

"Which includes you."

" — Allis', the baby's, mine, Mom's — "

I moved directly in front of him. "But according to Planck, isn't it possible that each world has entirely different properties?"

He said, "Exactly."

"Not exactly. *We* share the same properties — "

"Say, what?"

I laughed, remembering that when he was younger he'd mimicked Cosby. "We share the same properties, kiddo, what we have of the world, such as it is, mistakes, little angers. We're in the same world, okay? You're not abandoned. Okay?"

The cab was shooting south on Central Park West, a yellow blur. The driver saw us, hit the brakes and banked into a U-turn. We ran across the street to the car. "I hear you," Glenn said, getting in. "But Yellow Springs really *is* another world."

"If you say so. Take care."

"S'long," he said.

Other worlds, another world. The kid. How was she? He? Was Monica still out there? How many guys has she had in nine years? Say five a day for nine years: 14,600 guys. How's she / he taking that? *Is* she still out there? Even if you've got your kid relatively close, look what happens. Crap. No, shit. What's Barcelona like now? Franco's middle class he's building? *That* must be some world.

("Fine-looking boy you got there, Mr. Douglass.")

Forget it. Let him / her go. Tough, like Monica. Will survive. Another world. Another language. Another culture. What's her / his name? God. Did he / she *even* live? Have I created a world which he / she in fact doesn't inhabit, having been flushed down a toilet or buried under a rock in some park? No. Must be alive. *Know* there's life a full nine years grown.

Julio was holding open the elevator door. He regarded me with something like concern on his face.

"Your floor, Mr. Douglass. I was sayin', you've got a fine boy there. The big one."

"Uh, yeah." I started to add "Thanks," but Glenn and the way he was was mostly accident, perhaps even an illusion. Should I say thanks for something I didn't do?

I said "Thanks" as I got off.

Two weeks later I was still thinking about other worlds from the fiftieth floor of the *Passages* building. It was after four in the afternoon and Manhattan was already dark and pitted with lights from office and apartment buildings. Behind each window, I romanticized, was a different world. I was standing in one of them, a floor occupied by three cozy little apartments. It was very convenient for the *Passages* people. I wondered how one got to reserve an apartment for a night or for a weekend, and from what rank they came.

Maude Tozer bustled behind me in the kitchenette, fixing drinks. A "small" dinner was almost finished cooking in the microwave oven. A bottle of wine sat in ice in the wine bucket. The small table was set and a languid fire burned in the fireplace. Behind me Maude was saying, "During the day we have people to serve, but at this hour, which I prefer myself, they've gone for the day. I like to do these things. The idea of servants still upsets me."

She approached, smiling, holding the drinks. I had tried to have her do this earlier in the day. It's really no good conducting literary business, especially with a woman, so late in the day. It's all right if you're single.

The drink was strong, like the ones I used to fix for my dates. Hummm. "Do you do all your interviews up here?"

She laughed. "Let's sit down." When we were seated across from each other in front of the fireplace, she said, "No. It depends. Some people don't like to come into the city at all. Others, I feel, don't deserve or don't rate the *Passages* red carpet treatment. Sometimes the apartments have been booked solid for weeks."

I wondered if she booked and then found someone to interview.

"What's that you have with you?"

I held it up. "A tape recorder. I figured you wouldn't mind if I taped your interview."

Her smile was brighter. Her teeth seemed to gleam.

"Ha, ha," she said. "Clever."

Passages was notorious for the slant of its quotes, the viciousness of its writers, the venality of its editors. But it was one of those publications writers believed they needed to be reviewed in or interviewed in. It looked good, but it had the clap. You wouldn't know that until later, though, when it hurt.

Maude was up fixing more drinks. She liked the sauce, people said. "I hear," she said from behind me, "that you and Sandra Queensbury used to be quite good friends."

"She edited an anthology I did for her."

"Well, yes, of course. Everyone who was friendly with her *did* something for her — a book, novel or nonfiction, a collection." She was back now, handing me the drink. I glanced at her pad and pen beside her chair.

"Do you have to get home?"

"In good time," I said.

"That's good, because I don't like to rush."

I said no, no rush and then, "How many black people do you have working at this outfit?"

"What?"

"You had one black editor, I think that was his title, ten years ago."

"Oh. Who was that?"

Maude had a nice voice; pity that was all. I mentioned the name.

"I wasn't here then. We do have one editorial assistant who came when I did."

"He's still an editorial assistant?"

"She." Maude rose. "One more and I'll serve the dinner, okay?"

"One more?"

"Just a little one," she said.

"I want to save room for the wine," I said.

But she was refilling the glasses. "Do you," she said from behind me, "fool around?"

I turned. "Fool around?"

She came back with the drinks. Her fingers rested on my hand. "Come on, Cato."

"I don't understand what you mean." She looked hard at me to determine if I was fooling. I wanted her to think that perhaps I had not heard the term; that there did exist that great cultural difference between us, as many white people believed. "Really," I said.

She sipped her drink as the sound of the buzzer on the stove echoed through the room. Her look was vaguely troubled. "I mean," she said loudly, enunciating every word, "do you fool around *with women* the way you did with Sandra?"

"Oh," I said. "That. You mean, would I fuck you, right?" I glanced around in mock bewilderment. "I thought you were doing an interview. [And I had until I walked into this penthouse.] But you really want me to fuck you, huh, Maude?"

"Has that thing been on?"

"The tape recorder? No. That was for the interview."

"Are you sure?"

"Take it. Play it."

She almost snatched it out of my hand. She jammed buttons, then placed it to her ear, turning up the volume when she heard nothing. She pressed the buttons again, watching me closely. When she was satisfied, she handed it back to me. I noticed that it was running. I said nothing as I placed it beside me.

"Well," she demanded.

"Well what, Maude? If I say it, will you repeat it after me?"

She waved a hand. "This is getting silly. You're not a hick. You know what this is all about — "

Sure. The exercise of power. The power to fuck whom you wanted or kill whom you wanted, when you wanted to, or to withhold whatever you wished to when you wanted to; it was about racism, which as Maude defined it, meant that, though you looked and smelled like a cross between Grendel and Quasimodo and you were a white woman, a black man would want to fuck you.

I rubbed my hand across my forehead. It was the intellectual way of scratching the head. She got it. Her smile was warming.

"Let me get this together. No fuck, no interview?"

"If you want to put it that way, okay."

"Yeah. But what would really turn me on, Maude, would be you saying, 'Cato, fuck me. I want you to fuck me.' "

"Aw, c'mon. Really?"

"Yeah."

She slid off her chair after a hesitation and came to me on her knees, flushed with the booze. "Okay, Cato. Fuck me. I want you to fuck me."

"And I'll give you the greatest interview that's ever appeared in *Passages,*" I coached.

"And I'll give you the greatest interview that's ever appeared in *Passages.*" She laughed. "Maybe two or three fucks."

I sipped my drink.

"I know I'm not attractive," she said. "In this business looks are almost as important as in Hollywood. But I can make love, Cato. You won't be sorry." There was a sad bitterness in her voice.

"Do you do this with a lot of authors, Maude?"

I considered her an unattractive woman with secretly large appetites. In a society drunk on beauty, youth and sweet breath, she was way out of the running. What morning had the reality sunk in when she stood before her mirror; what night had truth come when a polite suitor fled as she quickly opened her apartment door to let him in? I felt a disturbing pity for her. But she was exercising what power she had. The wind was pounding softly against the windows. The heat seemed to be oozing out of the place. The bottle of wine slipped in the bucket. "Cato," she whispered, "let's do make love." She rolled her great (thyroidal, I thought) eyes up at me. "Please."

I touched her hair. "Why don't you go start dinner. I've got to go to the bathroom. We've got all night, Maude."

She sat back on her haunches. "Really? You do have time?"

"Yeah. Go ahead."

She staggered up and went to the oven. I went toward the bathroom, carrying the recorder, but slipped open the closet next to it and tried to get my coat. The hanger fell clattering to the floor and I looked across the room toward Maude, who, dumfounded, was staring at me, my coat half on, the tape recorder in my hand.

"You, you," she started as I opened the door, thrusting the recorder in her direction. "You nigger!"

And I was out and in the small, benched elevator that would take me down to the lower floors and oblivion as far as *Passages* and Maude Tozer were concerned.

"Everything all right, Mr. Douglass?"

"Julio, lemme ask you somethin' — would you fuck any old woman, *any* woman?"

"No, sir, Mr. Douglass. Then you are not a man, you run around boom-boom, poom-poom; you are an animal, *entiende?*"

"Claro, hombre, claro."

"Tiene una buena mujer y dos guapo hijos. Dig it, I know you're not gonna fuck up."

"No. G'night. Thanks."

" 'Dios."

Allis would be pleasantly surprised that I was home so early. I let myself in, clicked the dead bolt, locking out the world, and leaned against the door, breathing in the familiar scents of the apartment. Sometimes when I had appointments with women editors, publicity people, agents and reviewers, there was a questioning in her eyes, but rarely an asking put vocally. I was thinking of this before I heard the whispering voices, the intimate little laughs, coming from the bedroom. I stiffened, my mind filling with the most insidious possibilities. I was being betrayed; I was being cuckolded. My breath left me and, as it returned after a second that seemed far longer, Allis called out, "Is that you, darling?"

"Yeah," I growled. "Who's with you?"

"Pop."

They tiptoed out of the bedroom. He was carrying Mack, whose eyes fluttered on the edge of sleep. Mr. Greenberg looked older than his age. "I was in the neighborhood," he explained. "So I dropped up. It's time we met."

Allis kissed me. "Got away quickly, eh? I was going to give you another two hours. I know how those interviews and meetings run."

"Sit down, Mr. Greenberg." I whipped off my coat in an ecstasy of relief and embarrassment. I said to Allis, "We got through in a hurry. We didn't like each other."

"But will the interview run?"

"I'm pretty sure it won't." She was disappointed.

"What did you get on the tape?"

I shrugged as I set it on a table. "It was all so lousy that I erased it in the subway on the way home."

"Well," she said, "who needs *Passages* anyway?" She turned to her father. "Want me to take him, Pop?"

He didn't answer right away. She said to me, "Pop said he looks Sephardic."

"Hey," I said. "It's really good to be home. Out there, it's a jungle."

She didn't seem to be paying too much attention to me. "Oh." She was moving closer to her father. "You got a special delivery, honey. A teaching job. Name your load and twenty-five grand to start."

I didn't see the letter. I was waiting for her to get it. But she was saying to her father, "Your son-in-law, the writer; your son-in-law, the teacher." There was a challenge in the tilt of her head; her voice had the sound of pride in it.

Mr. Greenberg with a sudden thrust handed the baby to her and stood, turning first this way and then that. He pounced on his coat and hat. Mack started to bawl.

"Pop," Allis said. "Pop, what is it?"

I think she knew. She didn't move toward him, just stood frowning, with Mack against her shoulder, patting his back. She was mashing her lips together and I realized, though I had never seen her this way before, that she was angry; that if the sun had bumped against her in those moments, glaciers would have formed upon its surface. He backed across the room to the door, holding his hat. Tears streamed down his face. He kept opening his arms and letting them fall against his coat with soft, helpless sounds.

"I can't," he sobbed. "I just can't." He opened the door and closed it gently after him.

Allis was draining of color. I took the baby. She ran to the door, snatched at the handle, leaned out to shout something, but couldn't; she slammed the door, left it shivering for seconds on its hinges. Somewhere within the walls, the regiments of roaches must have started and wondered; down

228

the hall, people must have wondered. Allis ran screaming past me into the bedroom.

I put Mack in his crib and went to her. She lay twisting on the bed in an awful sucking silence. Her lips were blue. Carefully I bent over her, afraid of her anger and where she might send it spewing. "Allis? Baby?"

A humming sound oozed out between her clenched teeth. "Hey," I said. "Allis."

I wrapped my arms around her and drew her to me. "It's okay, baby. We can handle it." I squeezed her until she couldn't twist, until the humming sound stopped, until the stiffness left her body and she slumped, crying quietly, in my arms.

Mack, ignored, cried himself to sleep in little sobs. Allis took a deep breath, slid out of my arms and went to sleep.

I slipped Mack out of his soaking diaper, oiled his bottom, powdered it and pulled up his cover. I went into the other bedroom, still mine for the while, and quickly answered the letter from the university. Yes, I was interested. Could I have more details?

Maybe it was time for a change of pace in our lives.

I DID NOT WANT to have lunch with Ike. I was immersed in my own life. The word was that Ike was now clean and working hard and had a new contract with a Boston house. Still, his rehabilitation was not something I was terribly concerned with. Not now.

Allis was still moving about the apartment like a shadow, light and filled with silences. When she spoke it was with a heaviness. Her smiles were wan; her touches, absent-minded flutters. I stumbled on her solitudes: staring at Mack, staring at nothing, staring out the window, staring at me.

"We have a baby to care for," I said, and she nodded and bared her breast, having forgotten that she had only moments ago nursed him.

"It's nothing," I said. "We've got our lives to do things with," I said.

"Yes," she said. "I know."

But she grieved through the week, and my anger grew with her inability to grip the realities. And I smoldered.

And told Ike okay.

I was angry with Mr. Greenberg and pissed because I wouldn't let Allis see, feel or hear it. And I was pissed that she didn't respond to my silences — which were also an expression of anger. I went to lunch angry, sizzling at Mr. Greenberg, scorched because there I was once more, hung up between things, love for my old lady and hatred for my father-in-law — neutralized by both. I seethed in the righteousness of my anger, wrapped it in my generations on these shores as contrasted to my father-in-law's relatively late arrival. Who *was* he, with the grime of Ellis Island embedded still in the creases of his being, to jar *my* life, to fuck up the head and heart of my wife, who had been his daughter?

"I hear," Ike was saying against the background of chattering glass, china and silverware, against the hum of voices and the soft movements of the waiters, "I hear that a group of Ivy League nigguh professors have come up with *'real'* black writing, better than our 'protest' shit."

"Yes," I said. "I heard about them. Is that what you wanted to talk about?"

"No."

"What, then?"

He reared slowly back in his chair and set his knife and fork down carefully. "I hear you've been talking about me."

I looked up from my shad roe, wondering. Rumor is like a disease in this business. Nothing is ever set right.

"What is it I'm supposed to have said about you, Ike?"

"Humph!" he snorted. "Now you don't know, huh?"

"I don't know what you're talking about, man!" The words were coming out like steam. "Hey, I don't even *think* about you, let alone talk about you. What the fuck could I *say* about you?"

"That I couldn't write. That, like a lotta cats out here, I'm just riding the black wave, jiving editors."

He was leaning toward me now.

"*Who* told you that?"

"Never mind. I believe him."

"Never mind, my ass. You drop some shit like that on me and tell me to never mind?"

He didn't blink. "Yeah. I believed it then and I believe it now."

He moved closer with a crash. Heads turned and turned away again. I straightened up against the wall.

"You think you're hot shit, doncha, Cato? Got a big contract, good press, white chick for a wife — you doin' all right, aincha, nigguh, right up there with Whittington and Huysmans, stompin' on our fingers — "

"I don't know what you're talking about, Ike." I dropped my right hand to my lap.

But nothing was going to stop him. He leaned across the table some more, his voice rising. "Yeah, nigguh! I believe it! They don't give people the kinda contract you got unless you're a Tom, unless you agree to do the brothers in — "

I spoke softly, hoping he would lower his voice, but the steam was still in mine. "You motherfucker, you never read *Uncle Tom's Cabin,* or anything else, since you wanna rap that way. Don't pull that Tom shit on me, you junkie motherfucker — "

He seized my left wrist. His eyes gave off glazed yellow flashes. He was, I realized, crazy, crazier than the junk had ever made him, jealous crazy on rumor and the fear we all had that we were vulnerable to flushing away at any moment.

"Man, let go," I said.

He sneered. "I ought to kick your ass right here. Now, nigguh. Now."

The gin on his breath stank, mixed as it was with scampi. He rose partway and leaned farther over the table. The waiters melted into pairs, watching us. People close to our table were looking the other way and eating rapidly. (Where did those niggers come from, anyway?)

"If you don't sit down and let go my wrist," I whispered, "I'll blow you against the wall across the room." I tapped his kneecap with the gun; tapped it again, realizing as I did that I wanted him to keep coming, that I wanted to hurt someone badly. Who? Didn't make no never mind to me. "Just keep on comin', motherfucker," I whispered, his eyes now locked with mine. I tapped him again. He loosened his grip and slid back down.

"That's real?" he asked hoarsely.

"Touch me again," I said.

He made a smile. "You wouldn't."

"Wanna bet?"

He whispered, "Are you crazy?"

I shook my head and signaled for the check. The waiters and patrons would be happy for us to leave. "*You're* crazy," I said as I signed. The waiter whisked the card and check and walked rapidly away. "You believe whatever the hell you want to, man, hear? But you just stay the hell away from me."

He was following me to the checkroom. "You wouldn't have, would you, Cato?"

In the street I started to shake. My legs had gone to rubber. I kept hearing a growl, then a snarl. I looked around for the dog, but saw nothing, and after a block I didn't hear the sounds anymore and my legs were sturdier and the trembling had almost stopped. My stride was carrying me down the middle of sidewalks, and people were veering away from me as though I were the prow of a ship and they were waves. In the angle of a store window I saw my reflection. I was murder, was death, was the sudden New York end. Yet I had communicated something, had shaken my rattles, had barked, had readied my needles, and they were sensing it and moving away, careful not to bump or jostle, taking note of the large FRAGILE / DANGER sticker showing on my body from head to foot.

THEY KILLED Martin King.

I imagined that back home winter was breaking that first week in April and Central Park was starting to green again beneath the still climbing sun; I saw the benches along Central Park and Broadway filling once more with the winos, junkies and the aged. I could imagine that and also sense the frenzy back there, what with Vietnam finally arriving on everyone's hit list, the Weather Underground active and the many Days of Rage.

America was a nation of slogans:

Black Power!	White Power!	Red Power!
Brown Power!	Yellow Power!	Jewish Power!
Italian Power!	Irish Power!	Polish Power!
	Pussy Power!	

Before we left the madness, the ethnic bumper stickers had sprouted like fescue upon the rear ends of cars, and American pluralism was gaining desperate credence.

They killed Martin King. I was down at the docks, the poor side of the Carénage, to buy some fresh tuna from the fishermen whose boats were entering the harbor. I'd left Allis and Mack at the Grand Anse beach.

A man was sitting on a cluster of pilings, holding a transistor radio to his ear. The crowd of mostly women chatted and laughed as they unfolded their plastic bags, into which they deposited their pieces of fish. The man with the transistor shouted something, waved his hand as if to still the crowd. But it gasped (some had heard him the first time) and moved closer to him, a small sea of dark faces, legs, elbows. The crowd moved closer and then stopped, as if just outside a circle inside which they dared not step.

"Mar-teen Looter Keeng! He just was shot!"

"Wha?"

"Wha you say, mon?"

"You surely be jokeen, Alistair — "

"No, no, lis'en, lis'en — "

He held the radio away from his ear toward us and turned up the volume. The entire Carénage, clear to the other side, where the fine shops were, grew quiet, or seemed to.

"He is dead!" the man with the radio shouted. "He is dead!"

A shout went up. People turned to each other, uncertain.

"Where this is, mon?"

"Memphis, Tennessee."

"Lord!"

"Dot dere is one crazy place. Hey, you, Mr. Douglass, what you tinka dot, huh, Mr. Negro American — "

The women rose up in my defense.

"Hush, you now, Hubert! Don't be de fool now. Can't you see de mon's cryin'?"

"Shame, Hubert!"

I had backed away. I looked down at the earth for some place to grab hold of it and hurl it deep into space. I had never felt the compulsion to kill the way I felt it now; it was like having to have an orgasm. I sat down. I felt their eyes on me. Little waves splashed against the moorings. The battered gray boats of the ragtag fleet seemed to be coming in faster now, their crews calling to each other:

"Dey have shot Dr. Keeng! Dr. Keeng's dead! Dey have shot Dr. Keeng dead!"

I returned to the Cortina and drove for a mile on the right-hand side before I remembered to move to the left.

Allis, holding Mack in one arm and his stroller filled with beach things with the other, was waiting near the main entrance to the beach. She ran toward me, screaming, "Did you hear about King? Did you hear? They killed him, Cate, they killed him!" She was crying in rage. I got out and helped them in.

"I didn't get the fish," I said.

"To hell with the fish," she said, and cried again, banging the dashboard with her fist.

When we got to our rented house on Mustique Bay, I went directly to the radio and began switching from band to band. I fixed drinks and listened.

We had come to these islands, these remnants of mountain peaks, on the edge of the southern end of the Puerto Rico Trench, over a mile and a half down, to escape, to work and to renew ourselves from the effects of the rampages of public and private disasters that were shaking our lives to bits.

Paul and Betsy had gone to France, to divide their time between Paris and La Ciotat. We had not managed to get together before our mutual departures. Paul apologized for being so busy.

Slowly, then, the pace of life much changed, the sight of people devoid of the tensions and ferocities of the blacks back home, and the ever-present sun and sea — all these brought us back to each other. Allis took the sun well, daily growing darker and darker until those parts of her body that remained covered — parts of her breasts, pelvis and upper buttocks — were startlingly white in contrast. She rarely mentioned her father, but when she did, it caused pain no longer.

Mack was growing fat and learning to swim. When I finished working for the day, we moved to the beach.

I took long, leisurely swims, sometimes out as far as where people were making love on the decks of their boats. ("Hi. Mind if I rest just for a minute before I start back to the beach?")

We read the papers and the magazines and listened to the radio and felt pleased that we were away from the insanity at home. We did not try to hook up with the other Americans there, black or white, though we were often asked for drinks or dinner.

But today, back home, they killed Martin King. We sat as the night came down, not hungry at all, listening to the radio, and I kept thinking: *I don't belong in this time. Why am I here? To do something? What shall I do?*

I was glad when Glenn called. "You heard?" he asked.

There was something odd about his voice.

"Yes, we heard. You okay? You sound funny."

"Really? Maybe. I feel sort of exhausted since the word came — "

"Where were you?"

"On my way to *our* section of the cafeteria."

I laughed softly, remembering all the people who'd ever fought against having an *our section* that was imposed on them by "law," and there were the kids, *our sectioning* right on.

He said, "What's funny? Where were you?"

"Down at the beach; no, Allis and Mack were at the beach. I was at the docks, getting fish for dinner."

"You're not sure where you were?"

"I'm sure now. They catch anyone yet?"

"Hell, no. You kidding? The folks've started to burn Washington, from what I hear, and Stokely's told them to get their guns."

"Have they?"

"It's too early to tell, Dad." There was a pause. I felt suddenly and acutely guilty of something. At first I didn't know what.

Glenn sighed. "I don't know what to say, but I wanted to talk to you. Listen. It's all coming down to color, isn't it?"

Then I knew why I felt guilty. I hadn't prepared him enough. His voice told me that he wasn't tough enough. He hadn't grown up reading about lynchings in the *Chicago Defender,* the *Afro-American* or the *Pittsburgh Courier;* white men had never shot at him; he had never been segregated because someone else wished it. But he wasn't alone; there was an entire generation of young blacks who would never know those things, which was all right; yet had they been *told* those things enough, over and over and over again, so that every beat of their hearts was a punctuation mark in the litany of our time in America? "Yeah, kiddo. I do believe so. A lot of people have been saying that for an awfully long time, though. Nobody wants to believe them — "

"Goddamn it — *why?*"

"Color carries an imposed history. Shit, son, I don't know."

His voice was shaking a little. "I'm so mad, man, *mad.* I could kill the first honky comes in sight."

I said, "Careful, Glenn."

"Did you tell me it was gonna be like this?"

"I tried. Maybe you just gotta experience some things."

Allis was standing beside me now in her favorite telephone position, one of my elbows sandwiched between her breasts. She stood still, staring down at the floor.

I went on. "You remember once we were talking about Bontemps' *Black Thunder,* talking about old Ben, the house servant, how he wanted to be free, yet wanted to be comfortable? How he wanted to squeal, but knew in his heart he couldn't?"

"Yeah," Glenn said with an angry rush, "but he did squeal on Gabriel — "

"So did one of the toughies, Pharaoh, remember? What I'm getting at is that Ben did say, because he understood and also understood that he couldn't cut it, *There ain't nothin' but hard times waitin' when a man gets to studyin' about freedom.* I remember talking about that line because, man, I couldn't get down with you all the way. And even if I had, would you have believed me? Listen, I gotta pay for this call. You sure you're okay? Allis wants to talk to you."

"Glenn," she said quietly into the phone. Tears glistened in her eyes. "Glenn, I know how you must feel. But I really want you to know that *I* am not white; I'm a Jew. That's something else and I'm not going to take refuge behind color — what?" She smiled and glanced at me. "He really, really is all right, honey. A little down, both of us, and the people on the island, too. Stand back from things a little for a couple of days, okay? Here's your father again."

"I guess," Glenn said, "whether you liked the man or not, when they killed him they killed a little of all of us."

"I guess that's what it is," I said.

"G'night, Dad."

"Night, son."

The island was now tainted by the news and we decided to leave it and so went by boat, stopping at Petit Martinique, Petit St. Vincent (rich, awfully rich, where big private boats docked and private seaplanes landed and where, if you wished it, your haute cuisine was delivered from the main kitchen to the dining room of your ten-room "cottage," and where no one was supposed to be except the very wealthy and their servants — concubines, pilots, captains, waiters, chambermaids, cooks, sommeliers and telephone operators) and on to that island with the loveliest of names, Carriacou.

We got a house in Tibeau, not far from Jew Bay. Jew Bay? We had to discover the origin of the name; we would also try to find out where Negro Island, in Bar Harbor, got its name. (We never did, though through the years we discussed the names, and how they came to be, as if they were some well-liked dessert that we didn't wish to devour too quickly.)

A long letter arrived, forwarded from the main island from Paul and Betsy. They had been to Israel in the wake of the Six-Day War and were now back in La Ciotat, distressed at the news of King's murder and unhappy that they, like us, would be returning home soon.

Allis had been sending Mr. Storto picture post cards, and finally in response came a long scribble of a letter from him. The first, he said, he'd written in fifteen years.

On Carriacou the people still killed goats and poured water on the ground to ensure good luck to a venture; people still claimed to be Mandingo or Yoruba or Ibo; still greeted you in the morning with *ekaro* and welcomed you with *ekabo*. There were still *esusu* societies, and people played the ancient games of adji, boto or wari. Some nights the generations of drummers, using nail kegs stretched over with goatskin, played down the night, their drumbeats clambering over the surf smashing in from the windward side.

From our hilltop at dusk we could see the fishing fleets putting out, each splitting off from the main body until one fleet, spotting the schools of fish, started up signal fires, and then all the fleets, nets ready, converged like ants on darkening glass around the fires. We were watching them the Tuesday before the weekend we were to return to New York; watching and thinking how simple, clean and cooperative it all was, and how the fishermen had been fishing that way long before the first caravel pulled in along the West African coast. It grew late. All we could see were the signal fires from the boats. Mack lay under his netting as much at peace in the limbo of his sleep as he ever would be.

Allis and I were naked, tall, cooling, lime-filled drinks in our hands, savoring the moment when, finished with them, we would turn to each other.

I saw headlights, long, cold beams coming up the hill. I watched them without wonder, believing they would be going past. But, no. Like the flashes from the muzzles of twin-mounted Bofors, they swung squarely around in the driveway, flashing on the ceiling. The car stopped and the driver got out, leaving the engine running, leaving the ceiling stabbed with light.

"Corion," I said. Corion Jones was the bartender at the Mermaid.

"Must be bad news," Allis said, leaping up and running for the bedroom.

We had no phone and we no longer played the radio.

I pulled on my trunks and went to the door.

"Cato, Cato," he said. "They have killed Robert Kennedy. Give me one of those. Why didn't you get a house with a phone?"

I poured him a mostly gin and some tonic. Allis came out in a robe. "They *killed* Bobby Kennedy?"

Corion took a long swallow. "In Los Angeles. He won the election out there — "

"You mean primary," Allis said.

"Whatever," Corion said, shrugging. "They killed him."

I fixed another drink for Allis and one for myself. I looked at the signal fires out on the ocean.

"They caught the man who did it," Corion said.

"Who was it?"

"I think they said he was an Arab."

In the shadows Allis and I stared at each other.

"He said he did it for the good of your country." Corion chuckled and finished his drink. "Some place," he said. "America. Whoooo-boy!" And he left. We watched him back out, the lights sliding off the ceiling as he did, and drive back toward Hillsborough.

("Have General Graham call me. I want him to say it to me. I want to hear a general of the U.S. Army say he can't protect Martin Luther King, Jr.")

"What," Allis said in the darkness, which now seemed even darker, "in the hell's going *on* back there?"

"Shhhhhhhhittttttt," I said. It was not a response to her question. I didn't have an answer; it was just something to say, a single, sibilant word with stop to express almost everything.

"Shall I turn on the radio?" Allis looked like a ghost, even with her tan, there in the darkness. I turned to the sea again.

"*Shall* I?"

I didn't realize that my hesitation had to do with not wanting to be overwhelmed by misinformation; with not wanting to be lured into frames of thought that veered me around the realities. "Oh, to hell with it," I said. "If you want to, go ahead." There. I had shifted the blame to her.

"Don't you want to know more?"

"They aren't going to tell us more! They never have and, goddamn it, they never will, and people'll continue swallowing their shit just like it was candy! Go ahead, turn the thing on!"

"I am! Stop shouting!"

"Fuckers!"

Allis could find nothing but music. She said, "Do they really think they can get away with this, too?"

"They have. You'll see. Aw, shit. What a time to have to go home."

"Where else, babe?" she said. "Let's go to bed. It's very late."

We lay, lust turned to listlessness. "The time went so fast," I said.

"Was it that the book went so well or the things that've happened?"

"Both, I guess."

The stars seemed close to earth there, too, just hanging above us, companions as we rushed quietly through space. Everything about us was perpetual movement, yet nothing fell off; everything stayed fixed. The experts explained it: "gravity." On bright, sunny mornings, my mother would push open the kitchen window, just over the sink, inhale deeply, smile and say, "O Lord, our Lord, how excellent is Thy name in all the earth!" That phrase now seemed more fitting than "gravity."

"Cate. What are you thinking? I hear you thinking."

"About mysteries."

"Mysteries?"

"Ordinary mysteries, like how the stars manage to hang up there the way they do."

"Oh. If and when we ever get to the moon and back, do you think it'll make a difference? I mean, spiritually or whatever?"

"I wish I knew, kid. The track record ain't too good."

"Poor Ethel. With all those kids. Somehow, though, I wonder if Bobby would've made a good President. I mean, good enough for the times."

("Have General Graham call me. I want him to say it to me.")

I turned over. "I've a feeling that no one knows just how much shit and how little power goes with the job until they get there; then they become absolutely paralyzed with the immensity of their mistake in wanting the goddamn job in the first place."

"Maybe we ought to be voting for corporations instead of individuals."

I laughed. "We are, honey."

"Yeh. Shot down the World Federalist movement, then picked up all the ideas — or was the whole thing theirs?"

"Listen — you wanna?" I figured she did because she was talking so much.

"You?"

"Not really."

"I should shut up?"

"Well — "

"Okay."

We were back. We were rushing down the ramps like everyone else, fearful of being stuck in a long line, afraid there'd be no taxis. We rushed, clutching Mack and the handbags, working up a good sweat, hating to be back, yet excited that we were. I was already thinking of the apartment with the windows thrown open to admit a breeze, if one existed, and the Puerto Rican music that echoed up and down the block during the summer. We were not first on line, of course; that took a certain ruthlessness, a recklessness, that seemed out of joint with the goal obtained. Panting, we drew up before a sign that read:

ONE FAMILY AT A TIME

Customs.

When our turn came, Allis moved forward to the officer, and I, carrying Mack and a single bag, trailed. The customs officer looked up, this gray-uniformed man, and saw me closing fast behind Allis. His chin came up, his eyes blazed and he said in that sharp, official way all these people have when, finally, they have the opportunity to pounce on their betters, "Can't you read the sign?"

I kept coming, perhaps even a bit faster, bumping Allis, and placing Mack squarely down upon his counter and easing the bag down to the floor in the same motion because I wanted to be very close to him. "We can read the sign," I said. "I think we can read it better than you." But he had already found himself caught out in that ageless web, and it wasn't fashionable these days to be discovered. His neck was reddening; the color moved, like the ink in a thermometer, to his ears and then diffused like a stain over his face. My hands were trembling. He had dropped his eyes. Christ, I thought. They didn't want to let you get out and once you managed that, they seemed not to want you back in. Was there something out there that was contaminating?

The officer nodded. "I'm sorry." Allis' hand closed over mine. Her grip was firm. Its strength surprised me.

"Stupid," she said, aloud. He continued to flip through his book. I wondered what codes had been placed against which names and for what reasons. "Some welcome home," she said when he had finished and passed back our passports. I glanced up the line of expressionless faces behind us and wondered what they were thinking. Allis pulled at me.

Another desk, and then out into the bullpen, where sweating men, trying to be polite, asked where you'd been, though the passport told them, and what you had to declare. I'd already unlocked our bags; they had been mockingly accessible. "Okay," our inspector said, "you can go." He hadn't even asked me to open them.

He stuck the stamps on the bags. Allis and I looked at each other. "Wait," I said. "You mean we're free?"

He was a plump man with a round, dark face. His gray hair was matted down with sweat. His smile was quizzical. "Free?" He waved us away. We were home again, angered and surprised by its rapid contradictions. But, then, it is always the returning, the meshing back in.

I was afraid that bad memories would start again for Allis, and I was not sure what I would do. When she spoke of Mr. Storto, I understood what had happened.

"Mr. Storto hasn't been to visit us at all, Cate, since we moved, and I think it's time he did. I'm going to call him."

She did. The arrangement, as it turned out, however, was that we, *en famille*, would call on him. There had been, I gathered, as we cabbed down a couple of days later, profuse apologies on both sides for having been out of touch, and a great deal of talk about the baby. Mr. Storto was waiting outside in his old place, near the streetlight, all dressed up, his medal on his suit. He was happy to see us, his pleasure boundless. We had at last surmounted the bullshit of phrases like "will be in touch" and "let's get together," etc.; we'd made it. And Allis now had a surrogate father.

There was something comforting and old-fashioned and solid and correct about that afternoon. We had a marvelous antipasto and some country red and his beloved Italian ice. Mr. Storto held Mack and asked after Glenn. He showed me a photo of his cousin who had died in Spain fighting with the Garibaldi Brigade. We talked of big things in small ways —the assassinations, the Rebellions, the coming election, how the Village was changing, Vietnam. He still slept during the day and prowled the building and the block at night.

Allis, as if she were home, took it on herself to make the espresso. Mr. Storto liked the cards she'd sent to him. What were the people like, he asked; poor? Nice, though? Too many people had been poor too long, he said; couldn't the big shots see that? Didn't such a condition make them glance over their shoulders all the time? I teased him. He, after all, owned the building. Why was he on the side of the poor?

"If I knew back when I got the place what I know now," he said, "I'd have got myself a farm. Nothing but headaches. Taxes. Inspectors — crooked, too. The meter-reader, he wants grease; the garbage people, they want grease; the postman. Man comes with a bucket of cement and bottles of water to mix it, an' the first thing he wants to know is if I own or am I the super. I tell 'im I'm the super." He cracked his knuckles. "What the hell, the worker gotta cheat to stay up. I own somethin', well, I'm supposed to have the dough. I never once work a job where workers didn't try to slow it down, not give hundred percent, because they know no job ever pays what they're worth. It's all rigged, like the mob rigs things, y'see. The working man's smart. He don't put this screw in outa spite, he do this outa spite; what else can a man do? So, I know, 'cause I'ma poor man, too. Looka this place. Does this dump look like where a rich man lives? An' the rich don't know the poor. I know 'em, 'cause I'm poor." He shrugged himself self-righteously. Allis, standing behind him, patted his shoulders, then poured his coffee.

"You still like it up there?" he asked when we were ready to leave.

"It's close to the Park," Allis offered.

"Ah, sure. Get the baby out. Sure, sure."

"You'll come to see us?"

"Sure. I promise."

"When?"

"Well — "

"Next Sunday. We can all go sit in the Park." She had said it with finality. Mr. Storto looked at me.

"You better come," I said.

Allis emanated peace on the way home, and I was glad for her and proud of her in that way it is so difficult to speak of, for it is like suddenly coming on a secret, very private, part of someone.

I kissed her.

"What's that for?"

Her smile told me that she knew very well what it was for.

10

I DELIVERED *Circles Round Saturn* to Maureen Gullian. We were to have lunch with the president of the company at Latoque Blanche. "He wants us to pick him up at his office," Gullian said. She patted the manuscript. "I'm dying to read it."

The literary game of musical chairs had brought Jock Champion to Twentieth Century Forum only six months earlier. He had been nearly everywhere else in publishing, each move being a step up. Now he was president. He was on the phone. He winked at us and gestured toward chairs.

"Well, yuh. He'd be all right. Okay. You got my vote on him. Goddamn it, we do need an improvement over there, and I hope he can pull it off. Otherwise, let's go to the well again."

He hung up and swung around toward us. "You brought in the new one."

"Big one, Jock."

"That's great. We think the trend is back to bigger books." He stood and pulled on his jacket. His pants had cuffs. His suit, I guessed, was British-made, a shade rakish, with nipped-in waist, hacking pockets and double vents. I wondered on which side he wore the codpiece. Otherwise, Champion was cool and correct in his suit.

"That was Marsh over at the paper," he volunteered. "They got major publishers' approval on the new books editor."

"Including yours, too, I take it," Maureen said.

"You betcha. I wasn't about to approve any more of those assholes they keep flying up the pole."

We drifted out of his office and through carpeted halls.

"What's that over there, in that section with the drapes drawn?" I asked.

Jock and Gullian smiled at each other. Jock laughed aloud then, and said, as we strode by, "That's what we call the War Room; Gleason runs it. Probably in there with his girl, Nan Tyce. That's why the drapes are drawn. Shall we run over and peek?"

"No," Gullian said.

To me Jock said, "She never wants to peek. Nan spends so much time in there that she probably knows how to — "

He broke off and picked up his pace.

"So," I said when we were out of the building, walking toward the restaurant, "just who is the new books editor?"

"Shelly Popper. Know him?"

"Not really. Met him once when he was reviewing for the *Voice*." My mind was on this arrangement whereby people on the paper called publishers for their approval of candidates for books editor. Perhaps I was foolish. I figured the books editor worked for the paper and therefore no outside approval was required. How many others had been rejected and why? What made Shelly Popper okay, the publishers' choice? Did he even know what had gone down? They say the wife is the last to know about the affair. Maybe we all get to the place where we'd rather just not know.

Champion's table was ready, the perspiring maître d' rushed up to tell him. Champion chatted briefly with the waiters about the lousy summer weather, the mood of the chef, and ordered pâté ("Really great stuff, Cate") and our first round of drinks.

"I got a call this morning from *Life*," Gullian said, tossing her head so that her hair came whisking around in a soft, dark rush, which Champion's eyes followed.

"Yeah?" he said. "The pâté stinks today. From Brance?"

"Yes. He wanted to know if Cate's a nice guy."

She set aside her pâté and began to nibble at a breadstick. The pâté was lousy.

"Sure he's nice," Champion said. "Aren't you, Cate?"

Gullian broke in. "I told him you were nice. Had a family. Devoted husband and father. *Very* serious about your work."

"What the fuck does being nice have to do with my work?" I looked from Champion to Gullian. "He didn't mean nice nice, did he? Not a wave-maker, not militant, a weshallovercomer — "

Champion was waving his hand. "Aw, these jerks. You know how they are. Call him tomorrow, Maureen, and bug him. Bug him good." He smiled. "That certainly wouldn't hurt, to bug him into doing a big spread in *Life,* huh?"

I ignored him and turned to Gullian. "He asked about Allis, I suppose?"

She stopped chewing suddenly. It was as though I'd reached across the table and smacked her right in the chops. She went pale. Her eyes emptied of all guile, all embarrassment. "Yes," she said. "He did."

"So much for your big spread, Jock." I didn't wait for him to signal the waiter; I did it myself. Champion waved his finger in a circle. The waiter nodded and left. When the drinks came, I lifted my glass. "A toast." Champion and Gullian held their glasses toward me. They were bewildered. "A toast to being nice; to being the right kind; to pleasing everyone."

As I drank I looked across the table at Champion. Surely, if he could okay Shelly Popper, he could pull *Life*'s coattail. Yet he wasn't about to, and I certainly wasn't going to ask.

"To the first of several," Gullian said.

"My glass is empty," I said.

"God, no," Champion said, waving to the waiter. "We want your cup to runneth over."

Just then I remembered that I didn't have the gun; that I had not carried it since we returned. Stupid! I thought. Forgetting like that.

For it was, after all, the season of the Long Hot Summers, of Poverty Programs (phrases that slipped on and off the ink of the presses to be pulped and washed clean and formed into clean slates or pages again), of do-gooding on a national scale.

Colleges and universities were starting, reluctantly, to beat the bushes for the Asian–Hispanic–Amer-Indian–Afro-American faculty members they thought were hiding. Ethnic Studies departments sprang up like pissweed — so quickly that the various heavy weathers of the near future would pound them into oblivion.

Newspaper, magazine and book editors took to the phones, scouring candidates who could man the desks in their outer offices so that visitors would notice them. (Amos Bookbinder was not nearly enough, and no one knew about Jeremy Poode.)

Foundations plunged cleverly into the bash, offering funding for this or that — actually, peanuts for them, but worth a good mill or two in public relations, given the time. Thus, an array of institutes, academies, centers and colloquia were established, and the artists and intellectuals belonged to these.

But there was also money for the "communities," the "neighborhoods," the "areas." In short, there was money to wallow in. So much, that it called to mind the cartoon of a fleeing man popping big bucks out of his pockets to persuade his pursuers, close behind, not to chase, capture and perhaps kill him.

Thomas Nast, had he been with us, would have drawn such a cartoon.

It didn't matter that the money was "white." Who else had money, anyway? We had it coming for slave labor; this was reparations money and it was about time. How could there be any strings attached?

Out of these events and organizations came what was called a "dialogue." If indeed such an exchange of ideas did take place, it was of short duration.

Not immune to these events, I had accepted a membership in the Center for Black Arts and Letters. It was fashioned after the Center for Democratic Studies. Our sponsoring foundation was the Coalition for the Development of Western Institutions — an outfit so rich and with business origins so crooked that both Gustavus Meyers and Ferdinand Lundberg had been on its case. Big Oil was behind the coalition.

We took offices on the upper floors of a new high-rise on Third Avenue. Our directors jetted into New York from all points of the compass to hold their meetings. They took suites in the Waldorf-Astoria. We held lavish parties and made awards to black artists and scholars most white people never knew existed.

If the establishment had disgraced an individual in one way or another, for some thing or other, we embraced. The Coalition for the Development of Western Institutions could have stopped us, simply by withdrawing its funding. But we had deluded ourselves into thinking that we had grown so quickly and powerfully that CDWI dared not challenge us!

(Ah, but that was the major discovery of those times: we came ultimately to the understanding of everyone else, but not of ourselves.)

We watched while PEN and the Authors Guild hurled themselves into the postures of radical thought and action, only to come up with Prison

248

Programs, which, after all, nurtured those who presented little in the way of either challenge or change because they were locked up, anyway.

And there was, also, that whirlwind, off in a corner, that had been created by the larger storm, the Black-Jewish Thing, which broke open during a meeting in Westchester, with blacks shouting that Hitler had been right at about the same time Jews were shouting nigger.

Paul and Betsy were returning, and I looked forward to seeing him; he was a part of my past that, in contrast to the present, seemed blessedly stable and unadorned with cunning and clever twists. Paul was what he was.

11

DID I wake you, Cate?

It's Betsy and it's two in the afternoon and I do not take naps in the afternoon. I say, No. How's it going?

I'm okay, thanks. It's not as if I had to start pulling things back together. It's more like having done a favor for an old friend.

I'll bet it's different for the kids, though.

Yes.

There is a pause, the one that always comes when people who don't usually telephone you call and know that you're wondering why they did. When Betsy broke up with Paul, she did not come to cry on our shoulders. Instead, she cut loose everyone who'd ever had anything to do with him, as if we all had the plague.

Uh, Cate — I wonder if I could come over and talk with you.

About Paul?

She sighs. The sound comes over the phone like a small bird falling. Yes, it's Paul. Would you mind?

I say, No, and let the silence come again.

Don't you wonder, Cate?

While I'm searching for an answer, she says, I don't know what to tell the kids.

I don't know, either, but, hey, you want to talk, come on over. We'd love to see you.

She says, with haste and a shading of haughtiness, I don't want to be a burden, really.

You wouldn't be.

What's there to talk about, Allis says later.

Maybe it'll help her. I don't know. What could I say, No?

She pats the side of my face. Poor Cate, she says.

I find myself shaking my head.

What? she asks.

In college he was so sure his heroes would never do that, and, by extension, that he wouldn't either.

If he'd left a note, would that have satisfied you and Betsy?

I wasn't married to him.

She snorts.

But maybe, I say. A statement. A curse. Something. Like George Sanders.

Sanders did himself in in the Hotel Don Jaime Rey not far from Sitges. From the main road the hotel looked like a medieval castle. The walls were thick and the rooms were tiled and the windows were small. Sanders had done it in one of those rooms. But he'd left a note.

He left a note, I say, something like: I AM BORED.

That was something! I marvel every time I think of it. Not a whimper, not a defiant shout, just the cutting edge of the truth, which for him was that life had not sent its best into the arena where he was squared off to meet it.

Amos' wife left a note with only three words, too, Allis reminds me. You said it was mean, spiteful, vengeful.

It was, I say. It really tagged Amos. For the rest of his life. You look at him and you see the words of her note burned into his eyes.

Allis says, But what brevity, clarity.

We are at my desk in the corner of the bedroom. She leans over me. Her breath beats like tiny wings against my face. Let's not talk about it anymore, she says. Save it for Betsy.

I push the pages in place in the *Unmarked Graves* typescript. Allis smoothes the title page. It does not need smoothing. Together we stare at the pile of pages, some three inches thick. I drum on them with my fingers. I have not had a manuscript rejected in twenty years. I think I am still shocked. I have no excuse for feeling this shock. I know the countryside hereabouts, and the main roads, high and low; I know the byways, the grass-turned, dew-spilled tracks.

I am in shock, I think, because I want the outer edges of the possibilities; I want what must surely come, never to come. My vanity urges connection between these immensities.

I know I have said and thought it a thousand times in just the past few days since Paul's death, but I say it again: I wonder what he wanted when he called, and if talking would have helped.

Closer to me, she murmurs, The old common denominator. The metaphor of Paul's America.

Good paraphrase of Wright, I think. I say, The old retainer.

Retainer?

One who retains. A service to a household. A device for holding things up, you know, like a retaining wall? But I never wanted to, baby, or to be.

She replaces the pages. I know, she says. The problem is —

What is my problem?

You simply can't help making *eye* contact; that's always been your problem.

I laugh and laugh and laugh.

She gives me a soft shot in the back of the head. You *know* people aren't supposed to really *see* each other when they look at each other, darling.

Betsy wants answers she cannot have.

We have invited Amos to join us, figuring that he may be able to help her and even himself after all these years. He is still at Phaeton, not doing very well, the rumors say, for niggers are out of style now.

So there they sit, two representatives, they may well be, from Suicide Survivors Anonymous. Dorothea Blue-Sky could have come, or Caitlin Thomas, but they would have been in slightly different categories.

It is a tough session. I knew it would be from the way we started drinking. No white wine for us. No spritzers. No Perrier. Booze, maybe with spits of water.

By the time we get to the table, we're off like shots. I am glad Mack's away at camp. The conversation's too intense. Allis would have sent him off to his room, and he would have been relieved. And had he been here I would have resented Betsy's putting all that weight on him, when she didn't even bring her own kids. Of course, Amos no longer has kids to bring anywhere.

Maybe, Amos is saying, what he really wanted was to get back with you, Betsy.

I don't think so.

Did he ever talk about it? Allis asks.

Sometimes, when he was drunk.

Maybe he *needed* to be drunk to talk about it, Amos says, but wait. Let's back up. You wanna talk about what caused the breakup? I mean, you don't have to, but you're looking for —

Betsy is pensive. Then she says, He changed.

Our silence is not helpful.

There was a *drastic* change, she says, looking at me. Didn't you notice?

He was in the process of changing, Allis says.

But I mean, all the crap going to his head. He believed it.

It's hard not to, Amos says. He chortles. All the publicity, interviews, *appearances,* questions, letters, phone calls . . .

I say, Paul badly wanted to be a great success as a writer.

That's just it. His only *good* book was *The Burnt Offering.*

Even one these days is a triumph, I say. I don't know if I believe it, though.

At first, when we were alone he was truly embarrassed by it. He insisted, Cate, that you were the better writer. His uneasiness was real then. One day it was gone. I never even missed it for a while. It was a very fragile and beautiful thing before it went, aware, completely in touch with what real writing was all about.

Yeah. It can turn a man's head, all right, Amos says.

Then there were those women! Betsy lights a little cigar.

Amos flashes a look across the table toward me. Allis sees it; she misses nothing. Her personal recollections, however, do not even begin to show through.

Selena, Betsy says, ruefully. Marianna Wayland. Elizabeth Tottenham. Maude Tozer. Maxine Culp when she was about to quit agenting and became a literary expert on geriatric fuckings —

The risks of the business, Amos says. Art is cock.

Betsy is sullen and, having finished off the wine, has pounced on the cognac. Yeah? Then how come Cate didn't go through those trips, Allis? Or did he?

The honest-to-God truth, Betsy, is that I don't know.

Amos stumbles over a chuckle; he remembers too much.

Betsy studies first me and then Allis. I know Allis is thinking of Raffy.

Does all this add up to why? I ask. I don't want to linger around this end of the conversation.

You, Betsy, Amos says, do a little discoing out there?

She disposes of the question quickly and surgically. No. I've never, ever, enjoyed making love.

There is nothing for any of us to say.

Betsy shrugs. So sue me.

This next silence is too much for her. I never knew why, she says. If I was making Paul happy, or anyone before I married him or after we divorced, that was enough for me. Not enjoying it didn't make me want to be a dike or make me want to be loved by one.

Very, very gently Allis asks, You and Paul ever talk about it?

He never knew.

Allis persists. Maybe he did. Wouldn't that help to explain the women?

No, Amos says, as if on some pedestal from which he views both past and present. The women come with the package. Or the men.

I was glad to see him when you came back from Europe the first time, I say. Remember? We'd just returned from the Caribbean. This place was such a mess then, with the Rebellions, the assassinations, this movement, that movement. I needed something familiar, an anchor.

But *that* didn't last more than a few hours, as I remember, Betsy says.

You can't spend the rest of your life wondering why he did it, Allis says. We'd been out of touch a long, long time.

Betsy wibbles her ash into a tray and nods. I hear you, she says, and winks a congratulation at Allis. Yeh, I guess I did enjoy some of the good, high times with the special people in the special places. Yes, Allis, guilty. But when I found out where I was, I guess I was too ashamed to admit that being Mrs. Paul Cummings or Kaminsky or whatever had its grand moments.

People are already talking about books on Paul, Amos says. Proposal came in just the other day. The committee liked it, but they'll sit on it a while, just so it doesn't look too crass. Editors and authors will be calling you.

My former editor thought I might — I begin and then wish I hadn't, for Amos has bent halfway across the table.

Former editor? You've left Twentieth Century?

They left me, I say.

Got you. What kind of bread you want? Is it a novel?

Hey, man, you don't hafta . . .

A shadow dances across his eyes. Let me see it, okay?

Sure. You can take it with you tonight, I say. But he's just remembered that times have changed; that mostly what he does is sit in an empty office with sharpened pencils beside a cleared blotter. He makes a lot of phone calls and takes extremely long lunch hours. Phaeton does not know how to fire him gracefully. His opinions no longer count at his committee's meetings; his vote is discounted. For a moment I can see him in a last, drunken hurrah, trying to sell a Cato Caldwell Douglass novel to a firm that, like all the others, has closed the door quietly and firmly against, well, not against black writers (they are saying), but their themes!

Now we smile at each other. They are the old smiles of men who have recalled the nature of the game and all the nuances, and precisely why it is played in the first place.

I really would like to read it, Cate, he says.

So take it with you.

Betsy and Allis have been watching and listening; Betsy doesn't understand. Allis, of course, does.

Betsy stubs out the cigar. No ideas? Well, what the hell.

Before the silence can land, Allis says, as hostesses have said for millennia when it's time for the company to get the hell out, Who wants coffee?

We drove out that time to meet reality and it was in West Hampton, with Paul, with Betsy. But it began with just the visit.

They were renting a house for the summer and hadn't even stopped by their apartment when they arrived back from Europe.

"Whatever happens," Allis said, "it'll be nice to be at the beach for a while."

"What's supposed to happen?"

"I don't know," she said, "but something will. Words."

"Nah. It'll be good to see them."

"I want it to be a good visit."

"It will be," I said. "Hey, it didn't take Betsy long to get pregnant, huh? Ole Paul rang the bell this time. Maybe it was the French water or the Israeli wine."

"Cato." She disapproved, but with a smile. "Didn't he want children before? What about Claire and his first wife?"

"Janice," I said. "What could I know, babe? We never talked about kids."

We were on the Long Island Expressway, that engineering miracle that had somehow managed to make itself obsolete even before it was begun. It was, this summer day, wall-to-wall with cars outbound and inbound, a river of berubbered, beglassed, metallic money; the sheer amount of wealth creeping along astounded; the margins of profit amazed. For here was the very stuff of motor vehicle departments, insurance companies, automakers, steel companies, glassmakers; here on this panting, multicolored ribbon were all the parts that would suffice to keep a hundred thousand mechanics in three squares a day and more; oil company executives must now, at this very moment, be smiling at the fumes pouring into the air, the clouds of which must certainly indicate additional use of gas and oil. Sheriffs and state police had no fear that they would not make their quotas of summonses for the day; they had only to sit and wait for their radar to bleep the swift passage of one of the thousands kicking fifty-five in the ass to make up for lost time. These same radar trackers would also clock trees zipping along at ninety. But this snorting river of metal and glass was also providing a summer job for Glenn.

He was working in Detroit on the Ford assembly line with a friend from the Bowling Green College basketball team. I wanted Glenn to know what work was like; wanted him to know and smell his own sweat, not from dunks nor from clever passes that seemed to originate from within his scrotum, but from the exertion of having to do what he didn't have to do so that he might come to understand, for a little while, what his ancestors had had to do every day down through their generations. And for free. (But, being young, he'd wake after a short nap and dinner, and be out there hitting the bricks.) We'd see him toward the end of summer.

Paul had put on weight. Strangely, I felt it when we embraced before I saw it. His hair was longer now and his movements less tugged by anxieties. Betsy was proud of herself; her smile asked, Isn't this something? She grasped for Mack.

"And," Paul said, passing out the drinks he'd fixed, "we're going bingo for another as soon's the coast's clear with this one."

"We're not getting any younger," Betsy said. "We don't want to have the place filled with mongoloids. What about you two?"

"No," Allis said.

Paul looked at me. "I've already got two," I said.

He snapped his fingers. "That's right. But Glenn is just about grown, isn't he?"

"He's only just finished his freshman year," I said. "We were older when we went."

"Okay," Betsy said with a smile. "He'll be a kid for a while longer then, if you want. Well! What do you think of this place? Isn't it great? A motorboat comes with it, but we don't know how to drive it."

"I just want to lie on the beach," Paul said. "To hell with the boat."

"It's great!" Betsy exulted. "It's almost like being in La Ciotat, but of course we weren't on the beach there. That was always a special trip, when Paul got tired of working — "

"Just think of it, Cate," Paul interrupted in his own blast of enthusiasm. "Didn't we always want this? Work a few hours, lie out on a beach somewhere and have a few cocktails later, good dinner out or go to a dinner party and just rap? God, it's great!"

His hands gripped my shoulders. They tightened as he spoke and then, with some flash of recognition, they loosened, and the grip became embarrassed pats. "Hey! I haven't held the kid yet, Bets." She passed Mack over to him. Paul held him close and cooed to him.

Allis and I changed and we all shuffled out to the private beach on the bay, carrying drinks and snacks and talking about the things that'd happened to us since we'd last been together. Paul and Betsy talked of France, of course, and we talked of Grenada.

"But the high point was going to Israel, man. My God what a people! Can you believe what they did to the Arabs in just six days?"

"We went on a tour," Betsy broke in. "Up along the Golan Heights — was that where it was, honey?"

"Yeah, yeah. And for miles all you could see were these trucks and jeeps, brand new, man, *riddled* with bullet and frag holes on their sides. The Israeli Air Force shot apart a few million dollars' worth of Russian equipment like that!" He snapped his fingers.

"And do you know what? The Israelis will take that stuff and fix it up and put it right back into service with their army. Too much!"

"And," Betsy said, "as we went around the country, they showed us where the Israeli land ended and the Arab land began. Fields cultivated on the Israeli side — "

" — rocks and stones on the Arab side," Allis finished. We guessed just about everyone in New York had heard that by now. It was like saying, There is where the Upper West Side ends and Harlem begins; or There is where Little Italy ends and Chinatown begins.

Betsy was nodding her head in vigorous agreement with Allis. "Yes!" She had missed Allis' meaning.

"The place is so alive — so vital," Paul said. "The very air shudders with activity." He smiled.

"And the Negev," Betsy said. "It bursts with color — "

"It won't be a desert much longer, honey." Paul snorted. "They're even bringing that back, with new watering methods. Think of it, Cate, cities that were gone by the time the Romans arrived are being restored:

Arad, Ashdod. They are truly a remarkable people, if I do say so myself."

Betsy smiled at him.

"You two should go," Paul said. He glanced at Allis; the look carried a mild reproof.

Allis shrugged. "Maybe. One day. Who knows?"

Paul stretched luxuriously upon his towel. He placed Mack beside him. "Everything," he said, "everything they do is just at the right time and in the right place. Eichmann. That showed the world."

"Strangely," Allis said, "Eichmann standing there in his bulletproof cage, with the side of that thin, thin mouth pulled down, evoked, whether one likes it or not, some sympathy edged in horror. He was visible; his victims were not — "

"Aw, c'mon," Paul retorted, with a harshness that made me twist. "*That* goddamn weasel? I hope Wiesenthal catches them all. Leave it to the rest of the world, forget it. Get 'em all, every fuckin one of 'em; hang 'em, gas 'em, shoot 'em. Never again, goddamn it, never again." He turned accusingly toward her. "Didn't you lose some relatives?"

"Yes," Allis said. "Yes, I did."

"We shouldn't forget," I said. "We're taught to forget too many things."

But Paul was sulking in his righteous wrath.

Betsy said, "We all have things to remember, darling. Should my Irish part forget what the British did and are doing to the Irish?"

"Hah!" Paul said triumphantly. "The IRA's doing exactly what we're doing."

I smiled, and Paul asked, "What's funny, Cate?"

"Hey. Once we were talking about slavery and the slave trade — or I was — and you said we'd all be better off putting the past to rest. But you really meant *my* past, didn't you, not yours?"

Betsy broke in quickly, like a cavalryman riding to the rescue. "Aren't we, all of us, victims? And the past is a whole, a collective, linked, direct and indirect experience, Paul? Jews hardly ever talk about how well they did, living in the Arab-Iberian society, do they? Of course, that ended when the Christians kicked them both out."

"Few people treated us better, Paul," Allis said.

"I was talking about the crimes against Jews carried out by the Germans," Paul said.

I drew a deep breath and tried to signal Allis and Betsy that perhaps we should change the subject. But one last thing insisted, pushed and arrived: "Crimes against humanity didn't begin with the Jews and they won't end with the Jews. What happened this time around was technology.

258

Photography. Wire recorders. Radio. Duplicating systems. Almost instantaneous transmission, once the facts were disclosed, so you became fixed in time for a lot of people to remember, for many people to see. Other victims had to make do with not so hot photography, paintings by Goya, drawings — ”

“Maybe,” Paul said, “black people ought to build their own Yad Va’Shem in Jamestown Harbor for sixteen nineteen — ”

“That’s almost a hundred years too late,” I said.

“Why? Why? Why are we talking like this?” Allis demanded, reaching out for Mack as though to protect him. “Why does it always have to be blacks or Jews, Jews or blacks?”

“Metaphors, baby,” I said.

“I’m not a goddamn metaphor. I’m Allis Douglass.”

“Hear, hear,” Betsy said.

Something like waves of heat from concrete filled the air between us. Paul got up for more drinks. Betsy and Allis took Mack into the water. I watched a twenty-five-footer pump down the channel to the sea.

We were back together in another few minutes, Paul passing out drinks with a great flurry, Allis and Betsy drying off Mack.

“So,” Paul said. “What’re you working on now?”

“Nothing. Just delivered a novel to Twentieth.”

“Great,” Paul said.

“But he’s already into another,” Allis said.

Betsy said, “How nice. You know, David Susskind’s picked up an option on *The Burnt Offering* for the movies.”

“Marvelous,” Allis said.

“Fantastic,” I added. The game had begun. “Who’s to do the screenplay?”

Paul said, “They want me to take a crack at it.”

“Here or out there?”

“There,” Betsy said.

“Did you know that the Swedes, the French, the Dutch, the West Germans and the Spanish all have picked up the rights to Cate’s last?”

“That certainly won’t hurt,” Paul said. “Won’t hurt a bit.”

“Cate,” Betsy asked, “do you know this guy Brance from *Life?*”

“Only indirectly. Why?”

“He’s coming out next week,” she said with a theatrical innocence. “Wants to do a spread on Paul. Just thought you might know him.”

Allis stood Mack on his feet. He swayed there. “Jill Krementz is to do the jacket photo for Cate’s new book.”

"She's doing Paul's too," Betsy said.

Then we were silent, listening to the wind slipping through the rushes, and the waves lapping against the beach as the tide moved in. The echoes of all we'd said and all we'd meant were like a swamp of sea gull shit.

I said, sitting up, "We've known each other too long for this bullshit." But then I wondered. "Haven't we, Paul?"

"Hell, yes." He poked in the sand. "Yes," he said again. "This shit is like a disease, isn't it?" He stood and bashed the heel of his foot into the sand until he'd made a pit.

"Listen, Cate: Will the teaching hurt your work?"

"I hope not."

"Don't let it, man."

"No."

He seemed to want to say more but did not. We sat enshrouded in our silences, benumbed by the knowledge now plainly obvious, so much so that we could no longer delude ourselves, that our friendship existed only because of the tension caused by the enmity of our kinds. Like matter must beget antimatter; like antimatter simply cannot be without matter; we were particles of a scheme, magnetized, in motion, quarking under impetuses not quite our own.

12

THIS BRANCH of the university was private. The children of wealthy parents attended, slipping in and out of the hollows and trudging assuredly over the hills of the near–New York City countryside. The place was toughly bucolic; one could discern, almost without trying, nearby traffic rushing into and out of the city or, in the evening hours, hear it lapping along the interstate. The isolation was more imagined than real.

If the rich had always been different from the rest of us, then their children were trying hard not to be. Their allegiances were with the times: smelly clothes and Afro cuts. They liked rock music, of course; there was little other popular music so readily available. They drank wine and smoked the grass — ditchweed, mainly — that some jive townie had sold them at exorbitant rates while claiming it to be "superbad." About their courses of study the students were quite nonchalant; grades did not mean nearly as much as their family names, and they had come here, after all, because there was some understanding about the names.

A few black students were in attendance. Those who were not on scholarship scrambled frantically to create and maintain distances from those who were. These last, to a girl or boy, were from the streets of the city and were "down," wearing hats in the classroom and blocking narrow stairwells to give each other the most intricate handshakes or to pound their upraised fists on the air near their heads in emulation of John Carlos and Tommie Smith. They were all good dancers, and thus the males ran rampant through the "liberal" white coeds while invariably proclaiming BLACK POWER. Now and again one met serious black couples, quietly outraged by the racism they alleged had invested the campus. The males, with some caution, picked me up as a "brother." The females, sloe-eyed and wise, seeming to hear things with their eyes and see things with their ears, drifted about the campus, into and out of classrooms, with, very infrequently, white boyfriends and more frequently black boyfriends; I was not "brother" to them. I never knew what I was.

My colleagues were friendly, bending easily with the times that had cast me into their select company. They were poets and novelists and American literature specialists; this one had Melville, that one Hemingway; this one James, that one Crane; this one the Fugitives, that one the Lost Generation . . .

But at least I was *in touch.* We were out of the isolation of raising our child and of licking the wounds imposed by family, and we were back in the middle of things, where cities went up in flames, where national leaders were knocked off. To be *in touch* was really to be with students, I thought.

Allis had returned to fund-raising as a consultant, picking and choosing her hours so that she could spend the most time with Mack. A woman named Mrs. Lee, a thin, anxious grandmother, came to care part time for Mack. My own work was taking shape under the title *The War Has Already Begun.*

And Glenn had returned to school. His friend from the assembly line, a six-foot-eight-inch weed — Jed, by name — was transferring to another Ohio school to play Big-Time Ball so that he would have a better chance of getting a shot with the pros. He had now a scholarship that had brought him a Chevrolet Impala. After he red-shirted a year, he thought they'd probably give him a Hog to wheel through his junior and senior years. Jed was a poorly spoken, innocent and gullible boy, totally confident that his basketball skills would place him on top of the world. Nothing else mattered — rebellions, assassinations, Vietnam — nothing. I feared his being hurt by the hardball players.

There were times during their four days with us when I walked into the living room to find him sliding from pivot to post, swinging his body this way and that, head jerking left and right, looking for the imaginary ball, the imaginary open man. Glenn watched with not quite a sneer, for he was envious of such dedication, such confidence.

"Two seconds!" I would yell and watch him uncoil, scrape the pads of his fingertips softly against the ceiling and hear him say (his eyes following the imaginary ball as it arched over imaginary outstretched hands), say with the awesome certainty of athletes completely in tune with their bodies, "*Swish!*" Glenn would applaud.

They were gone now and I was moving through the university, pleased that it was not draining my energies. No doubt there was some small wonder at my being there, one of three black faculty. But the old rich know more of the whys and wherefores than most of us. There were no riots, no insults (that I could detect) and only one student, a female, who asked during her usual acerbic conference hour, "What are *you* doing here, anyway?"

She, alas, had tipped her hand; she was new money, obviously.

There were, of course, the tales (sometimes legends) of writers who'd run through the coeds like Zeus through a flock of swans; and there were the novels whose dénouements hinged on the coed-professor relationship. The campus hummed as much with the movement of eyeballs as with the passing of gossip.

There was an entire literature on writers on campus; thus there seemed to be no reason for what happened.

The second semester began with great promise. My European publishers were pooling their resources — each had proclaimed a singularly impoverished budget — to bring us to Europe during the summer to promote my books. Paul had come and read, along with other poets, mainly, and novelists, who through successive springs and falls "do the circuit" in much the same way another generation had "done Europe."

March winds like a troop of chasseurs whirled around the campus, over which students, bundled like Teddy bears, walked past my window.

I was working at my desk in longhand because I didn't want my colleagues apprised of my presence, for the door was still open for the wandering student who might want to talk or drop off a late paper. The sound of a typewriter is an insistent reminder that a loner crouches down the hall and that he or she may, at that very moment, be composing a fiercely brilliant paper, a book, a proposal, that would leave the listener of that peckapackapucka in shadow. I wrote in longhand.

I felt a presence, a lightness, inserting itself into the shadows of the doorway. I looked up. There stood a female student, her books held against her breasts. She was vaguely familiar, perhaps one of those two or three black females whose mouths lifted in slight smiles of greeting as I moved about the campus. She had been studying me for some seconds. Now she smiled, and in some way it was like the sun breaking out after a four-day rain. "Professor Douglass?"

"Call me mister. Or Cato. Come in?"

She drifted forward and sat down with a rustle in the straight-back chair. I waited. I looked at her face. Do faces really tell what we are? What's Hollywood done to our realities?

"I'm Raffy Joplin," she said.

Then I remembered the rumor that the daughter of Ralph Joplin was on campus, that Joplin was studying the syncretisms of religions and theater in Baía; that his plays were said to have run out of popularity in the United States. Well, I thought, he had at least done well enough to have sent his daughter here. *I* had liked his plays.

"Hello, Raffy. How's your father?"

"Do you know him?"

"No. Just his work."

"Oh, he's marvelous," she said with an expanding smile. "He's just written to me about Carnaval in Brazil. That's where he is now."

I nodded. My voice wouldn't come because I was chasing the echoes of her inflections; they reminded me of the touch, the warming touch, of gold molded by African craftsmen, and I was conscious of a sudden warmth spreading through my body, as when the acupuncturist's needles, precisely placed, open up blocked channels to restore dark and light, sweet and sour, fast and slow, to proper balance.

"I'm glad to hear that he's all right," I said finally. "He's a wonderful writer."

Shyly she said, "Thanks." Then: "Am I supposed to say that? I never know how to respond when people compliment my father." She heaved a sigh, her head turned chastely to one side. "Anyway, indirectly, that's why I came. I'm in Anthro, but I think I want to write, too. I'm not enrolled in any of the writing classes, but I wondered if you could, please, take the time to look at some of my stories and tell me if they're any good."

"Have you let your father see them?"

"Not yet. I know he'd like me to write. But I also know that he despises the system that controls what writers produce."

"Ah, I see." She looked like Sarasvati, of poetry and music. "Are you a junior? Senior?" It was suddenly and strangely urgent that I know how much longer she would be around.

"Senior." She sounded apologetic.

Within, I felt an explosion of tension. "Oh! You're finished in June."

264

She smiled proudly. "Yes, thank God."

"And then?"

"Michigan. University of Michigan. Graduate work."

"Ann Arbor. Well. Listen: Do you have your work with you? Yes? Why don't you leave it and come back, oh, whenever. Or call and we'll set up a time to talk. All right?"

Raffy was beaming as she leafed through a folder and handed me a batch of neatly typed and clipped stories. This once I would not have cared had they been handwritten. But, I thought, score one for her. "I really appreciate this," she said, standing. "My father's always liked your novels . . ." She stood there, holding the books against her body; her eyes roamed away from me and then back to my face. "Maybe I can do you a favor in return." She smiled. There seemed to be something behind the something already in her eyes.

"Well," I mumbled, "I'm sure you can. I mean, I'm sure of it."

Was she laughing at me?

"Bye. I'll call soon," she said.

I understood now why my male colleagues stayed on here and suffered low wages, divorces, remarriages to former students and divorces and remarriages again.

I lingered in my office, during the days following, longer than usual; my eyes sprang open to watch the coeds passing my window. I pawed through the campus dorm directory looking for her name and address in vain. Then, after a week (I'd read her work that same afternoon), when I'd relegated her into that corner of the mind reserved for students you wondered about, she called.

"I wanted to read your books — some of them, anyway — before I came. May I come today?"

"Today — ah, sure." I had wanted to ask: Right now?

It all would have been so perfect if she had been a good writer. She wasn't. Her father must've known. Her work was like the paintings on velvet seen at art hustles in various towns or cities that occur with the onset of spring — flashy, depthless and with much flourish.

She sat down. "Well, what do you think?"

I said, "I thought they were good stories."

She brightened and shifted to the edge of the chair. She carried no books with her this time, and she appeared fresh and lean. "Really? I thought you wouldn't like them."

"Why not?"

"I don't know. Something about you."

"Well, Raffy, they do need some work."

"Of course. Will you help me?"

That smile again.

I shrugged. "Help? I don't really teach writing, you know."

"No?"

"No. I try to teach the habit."

She laughed merrily, flashing neat rows of white teeth. "Then why is it offered?"

"Because people think it can be taught."

"But why do you teach it if it can't be taught?"

"To find the people who can write, I guess. To help them. To meet them. Kindred spirits, and all that. Do you write poetry, too? You must."

"I do write poetry," she said, tilting her head in appreciation of my discovery.

We sat in a brief silence, smiling at each other. "Why did you want to read my books?"

"To know you."

"Is that important?"

"It wasn't before I first came to see you."

"Ah," I said. We did not look at each other. "Have you had lunch?"

"No," she said. "Have you?"

"No."

"Then let's go have some lunch." I got up. She stood, waiting. "Here're your stories."

She looked quickly at the typed comments, then rolled them up. "Where shall we go? Off campus?"

"Okay."

"I can make you lunch."

"Okay." I closed the door. "You a good cook?"

"Sure."

We walked slowly over the campus the way two young people do when they like each other, turning easily to talk and smile. I had noticed this from my window and, remembering what it looked like to others peering through windows, I tried to assume a professorial gait, whatever that was, and I shortened my stride and tightened my smile and tried to talk seriously about writers and writing.

Yet I was in awe of the ease with which this thing was taking place. Though writers will never admit it, there are certain events they assume must happen to them, or certain things they feel are *due* them, perhaps in return for what they imagine they have themselves given to the world

266

at large. Yes, I felt I had this coming, but I was also wondering why I was there, why I'd let myself be there, whether I was like the cliché, getting old enough to desire to press my flesh against, into, younger flesh in the hope that, like the fountain of youth waters, it would make me young. Or was this a vague revolutionary impulse, a cementation of racial blood from which I was now legally absented . . .

She lived not far away, in a small cottage of which she had one half — a studio flat. It was done in greenish yellows, like the first deceptive sprays of forsythia that offer some confusion with languid spring sunlight. She herself was the gingerbread-brown counterpoint.

The ease, I thought again, a flaccid warmth growing inside my thigh. My generation, in most instances, had had to run through the maze, finding some exits blocked, others set with shock, making do with thinking how *close* we'd come — a desperate finger hooked on the elastic band of the panties; a far more desperate finger sliding through the wet, all hopes that its touch, its insertion in the proper place, would bring a frantic dropping of everything . . .

"Have a seat." She smiled as if she knew that I wished I had a pipe to clench between my teeth.

"Nice place," I said. I was sitting on the couch that had to pull out to a bed.

She placed a casserole in the oven and poured some wine. It seemed to have been already opened and breathing near the sink. All ready and waiting. I took the wine and looked at her pictures while she set up the folding table. I wondered if the diaphragm case on the end table was empty.

"My mother," Raffy said, coming over and pointing. "And my aunt Iris."

I had heard of Iris Joplin, the expatriate singer. Raffy was telling me that Iris no longer liked Europe and was planning to return to the U.S. While certainly not nearly as old as Alberta Hunter or Eubie Blake (more like Sarah Vaughan, who was making good in her comeback), Iris thought that perhaps she could arrange something with her old friend Bobby Short. Anyway, she wished to return.

"Do you," I said, tapping the diaphragm case, "have that in now?"

She had started for the stove and stopped; her eyes followed my finger. "That? Yes." She turned away again and pulled the casserole out. She smiled over her shoulder; it was teasing and seductive and something else I was not able to identify. I walked over.

"For me?"

She moved the casserole to the table. "Yes, of course. Ready to eat?"

"Sure." I sat down. She filled my glass again. The ease, I was thinking. It was too easy. No. That was the way things were today.

"How do you like it?" Raffy asked. It was macaroni, cheese and ham.

"Good, very good," I said, though in fact it was quite ordinary. That surprised me the way her stories had.

We talked of people on the campus, her father, the black students, and we ate and drank more wine and then, with nothing more to say on those subjects, I helped her to open the bed. Facing each other, admiring each other, we undressed and slid into it.

That, too, was disappointing. But she didn't think so. There was a curious disjunction between what she thought she could do and what she actually did. She did not perceive this. She lay breathing heavily, watching me.

"Fantastic," I whispered. What else was I to say — that she was too frantic, that she was inept, that she had shattered my concept of how young, very pretty women made love? Seeking a distraction, I reached over and took the diaphragm case. I opened it. There was a diaphragm in it. I went limp and cold and then angry.

"What's this shit?" I held the case toward her.

She laughed. And laughed. And laughed again. "Don't worry," she said when she'd caught her breath. "It's all right; a safe time of month." She laughed me out of her flat.

Two weeks passed, and I was starting to feel relieved that I had not seen her, that she hadn't called. It was over, I told myself. It'd been a brief excursion into the unknown; a skip through the snakepit; material that Ken Kesey would have come back from his cow farm for. A student was finishing up her conference hour — it'd been a bit longer than an hour — when the phone rang.

Raffy said, "No conference hour should last that long."

An avalanche crashed into my head, and foolishly I found myself explaining: "Oh, she just wanted to talk about some things — "

"Are you sure, Cate? That's all? I know that Melanie."

She'd never called me Cate before. I was afraid; I was pissed. "What did you think we were doing?"

"You know." Her answer had come after a sly pause.

Bits of things ran suddenly together. I put the phone down and went to my door and opened it. I glanced down the corridor to the phone booth. Raffy was there, the phone still to her mouth, but facing me, a storm so violent on her face that it destroyed any vestige of the Indian goddess of poetry and music. With angry motions, I signaled her. She

268

hung up the phone and swept toward me, past me, into the office. I closed the door and hung up the phone. I didn't dare believe what was happening. "What was that all about, Raffy?"

"I see the way you look at the women around here!" She whipped back and forth.

"Hey, you're imagining things. I wasn't doing anything with Melanie." She paced around my office. "You aren't jealous, are you, Raffy?"

She stopped suddenly and smiled. "I'm not jealous, just crazy."

"No. Mixed up, Raffy. Let's straighten it out: it was tremendous, being with you, making love with you, but it was eminently transitory — it couldn't be otherwise — and I do value the memory."

"Memory, my ass," she said. "Suppose I get pregnant?"

"Oh, come on."

"It's not over, Cate. I won't let it be over."

"It's over, Raffy. Over." She thinks, I realized, we had a solid thing going. My God! As traditional as ever! She pretended she wasn't! Could I expect to find her around the corner of every campus building, or behind every tree now greening with the soft April rain? (April, that was her mother's name.) Would she be at the terminal end of every flight of every Frisbee that sailed over my head? All on the basis of *one* lousy fuck? "You'd better go, Raffy. Yes, I think it's better that way. When you're in a better mood let's talk — "

She stopped as though she'd run into a wall.

"You're putting *me* out?"

"I'm not putting you out. I just want you to go now."

The *ease,* I groaned as she went past me like a shot, screaming, "Nigger, you're gonna be sorry you ever touched *me!*" She went down the hall like a squad of storm troopers and broke the glass in the door when she slammed it. I hoped that my colleagues who shared the floor with me were out, to lunch, to diddle coeds, to drink, even to class.

I remained still and listened. There was no minor hubbub of people sneaking into each other's offices to:

"Did you hear that! What that Joplin girl said to Douglass! She all but said they'd slept together!"

None of that.

I pried open my lunch — a tuna fish salad sandwich on whole wheat bread, peach yogurt, an apple — which Allis had packed for me. I'd realized that if I brought lunch, I could work and eat; in the cafeteria it was just eating and talking — and the prices of truly mediocre food climbed every week.

But I didn't work. I ate and thought, ate and worried. Which linked events had produced such a fashion-model beauty with such a fucked-up head? Was this a part of the cost for Ralph Joplin's success, such as it was? Had he ever, as a writer seeking his "due," been involved in such a situation? What was wrong with me that I hadn't been able to foresee this godawful consequence?

If, *if* Raffy called Allis during the flux of her madness, how would Allis take it? *God!* Had Allis ever been presented with what appeared to be such a golden chance? Had she climbed the mountain because it was there the way I had? Would she?

Madness should wear a sign or carry a bell, as lepers used to. That was God's curse — that the mad shall look and behave just like anyone else until they behave insanely. Ah, Lord!

Maybe — No. No, you couldn't take her by the hand and lead her to a shrink; you couldn't send a little unsigned note to her father or mother. A talk with the dean? No, no, for the question would most certainly arise: How is it that you know?

Who then would save this maiden, remove her gently from the abyss where tradition and change whirl about in deceptive downdraft? Those, obviously, who *know,* who know. But where were the others whose presences were implied by the case and what it contained? And, after all, I asked the lengthening shadows in my office, am I my sister's keeper?

A letter!

All my instincts surged at the thought of a letter, comforting in tone, cunning in concept, that would allow her to let me carry her to a shrink. But then — *then* it would be in *writing!*

No.

The tuna fish, the yogurt, the apple congealed into lead in my belly, and I remembered the surgeons talking about the autopsies they'd performed at slow moments during the war, and how they'd found whole dinners of boiled beans or K or C rations, completely undigested, in the stomachs of men killed in combat. Whole dinners.

Three days passed. I sat at my machine in the corner of our bedroom. Nothing came. The paper filled with words, but they meant nothing. I destroyed them and thought of Raffy.

Allis and I went to a dinner party on the evening of the third day, and when we returned, I took Mrs. Lee downstairs to a cab. When I got back, undressed for bed and started to slip in, Allis, who'd been in the posture of sleep, flung back the sheets.

"Surprise!" She was nude. (I had said in passing only the week before that some of the fire seemed to have slipped away from our sex life.) "C'mon, bay-bee. Fire away."

270

We laughed and made love and realized that the fire was a slow, long-burning one, and afterward slept in each other's arms, where we remained until, at some soft, darkly quiet hour, the phone rang, and Allis said, still in sleep, "Uh, uh, uh," and I suddenly had the instrument in my hand, saying, "Uh, uh, hello," and was listening to the breathing on the other end, not so much heavy as defeated, while Allis was saying, still sleepy, "Who'sit, honey, who'sit?" and Raffy, as if in a tomb, was saying, "I'm dying, Cate, pills, I don't wanna die, pills, save me, help me," and I was saying in fear and fright, "Who *is* this?" with the proper amount of indignation, aware now that Allis was close to being awake and peering at the luminous dials on the clock as I said, "But why are you calling at this hour?" while she continued, "Help me, please help — "

"Who the hell's that?"

And then the phone went dead. "A student," I said.

There came, just that swiftly, with the whirring of the clock, an anticline in our lives, but I was dialing the operator. "Operator. Emergency. The police in Slick Falls."

"What's the matter?" The tone was that of a teacher trying to bestir a sluggish class.

The operator was saying, in one of those ethnic voices that zips through the wires of the eastern seaboard these days, "Dial 555–1212–923."

"Who *was* that? Look what time it is."

"A student," I said, dialing. "She's taken some pills — operator? Emergency. Give me the police. A student at the university's taken some sleeping pills — "

"Do you know her? Was she one of yours?"

"Two-two-two Elm Street. Right across from the campus." I was out of bed, reaching for my clothes.

"Where're you going?" Allis asked. She was sitting up in bed, her breasts with their neat round pink nipples hanging over the sheet.

"I'd better go."

"Who is she, Cate?"

"Just one of the students on campus. I know her father. He's out of the country, mother's out of town — "

"But I don't understand," she said, which was what she always said when she understood perfectly, and just as I was about to leave her as I'd never, ever left before, "Why did she call *you*?"

I feigned a mixture of exasperation and irritation. "Oh, they bring their goddamn problems to me."

I was at the bedroom door. Because the light was behind her now, I could not see her face, only her silhouette, the spray of her hair that was like a small corona.

"I see," she said.

I hesitated. I did not ask what it was she saw. "I'll be back as soon's I can," I said.

By the time I arrived at Raffy's flat she had been carried to the hospital. She would be all right, a cop told me. It was spring, and every spring something like this happened at the university. You could count on it. The dean arrived and when she saw me, she sighed. "Cato, why are you here? Don't tell me. I can't imagine what you told your wife." She was a woman my age. She wore a merry widow corset even at that hour of the morning, and was made up. She said, "You know, they're wise old women disguising themselves as babies. Sometimes they confuse the roles. I don't know why it is that intelligent men can't understand that." She sat down wearily on Raffy's still-rumpled bed. "Theirs is a different world. Go home to your wife, Cato. I'll send a letter or something to make it all right. Go back to your books. Be happy you have them both."

Back in the car and driving into the city beneath a lifting gray morning sky, my stomach twisted like the knots of a hangman's rope, I slid into jagged disphoria induced by the events of the night now being punctuated by the click, click, click, click of the wheels as they passed over the lines in the concrete roadbed slabs. My heel touched the gun on the floor under the seat, and I thought, Who needs *that* to wound or kill.

"Is she," Allis asked at breakfast, which I'd fixed because I was already up, "is she going to be all right?"

Her face — it had angles and sometimes sharpnesses — was composed into harder lines than I ever could have imagined.

"Yeah. She'll be okay."

She busied herself with Mack; bright little cooings as she enticed him to eat. "Who was she — I mean, her name?"

"Raphaella Joplin."

She became motionless. "The playwright's daughter?"

"Yeah." I was surprised that she remembered we'd seen a couple of Ralph Joplin's plays.

She tilted her head back and seemed to squint into the sunlight now coming through the window. "She couldn't be more than twenty or twenty-one."

I said nothing, but I saw it coming, like the leveling of a rifle barrel.

Her eyes, more green than gray in the morning, sort of flipped slowly over to fix on mine.

"Cate, were you involved with her?"

"Not in the way you're implying."

She seemed to breathe a sigh of relief. "How then?"

"Her writing. She wanted me to look at it and make some comments. We talked about it. That's all."

"Is she any good as a writer?"

"No," I said.

"She have a boyfriend?"

"I assume so, honey."

Then she said, "Are you all right?"

I nodded. "Yes."

"You know," she said, "the reason strangers always seem to pick you out to ask directions of, and the reason bums all gravitate toward you, is that you look at them. You make eye contact, and you can't do that with people, honey, because when you do, something goes click! and they have you and then you feel shitty when you try to be gruff and shoo them off."

"But how can you not look at people, Allis?"

"I don't know. But when you do, something goes wrong."

"Yeah. Maybe. Were you worried?"

"Me?" she said. "No. I wasn't worried at all."

We had never been so married as at that moment.

13

WE WERE SQUEEZING in visits to an ailing Mr. Storto, who had never been able to bring himself to travel north of Fourteenth Street and whose apartment now always smelled of Ben-Gay or Minit-Rub; to Paul and Betsy, back from the Beverly Hills Hilton, where, I gathered, his attempt at screen-writing had been a near-disaster ("Those people out there are not to be believed, man!"). He was working well on another novel, *Isaiah's Odyssey*. We had dinners with Maxine Culp and Maureen Gullian and various editors of literary publications, all of whom seemed to be cranking up for the fall publication of *Circles Round Saturn,* which would have my name above the title, and there were the usual meetings with the publicity people and the art department folk.

Raffy, although she had not returned to classes, would be graduated in June. At this section of the university they took care of such details. I'd heard that she would spend the summer with her mother before beginning graduate school.

A lightness returned to Allis; her humor was vibrant as she regaled me with tales of her fund-raising activities, the idiocy, the greed, the cunning always displayed. She looked forward to the trip, even with an active eighteen-month-old child and an erring husband. We hoped *The Hyksos Journals* would do better after our swing through Europe and, though it

274

would be jive, it was the kind of jive that writers love. It would be, too, a holiday, and the distance it would place between the university and me was more than a blessing. Furthermore, while Paul had had Hollywood, he had not yet been invited to do the European Grand Literary Tour.

Now when I look back on that season in my life, it seems to be not quite a blur, but a series of images speeded up as though there were details the projectionist did not wish me to see too clearly.

It — that season — begins with our departure, and it is framed by the smells of taxis and cars and airports and jet fuel and the smells of hotels. The Cumberland in London, the Anglais in Stockholm, the Raphael in Paris, the Palace in Berlin, the Majestic in Barcelona, the Amstel in Amsterdam, smelling, yes, of imitation Aubussons and kippers and kidney pies and butter-rich foods and sausages and cassoulet, paella, hassenpfeffer, and the gas-fume smell of the cities, the river and ocean smell of those cities, the colognes and perfumes, the wines, the bathrooms, the sun-scorched gardens withering in their formality.

There are close-ups of the Europeans staring at us, some amused, some genuinely amazed, some merely interested in this zebraic couple with the "hybrid" child, a generally European uncoolness that even their dark "guest workers" — present-day serfs — have not dented. But the publishers and editors are always polite, always shallowly obsequious ("This is an American Artist"), and there is in all their offices, not much changed from the dark, paneled caverns of the nineteenth century, a dubious gentility of Old World quality, not anything like the chrome gleamings of both folk and furnishings in American publishing offices.

We go to small press conferences with editors serving as translators, where necessary, and to the parties where we meet other writers and translators, the Fulbright Scholars, the embassy or consular staff, and where there are displays of the novel, together with huge photos of me looking antiartistic, calling to mind some of the late-eighteenth-century steel engravings of African savages by John I. Senex.

There are always the questions:

Do you know Elliot Huysmans?

Do you know John Greenleaf Whittington?

Did you know Richard Wright?

Why is there so much violence in the United States?

Do you consider the civil rights movement to be successful?

Do you anticipate more race riots?

All of this, of course, against the recent past, when Nixon, wearing a white hat and riding a white horse, masked, but not for the same reasons as the Lone Ranger, had galloped through the campfires of the natives of Newark, Detroit and a hundred other reservations — or promised to.

And:

Are interracial marriages popular in America?

What are you working on now?

Do you know James Meredith?

Do you know Stokely Carmichael or H. Rap Brown?

Do you like

> England
>> France
>>> Sweden
>>>> Germany
>>>>> Holland
>>>>>> Spain?

When do you think the U.S. will have a Negro President?

Do you consider yourself to be an example for other American Negroes to emulate?

There are many Negro soldiers in Vietnam. What will happen when they return home?

Wherever we are, the questions are the same. My responses depend on how much I've had to drink, how tired I am and the degree of superciliousness of the questioner. Europeans possess conveniently short memories, concerning what they do not only to each other, but to everyone else in the world as well.

But we manage. By the time we are in Barcelona, it occurs to me that we have not mentioned my past there. Given what had just taken place back home, it is perhaps the wisest thing to do. This arrangement goes well until the day we are leaving for our final stop, Amsterdam; we are now as eager to leave as we were to come.

I sit downstairs in the lobby. The lobby looks out on the Paseo de Gracia, but now its grand promenade in the center of the street is filled with parked cars. I am finishing up some notes for *The War Has Already Begun.* Allis is upstairs doing a last-minute thing with Mack, who has taken the trip, even with the succession of strange nurses, far better than we have. Our bags are sitting on the floor beside me.

The hotel manager rushes over and, with that excess of courtesy that used to be the mark of gracious Spanish hotels, congratulates me on the articles that have been appearing in the papers during our stay. He hands me a manila envelope. I assume that it has come from my publisher and contains clippings of articles. I thank him and open it.

It is a photograph, wrapped in tissue, of Monica, a dark-skinned pretty little girl with a whimsical smile, a larger, more manly version of Federico García Lorca Jones, looking very much like his grandfather — I see that instantly — *me* between boyhood and puberty. Monica's face has a softness now; I recall it being sharp with the edges of hunger and desperation when we first met, the eyes sad and heavy . . .

I rush to the desk and ask the manager who had left the photograph. He tells me that a chauffeur, in uniform, driving a Mercedes-Benz, brought it. He glances at the photo, takes it, studies it and hands it back. He tells me that she is the wife of the representative from Fernando Po. He does not recall her name. She does charity work and is considered to be a person of the highest character.

I return to my seat and stare at the photo. *I* have a mischievous look that is not quite concealed by the smile about to be formed. Words come, lightly, rushing through my consciousness the way a chipmunk, looking like a leaf blown against the wind, runs across a road: *You, as you pass, your self must sow* . . .

Monica has a slightly haughty look to her. The camera has caught the glint of jewelry in her ears and about her neck. Her hands, placed casually upon the shoulders of the boys beside her — the girl is in front of her, centered — display diamonds and a wedding band.

In the white shirt, tie and jacket, *I* am reflecting the tradition of the middle-class European schoolboy. *My* eyes beam with light; in them I see that all things are possible, that there is nothing wan or defeated in them. My head booms with the refrain: *They made it! Yes!* It is all there, the symbols, and in the faces, the attitudes of their bodies. I feel like crying. I must do something not to cry. I flutter the photo, and as it waves up and down I see writing on the back. I turn it over and read: "Federico is a good student at school. Alejo Cato is already a little poet! The other is Teresa. Good luck, Cato! Monica Donoso."

I go to a phone to call my editor at Amaya. I ask him to get their address and send it to me, and in the privacy of the booth I cry.

14

"LET GO! LET GO!" Mack screamed. He twisted around. "I can do it, Daddy; let go!"

He had grown into an active, lusty, demanding boy. I had removed the training wheels from his bike at his insistence. Why not let him finish what he thought he could do? The bike was, after all, a birthday present.

"Okay!" I yelled. Allis trotted anxiously at my side.

"Oh!" she said.

I scampered a few worried paces after Mack and stopped; Allis bumped into me. She grabbed my arm and we watched him weaving, shifting his balance, until at last he straightened, pumped hard and was off, a great dazzling smile on his face. Not much more in life would be so clear-cut a triumph, I thought. Enjoy, kid, enjoy. That's where the past few years had gone, really. Never mind the work, the college, tracking Glenn's progress, the trips. The time was measured from Mack's last diaper full of shit to his riding away from us on a two-wheeler his first time on it. He was five.

Allis was saying, "Look at him! He's done it!"

We smiled. Mackland Douglass had just gained his second out-of-home victory. The first was that he took to nursery school without any problem.

We walked to a bench where we could sit and watch. It was mild for November, and Central Park had filled with people. They sat on the edges of the benches, looked warily around and seemed to be relieved when the cops came by. They complained (one could overhear them as they sat on other benches) about the high prices at Foodtown or the A & P, or how they always got their gas tanks filled in New Jersey before returning to the city after being away.

"They're right," Allis said. "Things are changing."

She had a way of sitting with a book or a magazine while at the same time drinking in all the conversations that flowed about her. "It's changed an awful lot since we moved up here."

"It's been five years," I said.

Glenn had graduated and was going to Iowa. His friend Jed had quit school in his junior year to take advantage of the hardship draft and was now in his second year with the Lakers — living, Glenn said, like a Hollywood star. Glenn had visited him over part of the summer, and that had set him to work on a novel about Jed, which he was calling *Jumper.*

Paul's novel *Isaiah's Odyssey* was published with tremendous fanfare. There were ads for it all over the place. *Publishers Weekly* had called it "a sure bet for the National Book Award." Paul's photo was on the cover of *Passages* and *Newsweek,* and there was a big story in *Time.* Selena Merritt did a page one review for Jeremy Poode's paper, while Poode himself did an inside interview. Shelly Popper also ran a page one review by Colin McInnes, who'd done *The City of Spades,* and Mark Medowitz returned to writing long enough to do a centerfold portrait of Paul in the *Village Voice,* and we got up early one morning to catch Paul on the "Today" show with Barbara Walters. She interviewed him for thirteen minutes. I counted, because, with two other black writers, I'd been on her show for nine minutes.

(You are picked up very early by a considerate chauffeur, who is dressed in a black suit, tie and cap and a white shirt, and are driven in a sleek limo to the RCA Building on Forty-ninth Street, where everyone appears to be waiting anxiously for you, and you are settled in an anteroom with a TV monitor and given coffee and Danish or juice and slipped the release forms to sign, and then they rush you into a studio, where Walters — with someone else — surrounded by cameras, sound men and directors, floor managers and assorted assistants, rush together from one corner of the studio to another, doing a commercial here, updating the news there, and finally, like a small, panting, sweating herd, wired and emitting light, they settle before you, and Walters' first question is about still another black writer who isn't even there.)

I had, of course, received a copy of the novel and a long letter from Paul, explaining why he'd written it and what he'd tried to do with it. There was a blurb on the jacket by John Greenleaf Whittington. For Isaiah was a black man. After all, Stowe had done it, and Melville and Van Vechten and Stein and Bellow and Mailer and Malamud and Updike and Holmes and Styron.

It seemed to be *de rigueur* for many American writers. It was rather like the old Egyptians telling the rest of Africa's story or the Greeks telling the Egyptians' story or the Romans telling the Greeks' story, etc. No one seemed to put much credence in the teller who told his own tale. Maybe for Paul and the others there was no other story worth telling. Anyway, he did win the National Book Award with *Isaiah*.

Now there was Paul, who after all this time of knowing Leonard and knowing me, had missed our essences, capturing instead, unlike some of the others, the Mau-Mau, the Panther, the militant, the revolutionary, the supercock, without providing him, Isaiah, with the motivation, the reason, for being the way he was; without seeing himself in the portrait with Isaiah the way we all were, just as we all move through the same atmosphere, loving and hating and making love the same way. I had not known until I finished the novel to how great an extent a part of my life had been given over subconsciously to teaching Paul — this time I was the master and he the pupil — an upper-level course in the Real World of Race. Isaiah was a poet, based partly on Leonard, partly on me. (I could not have been wrong.) He rode the Freedom Buses into beatings; he marched with King and had many discussions with him about racism. As he is reciting Sterling Brown's *Strong Men* to a group of civil rights workers on the Tougaloo College campus in Mississippi, he's shot dead by the White Citizens Council. A roaming poet called to the movement by the "essential rightness" of it, Isaiah has a number of affairs and whispers to his women while making love to them: "And there shall come forth a rod out of the stem of Jesse, and a Branch shall grow out of his roots." (Isaiah 11:1)

As Paul's private teacher-tutor-friend, I had failed. Or he had been a poor or unwilling student, or there had been some kind of barrier between our communication.

It was frankly difficult not to be envious. White writers were always running off to Africa, literally and fictionally, to mine for gold. My novels, *Circles Round Saturn* and *The War Has Already Begun,* hadn't even gone into paperback editions, and this was in a time when a good fart could bring fifty biggies without too much trouble.*

We didn't have a chance to talk after his book came out. He was doing a lot of traveling and they were thinking of moving and their two kids kept them busy.

But quite by chance we did meet, at Le Périgord. I was dining with Maxine Culp, who once again was trying to describe for me the "new novel," since, she intimated, it was becoming harder to sell my work. There was a trend riding down on New York, she said. "Books have to be like television shows. They've got to have the same format."

"You mean ninety-six minutes of more or less real stuff and twenty-four minutes for commercials for a two-hour show?"

"Exactly. Hard spots and soft spots. Television has fouled up peoples' attention spans. And the characters can't be subtle; they've gotta be up front and glamorous and tough and, yes, one-dimensional. That's just the way it's getting to be, Cate. No — *thinking*. Cliché, if you will. The good guy, riding high, has a fall. Hell, we know he's going to survive, but how? What new agonies can you come up with to make the eventual triumph all the sweeter?"

"Shit."

Maxine shrugged. "What can I tell you, babes?"

But I was watching a small, jovial bunch pushing into the restaurant, stringing out around a corner, where a large table bore a RESERVED card. Alex Samuels, Bob Kass (beardless, puffy pink, in from Hollywood, I guessed), Mark Medowitz, Jeremy Poode (I'd figured that the two fine ladies were for Bob and Mark; Alex traveled alone), and Selena Merritt and Paul and Betsy.

"Anyway," Maxine said, "I don't like the way they're handling you over at Twentieth Century Forum — " She turned to see what I was watching. Slowly she turned back to me and picked up her drink and sipped it. I felt somehow the way I had when as a kid I heard about a party to which I hadn't been invited.

"Celebration," I said.

"Must be that Book-of-the-Month Club deal," Maxine said.

"Ah," I said.

---

* *Circles* was about the reaction on Earth to a visit from beyond the deep space of Saturn by black people who lived out there. *The War* was about the unofficial declaration by the unofficial National Police Force that the random violence in large U.S. cities, in which substantial numbers of young black people were involved, was really a prelude to *The Race War* predicted by Ronald Segal in 1967.

"Paul got a bundle. They've spotted you," she said, lowering her head, "and they're on the way over."

"Cate!" Betsy was bent over the table, kissing me. Behind me, Paul had gripped my shoulders. "How you doin', man? Guess who's in town? Kass! Remember Bob Kass?"

Grinning, Kass extended his hand. "Cate, it's good to see you again. You've been writing up a storm, man."

Selena, Poode, Alex Samuels, the girls, gathered around, too, and we chatted quickly, effusively, embraced, shook hands, introduced around. Paul said, "Why don't you two join us?"

"Love to," I said, "but Glenn's coming in and I've got to get back."

"It'd be nice," Paul said, "if you could." The others drifted back to their table. He looked uncomfortable standing. He said almost in apology, "Shit, Cate. I'm lucky."

"Aw, no," I said.

"Yeah. You know it. We'll talk soon, okay? Maxine, take care."

When he'd gone, Maxine said, "Is Glenn coming in?"

"No."

"I didn't think so."

"Neither did Paul."

We never saw each other again.

15

"WE'D BETTER get going," Allis said. She'd just glanced at her watch. "I've got a lot to do before tonight and you have to leave early."

We were attending the annual awards dinner of the Center for Black Arts and Letters. Tonight we were going to award posthumously the CBAL literary prize to George Jackson, whose killing on the Coast had sparked the Attica rebellion.

The literary committee, of which I was chairman, two weeks ago had unanimously voted to make the award for Jackson's *Soledad Brothers.* Last week I'd put two days back to back and had taken off for Amos' place in the country to rinse out my head. I was climbing a steep trail, breathing hard but exulting in the vast woodland silence, when suddenly a man stepped out of a clump of white firs just ahead of me. He had moved so quickly and lightly that for a moment I thought I had imagined him. He wore a uniform and there was a badge on his jacket. I didn't know the area well and wondered how he'd got there without coming up the trail I was on.

"Are you Mr. Cato Douglass?"

"Yeah," I said, abruptly aware of the isolation in which we stood studying each other. What had I done? Why were *they* here in the emptiness of Amos' woods? My family! I thought. But I'd called Allis only an hour ago, before starting up. Not that, then. I watched his hands. Shit, if he went for his piece, I'd go for mine. A Western shoot-out on an Eastern mountain. Emmett Till, Medgar Evers, Martin King, Fred Hampton, Mark Clark, among dozens more, and now me. Why? What had I written in my books or said in my classes (he *was* there because of that, wasn't he?) that made them dispatch a hit man to get me?

"I'm Deputy Sheriff Castle. I've got an urgent message for you from Dr. Jasper Mansfield."

Mansfield was the director of the Coalition for the Development of Western Institutions.

"Yeah?" I said. He was, like me, wondering about the mechanism of events that had sent him into the woods to find me. He took a folded paper out of his pocket and gave it to me and started back into the woods.

"That's all?" I moved a couple of steps after him. I could see the trail he'd used.

"Yessir," he said, without turning back.

I sat down on an outcropping of rock and listened to my heart banging away. My hands were shaking. I opened the paper.

Vigorously oppose granting Jackson CBAL lit award. Will cease funding soonest if done. Board directors adamant. Call soonest. Mansfield.

Word of the committee's action had got to Mansfield, who had then called our president, who then had called my home minutes after I'd called Allis. The president called Mansfield back and Mansfield had utilized his own communications system — the county sheriff's office.

Now it was early evening. Mack lay before the television set, basking in his achievement. Allis was getting party-pretty and I was leaving for a meeting with the literary committee, the president and the officers of CBAL. It was showdown time.

We gathered, gowned and tuxedoed, in a private room down the hall from the grand ballroom of the hotel we'd hired. Almost never before in history had so many black artists come together for so singular a purpose — to honor our own, who had been chosen by us, not others, and to speak our words of praise and encouragement. From the start some had felt it to be a mistake to accept any help from whites, fearful that just what was happening would have to happen. Others recited the dreary history of previous failures, mainly for financial reasons, of attempts to form similar organizations. We had all cited the lists of other ethnic groups that had managed to cohere about the issues that concerned them — or had seemed to.

The president and the officers appeared. The president was a preacher.

284

It was rumored that he wished to use his position with CBAL to secure for himself a position as U.S. ambassador to an African country. Any African country.

"Jackson gets it," I said.

"Jackson," Mae Smithers said. She wrote children's books. "We don't have any problems with that at all."

The other committee members said, "Jackson."

The president rolled his eyes upward and sat down heavily. He closed his eyes and then opened them. "I understand where you all are coming from," he said. "But, if CDWI pulls out, we're dead. As Jackson is now. What's the goddamn point you're making?"

One of the officers said, "He was just a small-time punk who got caught and became a folk hero. The kind of man none of you would want in your house."

"Jackson," we said.

"We've got a responsibility to all those other black folk who need encouragement and help, to those nobody ever cared about but us. Think of them. Jackson's *dead.*"

"As long as we think we need their money, they'll pull the strings," Mae Smithers said. "That's what money's all about. Didn't we know that? If we void Jackson this year the way they want, who will they void next year or the next? When do we start saying no?"

The president snorted. "When you're ready to sacrifice and spend your own money — no! no! — I don't want to *hear* that old refrain: black people don't have any money." He leaned forward. "You do what you have to with what you got." He emphasized every word as if reciting poetry set with iambic pentameter.

"Jackson." The name seemed now to embody considerations of the most imaginable range.

Whittington slipped in and took a seat.

"You know what Jackson would say if he could," one of the officers said. "Outslick the pigs. Use them, use their money — "

"That's what *you* say," one of the committee members said. There was laughing. "Jackson knew that everything carried taint."

Stung and exasperated, the president got up, his spare, tall body tightened with anger. "You revolutionary niggers have sure fucked up this gig!"

There was one frightening second of silence in which we must have pondered whether what we had done was right or wrong. I started to say something, but Whittington had leaped to his feet. "Yeah? Well, maybe it needs some fucking up. And maybe we will not be together for the next five hundred years; it may take us that long to learn, but goddamn it, Lem, we're going to give that award to Jackson's mother, to hell with you and CDWI. Attica's happened out there. Maybe he was a crook, but he wrote something that touches us all, black *and* white. And if white people don't recognize that, we certainly must. They killed him like a dog, just the way they can kill any one of us any time they want. Our vote says no; no, they aren't going to do that anymore. Jackson."

"Gentlemen and ladies," the president said, "it's been nice." He stalked out, followed by the officers.

The guests and the honored didn't know as they danced, as they ate, as they applauded the awards, that this was the end of it, of CBAL; that this, too, had been stifled, like so many other ventures.

Like boycotts, prayer meetings and marches, like voter registration drives, like community action groups and community school boards; like writing or painting or playing music, like working to the tune of the Protestant ethic, like —

The jungle has vanished. Still, I'm holding my M-1, and my fatigues are heavy with sweat. I am running down a dark corridor — another one — toward sunlight. I am running as fast as I can, faster, even, my canteen, belt and bush knife beating up blisters in my sides. I'm almost there, impelled by a nameless fear, and just as I reach the threshold, the sunlight vanishes and a darkness without dimension is suddenly there, like something solid and malevolent. I fire at whatever it is, and the bullets ricochet. I whirl and run to another slot of daylight and the same puzzling thing happens; it happens again and again and again. And then as I am racing once more toward yet another opening in what I now realize is a maze, I understand somehow that this is the last, the final, the ultimate opening. I am running with incredible speed. Grenade rings click like castanets on my belt. I sense on this dash that I'm racing against time. I am shouting and cursing as loud as I can; my shoes, barely touching the surface, make booming sounds.

"Honey — ho*ney!* Wake *up!*" Allis said. She was crouched over the lower part of my body, holding my feet.

At the same moment, Mack came running into the room, shouting, "What's that noise? Mom, Dad?"

"Dad had a bad dream."

286

I sat up and groaned.

"It's all right, Mack. Go back to bed," Allis said.

"No," I said. "Come here, Mack."

He came to the bed and I embraced him, hard. "What's the matter, Dad? Are you all right?"

"Yeah. Go back to bed now, okay?"

"When I grow up," he said, "am I gonna have bad dreams, too? I don't wanna grow up if I am."

"Anybody who can ride a bike the way you can won't have bad dreams. Go to bed."

He kissed me and went out, looking backward.

We lay then, face to face. She studied me while I watched her eyes move. "The nightmares you have," she said.

ENDINGS

1

ALLIS' FATHER died. He had hovered through our lives like a fog, with word of his health, or lack of it, seeping into our apartment: a hesitant call from Amy or some other relative, who always suggested that Allis not call him because it would make whatever illness he had at the time worse. Then nothing, until Amy called with word of his death.

Allis had missed the holidays. She was pleased when we were invited to seders — ecstatic when they were first seders. And at Chanukah Mack received his presents, while Allis hummed *A Partridge in a Pear Tree*. Holidays just seemed to run together, Chanukah and Christmas, Easter and Passover. We threw Mack pellets of Blackness and Jewishness. They were his heritage, even if his society would undoubtedly make him the recipient of but one.

Then Amy called.

We went to the funeral and defiantly occupied the family pew. Allis did not cry, but Mack did. He sensed, I think, that something was terribly wrong. We hadn't talked to him about Allis' father; that was to come later, when he would understand such things. Yet there he was, Mack guessed correctly, there in that *box*. Something had passed through his small life and departed before he was even aware of it. That must have frightened him.

Amy was married now and had three kids and was almost three times the size of the woman after whom I'd lusted on that summer afternoon so long ago. Allis carried her figure as though she were twenty — and the relatives must have hated her for that, too.

We drove to the cemetery and Allis, who still had not cried, threw in the first dirt, this only child, and walked fiercely from the grave, Mack and I trailing, and got into the car. She now seemed angry enough to have slammed the door and popped the window, yet she closed it with the greatest care.

"You okay?" I asked as we rode away.

She nodded.

Mack settled in the back seat to take a nap; that was easier than reading.

My thoughts wandered over classroom lectures and piles of papers yet to be graded and *The Pushkin Papers.* That was the title of the novel I was now working on. Teaching does that to the writer, pulls him or her in twenty different directions while insisting that the writer remain superbly sane.

Allis was still silent, and I didn't talk. Grief is a personal thing; everyone who tries to edge into it is a stranger, an intruder.

We were inching along in Long Island Expressway traffic and Allis said, "I'm going away, Cate."

"What?" I was sure I hadn't heard what I'd heard very well.

"I'm going away. I've got to."

"What're you talking about?"

"Going away. That's all."

I considered what she'd said. "Just like that, huh?"

"Yes." She didn't look at me.

"Did I do anything?" I said.

"No. Not lately."

"Then, why, Allis? Whatever it is we can work it out, can't we?"

"I — want — to — go — a-way," she said, bending toward the dashboard with each word.

I think I sighed. Maybe, I thought, it was too much. All the fucking hate all the fucking curiosity all the fucking anxieties all the fucking energy protecting your wife from insults and all *her* energy protecting you from the same. Maybe she was right. Enough was fucking enough. We'd given it a goddamn good shot. There came that time when they had you backed up on the beach with ten thousand miles of ocean behind you, like that guy in the pocket magazine.

"I wish you wouldn't, honey."

"I've just got to."

"I'll take care of Mack, then."

"Yes, I thought you would."

We drove on. Anger whipped at me, and my own grief and self-pity. She was deserting me! She had let *them* beat her. Shit, then maybe she *should* go. Mack woke as we drove down our block, woke up to a car filled with vibrating angers and sadnesses. Upstairs he watched her pack.

"Where're you going, Mom? Dad, where's Mom going?"

His eyes were haunted by the expectation of still another disaster.

"Business trip," she said.

"Mom's got to take care of some things for Grandpa."

"He's dead."

"That's why."

He said, "Well, when — " I led him from the room.

Allis came out with two bags. She set them down and kissed Mack. "Back soon, honey." She picked up the bags again. I moved to open the door for her. I raised her face; we kissed lightly, and she was through it, into the hall. I closed the door and went to the window, where, shortly, I saw her down on the street, hiking toward the corner, her back bent with the weight of the bags, but walking firmly.

She really went, I thought. She's gone.

Mack sat rigidly before the television set. "When's she coming back?"

"It's just a business trip, Mackie. In a couple of days — "

"Then why'd she take *two* suitcases?"

"Because — "

" — and she didn't even take her briefcase!"

"Uh — "

We struggled through what was left of the day, and I finally took refuge in my corner of the bedroom and pulled out *Pushkin*. Mack came in twice, interrupting me. I was up the night, working. I canceled my classes, told the department secretary I was ill. Could anyone cover the class for me? No, I told her; it was too late. I called Mrs. Lee to work something out for the next day and then got Mack ready for school, after a breakfast of cereal and toast. His face was somber when he left to walk the three blocks. His first days there I had slipped out of the building behind him — he had insisted on going alone — ducked in doorways, scanned traffic and every suspicious person who passed him, and sweated and shat until he was safely inside the school. And I did the same when school was out. For days I did that; for days. Now he did it truly on his own.

Alone, I let the exhaustion come; with it came new thoughts. I hadn't asked Allis where she was going. Maybe I should've pleaded more with her to stay. Could she have wanted or needed that? Why hadn't I? Money; had she taken money? Well, she had her own and the plastic.

There came the click of an afterthought: it wasn't like her to just walk away from Mack . . . God! Why hadn't I *stopped* her? I saw her morning face across the table, relaxed with sleep just broken, free of the little furrows and lines that came as the day wore on. I'd been involved with *Pushkin,* Paul's triumphs, my own career, classes — why had I let her walk deeper into the pit into which she'd fallen with her father's death?

I fretted the day away and put on a Chico Marx grin when I heard Mack at the door, and assured him that she would be home in another day or so and that, yes, she had called. He watched "Sesame Street," but he didn't laugh as he usually did. By the time we'd had dinner and he'd bathed and I'd read to him, my face was stiff with the grin. When he was asleep I realized that the grin must have worried him, too.

I worked that night, also, but not well, and I drank more and watched television. I thought of the "book things" I'd go to now, even though I hated them, and of the unending line of coeds I would entice to the apartment — that would show Allis!

I returned to the typewriter, leaned on it and closed my eyes. I thought of Alexander Sergeyevich Pushkin and his forebears who had been slaved out of Africa into Russia, and how his grandfather had become the pet of Peter the Great, and he himself a favorite of Czar Nicholas. *The Blackamoor of Peter the Great.* He'd never finished that novel; perhaps it was too painful. ("I am the ugly descendant of Negroes!") What parallels! I imagined him in the waist-deep snow of a park near the Kamennostrovsky Prospect that morning, with pistol in hand facing Baron Georges-Charles D'Anthès in a duel. Georges Heckeren. Pushkin's wife, Natalya. Indiscretions. Insults. I seemed to see and feel Natalya stroking Pushkin's fevered head, the head that topped the runty body that D'Anthès's ball had shattered. How gently she now stroked this father of the language! And he, in delirium, remembering how he had taken the ball, gone down and then, calling as D'Anthès walked away, "Wait! I feel strong enough to take my shot," and firing, hit D'Anthès in the ribs and arm and was not sorry he had not killed him.

A countervibration. I moved, then started up, bumping the machine and hearing the keys go *click click clung,* stuck, and the margin bell. I grabbed the hand as I whirled, the hand that had been stroking the back of my head, and saw Allis, drained and weak and her eyes brimming with tears.

I held her and she cried as an old, wide stream flows, without sound except for a burble here and there. We stood and held on to each other for dear life, as though God in some ancient vengeance was zooming out of deep space to punish us: *Pushkin* lay every which way — on the floor, the desk. And the typewriter keys remained stuck in their *clung*.

"Where you been?"

"Israel."

"Where?"

"Israel. As soon as I got there, I came right back. I heard you," I thought I heard her say. She fell on the bed. I looked down at her and felt her exhaustion.

"I shouldn't have let you go," I said.

"No. But you couldn't have stopped me either."

"You want to tell me why Israel?" Fleeing back, taking refuge in, I thought, suddenly pissed, Jewishness, whatever that was.

"I can't. I mean, I don't know. I mean, I do, but it doesn't really work that way for me. Is Mack all right?"

"Sure."

"I'm tired, very tired, honey. I want to sleep. It's so good to be home." She closed her eyes. I stood, still looking down at her. "I'm sorry," she said, her eyes closed. "Why did you think I went?"

"Your father's death. Our marriage. Maybe it's all too much — "

She tried to shake her head against the bed. "My father, maybe. Us, never. Never. I knew you'd think that as soon as the plane took off. I knew it. You were wrong. I love you very much. I hope you still love me." Her eyes had not opened.

"Yes, I do, kiddo. I'm glad you're home."

I lay down beside her and felt the warmth of her body. It was a good feeling.

Allis began to breathe deeply. I stood and watched her. Ordinarily when I moved in bed I could hear her breathing pattern change, as though some deeper part of her were listening, as though she felt invisible things in the atmosphere near her. Suddenly, her breathing became rapid and shallow. Was she stumbling along close to the edge of something in her darkness? Fascinated, I moved closer to the bed and watched her more closely through the muted light. I straightened and went into Mack's room and saw him in the tendrils of streetlight that filtered in along the edges of his window shade, his arms thrown back above his head, his sheets wound across him. He seemed very trusting, very vulnerable. Softly, I unwound his sheets and pulled them up. I went out and fixed a long

295

drink in the kitchen and tiptoed back into our room, treading upon *Pushkin,* whose pages were still scattered on the floor. Pushkin: an enemy of the aristocracy, some said, and God. How had he moved through the night, his last night as a whole human, a whole poet? I looked and listened again to Allis. Her body was in a curve, end suggested toward end, and her hands, clasped together, rested near her face.

I slid through near-darkness from room to room, trampling *Pushkin,* feeling carpet and then slick oak-wood flooring underfoot. I felt both like a spy creeping around the edges of their consciousnesses and like a god — Morpheus — prowling carefully through their dreams, ordering them, and I was thinking this with still another drink in my hand, and had not noticed the precipitous break in Allis' breathing, when she said, "Why are you staring at me?"

There was fear in her voice. I quickly sat down beside her and stroked her hair. "No reason. I was just filled with wonder that you went so far and came back."

"How long did I sleep?"

"Only an hour."

She turned. "I'm too tired to undress. Come to bed."

"I'm not sleepy."

She turned back to me. "Don't be angry, honey."

"I'm not."

"Yes, you are."

"Well, why in the hell did you go?" It came out a snarl. She blinked in recoil.

"Guilt — "

"For our marriage?"

"Yes."

"Thanks a lot."

"Not *for* the marriage — "

"What then?"

"For not being the way he wanted me to be — I'm tired, Cate — "

I *knew* all the answers, yet I insisted on her speaking them.

"Me, too." We did not talk for a minute. "Sorry," I said.

"I wanted to do something for him," Allis said. "Give him something; bear witness. I don't suppose you do something like that without hurting someone."

Her hands fluttered wearily on my face. "Do you?"

"No," I said. I did not say that I also had been scared of my life, of Mack's life, without her.

"Can we fight in the morning?" She turned again. In a drifting voice she added, "Okay, Cate?"

She took a very deep breath and it rushed down her throat and windpipe and fluted through her nose in a mighty, indelicate snore — PPPPSSSsssssssssssZZZZZaaaaaAAAAAAAaaaaaaa!

I picked up the sheets of *Pushkin* and under the desk light arranged them. I finished my drink and checked Mack once again and then, fully clothed except for my shoes, fell into the bed beside my wife.

2

A PART OF ME went to my classes the next day, another part stayed with Mack and his delight at Allis' return (we shared this); and, strangely, her departure and return lent tone and new color to the novel through which Pushkin was moving. The difference between an Afro-Russian of the early nineteenth century and an Afro-Anything of historical time ultimately was very small. And still another part of me leaned out toward my students.

These were unlike those at the private branch of the university. I had transferred to this, the public branch, feeling that my true allegiance was to these ethnically fragmented and blue-collared masses. The rich didn't need me, in the correct sense of the word; the masses, I concluded, did.

There was, of course, a trade-off in the transfer. For the administration of this branch, I was, except to a few, unequivocally the showpiece nigger; there was no question as to *who is that nigger?* The answer was everywhere in bulletins, notices, memos and the college paper. This is a nigger who *writes!* In exchange for making the administration look progressive and affirmatively correct, I was given a senior appointment and a neat schedule, which caused (how could it have been otherwise?) considerable antipathy toward me from the assistant and associate professors who were plodding or conniving toward promotion and tenure, which had been mine when I stepped through the door.

At the private branch of the university, though the faculty well knew that I was a Token Negro, they accepted me with a modicum of equanimity, and even on occasion invited Allis and me to their homes. Some may even have felt that it was right for me to have been there, okay for me to insert, just by being present, a little pepper to the salt already on the table. What struck me as being most curious about the matter in both branches was that no one believed I understood what was going on; that I couldn't read between the lines of memos or see around corners or correctly read their eyes or the tones of their voices.

Nor did they seem to understand that I knew what they'd successfully concealed from a multitude of people: the awesome, stunning, horrendous condition of most young Americans who had been, up to the point where I met them, poorly educated, miseducated and / or programmed not to know very much about themselves, their nation or the world. The plan seemed to be to keep them precisely that way. There were two massive barriers — most of the teachers and the teaching, and the thorough and wayward preconditioning of the students.

Of course, most of the students had never studied with a black teacher and therefore, despite the sparkling ambience that indicated it was quite all right to do so, were, at least for the time being, suspicious.

(Who's *that* turkey? Who's *that* nigger? Hey! What's the name of *this* game? Professor *Who?* Dude don't look heavy to me. Ain't this sho nuff some shit? A *brother!* What, goddamn it, can a *black* man teach me? My, my, my, this teacher shouldn't be so tough; after all . . .)

They didn't trust Open Admissions any more than they'd trusted anything else in their battered lives, but they wished to, yes; within each of them there existed that pinhole of hope that there were still lyrical possibilities they might experience. So they congealed in the classrooms like a multicolored swamp, or flowed like an unnamed South American river, thick and turgid, through the hallways, now bright, now heaving and menacing.

These Afro-Americans, Puerto Ricans, Colombians, Ecuadorians; these East Indians and West Indians and Haitians; these Italo-Americans and Middle Europeans and Chinese and Japanese and Arabs and half-generation Greeks; these last of the shanty Irish, Jews and Portuguese — they all wished. Not infrequently, the students could have been the parents of the teachers, for we were also splintered by age. Old men and old women tottered through the halls, their faces bright with expectation and self-adulation. This branch of the university was like the last train to the Dream, the Mirage, the Illusion, and everyone was climbing aboard; no one wanted to be left behind, not even the policemen, firemen and sanitation men who were wringing out the last of their G.I. Bill benefits for service from the Korean War through Vietnam.

It all looked good; the administration's statistics must have sparkled and brought tears to the eyes of the old-line liberals who had not yet deserted the frigate. But the men's rooms' walls (and for that matter, I assumed, the ladies') concealed from the not very inquisitive eyes of the administration and the Board of Upper Education a very old condition:

Down with niggers! Lynch niggers! The KKK is cuming for all niggers at this colege. Jews eat shit! Suck my dick! (Love to!) Kikes! Porto Rikans eat coconut-flavored monkey shit! So's yer Mama! Piss in your hat, Greek! Ginny fuckers! You all eat shit! West Indians stink! Chinese eat crossways pussy! (Love to!) America for whites! You can have the motherfucker, honky! Down with niggerdom! And up your ass! Call Richie: 935–3344 — anything goes! Yeah, but where? Down with Open Admissions! Hitler was right! Not right enough! Here I sit, broken hearted . . .

It had been discovered that about two of every ten students could write the English language well enough to be understood, which was the primary reason for launching that vast vessel, *Remediation,* down the ways. It was also decided that creative writing, telling stories — their own, someone else's — or just *creating* them, would help unlock the great door to writing expression and comprehension. Since there had been a heavy emphasis during the Rebellions on the strength and durability of the oral tradition, most students, whatever their background, approached any kind of writing with distinctive reluctance, if not open hostility. There are ages that demand great speakers and those that demand great writers. We were in the latter, still dribbling down from New England, "a culture so exclusively one of books that it had grown incapable even of appraising the worth of other modes of expression." And this at a time when few books were read. Visions must have lingered in the heads of students of the Great Rappers: Jesus, Mohammed, El Cid, Martí, Lenin; of stump and pulpit oratory, of griots and walking repositories of dirty limericks, of George Patton, Churchill and Hitler, of Darrow and La Follette, of King.

We insisted that they learn to write and to comprehend what was written.

I worried about them; I worried about reaching and touching them. They'd been hurt so much and so often that I could see the anticipation of hurt once again etched in secret lines on their faces. I carried them home with me and they warred for my time with my family and my real work, and when the battle became too much, too hot (I could smell the wires burning), I decided to keep notes so that later I could write a book about them and the university — which my colleagues believed I was doing anyway.

I'd explained this to Allis, and she too thought I should keep notes until I had the time to write about it. In the days following her return when I fretted over her and we beat our way back to each other, I started to catch up on the notes. They were there, right at the top of my skull:

The new main building, rebuilt around the shell of an old factory, is all yellow, red and white inside, filled with the bright sunlight that floods through the skylight on the roof of the main corridor. Outside, the building is a smooth, brown structure. There are no windows. It resembles, almost, a prison. It is curious these days, how many buildings are constructed to reject, rather than embrace, nature. I can understand why the most modern buildings in photographs from Israel look like fortresses. But who is the enemy here?

It is the final day of September, the starting day of classes for the new school year.

We have already had some faculty meetings at which the president and the dean of faculty spoke. As usual, there is a shortage of money; both officials address themselves to that situation. They are relying on grants; we're supposed to think up gigs that will bring in the bread. They also talk about standards. Increased enrollment. "Our" students. The teachers ask their usual questions, foremost among them how they can handle student evaluations of their teaching. Students, of course, can state on official forms whether they rated their teachers good, bad or indifferent. Teachers do worry about the evaluations because the university administrators can use them to deny tenure, promotion or reappointment. It makes no real difference what the forms say: interpretation and by whom is at the crux of all.

A couple of low-level administrators have been moved up to deanships. It is said that we once had so many deans that even the student paper finally complained. A year or so later, a purge of deans occurred. It was a matter of the budget.

After the branch-wide meeting, there are a series of Professional Development workshops. I have never figured out the worth of such meetings. But I go to a couple. One is about videotaping a teacher in the classroom. She says that, on replaying the tape, she was able to see why she was not reaching certain students. She says this with great flair and sincerity. It is bullshit, Doublespeak, but the administrators are all smiles. The second workshop is even more of a tap dance. I don't stay there long, either.

The English department is meeting this afternoon. I check to make sure that I have a desk, typewriter, chair, file and bookcase. You have to double-check everything. Budgets make things vanish. And people.

With holidays and the exam period, classes will run here something just short of ten crowded, intense, gut-churning weeks. We are on the quarterly system. During this time, students who have learned little or nothing during twelve or fifteen years of previous schooling, will be expected to become (but not really) proficient in writing and comprehending the English language. Some will have the Fundamental English requirement waived and will thus escape twenty weeks' study. They will have to take Basic English for one quarter, ten weeks; but clearly, we simply cannot undo in ten, twenty or thirty weeks what has been done over a span of fifteen years. Our mandate, however, is to try.

Both the public and many of the students believe that the branch population is composed mainly of the various colored peoples. The university has done nothing to dispel such thought. The ethnic population, however, is 44 percent white, 32 percent black, 11 percent Puerto Rican, 4 percent Oriental and 9 percent "other." Sixty-seven percent of the students are female, 33 percent male. Fifteen percent are not U.S. citizens, and 68 percent come from families earning under $10,000 a year.

The heat and air conditioning are controlled automatically through a central system that, on this extremely warm September day, is overheating. It is a brand-new system; taxpayers have paid hundreds of thousands of dollars for it. It does not work.

Everything is chaos: rosters, room assignments, departmental guidelines (which are changed every year), phone hookups, secretaries, book orders — all these undone tasks and missing people and equipment fail to daunt anyone's spirit. On the first day, all things are possible, all things. Even the question of parking, at $55 per quarter, elicits no grumbling. For three quarters of the year, it will cost the faculty 165 smackers.

I don't know what the administration does with the parking money. I park on the street. There were no such charges at the private branch of the university.

I warn my students that, though they may have taken rinky-dink courses with rinky-dink teachers, I and what I teach will definitely be different. I pass out the class outlines. You must establish your class regs early on; perimeters must be fixed. You tell them what pages to read, the number of papers due, your office hours — the usual. (One teacher, who is taking his case to court, was fired because he did not affix to his office door, or pass out, his office hours. I think they just wanted to fire him.)

I have loaded the students with paper. The university generates a lot of paper. If other universities generate half as much as we do, there won't be a tree left standing in the United States in another century. I would be a very rich man if I sold paper to this institution. It snows paper in this place.

Mike Z. is clever; he wears a backpack to put his student papers in.

Did I say it snowed paper? No. What we really have is an avalanche.

I admire most of the authors who have undertaken to write textbooks that purport to show people how to write and understand their language. There must be at least fifty on the market. And I envy the publishers that have made millions producing such books. If I could paste together such crap, think of it: Allis and I would be stinking rich!

Perhaps all these fine textbooks on how to teach basic skills are invaluable elsewhere, in other colleges. But we are limited by time and the structure of the branch programs to weeks — not months or years — so these books do not work. Those students who do manage to get through the remedial courses do so only when compared with their peers — who have done worse — not with the great, demanding outside world. Very few of the students have had good secondary educations and so the task set for college-level teachers all over the nation is all but unachievable. One must ask what all those secondary teachers — many of those secondary teachers — have been doing for so long to have produced these generations who often cannot work at their grade and age levels.

One of the answers, I am beginning to believe, is bureaucracy. Forms. Filling out papers. Meetings. School boards. Going through channels, which are wide, deep and treacherous. Things must be done by the book. One must make copies of memos and letters in order to *prove* that a thing was done. It's the old army game: CYA — cover your ass. Generate paper.

Teaching may once have been a career. Today it's just a job, and within certain systems the salaries and fringe benefits are unequaled. Who would wish to lose these? Who in a tight teacher's market would protest the system that is more involved with politics and bureaucracy than with education, when one has a family, a mortgage and maybe even a track on tenure?

My colleagues in the English department are mostly Ph.D.'s, and those who are not are always being urged to complete their work for the degree or to publish or both. The Ph.D.'s are of course specialists — but nearly all of them teach remedial writing, and they do it on the whole without too much complaining. They know that no one without a Ph.D. will be hired, and they also know that there aren't too many colleges around the country with vacancies in English departments. The kids seem to have caught on to the bullshit, and enrollments in English departments are dropping like frozen eagle turds. But there must exist a basic tension between these doctors of philosophy and their students. The teachers must once have dreamed of teaching wholly or nearly literate students on campuses wide with green lawns and proud Gothic towers, all overseen by benign administrators eager to shower prestige upon them. And why not such dreams? They studied long and hard at great expense in time, money and stress. Now, here they are, some "retrenched" at other colleges and then "detrenched" here. If they are happy, it is only because they can now feed their families, but at the end of a difficult week, bent with exhaustion, their nerves shattered by the deluge of papers, student and administrative demands, it is easy to see by the look in their eyes that just having this job is but a small part of being happy.

I have an ex-con in one of my classes. This is not the first time; the branch is involved in a prison program. This guy is in his thirties, does not attend regularly, does not do his work, but still manages to exude a sense that he is being injured. He does, however, make all the student dances and is considered to be a student leader. The students seem to forget that he is a grown man. He mentions, as many cons do, "taking a fall." This is really to intimidate students and faculty alike. He blames his problems on personal troubles, and I suggest that he see his counselor. We have lots of counselors but perhaps only one out of every ten of the six thousand students knows who his or her counselor is.

Speaking of con, the students have plenty of it, allowing their parents to die each and every quarter to explain absences.

Mabel is not one of these. She is in my Creative Writing class. Mabel is a young married, with two kids. She is vivacious and she teases. She gives me lingering looks and sits too close to me when we discuss her poetry, which, if not all that great (she is still learning to maintain metaphor, build on it, and to tighten her lines and focus imagery, and to *know* things), is radiant with *soul* and an often irritatingly buoyant view of life, trillingly broadcast over the campus, through the halls. I have given her to read Tolson, Hughes, Hayden and Brooks, and I have given her tapes to listen to. If I had not had the experience with Raffy, I would have an experience with Mabel.

I envy her husband and fear for him. Mabel is so hungry to know and to write. She will not be subservient; she will know and she will write, whether she is ever published or not.

My black students worry and puzzle me. With but a few exceptions they have all been singed, seared or severely burned. They have cooled their bop; they have muted the con, and when they have to, they buckle down.

Most students, at least after the first year, approach their studies with the airs of players in a game. They aren't remotely serious, but then most students are not serious people and college *is* a game. White students do better at it because they've more innate, subconscious practice. They know what the game's about. Black students know a game's being played, but prefer to disbelieve the Ashanti proverb *It is the fool who proclaims the insults are not meant for me but for my colleagues.* They don't even work hard in Black Studies courses, perhaps because they have absorbed white reservations about their validity.

To see them is to understand (how bleak is the view!) how effectively — God, how very effectively — racism in all its relentless, insidious forms, education foremost among them, has hacked and stabbed and butchered their psyches. They enter the game and know they will not win. What's to win? How *can* they win? They pierce the bullshit and tread water, waiting, hurling tired old sixties' phrases hither and yon in the classrooms. They wait in the corners of time like spiders, Anansis, hanging from slender threads sent swinging back and forth in any kind of wind.

White teachers seem to be giving even the most ineffectual black students A's and B's. If the teachers are not throwing around A's, some of them seem to go to the other extreme: a nonwhite student could not possibly earn more than a C in a course. Yes. But these black students who are sliding on shit depress me. I see them a few years down the line, having smacked the wall, backing away, murmuring, "I be goin' to figure this out." It will be stress time again and the level of frustration and anger will have to be a thousand times higher than it was in the sixties. ("But right now," Glenn had said, "with equal opportunity and affirmative action and this and that, you can't walk anywhere downtown without the head hunters from the big corporations boiling out of their company cars to put the arm on any black cat who looks good in a three-piece suit and has been anywhere *near* a college. They don't care if he can't talk or write. Just stick him near a door so people can see him, and trot him out for the company pictures in the advertising." Glenn, though his book isn't yet finished, sold it just before graduating. We celebrated with lots of champagne and then he and I drank up and down and across the Village, where he has moved. He doesn't seem so much like a son now, but another man of whom I am very fond.)

I was asked today why I kept all the books publishers send to college teachers, and I said that I just liked having books the way some people liked having money. My colleagues advised me to put all the books in a shopping bag and carry them down to Barnes & Noble and sell them.

I mentioned to a colleague that I think the dean of faculty uses a hidden tape recorder, like a President who was all over the news not so long ago. The dean takes no notes when you talk to him. He seems to listen intently (though nothing ever comes from the meetings). The next time I go in to see him, he takes notes on a yellow pad.

There was a shoot-out in the cafeteria today. No one seems to have complete details. One student was shot in the leg and he limped away. The security is beefed up. The guards wear guns. Guns? In a college?

The branch has no money, say the deans, to send participants to the Modern Language Association annual meeting in New Orleans this year. They suggest that those who were invited to serve on panels pay their own way. Colleges look for, indeed need, the prestige their faculty members can bring to the institutions by participating in such conferences. The deans press faculty to present papers, and some of the faculty *need* to present papers to stay in the struggle for promotion and / or tenure. It's all extra work for the faculty as well as extra expense. But they do it. Colleges get puffed and professors get a blurb in the annual report.

3

"HONEY! Pick up the *phone,* will you! It's Roye Yearing!"

I stared at her and wondered why she was shouting. She stared back. I felt like a stranger who had stumbled into this corner of our bedroom and seated himself in this chair before the typewriter and a sawed-off, propped-up door that was a desktop. I forgot, and it bothered me, what I was doing. "Who?"

Yes, I thought. The phone; it was sitting right next to the typewriter. I had heard a sound.

"Roye Year-ing! Who'd you think, one of those bitches?"

I wondered again why she was shouting and looking at me so strangely. "You don't have to shout," I said. What bitches?

Allis backed away. "What's wrong?"

But I was on the phone. "Roye. Hi. Can you do it?"

He said he could. Allis eased out of the room.

Roye had published three very good novels between, I'd heard, drinking himself into oblivion and drying out. They had cast him, nevertheless, into that special literary purgatory where, while highly esteemed, he was ignored.

He was saying that he could join the Writing Festival the university was allowing me to plan in an attempt to make it look more like a college than a factory.

"What do you want me to do, Cate?"

"The usual. Read something already published or in progress. 'In progress' makes people think they're in on the delivery — "

"Oh, shit, I got something. I've always got something."

There seemed to be some great distance between us, a void over which our voices carried in echoes, like one of those coast-to-coast calls where your voice seems to bound out against the Kennelly-Heaviside layer and drift languidly back. It wasn't the connection. "We can give you four bills," I said. "None of that high-brow, low-brow shit; everybody gets the same."

"Okay by me. You want something back?"

"No. Hell no."

"Just asking. You know how it goes sometimes. Hey, what do you get these days? You mind my asking? I know we're starting to sound like a couple of whores — "

"Aren't we?" I didn't want to tell him, though, nothing was that great anymore. During the Rebellions the honoraria were ridiculous, often more for my two hours (or less) than my father earned in half a year. They had fallen to realistic levels. "I get about the same," I said, "and expenses."

"I don't suppose your buddy Cummings'll be there. Must be drinking with another crowd. Who else you got?"

"You're the first, Roye."

"Okay. You'll send me a letter, like official, huh, and let me know who else'll be there?"

"Why? So you can back out if you don't like somebody?"

"Naw. I wouldn't do that. I know people do it all the time, but I wouldn't." He laughed. "Shit, I don't get invited to do this too often. I can't be fuckin' choosy."

I hung up and tried to remember what I'd been doing. I knew what it was, but I couldn't get my head to say it. I had tilted my head back in exasperation when I became aware of Allis behind me, and, strangely, as soon as I saw her, I smelled dinner cooking. I turned.

"How's he?"

"Sounded okay," I said.

She came closer and sat on the edge of the bed.

"Are *you* all right?"

"Yeah, sure. Why do you keep asking?"

She had never sat so straight. "The phone, honey. It's right under your nose — "

And then I heard myself, again like an echo. "I don't have time anymore. I forget things. I don't *listen* to things. I didn't used to be like this. I don't know what happened or what's happening. I can't believe I didn't hear the phone or pick it up — "

"Take a leave from classes."

"What?"

"Take a — "

"Yes! Why the hell didn't *I* think of that? Jesus Christ, I'm not *locked* physically into the goddamn place. I could finish *Pushkin* and start on this other thing — "

"*What* other thing? You didn't tell me — "

"Something running around in my head with the name *Unmarked Graves* . . ."

The ideas, at first benign as butterflies, monarchs perhaps, having come such a long way, such delicate things that their migratory patterns are disbelieved, and then they become as insistent as gnats, but they are only that, and in the solitudes the ideas come like anopheles, singing through darkness, yet solitude often equals vulnerability, and the ideas become little nudgings, small impacts, meteorites on an uncharted spatial body, but the impacts leave craters, shape, form, dimension, out of which some clumsy thing evolves and then becomes a myriad of furiously growing fetuses, demanding, within their term, form, voice, and they force themselves through the head, that enclosure wherein reside a trillion neurons, and there they swell, bloat, kick against the sacs of confining time and form of expression; they surge, insist that they must be set free, must be let out, and some, of course, surge more powerfully than others and their language can almost be heard, their color can almost be seen, their histories almost documented, as they clamor and clamor, like children wishing to help; here comes one bearing plot, another returning because motivation has been found wanting, here one rushes with characterization well-honed, while still another shouts, "Why not have me do this? Why not have her do that?" And others cry, "Yes, but first she must do this or say that . . ." And they keep coming without regard for time, sometimes early in the morning, masquerading as an urgent need to urinate, but they simply wish to test the purity of their being, and at the most unconscionable moments they send the mass of protoplasm in which they reside reeling through gazetteers, biographical dictionaries, atlases, all kinds of books, novels, even, having cunningly and finally triggered —

"CATE! Listen." She was on her knees beside me, the lovely swell of her thighs showing. "You have to take a break — "

"Yes, but if I can just hold together until the end of the school year — "

"What do you mean, 'hold together'? What are you saying? Listen, honey, there's Pop's money, and we never use what I earn — "

"It's not the money — "

"I know that, but it's there. Honey, you simply cannot do it all."

I did not know why there was suddenly a small, hard frown in the middle of her forehead. Precisely in the middle. "Dinner's ready. Shall I get you a drink?"

Mack had gone off to sleep quickly, as though escaping from something. Allis had collapsed in front of the television set. I didn't think she was watching Channel 13. Mack thought that was the only channel we watched. I stood hunched over the desk. What? I asked myself. Papers? Get a lesson together? *Pushkin? Unmarked Graves?* More notes on the branch? Pay bills? Do nothing? How often had that thought cropped up. How does one do *nothing?* A poem, perhaps? Was there something we should be talking about? Were there meetings scheduled for tomorrow? It would be nice to take a leave. Marvelous.

"What's the matter, honey?"

I had not heard her coming through the halls.

"Nothing. Just trying to decide what to do now."

"Do you know how long you've been standing there?"

"Sure. I just got here." Jesus.

She said softly, "It's been an hour, Cate."

Then I had done it. Nothing. For an entire hour. I looked at her; she seemed cautious about approaching me.

"An hour?"

"Yes."

"Are you sure?"

"Yes."

"Shit." I sat down. "You made that up."

Now she came closer. "Look at your watch, honey."

She was right.

Something was wrong with me, but I did not know what. I mean, I thought I knew, though I did not know precisely. What I mean to write is that I thought I knew precisely, but did not know how to translate it into the only language I knew well. *Mal au coeur? Mal de siècle?*

I needed a *langage,* a "deep talk," to explain it; I knew none even though I felt I did. It simply would not come. *Blues.* An inexplicable exhaustion. An icterus like a veil over everything.

My family, the world, and sometimes even I, stood at a distance from me, separated by some force field through which neither I nor they could pass. They seemed not to notice; I was, however, fearfully aware of the partition and wondered what it meant.

4

MY WRITERS CONFERENCE goes well. How could it not? Instead of ice water, I had had vodka placed in the pitchers. Maxine Culp — who, though still agenting (and apparently doing less and less — she is seldom in her office when I phone, and writers get restless when their agents are not around), has just published one of the new breed books, *The Sex Life of Senior Citizens* — agreed to come. She looks like a slightly aging vamp just redone for the new tits-and-ass shows that are beginning to bombard television. She is a great counterpart to Selena Merritt, who came, as I correctly calculated, because her publicity had fallen off a little. She's dressed in a style somewhere between the latest rock things and the newest fashion craze, disco. Behind the large place card for Paul Cummings the chair is empty. I guess I am still recovering from the telegram advising me that he couldn't come. There's something final, sinister, in his not calling me. I don't think I wanted it to be like this. Roye Yearing looks the same — gray and the way he would look, I suppose, emerging from a five-day drunk. We are displayed, all in a row like talking dolls. We first chat for the people. Then Maxine reads ("I am also a poet") some very bad poetry with a great deal of vodka-inspired fire and draws great applause. Roye lurches to the mike, gurgling and gargling in his throat as if on the verge of puking clear to the last row and reads from his fiction a biting, snapping section about an old woman being murdered in a corner of a subway station while a transit cop a hundred yards away, around a corner, prays that there will not be any action on his shift. Selena gives a solid performance, sliding to the lectern as applause dies for Roye. She should have been on the stage. Her pauses are chasms across which you are suspended until, almost whispering, as if in afterclimax, she brings you on across and lands you gently on the other side. Too much. She gets a rousing ovation. And I have to follow her. I read from *The Pushkin Papers*. Usually I do not read very well, feeling reticent about speaking words that are intended for inner ears. Some violation there, if you were not a poet, it seemed to me. But I confess to being completely drawn to the performances. Oh, I was not into the thunder-whisper routine of Selena, nor the cutesy-poo act of Maxine (who, I hoped, would not forget that it was I who gave her her first opportunity to read in public) nor a deadly serious, slightly nervous imitation of Roye. I don't know in fact what I did, but at one point my words seem to leap clear out across the audience, unencumbered by nasty little inattentions or anti-vibrations. Politicians and stage actors know the feeling; it is, I supposed, addictive. The audience is mine for moments; I own it perhaps even as Pushkin might have.

I hate to lose students. Some I see struggling with the work, sitting, or trying to sit, aloof from the class. I ask them to come around to the office — I have seen in their work perhaps a little blaze being buffeted by strong winds. But they don't come. I encourage: give them C's when they should have had D's, and D's when they should have had F's, but that doesn't work. Often I am angered by students. I digress to tell them about the *real* world and how it really does expect them to fail and how they are *programmed* to fail, and I try to explain that we are *both* accidents and that we'd better do something about it. Most often, nothing works and one day they simply are no longer in class, and I stare over at the empty seat — and feel very, very tired.

A large number of my colleagues, rushing through the halls or, if they are males concentrating on what they are doing at the urinals, see only my color and, thinking I am a student, rush by or finish pissing. Perhaps I am being charitable. One whom I will call Shorty, however, never uses a urinal if I am using one. He curls away into one of the stalls, often breaking off in the middle of a piss to do so. Maybe he's afraid that I will, like the field judge in a professional football game, call for a measurement.

The year approaches its end. We are all exhausted. We scream at each other at meetings. We dash to the nearest bar for triple martinis, which are gulped like cold beer on a hot day. A few people have been fired: the poet who one day taught his class in the nude, the fine young playwright who was functionally illiterate when it came to teaching, the four teachers caught in a daisy chain in the rear of the theater. There are exit exams to make sure the remedial students know what they were supposedly taught.

A couple of walls fell down during Della K.'s class yesterday. Fortunately they are made of cheap wallboard, so, though people were startled, they were unhurt.

It is the time of the year when students roam the halls and campuses looking for their teachers. They wait on long lines to get into their offices. They have suddenly realized that they are flunking a course. The student con is heavy. Plagiarized papers inundate the office. But there are some good ones, too.

Happy seniors roam the halls. I know most of them. They think they are ready; they have been led to believe that they are ready for graduate schools, work, whatever. They have accumulated grade points, yes, but they have not accumulated knowledge, for the most part, and much of that is our fault and some of it is theirs. The world will either devour them or absorb them; if they are absorbed, then they will not count on those coming after having much education either. Either way, we all lose.

When I was a kid and had a good teacher, I assumed that the world I would enter had to be like her or him, just plain good. Of course, I had been misled. After those good teachers they must've turned all bad. Most of them are here. They are broken down into cliques; they drift through the halls into one another's office to gossip, plot, connive. They vote in blocs, rejecting and accepting on whim, it seems, voting naturally for what they want, even to the extent of calling in people who are on sabbatical to give them strength. Ditto when voting for what they will not have. They stand astride the paths to promotion and tenure like a collective monster. We are not educating; we are exercising power or fending it off, just like everyone else. We pretend, however, that we are *not* like everyone else; we are scholars, educators, etc.

There is shock on the campus today. I know what has caused it. I heard it on the radio. Mabel was murdered by her husband last night.

Then he dismembered her — he was Set to her Osiris — with a chain saw and scattered her into the East River. He was caught doing it. Mabel might have been a fair poet, the kind who always has lines ready at community functions. She would not have been exceptional. What really mattered, though, was that she had the soul of a poet. I think now her soul is free. When she trills now over the heads of the oozing, multicolored swamp, over the heads of the turgid South American river, we will hear her only in our minds.

Some of my colleagues are talking about the murder. One laughs and says, "What else did you expect from these animals?"

5

I WANT to go away from it all, the branch, the books, the bullshit. I feel myself drowning in it, but I have no place to go to, no Israel, and I have been to Africa. I feel a great pain in a painless limbo — and this strange, demeaning exhaustion. I don't understand it. (But I do, I do.)

"There's no book in it," I said to Allis. "What could I say? How would I write it? And who would give a damn about a thirty-year-old woman who was black and wanted to be a poet?"

It was a week after Mabel's murder and we were sitting in the living room, the paper and a magazine opened to profiles of Paul Cummings.

Mack came in. He was uncomfortable with silences. "What's the matter?" His asking was cautious: *Don't tell me if it's too bad.*

"Nothing," I said.

He peered at me. "You look tired, Dad. You look tired all the time. Right, Mom?"

"Well . . . yes and no . . ."

"So nothing's the matter?" Mack said without waiting for an answer, and left the room.

Allis said, "You need to slow down, rest, honey."

"I'm all right."

316

"You may think so. You haven't been giving Mack a lot of time, either — "

"There's only so much goddamn time I can give to anyone — "

" — and you're always shouting at something or someone — "

"What is this?"

"I'm saying you need a break! Take a leave from school!"

"I keep telling you I am all right!"

She leaped to her feet and swept the paper and the magazine to the floor and remained there, crouched over, daring me to do or say anything about it. In measured tones she said, "Cate, you cannot see yourself; you cannot see how you are, and I am serious, damn serious, about you slowing down."

"Well, Allis, I just don't see — "

"For one thing, those nightmares of yours are coming more and more often. And Mack's right. You look like hell . . ."

"Okay," I said. "Okay. Lemme think about it."

So I bought a small peace for the rest of the evening, but I was also suspicious that Allis was right. If so, I wished to conceal from her what I considered to be a weakness. How could I have let all this shit get to me, eh?

I was still wondering about it when, later, Mack in bed, the doorbell gave off its harsh sound somewhere between a ring and buzz. We looked quickly at each other, wondering who it could be, which neighbor, which stranger from the street ringing at the wrong doorbell, which tenant gathering signatures for a petition not to go or to go co-op.

"Who the hell can that be?" Allis said and got up. I drifted along behind her. She snatched the door open and planted herself in the doorway.

Mr. Storto stood there, dressed all in black and holding a bouquet of street-corner yellow roses and a brightly wrapped bottle that had to be wine.

"Oh! Mr. Storto! Come in." She backed out of the doorway and he entered, an inquisitive little smile on his face. He was wearing his battle ribbon. Allis kissed him and he thrust the bottle and the flowers into her arms. He smiled at me; his glance lingered on my face.

"So, here I am at last."

I shook his hand and said, "Come sit down. So you finally came north."

"Yeah." He glanced around. "Nice place."

"It's all right. Can I get you some wine?" It was almost eleven.

"A little glass."

"I'll get it, honey," Allis said from the kitchen.

"You take a bus, subway or taxi, Mr. Storto?"

"A cab. It's been a long time. They're expensive."

"Yeah."

"How's the little boy?"

"Okay."

"Glenn?"

"Okay."

"You don't look too hot, Mr. Douglass."

"He's tired, Mr. Storto," Allis said. She came out with wine for all of us and the flowers in a vase.

Mr. Storto slapped his forehead with the palm of his hand. "You know, I forget that people go to bed — I'm so used to staying up — "

"It's all right," I said. "Here's to your very first visit."

Mr. Storto saluted with his glass and sat back. "Look, my friends, I'm gonna go back to Italy."

"Italy," Allis said. "But why?"

"Well, let's just say it's time for me to go."

I said, "Do you have family there?" He'd never mentioned family. He looked a little tired himself and thin.

"Naw. A couple of friends who went back. I decided that I didn't wanna die here."

"What's this dying business?"

He shrugged his great, bulky shoulders. "We all gonna die an' I'm closer to it than some people an' I don't wanna do it here, is all."

"Are you ill?" Allis asked. Her voice was gentle.

"I got a tumor in the belly. I don't wanna operation here. I'm gonna go home."

"This *is* your home," Allis said. I could see that she was close to weeping again.

"When?" I asked.

"Tomorrow."

Allis gasped. "But what about the house and — "

"I sold the whole damn thing."

"After all these years in America, Mr. Storto — " I began.

"Yeah, sure," he said, laughing abruptly, mirthlessly. "America. I came here an' worked hard, married, lost my wife, lost my boy to still another war, an' took his insurance money an' my savings an' bought a house, then a bigger house an' then a building — our building. An' that's all; that's my life in America. No book in that, hah, Mr. Douglass?" He

318

studied his glass. "So, I came to say goodbye. I'll write, I guess. Maybe not."

"We'll write," Allis said. She hesitated. "We didn't know about your wife and son."

"Some things, what's the good of talkin' about them? It'd be nice hearin' from you. Send me pictures of the boys, too, all right?" He got up slowly and stood solidly, studying the room.

"You're sure?" Allis asked.

"Sure I'm sure."

"Would you like to take a look at Mack? He's sleeping, but that's all right," I said.

"Yeah," he said, with a grin that was wan and gray.

We clustered around Mack's bed like three spirits, peering down at him in silence, and then we tiptoed out.

"Big," Mr. Storto said. "An' he's a good boy. It's said that Garibaldi was married to a black woman from South America." He mused. "I suppose there's more of it than we could guess. Did you know the Moors were as far north in Italy as Rome? Sicily, forget it." He looked around. "Well."

Allis went to him and he opened his arms. He patted her on the back. Even in my — what could I call it — *state,* whatever it might be called (and I was beginning to suspect that I was in some kind of *state*), I knew that Allis was thinking of fathers, fathers dying, fathers going, and as I looked at Mr. Storto's full and wrinkled face and the water starting to rise, slowly, imperceptibly, a hydrostatic leaking in his eyes, he said, "So. Here is a daughter and here is a son. A Jew and a black with an Italian father who could be both an' more." He patted her again. "Then why is this place such shit, where such bad things can happen?"

"I'll walk with you to the corner," I said.

"No." And he embraced me with a force that took my wind and then he stood back. "I know: muggers, junkies, thugs — but this is my city. Was my city, an' I'm not afraid, Mr. Douglass. Only those rats I told you about. Nothing else."

We did walk him to the elevator. When the door closed to take him down, he was standing very erect.

When we were in bed, I could tell that Allis was thinking of Mr. Storto. She sighed. She turned and twisted. Finally she said, "Are you awake?"

"Yes."

"I didn't know he was that sick. He didn't look it."

"I didn't either. No, he didn't."

"And a wife and a son he never talked about. Only his brother."

"I think maybe he didn't want pity, honey."

"I guess."

I wrapped my arms around her. "It means something that he came, darling. You know that."

"I know, but it's flaking off here and there — "

"What?"

I felt her shrug. "Life. People we knew. Things. Please, Cate. I do want you to take the time off. We're all of us so vulnerable."

"I promised to think about it, right? Don't fret."

In mid-June I did take my first leave from the university. I hadn't thought I'd have to. I believed that even with book orders to fill and lessons to plan and working on *Pushkin* and outlining *Unmarked Graves* and batting out a couple of article assignments, I'd have time to recover, as teachers sometimes do, and be chafing to hit the classroom once again in September. Time would have ceased to enclose me in a warp. I would hear the phone ringing, even a block away. I would no longer smell things burning that I could not find afire in the apartment.

It did not turn out that way.

Allis said that morning that the temperature was to go up into the 80s. But I felt cold. She was off to a conference downtown with some political P.R. people who wanted to raise money for their client. Allis had been doing a lot of that lately; it seemed to be the newest thing, and she preferred it to raising money for hospitals and private schools and churches, which always somehow seemed to miscalculate her 15 percent. On the other hand, she didn't much like the politicians either.

Mack would be going to a school picnic. He seemed to be as excited as I remembered being as a kid when it was time for the Sunday school picnic.

I remember feeling sharply lonely. I had the feeling as I looked out the window toward the Park (we had moved upstairs to a larger place and another few yards of Park view) and thought how green it was. I went suddenly from being chilly to roasting. Flames burned up and down my body. I could almost see them. My body was being seared and fried. I couldn't breathe. I stood there until I melted toward the floor. My flesh seemed to be dropping away from my skeleton, the way I once had seen flesh separate from the body of a Japanese soldier caught in the blast of a marine's flame thrower.

And yet things in the apartment maintained their usual inanimate serenity. I was at and was the center of destruction. I must have blacked out.

I heard Latin music echoing up between the buildings. I lay where I'd fallen, and listened, thinking that Allis and the weatherman had been right: it was hot today. I felt extremely tired but knew of no reason why I should be *that* tired. I rolled over and struggled to sit up. I don't know how long I stayed in that position. Allis found me like that.

When she asked in a tremulous voice what I was doing on the floor, I said, "Thinking." She knelt and looked closely at me. I didn't like what I saw on her face and I said quickly, "I think you're right. I'm going to take a leave."

Her look softened; the fright faded a little. She sat down beside me. "Let's travel," she said.

"No," I said. We were holding hands tightly. "I don't need any new experiences right now."

She considered that with bowed head, and looking at her neck, I wondered if she'd ever had an affair and with whom and if it had been pleasurable.

She said, "Well, let's go somewhere and stay for a while. Grenada?"

"No."

"Spain? France? They wouldn't be new experiences."

"No."

"Africa?"

"No," I said, and thinking I might be unreasonable, added, "I mean I just don't know, honey."

"Should we get a doctor?"

I had a frightful flash of Leonard. "Why am I thinking of Leonard?"

"Leonard Blue-Sky?" She moved closer to me, squeezed my hand harder.

"He knew something, Allis."

"What, darling?" She was going to say more. "Like something you're just starting to let yourself know?"

Aha! I thought. "Yes. That's it. I like you a whole lot, Allis."

She smiled. "You used to say before Mack came, 'Love ya today, baby,' remember?"

"Yeah. You wanna know why I stopped, huh?"

"No. I know why you stopped."

"Because you knew it, didn't you?"

"Yes, babes, I knew it. Look — should we?"

"What?"

"Get a doctor."

"Naw. We'll work it out. But you know too, doncha?"

"What, what do I know?"

I felt a small licking of small flames and smelled something burning. Then the feel and smell were gone. "That nothing's gonna change. That, after all, I'm not gonna matter and what I write isn't gonna matter — "

"No. You matter. It matters, and really, darling, I mean really, if that was not to be the case I don't think we'd be here. It's just that — just that these things don't happen the way we'd like them to happen."

I didn't know. I really didn't know that she ever thought like that, and yet in a way I couldn't describe I must have known that that was precisely the way she thought.

"Let's rent Amos' place," she said. Suddenly that seemed to be right. He was spending the summer in the Caribbean.

"Okay. That seems okay," I said. "I'd like that. Take a typewriter — "

"Sit in front of the fireplace when it gets cool at night — "

"—some fishing. Remember the bullheads we caught?"

"They were good, but you have to cook them."

"I'll cook them. You know I can burn when I want to. I'd really like that, honey. The sky's so full of stars at night — "

"What's the matter?" Her voice banged sharply against my eardrums. Had I caused the panic I heard?

"I am a little tired, kiddo." I leaned out of her arms to the floor. "Just lemme lie down. I want to sleep."

She got up quickly and began tugging at me. "On the bed. C'mon." I struggled on my knees to the bed and climbed up on it. I closed my eyes.

Hank Lowe was there when I awoke. That surprised me. How had Allis managed to get him away from Westchester, from Columbia Presbyterian, from Park Avenue? For a dozen years Hank had been prying me apart once a year from asshole to eardrum, from eyeball to armpit. We had done much talking. He had read my books, he said, and liked them. I signed them for him. There was always a point during the exams when he stepped slightly back and looked thoughtfully at me — a brief, sharp look — and then wordlessly he'd resume. His unvarying advice to me? "Get some rest, Cate."

So there he was.

"God," I groaned. "How much is this gonna cost me?"

"Hello, Mr. Wise-ass," he said. "You're taking a leave, Allis tells me."

"Yeah. She could've told you that on the phone."

"What're you working on now, Cate?"

"A couple of things."

"More like a dozen," Allis said.

"Do you have to?"

"I should."

"*Must* you?"

"I'll take it easy. What happened to me?"

He said, "You want bullshit?"

"Yes, of course."

"Stress."

"Stress. Sounds, sounds, well — all-encompassing. But I'll take it."

He was busy writing. "And you're going away?"

"Yeah, that's the plan."

"When?"

"In two weeks," Allis said. "Mack's finished with school then."

"Why do I feel so tired, Hank?"

"Because you are, that's why. You had any of those dreams about the war, foxholes, little old men, things like that?"

"Not lately. But I had a great one about God and me playing pool with the universe. I think it was eight ball, not points." I said nothing about the rest of the dream.

He started laughing and then I started, though I'd really had the dream, and then Allis laughed. "And you won," Hank said.

"Aw no, man. You kidding? God won. Five straight. But I was really learning when the dream ended."

When his laughter died, he reached over and patted my cheek. "Sounds like another book, Cate. I'm gonna leave you some pills. You come to the office tomorrow morning for a workup. I think you're all right. Maybe a few too many cosmic rays in the head. Gotta slow you down. Allis, you hear that?"

"Yes, Hank. I know."

"What're these fuckin' pills?" I asked.

"Slowing-down pills. The next time you play eight ball with God, ask Him. You come tomorrow. I don't want to have to send for you. Okay?"

"Okay."

ALLIS wasn't joking. In two weeks we were ensconced on Amos' mountain, having arranged for a flow of visitors with children so that Mack wouldn't grow lonely or bored with so much of the world staring him in the face. Allis had suspended all work until the fall, when we would have to be back anyway for Mack's school.

The second day, while we were out on the lake fishing, Allis told me that Glenn would be coming that weekend to spend some time with us and get into his book; that was to be a surprise. We would all be together. And that night, feeling again a sense of being alive and in touch with deeper things, we stared at the star-laden sky, picking out constellations, crying out at falling stars and marveling at the profusion of bodies glittering up there. As we watched, I told her about God and eight ball.

It's all a great pool table, Cate, God said. The cue stick — straight, true, balanced — is the will; it controls the cue ball, you see. The cue ball goes where I direct it — ignore the crude sexual implications, my boy — a little draw here, a little run there, some pull on either side of the center — just a little bit — and behold, it's done! The ball runs way to the end of the table. The balls, solids and stripes (he laughed and it echoed like fading thunder), consider them heavenly bodies rushing about the table of the universe in response to this stroke or that — force, gravity, or lack of it, if you will. Some balls collide, like so — clack! Others narrowly miss; still others carom from cushion to cushion — call those edges of space, if you want — and there are always balls that just barely kiss — click! — in passing. Some, of course, must be put away (and here he snapped off a long diagonal shot down the table), like that planet that used to be between Mars and Jupiter. Left pieces of that floating around — hit it too hard. Messy, but interesting. (Briskly he moved around the table, chalking his cue stick and pocketing balls. He had solids.) Rack! he called.

You see, Cate, the next rack all the balls are back. A new world! A new universe! Mosconi, Minnesota Fats, Cicero Murphy, Hoppe, they can tell you that playing pool is like playing god with the spheres in space. Otherwise it's a silly game, don't you think? Set them up and destroy; destroy and set them up; start all over again. You folk have some theories about that. He winked at me. He was already on his last ball. He had stripes this time. You're probably wondering, my boy — Rack! — why the eight ball is the black ball and the last to go, the ball you must not get behind. And the cue ball, white like the sun, is the contact ball, moving here and there through the changing system of spheres, and if accidentally pocketed — Scratch! — must quickly be replaced and a ball forfeited. Well, the system must have its sun or it isn't a system. The black ball is the stranger hidden in the heavens, a threat, a runaway planet, an asteroid hurtling out of orbit threatening everything. The Dark Prince hides behind galaxies, constellations and nebulae. One works and waits, pocketing all other balls before he is discerned. It must be that way. Pocket him by accident and you lose. Pocket him as planned — like so! Rack! — and you breathe a sigh of relief when he's put away. Only then can we have a new game, world, universe. The black ball demands more, is more, than we can imagine. (He laughed again and it crackled down time like lightning left over from a war fought in space a million years ago.) He sighted down the table toward the triangular-shaped stack, the eight ball in the center, and slid the cue stick through his thumb and forefinger; the other three fingers were a solid bridge.

Suddenly, he jerked a look over his shoulder, which was a shimmering mountain filled with sparkings. I followed his glance and saw (of course, I did not tell Allis this part of the dream) a young Japanese soldier aiming a rifle at me through the delicate webbing of the Brooklyn Bridge. He was firing. His shoulder snapped with the recoil, but I heard no shot, only saw words emerging from the muzzle of the rifle in a streamer like those towed by planes, and the words read, spilling out and curling effortlessly around great balls: WHO IS THAT NIGGER? WHO IS THAT NIGGEr? WHO IS THAT NIGGer? WHO IS THAT NIGGer? WHO IS THAT NIgger? WHO IS THAT Nigger? WHO IS THAT nigger? WHO IS THAt nigger? WHO IS THat nigger? WHO IS That nigger? WHO Is that nigger? WHO is that nigger? WHO is that nigger? who is that nigger? who is that nigger?

"Did you ever look at the sky at Bread Loaf?" I asked.

"What ever made you think of that place?" Allis said.

"The stars, girl, the stars."

"Yeah, look. It's pretty, but I'm not dressed for a long stay out here. Let's go in."

It was getting cold and a mist was rising from the cooling ground. I put my arm around her hip; she put hers around mine. "You take your pill?"

"I don't need it, honey."

"Do me a favor. Take it, take them."

Glenn drove up that first weekend. He seemed not to disturb the air, as he moved, quite as much as he used to; he had in some way perceived his vulnerability, I thought. He should have been still galloping on clouds, with his first book already under contract; and I thought his nostrils would be quivering with the still-distant smell of success. (Never mind what I'd told him. Who when young believes? Had I believed Langston Hughes? But Hughes had taken his tambourine to glory to the tune of Ellington's *Do Nothin Till You Hear from Me* — perhaps a more stylish way to meet the Big Pool Player than sending a note saying, I Am Bored.)

Glenn and Allis had had, it was natural to assume, some conversations about me, so there he was, trying not to be worried, while Mack, with that frenzied cool of a kid dying for company, dogged at his heels, wanting to have a catch, go for a swim, destroy snakes, put up a tent, cook hot dogs. Allis carried him off with her to shop, and Glenn and I were left at lakeside holding beer and fishing poles.

"This," he said, "is a great idea."

"You don't have to rush back, do you?"

"Naw. I can stay a while. How you doin'?"

"Okay."

"Slowin' down with the work? Taking next year off school?"

"Yeah, yeah." I had been concentrating on my line. I never understood why it was that Mack could bait with pieces of bread and come up with some biggies, and I couldn't get shit with caviar. I said, "Surprised you didn't bring someone with you. You're taking all this too seriously."

He laughed.

326

"You bring more of the book for me to read?" I asked.

He nodded. "Maybe you can help me with something."

"Me?"

"Hey, you sound like you never said that I ought to change this or move that around — "

"I know, I know. But this time you asked. I'm flattered."

"I figure you've written more books than I have."

We sat in silence, listening to the wind playing in the trees. I felt a great sense of comfort with him sitting beside me. Then he said, "I don't think I want to write another book. Just now, it's tough finishing this one."

I started to ask why, but he rushed words at me: "Jed's dead."

Jed had not played the past two seasons because of an injury. He'd returned to Cleveland.

"The Lakers didn't want him back and no one else wanted him. He was just a piece of meat. Couldn't find work — who wants a dinosaur cluttering up your place, you know. Not even as a playground director. Never saved anything. Tried to draw up and shrink in the ground so people wouldn't know it was him looking so beat — "

"No commercials, no color commentary for the games — "

"You kiddin', Dad? The white boys got all them gigs, damn near all of them. Jed was ashamed that he'd made it and then lost it."

"Never married, did he?"

Glenn snorted. "Having too good a time. I mean he wasn't making Wilt's money; still, it wasn't bad for a guy who couldn't count to one hundred and whose vocabulary you could almost put on a cigarette wrapper. A piece of meat, black meat; that's all he was. I tried to talk to him and he'd always say, 'Man, you right. I ought to go back to school and finish up, be somethin' more than a basketball player.' He always said that and then smiled and I knew he was shuckin', was too kind to ask what all my education had got for me. Shit, I didn't have a Rolls-Royce or a circular bed with mirrors on the ceiling or a swimming pool or instant recognition."

He sank into silence.

I said, "It was that ankle, wasn't it?"

"Yeah, it was, and it might have been all right but they made him play on it a whole season before he had to quit. I mean, he wasn't Wilt or Jerry West." He sighed. "Last week he suited up in his Lakers' outfit, took one of the game balls they'd given him when he was Rookie of the Year, and he dribbled right out on the highway and tried to stuff the

327

ball down the top of a trailer rig doing seventy-five." He shrugged. "And that was it."

I looked out at our lines running down into the water and then seeming to go off at angles.

"I feel like I put the whammy on him, Dad, and I don't know how to — maybe I don't want to — finish the book. It won't help anything or anybody."

"Yeah," I said. Something had sunk in after all, but I didn't feel good about it. "Finish. For yourself. That's most important. It's all a meat market, son. The thing is to try to stay off the hook."

Glenn had a habit of starting to speak, stopping, and then speaking again. It was as though thoughts came at him like lightning and some he had to dodge. "I wonder if it's not too late for good books."

He looked at me; I had not responded right away. "Can it ever be?"

"Maybe it always was, Dad. We just keep hoping."

"If you didn't write, what would you do, teach?"

"No."

"What, then?" I shouldn't have said that. Some old-fashioned cultural holdover had slipped out: one must do something.

"I think I wanna travel. Hire out on a ship, like Grandpa, like Langston Hughes, look at things, do that until I'm ready to write or settle down with something else. Sound okay?"

He didn't have to ask, yet I was pleased that he had, and he knew it. I envied his lack of encumbrances. I trusted the range of his vision because it seemed that something had sunk in after all. "That was an asking," I said. "You didn't have to."

"Well . . . the money for the education . . . things like that. Some folks get testy. They want you right out there in the marketplace."

"You don't owe me — us — anything."

"Yes I do," he said quickly. He became busy with his line. "I worry about you," he said after a while. "Can't help it."

"I'm okay, and I'm really gonna slow down."

"Go traveling. Allis wants that for you."

"I know. Maybe later. I've got a few things to finish up."

"Ever since I've known you, you've had a few things to finish up." He snatched open the lid of the cooler and took out two more beers. "What you've always needed was just a well-armed battalion instead."

I flashed on a father going and coming, coming and going, while his children waited to play with him, and I felt suddenly and abjectly apologetic. "Look — I'm really sorry — "

"Hey! It's all right! It took a little time, but I know where you're coming from. I've learned the lesson and that's why I wanna hit the road — the way you did."

"But where am I coming from?"

He laughed one of those nasty street laughs, like someone who's looked over your shoulder long enough to know your hand.

"Tear down the sand castle," he said. "Put it back under the water."

He was right. I said, "Mack has the same complaint." The abrupt bitterness that framed my words surprised me. "I'm always finishing up a few things."

"Oh," Glenn said, "he'll learn the way I did that there are a couple of things more important than playing with a Frisbee. Don't worry."

"I count on you to help with Mack, you know, if anything happens to me."

Yes, I had been thinking such things. Putting items in order, I guess it's called, and pondering once again how a society, in inverse importance, could make an individual more valuable dead than alive. Insurance. Seeing that the loved ones were provided for, etc.

Glenn looked at me and then stared glumly out at the water. "You didn't have to say that; that was a given, and that's why it's better for me to travel now instead of later."

The last part was so familiar. I said, "Thanks. But talking about life and death, continuity, yes, and travel, I want to tell you something important."

"Sounds ominous."

"No. You've got yourself another brother in Spain."

"Say what?"

Now I laughed.

Glenn took a very deep swallow of his beer, peering out at me over the can. "How old?"

"Around eighteen now." Glenn's face was without expression; it waited for detail to be carved into it. "I never saw him," I said, "only a picture some time ago." I felt compelled to say hurriedly "I looked for him — them."

"What's his name?"

"Alejo Cato Donoso."

Glenn said, "He ought to be a poet with a name like that." He moved his line. "Cato. The relationship couldn't have been all bad. Did you love the woman?"

"Allis asked me that and I said no. But I was lonely, so I guess I did love her. Then. And, as a matter of fact, he is a poet. His mother told me that in a note several years ago, and now my Spanish publisher tells me about his work."

Glenn smiled a great, beaming smile and said, "You leave your mark, Dad. Maybe a writing genius like me."

"Maybe. I have this hankering to see him. It bothers me, I mean, it really bugs me, but it was one of those things born out of night, and went into daytime and then went, period."

"It happens," he said. "Somehow, you never think it happens to your father — although, I gotta tell you, I always had an open mind."

"I want you to look him up. Talk to him. See how much of us is in him."

Our lines lay languidly, not even drifting now. I said, "I worried about him. Before I even knew it was a him. She — her name is Monica — already had a kid when I met her. In a way, it was like being back with you and Catherine. She was part African, part Spanish. When I found out about the other kid, she was gone. I'll give you the dough."

"Maybe I can hire out on a ship that stops in Spain."

"Yeah. Give it to you, anyway. Do you remember, were you pissed when I left?"

"Not pissed, but I remember a hole in my life, when I didn't see you."

"Well. I'm sorry."

He reached over and hugged me. We both stared at the water. The bass seemed to be having a very good time not ten feet from where our lines were. Glenn looked at his watch. "It's time for your pill."

Naturally, there were times that summer when the work seemed to want to wait. Some days when I was alone, Allis and Mack having gone back to the city for something or other, I would sit poised before the machine, my notes neatly stacked, yesterday's manuscript marked and ready for rewrite, and then would glance out the window. That was my undoing. For mile upon mile the valley opened itself to the sky, which pressed down into it. I would go outside and sit and stare at the serenity of the coupling, and I marveled at the foliage silhouetted against the heavens: some of it looked like the profiles of people I knew.

But it was the wind, I think, the wind that most hypnotized me. The wind said things; it said things in whispers, gusts and occasional roars. The wind had to know all. It had whipped around this Earth from the beginning, enveloping it as it moved through space. The wind had seen and heard everything: long-extinct beings communicating with !clicks, the Himalayas, the Alps, the Andes exploding up out of the plain while other ranges, now nameless, slid beneath the sea; it must have recorded the awesome sounds of lands breaking away to begin their inch-per-year journeys apart from each other; in reply what would the wind say about the sudden Cretaceous extinction of the great reptiles: They ate their own eggs? They drowned in a flood? God had been playing pool and when he destroyed the planet between Mars and Jupiter it spread deadly iridium over the Earth? Would this wind echo Akhnaton in his prayers perceiving the sun as Center, and was it now whispering as it slipped through trees and grasses, curled miniature tsunamis out on the lake, that all was now being brought to us by the people who stole everything from the Southern Tribes in whose sun-drenched lands gods were born? By the people who stole sextant and compass and grandly presented us with five hundred years of Holy Crusades and channeled the Renaissance northward, evolving Descartes, Hobbes, Rousseau, et al., and who brought you the first multinational companies and over-ocean trade in souls and bodies, who implanted ovenry in the tale of Hansel and Gretel and made Jack-the-Real-Culprit the hero — he who had stolen from the giant sleeping peacefully atop the beanstalk? Say what, wind, Typhon, Huracán, Zephyr, Tronada? This is being presented by the people who brought you the spinning jenny and the cotton gin, the steam engine, the Gatling, Spencer, Colt, the .75, .88 and the .105? And why not have developed the ICBMs and MIRVs after Dresden, Hiroshima and Nagasaki?

This wind had witnessed the passing of every one, including my mother's in her sun-bright bedroom, with her husband (they'd never divorced, only separated) riding one ocean and her son another, and it, in coats of sleet, had driven my torpedoed father to the bottom near Murmansk — strange place for a black man to die — and this same wind (had it never tired of seeing, hearing, doing?) knew the dark Moravian forests in which Allis' people had huddled, watching Catholics kill Protestants and Protestants kill Catholics, and knew that both together had killed Jews — this wind that had absorbed the billions of first-born sounds, always a cry of anguish and fear that the end of the passage was about to commence.

Chastened, I would then re-enter the house and settle down to tell my story, which seemed barely a pause between all the words, the infinite number of words, the wind could tell if only it were possible.

When I had finished my work for the day, in that vast forest silence stitched only by wind sounds, I reread Paul's books. "Why those?" Allis had asked when I packed them. I'd shrugged, truly not knowing why, except that if I wandered around in them, I might chance upon something that might explain us both.

And I did.

With the exception of *The Burnt Offering*, he had written absolutely dead things, without potency or life. His books were drills, exercises, promenades of the seeming manners and morals of the times, totally incapable of springing up armed men, as I believed books ought to do. If his works did preserve the essences of his will, his intellect, then I had no reason to envy him. We had simply moved through a second life, had once again reached puberty, when the glands, this time artificially stimulated (fame, fortune), produced a change that was not physiological. He had arrived at his religious certainty, after a false start. My certainty, racial, had been imposed. I rejected that imposition; Paul had no need or no wish to reject his. Toward the end of summer, when the dew became heavier in the mornings and white spider webs dotted the ground, when one came on shedded snakeskins and the late afternoons bit harder with chill, when I had finished all his books, I returned to my first conclusion about the leaking away of our friendship.

Simply, I was a reminder, proof, that the somewhat lofty values he held (within reason) could work only if he restrained or ignored me. Obviously, the two were interchangeable; they gained the same end. Given the situation, illusion could only persist, *insist,* if one caused the reality to be absent.

I was Paul's reality, finally, and who ever wants much to do with that?

And he, goddamn it, was mine.

Absurd, this bicamerality that turned each on the other while time robbed us both — as individuals, as groups — of unheard-of probabilities. I wondered if Paul had ever thought this way. I wondered, in fact, precisely what he was wondering these days.

One day when Allis and Mack had gone to the city and I was moving through my routine, the phone rang. When it rang here, it always startled; it was like a lance slashing through time itself; the ring was an anachronism composed of wires, bells, electricity, unimaginable distances, faceless operators and technicians. One wanted it to ring, to carry good news, greetings, information, but one was always startled to hear the ring insisting itself just under the sound of lazy winds gliding across the mountaintop.

"Hello," I said, hoping Allis had not had an accident or that the apartment had not been burglarized.

A fine female voice said, "Mr. Cato Douglass?"

"Yes, who's this?"

The phone startled, yes, but it was like the mail, holding magical qualities

332

for the writer; a thumb up, a thumb down, a rocket ride into the cosmos or a descent so swift and so deep that Dante's Inferno resembled a swim in three feet of water.

"Hold for Mr. Kass, please."

Kass? Kass? Oh! *Bob* Kass. *The* Bob Kass. He had been the subject of numerous laudatory articles about his leadership in the new Hollywood. He brought in new writers, new directors, took chances. I tried to grab hold of myself in midbound. Is there a writer whose heart doesn't bound just a bit at least when Hollywood is on the other end of the line? Listen: even Kosinski gave in. Take the money and don't go to see the film. What law says you have to see a lousy film made from your very good book?

"Cate? Cate, hi. Bob Kass. How're you, Cate, all right?"

"Okay. I'm okay."

"Listen. Paul was out here last week. He's your greatest fan ever, man, no shit, and he was saying that we ought to make films out of your books. And he's right, Cate, you know. We got all your books. I make sure the story editor gets every fuckin' thing you write, but I gotta level with you, baby. You're in the top class of American writers. You write your ass off, no shit. But, hey, we aren't doin' *anything* black; nobody is — "

"Hey, Bob, you guys out there never did anything really black, so what else's new? Is that why you called?"

He laughed. "Good luck, Cate. Say hello to Paul and Mark for me, huh?"

And he was gone.

I didn't have time to stew or to curse or to be angry. The phone rang again and I snatched it as though it were Kass coming across the ring to start the second round. I snarled, "Hello!"

There were startled sounds on the other end. "Hey, down boy. It's me, Maxine. Christ! I guess that was Bob Kass who just hung up, right? Your line was busy. He just called me. Said he wanted to talk to you personally. What kind of deal does he want? Which books? You didn't agree to do any screenplays, did you? Why are you pissed?"

"Hold it, Maxine, hold it. We didn't talk any deals. You know what he said to me? You wanna know what that cocksucker said to me?"

"Of course I want to know." The bouncy expectancy had disappeared from her voice.

"They're not doing anything black. Which was not news, but also seemed to indicate there wasn't much chance in the future either."

Her voice was incredulous. "He *said* that?"

"Yeah, he *said* it."

"Well, Cate, there's been a lot of talk — not talk — because no one wants to be quoted; no one wants to be ridden on rumor. But it's in publishing too, to a larger extent than you want to think. I mean people — they don't seem terribly interested in us after we leave Twentieth Century Forum Publishers. Darling, frankly, it's gonna be hard to sell you when you finish with Maureen and — "

"Wanna quit?"

"No, no. Just want to let you know up front. The business is changing. Remember, I told you — "

"Listen, Maxine, I may write shit, but I don't *knowingly* write shit and think it is art, and besides all your neat little formulas only work if you're writing that silly white- blue-collar shit; even that nigger-in-the-projects crap has run its course, so there you are. If you write what you know, the first law of writing, and what you know is what *I* know and some frightened people in New York and Hollywood don't wanna *know* what I know, then you're right where you should've been all the time: writing for yourself."

"Cate, Cate," she was saying, trying to interrupt.

"What the fuck, Maxine. I've probably got more out of it already than I should have, given the chickenshit situation. Listen. I'm goin' fishin' — "

"Is Allis there? Let me talk to Allis."

"She's not here. She's in the city with Mack. Something he wanted to do."

"Are you *okay?*"

"Yep. I'm fine. Bob Kass just put things back in perspective for me. I am A-O-K, as the super-honky moon-walkers say."

"One more thing," Maxine said. "I've started another book."

She sounded embarrassed.

"What's it about?

"Same thing. Sex and old age."

"Sex and Old Age Two."

"If you want. I got this tremendous advance. Fabulous."

"I know you won't tell me how great. I don't wanna know how great. I suppose you'll be spending more time with that now, huh?"

"Yes," she said quickly — almost too quickly, as though she'd been waiting for an opening. "I *am* dropping some clients, but you're not one of them."

"Shit, I didn't think I was. Loyalty. Longevity. All that."

She laughed. It was a thin laugh. "Sorry Kass had nothing to offer," she said. "Call me when you get back to town."

I bolted a few drinks before, during and after my dinner, then put on a jacket and went outside. I lay down and watched the night slide over, bringing with it a gibbous moon. As I lay, my mood shuffled from one of unspeakable sadness to one of dread. Perhaps the sameness of the conversations, the persistence of attitudes, the shallow ways of things, people. The joyful pursuit of hypocrisy by hordes of guisards. Back down the ribbons of tarmac and concrete that led to New York, there, in the city, editors and agents had trampled each other to death to be the first to offer that platoon of confessed Washington criminals obscene amounts of money for books (that would be ghosted) detailing nothing more than their deeds, victims and accomplices. There was no end to the books. Frank Wills had been shuttled into the obscurity reserved for his kind. In the big shell game of our time he had become the goat, the victim, Francis the Obscure, and those he had discovered had become the contrite heroes; aw! the continuum of bullshit was of course unbroken. I was sad. And I was afraid. I wanted out of this warp.

I thought of the revolver, upstairs in a desk drawer. I thought of its heft, its blunt kind of beauty, surcease. But I did not move. I stared at the moon and thought of the men who had walked upon it, men ten generations removed from the "human débris anxious for any adventures, psychologically armed with new facts," who had sailed rockets instead of ships and who, for a time, had garnered acclaim instead of anonymity. Only the machines had changed; only the ritual had been altered. Did I see an American flag listlessly drooping near the Oceanus Procellarum crater?

The chorus of peepers began to give way to the hoot of owls. Don't call my name, I thought; don't call my name yet; and then I heard an eerie howl, human but not, off in the distance, which distance at night brought all sound within cup of the ear. Big Foot? Poor Big Foot. How could there not have been a Dr. Zarkov or so who had impregnated female baboons with human sperm in the quiet corner of a lab here and a lab there, and had unwittingly chosen the right time when human and primate chromosome bands precisely matched and at that time, that exact time, overcame the two-chromosome difference between man and that beast because of sun or moon spots, falling stars or some other cosmological occurrence?

The sound fell into silence. Ancient Egyptian women of high birth were sometimes mummified with baboons, !clickers; and ♀ in the Papyrus of Ani is: her, homage, all, peoples, thee, upper, within, through, upon, face, over, at, for . . . Ra! preposition, noun, proper noun, collective noun. The first. Of course the ancients knew. I felt better. Now I thought of the gun in abstract, having nothing much to do with me, just an object to do my bidding, like, perhaps, a hoe commanded to work while I rested in the shade.

I was thinking of the ⌐ᴅ glyph when I saw, topping what I knew was the twin peak to the one I now lay upon (the start or end of a long-gone water channel), the lights of a car moving slowly but surely through the night. Allis, I thought, drives like that, and I longed for her so sharply that I knew when I went inside I would call. The car lights dipped out of sight and came back into view again, radiating lines 360 degrees off into space through my astigmatism.

Then I thought of a friend who had gone scuba diving with his son and daughter off La Tortuga. One moment they were swimming in sun-bright water and the next minute they were inside pitch-black submerged caves, one opening on another. He found daylight and surfaced, waiting for his children. He waited. He waited, squelching panic, fending it off. Time was running out. He submerged carefully. *They were his children,* and he entered the dark again, every neuron in his brain electrified, alert, screaming. The panic began chewing up his air and he knew that theirs too was short, about to go stale, about to be of no use whatsoever. They bumped into him as they were speeding breathlessly back to the entry point. They surfaced in the sunlight and drifted back to the boat, safe.

I got to my feet, assuming that the car would veer off into some valley, be swallowed by forest walls and limestone ledges, but it kept lancing light, brighter and closer, until I could hear the car itself, the pulsing of its engine, the mashing of its tires against the road. It rounded the curve down the road; the engine noise dropped off and then the lights swung up the driveway and spilled all the way down to the lake, and even before the car stopped, I realized that my wife and my son were calling:

"Cate!"

"Dad!"

And I ran to them. Somehow they had heard me and returned.

7

I THINK I was okay by the time we got back to the city and hauled all the luggage up on the elevator. Mack was eager to return to school and to see the friends who had not come to the country on a visit. (He does not appear to delight in the country the way we do.)

Allis was planning reluctantly to crank up her accounts; I was going to finish *The Pushkin Papers* — though Gullian did not seem to be eagerly awaiting delivery. I felt I had gained a second wind, as Glenn had described it from his running days, and gone right through the wall, scattering bricks to hell and back. I was more eager to work than I had been when I first arrived in New York.

I think I was better; the apartment seemed to be bigger. Usually, after I had been away and returned, it seemed smaller. Also, I no longer caught Allis or Mack or Glenn staring at me when I turned quickly.

Without waiting to put away the luggage, we attacked what mail had come since Allis' last trip down. (That had been when, having herself had this malady whose name is never called, this deadly dysfunction, and coming into view of the squared stalagmites of Gotham seared over, glucked with steam and grime, she somehow made Mack understand why they had to go right back, had returned to find me in the embrace of night, glyphs, fear and dread. "I heard you," she had said later as we held each other.) Allis seized all the interesting-looking stuff — the air letters and striped airmail envelopes from distant places and the important-appearing envelopes made of fine paper and bearing copper- or steel-engraved return addresses. Mack had grabbed his soccer ball and was already leaving, his voice resonating in the hallway in conversation with Julio. ("Is Tim home? Eric? Aldo? Billy?")

Allis tossed bill after bill in my lap, unashamedly, until we had two stacks of mail. She had also given me the books whose bags were uniformly vomit brown. I opened the one from Amaya, wondering. They were not scheduled to publish anything of mine soon. The bag contained a thin volume of poetry by one Alejo Cato Donoso, entitled *El Sol Sobre Una Colina Azul.* He was, the jacket copy advised, *Un Lorca contemperano.* I felt that I had been hit with roundhouse padded by a sixteen-ounce glove. "Look!" I said to Allis. "*Look,* and he's only fuckin' eight-*een!*"

Startled, she looked up from her greedy perusal of the mail. "Oh!" she said, taking the book. "Oh, your son!"

"Yeah, Alejo . . ." She ignored my outstretched hand and thumbed through the book.

"My God," she whispered. "*Eighteen.* Glenn and now this one. Jesus." She leaned over, the book opened to the title poem. "What's it say?"

I looked at the Spanish. "Uh, ummm —

> *I crept up behind the sun*
> *resting on a blue hill,*
> *laughing down in time.*

I'll have to study the rest of it."

We sat motionless, staring at the book. "A poet in the family," she finally said, seeming to taste the words, "and another novelist."

"I'm not sure Glenn plans to write anything more when he's finished *Jumper.*" Jesus, I thought, he's a baby yet.

"Why not?" She was torn between going back to the mail and digesting this information. "You've talked about it?"

"He feels bad about Jed. Thinks in some psychic way he caused it all to happen. He didn't *say* this, but maybe he feels guilty for being jealous of Jed." I was sure we were both thinking of Paul once those words were out. "He'll finish the final draft this fall," I said, "and then quit Office Temporaries and take off."

338

Allis was still looking at and fondling Alejo's book. "You really ought to go back to your poetry," I said.

She closed the book softly and shuffled halfheartedly through the mail. Then, almost fearfully, she said, "I have. But I could never come up with lines like Alejo's. I just don't *think* that way."

"But why didn't you tell me?"

She was back at the mail.

"You know there's no special way any writer should think, baby. You know that. You just keep forgetting. And it's what I've been discovering. I *thought* I was writing differently from all those other turkeys, cutting closer to the bone. But shit, you get sick, there's a kind of sickness, before you can really understand anything — the business with your father — you've written about him?"

She nodded, her eyes showing something I could not define.

"And Mr. Storto?"

Her head snapped around. "How did you know?"

I gripped her hand. "It's that that lets you figure out whether you're in a pit or on a peak; it's when you find *your* place in some dimension where you can function. It's like after the temptation of Christ, Jacob at Peniel, Buddha far from his pipal tree, suffering temptation, Mohammed on Mount Hira, see? That's why poets in Arabic are called Sh'ir; the poet is 'the Knower,' and how can a poet know unless she knows? And how can you know if you've not been sick with the way you were? How about that, Momma, some rap, huh? Sh'ir. Isn't that some fuckin' name? And here we're all saddled with names that don't mean a goddamn thing, over here, I mean."

She was looking at me in the way she used to look at me when I read to her a story I'd written, as though she was seeing something about me that she hadn't seen before.

"So you have no business being afraid or shy or even of letting me be the only writer in this house." I paused. "When I think of all you've come to know since Bread Loaf — "

I hefted Alejo's book. A finely crafted book has a very special feel to it, none of the sleaze that comes from handling tapes or film; a book is a bound essence, or should be, of something special. "I do get to read your new poetry, don't I?"

She smiled a pretty smile, all dimples, and said, "I'd be the fool to say no, wouldn't I, after all that?"

"Quite right, my dear."

She passed her stack of mail over and smiled at the floor in some inner happiness. I had an enormous sweep of pride. And then I said, "So look — what's for dinner?"

We both laughed.

I remember that autumn with amazing clarity. The weather had been remarkably good — dry and temperate. It went well with the feeling that people were trying to recover from the most recent series of debacles around the country and the world, the corruptions in high and low places, the merry-go-round of wars, small and bitter. I was over half a century old then.

That autumn, Elliot Huysmans published an article in *Ebony* — rather a surprise, for the publication was not known for its devotion to anything other than the popular arts — about himself and Norman Mailer.

Two years earlier he had been asked by "a major publication" to go to Zaire to cover the Ali-Foreman fight. Huysmans had been to Zaire when it still bore its "slave" name, the Congo. He had been, in spite of his host of literary coronas, the 372nd Regimental middleweight champ during the war in Italy. He had never written about boxing until the *Ebony* piece, but he knew it, from Jackson and Johnson, through Ketchel, Risko, Levinsky, Kid Chocolate, Louis, Armstrong, Graziano, La Motta, Zale, Robinson, Sadler, Pep, Gavilan, Basilio, Fullmer, Turpin, Cerdan — when it all seemed to fall apart until Ali howled and punched himself into the spotlight. Huysmans had the credentials, the savvy, and he packed his bags for Zaire. But then, through the "industry," came word that *Playboy,* ole supercrotch, had signed Mailer to cover the fight. Huysmans' "major publication" (it could only have been *Esquire*) canceled his assignment, an act that implied with an obvious heaviness of hand that white was right, indeed, *yes* indeedy, even in Zaire, even if Huysmans had a tarnished old 372nd Inf. Reg. 92nd Div. AUS championship belt somewhere behind his awards. That fall Huysmans stopped being a Negro and became Black.

We learned that Paul, like me, had delivered a new novel to his publisher and that it would be published at about the same time as mine, late spring. (I'd delivered *Pushkin* to Gullian over lunch at Lutece. She made all the proper sounds, the proper promises, the wham-bang predictions of success. I'd heard the litany before, and besides, I was well, so I enjoyed the lunch.) Paul appeared regularly in notes and items, snips and snaps:

he trundled a pushcart through Central Park with other well-known authors to help protest the high cost of books (high because publishers often made big — that is *thick* — books out of thin ones by using high-bulk paper, large type, wide margins and chapter pages begun halfway down); he got a double off George Plimpton at the big game between Writers and Artists in East Hampton; was a signer of various PEN and Writers Guild and Authors Guild proclamations protesting the imprisonment of writers in Uganda, East Timor, South Africa, Russia, Bolivia, Chile; he was the scheduled keynote speaker for the coming MLA meeting . . .

That was the autumn we bought Amos' mountain house. The city's sickness was deepening; perhaps it was a national and world sickness, the scrambling, scuffling, the scratching, the lack of even the most elementary graces or courtesies. People were killing each other over parking spaces; cops, scared witless, were now being killed as often as they had witlessly killed. In the gas lines, where the gas pumpers exercised their new-found power in a fashion that would have made Captain Bligh blush, drivers killed each other for places on line. Repairmen of cars, television sets, door jambs, etc., were no longer capable of repairing anything; they simply took your money. At least twice a month we had to return tainted meat or soured milk to the supermarket, and everywhere, *every*where, people waited on line to give sellers who no longer even pretended to provide service, let alone decent products, their money, and did it without too much grumbling, like cattle being led through the chute to slaughter. We bought Amos' place because something had changed, swiftly, it seemed, and irrevocably, and if people were aware of it, they did not show it. We wanted a place we could run to when Vesuvius finally buried Pompeii again, when Rome fell, when Dilmun died, when Memphis ceased to exist.

Most of all that autumn I remember that my family moved closer together, appeared to be on the verge of becoming larger. This was all the more underlined when Maxine Culp called to trade gossip and told me that Paul and Betsy had broken up.

About Alejo, I had made inquiries through my Spanish editor. The critics in Spain had treated him well; he was now "established," as they say over here. He lived, wrote my editor, in an old house up near Tibidabo that had a marvelous view of Barcelona away to the south. (I imagined that it was like gazing down on Hollywood from the hills above it.) It was rumored, said my editor, that Alejo's frequent house guest was Dolores Montefrio y Lucena, the flamenca dancer and Andalusian nationalist. Perhaps I had read of her? (I had not, but on, son, onward — and only just nineteen!) Alejo was also a candidate for the City of Barcelona and the Boscan poetry prizes. These were, I'd heard, awards for the Catalan clique, but hell, he was a Catalan!

Glenn, as if weary of working on *Jumper,* exploded through the final draft, battling his editor every paragraph of the way, collected the rest of his advance and was readying to ship out one-way on an Exxon tanker bound for the Persian Gulf. He would cook for ten men. ("On tankers they save all the room for the oil.") From the Gulf he would rendezvous in Cairo with Maija.

Maija. She had moved into his apartment that summer. She looked something like Angela Davis and was as statuesque as Miss Peggy Lee. I am quite sure they were not constructing young women so wonderfully when I myself was young. She was a painter (a terrible one, I might add), and, enamored of Mack and Allis, she had given them painting after painting until we had to suggest, gently, that she hold on to similar gifts until we got a larger place. I suppose she had caught me looking wolfishly at her too many times to have been enamored of me. Maija had a loft studio a few blocks farther south in SoHo. I could understand why Glenn had not brought her to the country that time; she was a great distraction.

From Cairo they planned to travel down to Luxor (where she wanted to sleep in a temple) and then across North Africa to Tangier and into Spain and up to Barcelona and Alejo. They would give him my letter. It pleased me that Glenn was going in the season I had, and that he would not be alone. They would see Gibraltar rearing mightily up out of the mists. I could almost envision the way they would see it, and I could nearly smell Barcelona, cooling down after the humid summer, and I pictured all four of them strolling through town or eating and drinking in the sidewalk cafés.

And there was Mack, an unrelenting *presence* in the apartment; he asked a thousand questions a minute about words and people and things. His curiosity exhausted me; his stamina made me worry. He wondered briefly why it was that I was black and Allis was white; he had wondered that before, out of mere passing interest. Maybe he would become an anthropologist?

Mack brought home snippets and gouts of his world, idioms and mannerisms and tales of shoplifting classmates, of kids rubbing dicks together in the boys' room, of little girls who wanted to "go with" him. He had guests and he was a guest for sleepovers and parties and flurries of outings. Suddenly he knew every Yankee's batting average, every NFL quarterback, every basketball player in the NBA. God! He went through sneakers like a hurricane through Galveston. Brand names of hundreds of items echoed through the apartment halls. Merchants and advertising people, faceless, distant, were our constant adversaries in battles we so often lost. Up to that point in his life, Mack had agreed to wear a tie with jacket and slacks but once — and then with sneakers. Andy Warhol saw us walking along Central Park West one day, *that* day Mack was dressed up, and immediately pounced on my kid's style.

A couple of times, rather weakly, as though halfheartedly performing a wearisome duty, Allis had suggested that he be bar mitzvahed when he reached thirteen. But he had already made up his mind: "Mom, *please*. I just want to be me, okay? I know I'm part black and part white, part Jewish and part Gentile, but I really don't want to be part, I just wanna be a whole *me*, okay?"

He was, then, aware and was dealing with that awareness. The revelation, though I am sure there had been others less succinctly uttered, gave me much pride.

And so did Allis. She was enthralled with her writing of poetry, the act of it, the process. Song and idea, idea and song, she constructed, word by word, line by line, until she could say: "I think I've finished. See what you think."

There were moments when, her back turned to me, I studied her body (for the millionth time); I thought I knew it well, thought I could detect intelligences rising from her slopes and curves, even the sound of her voice or the pauses in it. But there are things you can never see, only know and not be able to describe how it is that you do know. So I watched her and knew nothing, read her poetry and only then began to know nearly everything.

My contentment was luxurious, tending toward a benevolent concern for others less fortunate. It was true that I had detected in Glenn a fleeting envy of his younger brother's Spanish success, but it had motivated him to finish his own book regardless of the many editorial obstacles that had little if anything to do with his writing or subject.

I thought often of the Cummingses' breakup. Had they been the latest victims of the success syndrome? Or had it to do with religion? Would he be marrying again? Would she? I felt smugly superior to Paul, clearly and without the encumbrances of envy. For what mattered all the acclaim and attendant fringe benefits if you couldn't keep your personal act together? I wondered if Paul would be calling, or she, for solace from a familiar place. I was not sure I wanted that. And in any case, given the circumstances, I would be perhaps the last person he'd think of for comfort now.

On the eve of his departure for Norfolk, where he would catch his tanker, Glenn gave a party. We took a cab down, passing Mr. Storto's old building. We had not written and we had not heard from him. We carried into Glenn's a wisp of sadness that was completely disintegrated by five million decibels of disco music and snapping, wriggling young bodies, moving like the proverbial can of worms in that small apartment. Strobe lights pounded us as we sat subdued yet strangely excited by the noise and movement in a corner to which Glenn kept bringing people and shouting above the din: "Dad, this is So-and-so. So-and-so, this is my father and my stepmother . . ."

We watched Mack dancing with Maija, licking his little chops; watched him searching out other young women who thought he was so cute, and the slick little bastard was pushing *that* hype for all it was worth. Then he took his mother onto the floor, and then I took her and we jiggled and moved and swayed and, noticing that no one was paying any attention to us, abandoned our conservative motions and grunted and bopped and snapped our fingers and rolled our asses just like everyone else, and loved it.

The affair was, also, a book party; not the publishing of one, but the completion, and I wondered, as I watched my eldest son move about, if Jed would always be with him. That he would write again I had no doubt. We all work at our own paces. We fill our cups at different taverns and beat our drums for different marchers. He was my son. He would write again. And again.

I had foolishly offered to drive Glenn to Penn Station in the morning and, having reached the limit of my capacity to hold white wine, red wine and rosé wine, we left and took a taxi back uptown, where I slept restlessly (I had never had a son go off the way Glenn was going) and in the morning strolled with banging head to the garage and got the car, recognizing all the while the woman in me that had to see him to his *eunoto.*

Is there anything as forlorn as the remnants of a party? How different his apartment looked in the gray light sifting through the Village alleys. The detritus of the party lay all about, chicken bones ground into the floor, sparerib bones in ash trays, empty Colonel Sanders Kentucky Fried Chicken boxes greasy and crumpled, Astor Place gallon wine jugs half-empty with their poisons. All this Maija would clean up.

344

They both looked exhausted, but not quite out, the way young people do. They looked as though they'd wallowed in each other for what was left of the evening after we left. In the rearview mirror I could see Maija at his ear, his neck, nibbling, nibbling, and all I could think of was this shtunk whose ass I'd wiped, whose absence I sometimes cried over, whose hurts I'd kissed. And there he was back there, a man so sure of himself that he would be cooking for an assortment of Asians, Neapolitans and Texas honkies. Like one of the Maasi men: so bad they red-ochred themselves and wore beads. I glanced in the mirror and thought to him: I love you.

I waited in the car. Maija returned and sat beside me. She was quiet. I was quiet. I drove her back to his apartment and when she got out I told her to call and come by; that we would compare letters from Glenn until she left to join him.

Jesus, I thought, driving home. Ole C.C. is just about a father-in-law.

I REMEMBER that autumn vividly.

One day while we were still waiting for the first letter from Glenn to arrive from some exotic African city (some, I know, would think this a contradiction) — Dakar, Luanda, Dar-es-Salaam, Mombasa — I took the sign Allis and I had worked on together, with some of the cards I'd ordered, and strolled down to the Museum of Natural History. I jogged up the steps past Teddy and his Indian and African companions, white man's burdens, and headed for the Man in Africa and Mexican wings. They are practically around the corner from each other, so it is like sailing a current of ocean (as was probably done) to move from Africa to Mexico.

What was this sign; what were these cards? They were attempts to make people believe what they *saw* in museums, not what they read. The idea had come to me one morning as I was emptying my bladder. Strike back! Deposit the sign or the cards where the evidence of cultural theft and Western Doublespeak displayed themselves like flashers at the Metropolitan Opera. Allis approved; indeed, she was eager to see me involved in a venture that excited me. There was some risk, yes.

The Man in Africa Wing was unusually hushed; the light was filtered through discreet floodlights and the three-dimensional displays of people, instruments of work and play, and weapons. Teachers led clusters of children through — "Now, children" — in strong voices that would brook no questions.

Here and there men and women sifted through the dim, casting glances at each other and pausing now and again to appreciate the displays and to read the accompanying legends.

Most of the guards were black, just as at other museums in the city. There seemed to have been a subtle shift from hard-jawed white to black, Hispanic, and long-haired white in these positions.

I stopped before the display of the Hausa people. The spear never failed to attract me. It stood in a corner, simple, straightforward and splendid. Of course, there had been made much more hullabaloo over the Maasi spear, but there's really no comparison. The Hausa spear is all metal — iron and brass. The spearhead has no aerodynamic equal anywhere; its symmetry is superb. The shaft of the spear comes apart in two lengths with a twist.

The Maasi spear is broad-bladed, almost three times heavier than the Hausa, and the spearhead itself comes down almost a third of the length of the shaft, where it is fitted into various lengths of heavy ebony wood. The bottom part of the spear, which fits into the opposite end of the wood, is a four-sided shaft of iron ending in a point. Very heavy. Good for killing lions. I was glad I wasn't born a Maasi and that for my bar mitzvah I didn't have to go out and kill Simba.

They say that the Maasi spearhead is like the ancient Roman broadsword. They never say that the broadsword is like the Maasi spear. Iron was used in Africa before the Assyrians arrived there.

The spear had copper and brass circlets beaten into the shaft, which also was decorated with subtle X-marks and lines. I stood studying, and for some reason thought of John Updike standing in the garden gallery of Paa Ya Paa in Kenya. I became aware suddenly of a small man to the side and rear of me in the reflection of the display case. He appeared to be studying the spear, too. Or me; I couldn't quite tell. He was Oriental. The Hausa-Maasi and the Samurai. In Teddy's museum. Now our eyes met through the reflection of the simulated tropical light. I imagined him younger and in a real jungle, a 7.65 sniper's rifle at his shoulder. I smelled, quite sharply, something burning and I closed my eyes tight and thought: Goddamn that war. It had been the beginning and might yet be the end of me. It plagued like a disease whose onset was unpredictable, whose remissions were all out of sync. Then, it had been so easy, so right, so laudatory to kill strangers you'd been taught to hate. Slowly I opened my eyes and my heart burbled against my chest. For the man had disappeared and a guard was smothering a small burning piece of paper with the sand of the cigarette can.

I left the wing and went around the corner into the Mexican Wing, which was not as crowded and was vast, dark and brooding. I slid onto the bench beside the replica of the gigantic Olmec head of La Venta. I loved looking at that face. All of Africa was in it, all of black America. Constance Irwin and others had characterized such heads (there were others) as being sculptures of slaves. This was, of course, because of the Negroid features by which every anthropologist and KKK member swears. But who ever took the time to make so huge a resemblance of a slave? And, mind you, not one, but several, each approaching twenty tons. Who ever carved a slave looking so imperious, so anger-threatening, so monstrously sure of himself (and then made a cunning tunnel for a speaking tube up through the mouth to address the rabble of other Africans, Semites, North Europeans and Orientals, whose images of stone lay scattered from one end of Mexico to the other)? The face looked like Joe Louis', with the flattening nose, heavy brow and superbly full lips. And this guy, whoever he was, was not playing! His expression says, I don't want no shit from you jive-ass turkeys!

I slipped the waxed paper off the stickum pads. I pretended to write on the pad while I studied the hall, the few people who were studying the calendar, the position of the single guard.

I read the legend near the head and smirked: THE NEGROID APPEARANCE OF THE FEATURES MAY BE A STYLIZATION OF CERTAIN INDIAN FACES OF THE REGION THAT TEND IN THIS DIRECTION.

Lord! Anything, anybody, but a black man! For history tells us that Columbus found only Indians, but didn't Columbus himself say, "There are Negroes over there?"

Now everyone in the hall seemed motionless. I slipped off the bench, whipping out my sign, and attached it to the legend. I had returned, grinning, back to the bench when even in that dim place a shadow fell beside me. Startled, I looked up. A second black guard, now signaling the first, stood beside me. The first guard came striding down the hall like a panther out of the high valleys of Popocatapetl. The second guard planted himself beside me. I thought: Give a nigger a uniform and — shit! Would they arrest me? Think me a nut? Could I give them the "brother" routine the way my black students ran it, or tried to, on me? The first guard arrived, his face as expressionless as the second's. He had a tough, square face and a thick neck that reminded me of a lineman. Together they stepped to the legend and read it. They looked at each other, then stepped back to me and stared down like the Olmec himself.

The second guard had a guardsman's mustache. It began to crinkle up into his face in a smile. He winked. The first guard made a soft noise with palate and throat that sounded like !Kung.

"We've read your books, Mr. Douglass," said guard number two. "Do it at the Met in the Egyptian Wing and get one ready for the African Wing when it opens. Tutankhamen is coming."

His voice was soft, not quite a whisper and not quite normal tone. I was surprised. "No shit?"

"No shit," they said together and then melted away.

I got up to leave. I felt good, better than when finishing a book, certainly better than hitting the numbers, almost better than making love and far, far better than getting high. I left a few cards on the bench. They bore the same words as the sign.

"A landsman. Two of them," Allis said when I reported my encounter. "I guess you have to *do* something to make them pop out of the woods. Otherwise, you'll never find them."

"Yeah," I said. "But I wonder if the sign's still there."

"If only for an hour, that's something."

We were in bed, she propped up, writing in longhand. I glanced over. Her poetry. "How's it going?"

Her smile was great; her eyes danced. "Okay." She burrowed deeper into the sheets. "For the first time I like it, really love it, because I don't have to have them published. I mean, I don't feel the slightest compulsion to rush them to an editor, you know."

"C'mon, now. Really. Of course you're going to submit them."

"Oh, no, I'm not."

Her voice had gone hard. She sat up again and pretended to concentrate on the pad.

"And why not?"

"Because I don't want people I don't even know pissing all over me, that's why. You can take it, and maybe you want to take on the world. You do, you know. But I don't."

Some of my students sometimes smugly announced that they were not the least bit interested in writing for an audience; they wrote for themselves and no one else. I never believed them and told them so. Now here was my wife telling me the very same thing. She had not, then, recovered from the wounding at Bread Loaf; Bread Loaf and sharing my own experiences.

"You know that getting your butt out there's what writing's really all about, baby."

"Oh yeah?"

For a moment she sounded like a gang girl of old from Brownsville.

"Well," she went on, "if I die before you, you can have them published; not before, my dearest, not before."

"And you do," I said without looking at her, "take on the world with me." I knew, however, that in many unspoken ways she had always insisted on not publishing, had always rejected vehemently the idea that I let various poetry editors I knew look at the work she was producing. "And if you don't, babe, if you don't hang your wash out, what's it all about?"

Sullenly she said, "For me. For my own very personal pleasure. The way some people work crossword puzzles." She bounced around to face me. "God, after all this time don't you think I know what it's like out there? A pigeonhole for young poets and old poets; one for men, one for women; for the quote traditional unquote, for the quote experimental unquote; one for the Latin poets, one for the African, European, the Commonwealth, the former colonies, the revolutionary, the passive; and then there are the poets who *always* win *all* the grants and those who don't win any. I read somewhere recently that Sterling Brown was *a* black poet. He's been around a thousand years, long enough so people use him as if he were a subway — train or station — it doesn't matter. Can you imagine? Being wiped out by a lousy, stinking, one-letter indefinite article. Dismissed. And poor, poor Osip Yemilyevich — they were only two years apart in age, you know — poor Mandelstam — not bad for a dead Jewish poet. Darling, do you think I want to get into all that, at my age? And dealing with those swishy guys who don't like women, and with women who are into one kind of feminism and wouldn't like my work because I'm married, and then there's the jive-left women who'd like my work only because I was married to you — you know — the people who don't even *know* me at a party until we stand or sit together. Then it's OH! No thanks. But, yes thanks, Bread Loaf, and you, honey, for taking me away from all that idiocy, all the men and women I'd have had to fuck — don't look at me that way; it's true. You said it. Art is cock. And, darling, I really do suspect that you're where you are because you haven't been fucking around too much."

Quickly I said, "Whaddaya mean by that?"

She laughed, leaned her head into my chest and laughed some more. "Nothing," she said. I could see the wrinkles starting, just starting in her neck, and could pick out quite clearly the curled white strands mixed with the dark blond of her hair. I felt a soft, spreading sadness, together with a long, firm pull of pride.

"Put the pad away," I said.

She looked at me. "Honey, I am a little tired."

"So am I."

"I don't think Mack's asleep yet."

"Tough."

She was smiling when she put the pad on her table and turned to me as she slipped off her gown.

The letter was postmarked Cabinda.

Dear Dad (and Allis and Mack):

It took me four days to get my sea legs and to stop puking in the oatmeal. I'm okay now.

Strange how the sea rather than the land makes you miss people, places and things.

It was curious, passing over the old slave-ship routes. I thought I'd feel something. I didn't.

The crew's interesting. From all over the world. A couple of Africans. From where, I am not sure. They grin all the time and say yes to almost everything. The crew ranges from dregs to dreamers. That's not right. No good seaman could be dregs, at least not at sea. They all want to make money for different reasons, away from the crowd. I guess we're all loners.

They tell me this is a small tanker; it holds only a million gallons of oil. There are tankers that hold twice as much, built mainly by the Japanese, I'm told.

The smells are the oil, though there's none in her now, the sea and my cooking. But the air neutralizes them all.

I saw my very first Africans in Africa fishing off the coast of Senegal and again nothing special happened. I thought it would. They waved. We waved back.

What else? I seem to have a lot of ideas kicking around. But I wasn't going to write anymore, was I? Well . . .

There's really not much more to write about. Nobody's complained about my cooking, but they didn't out at Yellow Springs, either.

Gotta get a letter off to Maija. More, as they say, later.

Love, G.

"We have always been sailors in my family," I said to Allis at dinner the night the letter arrived. Maija had received a letter, too, and had joined us. I felt uncomfortably like a father-in-law instead of a letch. "Name for me," I said haughtily, "a famous Jewish sailor."

Allis was serving and didn't even bother to look at me. She said without a break in her motions, "Christopher Columbus."

"Really?" Mack said, his eyebrows rising to meet his hairline, while Maija politely said nothing. "I thought he was Italian."

"What's the matter with you, kid," Allis said. "You never heard of an Italian Jew?"

"Yeah," I said. "Mussolini."

She threw the French bread at me.

Dear Dad:
This should have a Dar-es-Salaam postmark. We're on the way to Mombasa.

We stopped at Cape Town, but most of us didn't go ashore. I felt bad about not going. Would you have? I thought of Gandhi, Luthuli, Suzman, Mandela, Paton, Mphalele, Tambo, and Sharpesville and God only knows what and where else. But, hell, I didn't go on any big marches back home either. I didn't do the voter registration drives. What would it have proved?

I mentioned the two Africans who were always grinning. But every grin ain't for glee. I think they smuggled aboard a guy in Cape Town harbor. There was a lot of bustling and eye-cutting among the crew. One of the Africans claimed to be so hungry. Would I please fix him extra rations? This was said, you should know, in such a way that I couldn't refuse, with all the charm of a super-Godfather. I think this guy was close to Tambo, heading for Dar, where, I've been told, for every African Freedom Fighter there's at least one CIA agent. These brothers have networks all over the place.

I don't think I'll ever forget these smells — the oil, the sea, the galley. There's another, Africa. It's a great giant reclining on the horizon, all green and brown and gray. We come from here? I'm trying to stick my plug in; it won't connect emotionally. I want skyrockets to go off, explosions to boom, the heavens to crackle. But there's only silence, nearly. The engines, you know. And the smells. The ship is like my history — *our* history — perpetually moving around the body, rarely piercing its core.

I love you all and I miss you.

G.

Allis whipped the letter out from under her pillow and read it to me. "He'll write again, don't you think?"

"Yep. Let me see it."

She passed it over.

"Was there anything else important in the mail?"

"You saw the rest of it, Cate. I thought this would be a good bed-time thing for you, hearing from your other son. How'd the work go today?"

I was reading, hearing Glenn's voice and seeing the east coast of Africa as the Chinese must have seen it, Duarte Barbosa, the nameless Arab and Indian sailors, and thinking of Africa's implacable silence behind the monthly discoveries that attested to its place in the world. I was finished.

"Yes, he'll write again. *Graves?* Went okay. I'll show it to you tomorrow. A section I want to finish." I turned to her. "I really liked 'Toast and Terror,' but now I'm going to feel self-conscious when I turn on the radio in the morning and unbuckle the *Times.*"

"*I'm* the one who turns it on, remember? Want the latest report on the candidate?"

Allis was working on the campaign for this asshole who wanted to be mayor of New York.

"Not really. But how far did he put his foot into his mouth today?"

"Up to his kneecap."

"What?"

"The city could save money by eliminating twenty subway stops in Harlem."

"You ought to do something with that poem," I said.

She didn't respond.

"Look," I said. "These jerks come and go every two or four or six years. They don't interest me. Your poetry does. I think," I said less forcefully, "that a work that deals with the terror that men must feel every morning when they go out to work touches everyone more than any politician's statements could in a century. It's a good poem. Maybe even a great one — shut up! How do I know? I don't *know* but I do. Maybe I know through feel — "

"No! And don't tell me to shut up!"

"Well, goddamn it, you were the one who said you have to *do* something to make the landsmen come out of the woodwork! You said it, and you've done it and all you want to do is to take refuge in something that happened to you twenty years ago. They *hurt* me. Yet you could sit down and record *my* hurts. Shit, you don't know the half of my hurts because I haven't let you see them and I haven't told you — "

"I have seen them! I've felt them. I don't think being a man is easy. I

353

think being a black man is, a functioning black man, is a stupendous achievement, you ass, marvelous. There! You made me say it! You think you can be with someone for the same twenty years and not know, you ass? I know what they've done and are doing. How could I not? Don't you think I *know?* What the hell's this marriage all about if it isn't about knowing? What's so important about publishing my poetry? Why are we shouting? You *didn't* have a good day, did you?"

I flipped over. "Aw, to hell — "

"Is this about being black?"

I raised myself up and looked down over the foot of the bed toward the door at the same time Allis did. Mack was sitting there cross-legged, as if he'd been there for a few moments.

"It's about being a man," Allis said.

"It's about being a woman," I said.

"It's not really about being black — or white?" he asked. A smile of relief waited in the wings of his lips. There were echoes in his voice.

"Well, gee," he said. "I get nervous when you start arguing."

"Mom writes poetry," I said.

"I know it."

"It's good poetry. You know, like you want to get things in the school paper?"

"Yeahhhh." He was looking at his mother. She was smiling. He was starting to smile.

"I just think that she ought to get her things in magazines and books; that's all."

"And she doesn't want to."

"Right."

"They're her poems."

I looked from him to her. "When they're good," I said, "they belong to everybody."

"Why?"

"Because they might make the world better, that's why. Good night. Get your ass in bed."

"You won't fight anymore?"

"We hardly ever fight, Mackie. You know that," Allis said. "Right? Give us a kiss. Good night."

It seemed a long time before we spoke again.

Then she said, "Can we talk about the sign for the Metropolitan?"

With some relief I said, "Yeah. I think we gotta forget about a lot of those people, like Hawkes and maybe Bibby, and 'Nubian' archers as against 'Egyptian' spearmen. It's gotta be about what people *see* or don't want to see. Yes. Let the other be."

"Yes. How about that quote you got from Desroches-Noblecourt, the colors of the people and gods in the wall paintings?"

"Perfect. Did you see the cornrows?"

"Yes! They seem to be the style now."

"Used to call them braids, plain and simple."

"Let's look at what he says about the colors in the wall paintings, okay?" She went quickly through her book rack and pulled the book. She opened it and read, smiling all the while: ". . . women's skin is always painted light or pinkish yellow whereas men's skin is red ochre."

I said, "That doesn't try to explain those obviously slanted-eyed yellow-colored girls with dangling pigtails, or the very black, and brown — "

"Red ochre," Allis interrupted.

"Right. Or the *kind* of hair apparently best suited for cornrows. Well, let's just continue."

She put the book back and slid down under the sheets. I turned off the lights. In the darkness I said, "You're sure, baby? Nothing nagging? No furtive little desire? No sense that you might be missing all kinds of acclaim?"

"No, honey. Honestly. Nothing."

"Then I'm sorry I've been insisting. Maybe I wanted it for myself."

"I thought of that. Maybe. But you aren't a failure, not in the terms we both consider right."

"Then why sometimes does it feel like it?"

"That's the whole plan, darling."

Yeah, I thought. Why did I keep forgetting that?

"IT'D BE GREAT if you could come to the national sales meeting," Gullian was saying, "to meet and talk with some of the men in the field. They know about you, of course, but they'd like to meet you. It'd be a tremendous help, Cate."

I agreed to go. Like an old boxer, I was looking for the edge; I sensed that they were cutting off the ring on me. Some boxers used the speed of their opponents to their own advantage; others came up with a new style just for that fight, a kind of rope-a-dope, if you will. So I went down to the Hilton already knowing as much as I wanted to know about book salesmen. If they had plenty of good advance word, they hustled your book; if the word came down from Jock Champion that *this* was the book to push, they pushed on pain of probable separation if they didn't. But the work of nearly all black writers was as suspect as it had been in 1940, when, somehow, the system let *Native Son* slip through.

A publisher might be coming out with a great book by an author who is black. The publisher of course plugs the book at the sales conferences; he has advanced too much money, maybe, not to. The salesmen who have come to New York, Chicago, Los Angeles, Miami, Dallas, San Francisco — anywhere people buy books in great numbers — are wined and dined and possibly even whored at the publisher's expense. Are they then

356

to question the greatness of this book? Are the salesmen not, as company men, visibly and excitedly in agreement with the publisher's assessment of the work? Of course they are. At the conference. When they leave, the book goes into a corner of the trunk of their cars. Who's gonna buy it? they ask themselves. The sixties are over, done with, and my booksellers and their customers have no interest anymore in black people. They're fed up with them, as a matter of fact. This would be in some cases a judgment unilaterally arrived at. The pages of the book begin to yellow and flake; the sleek jacket, once so brilliant and bright, turns lusterless in the dark. "Oh, there's no market for that book," the salesman advises his regional manager. But of course he has not tried to place the book, fobbing off on booksellers in the hinterlands various up-to-date versions of *Peyton Place* or *Gone With the Wind* in its stead, for he *knows* commissions will accrue on these titles. Some people with a sense of balance — teachers, perhaps, of the better sort — scream, phone, write and plead for a multitude of books by authors who are black; these books, however, have gone into and out of print with the speed of a message rushed through the old *pneumatique,* out of sight with a *whooosh!*

When I walked in, I felt like the fighter who knows he's supposed to lose, that he's in the bag, at the bottom of the latrine looking up. Gullian, with forced lightness, I thought, introduced me with that hackneyed phrase "distinguished novelist," etc., etc. She was nervous and her camaraderie was like the flit of a fly as she fended off bold lunges at her breasts and butt and parried whiskey-sheened lips with deft twists of her cheeks.

I talked about *The Pushkin Papers.* The salesmen shifted in their seats, whispered to one another. Then Jock came into the room and they gave me their attention, or pretended to. There were no questions during the question period. There was one statement by a regional manager: "I suppose after all the times you've come to bat you could stand to make a little money, right, Cate?" He scanned the room as if seeking support.

"Money?" I said. "Look, let me tell you that those people who've been writing jacket copy, and those interviewers and biographers, have got it all wrong, you know. I don't need money."

A stillness slipped through the audience like a knife through Blue Bonnet margarine. Jock glanced at Gullian.

Money. It was what they understood. All they understood. All they respected, and they were saying they would maybe give me a bit of it.

"Both my parents were doctors; surgeons, to be precise. So I've always had money, you see. They gave me my first Cadillac when I was sixteen and had come home from Eton for a part of the summer instead of joining them on the French Riviera. They thought I should have at least one American car. That was the same year Dad built a poolroom onto the house for me and bought a two-inch slate-bed pool table, upon which I still play from time to time with a good friend of mine whose name I won't mention because I know you're familiar with it."

There was a murmuring. Gullian was bent close to Jock Champion, who was talking furiously into her ear. She looked pale.

"It seemed somehow wiser when I began my writing career to concoct that background of the mother who was a domestic and the father who was a merchant seaman. I mean, it was expected, really, wasn't it? If I had come on with airs and a British upper-class accent and a splendidly tailored white suit, who would've believed I was for real?"

Jock was standing.

I said, pointing to him, "I didn't even let ole Jock in on the secret, did I, Jock?" I turned away from him. "To answer the question more directly, gentlemen, it's not money I need. I don't need *you* to make money for *me*. I just want all you cocksuckers, all you motherfuckers, off my goddamn back. You are not clever. You are not cunning. You are just small, greedy, frightened men, fit mostly to flush woodcock or pheasant or partridge from the heather on my moors in Scotland."

Jock Champion had sat down. Maureen Gullian sat beside him.

"Thank you," I said with a smile, my voice booming back through the silence from the speakers. "Thank you very much."

And I hit the road, humming, feeling good, feeling that I had at last washed myself clear back to absolute sanity. Therefore, it was nothing to walk at a brisk clip up Seventh Avenue, through the Park, to the Metropolitan Museum of Art, from where I could just see patinaed towers of the building where Paul and Betsy had lived with their children. I wondered how long he'd dreamed of living on Fifth Avenue.

For a moment I hesitated, thinking first to go to the second floor and look again at the Rodins and the Degas. No. Business. I strolled into the Egyptian Wing, down the corridors hung with replicas of wall paintings. A guard who was black sauntered through, his eyes catching mine. For an instant they seemed to dance, and he was gone.

There is a painting said to be from the tomb of Nakht (Eighteenth Dynasty) of three young women, loosely called, by some, entertainers; by others, a double-flute player, a lute player and a harpist. (A harp has forty-six strings; this "harp" has thirteen.) They all wear pectorals and beaded headbands, and they have intricate cornrows. They are a neat, rich brown — "red ochre"? Their heads are long and possess a modified prognathism; the faces are seen in profile, the style at the time.

358

What's unusual about the three women is that they all have blue eyes. The women in other wall paintings have brown eyes, and in the three-quarter rather than full-bodied studies they have pronounced, lusciously thick lips; the lips of the blue-eyed babes cannot be precisely defined. It's as though Lord Carnavon, James Breasted, Caton-Thompson, Champollion, Budge and whoever else was messing around there thought that a bit of the old Anglo-Saxon blue was needed, and slipped in to touch up the eyes.

Or maybe the mixed-bloods of the New Kingdom, just coming to prominence, were still unusual enough in certain respects (blue eyes) to be painted.

I affixed our sign so that it neatly covered the museum's legend, and started out. The guard had circled round and was at the exit, humming and clicking softly, pretending not to notice me. But as I passed him, still feeling a slight dread that he might be a traitor, he broke off his humming and clicking and said, almost without moving his lips, "Tutankhamen is coming." I let some cards fall out of my hand to the floor.

Out then. I slogged through the Park, though by now all the papers carried stories at least once a week of someone being mugged or murdered there. But it was still daylight and I took refuge in the belief that it was not my destiny to be ended in such an ignominious fashion. Anyway, suddenly I had other concerns. The book salesmen. Jock's look. Gullian's attempt not to look any special way. Literary death was not all that far away.

The silence prevailed, naggingly, and it would have been ominous had I not expected it. I went off to some nearby campuses to do some readings from *The Pushkin Papers* and *Unmarked Graves* and returned to find my daughter-in-law-to-be (I supposed) almost ready to leave to meet Glenn, whose letters had come from Mombasa and, finally, Tehran, to which he traveled after leaving the tanker at Kharg Island. (He mentioned that Fanon's works had been translated into Farsi and were being read everywhere.)

We gathered all the latest photographs and gave them to Maija for Glenn and Alejo and then, quickly, day pounding down upon day, it was time to drive her to the airport with her Arab, French and Spanish dictionaries, her hair freshly done, and her sleek travel bag, stickered and tagged from previous trips, hung over her shoulder.

A few days later, close to the end of October, Maxine called. "We have to have lunch." Her tone was brusque, without any of the small talk or the stroking that agents often apply to the egos of their clients. Of course, something was going on with TCFP.

"Pushkin," she said, "is in trouble."

We were in the Plaza. It occurred to me that it might be my last time there. "Whaddya mean?" I wanted the numbers, the complete briefing.

"That was a beaut you ran off at the conference. Maureen told me all about it. It's all over town, how you cut your own throat. You think those guys are gonna go out and push that book now?"

"Well, shit, Maxine, they never really did push for the others, did they?"

She ignored that. "There are things that you simply cannot *say*, sweetie. But, anyway, we know people in this town, so let's try to make *that* work."

"Like how?"

"Let's get a typescript to Paul Cummings — "

"We're out of touch." I demolished the last of my lamb chops. She watched me chew it.

"Listen, Cate. I can get in touch with anyone. You want to do it?" She didn't wait for me to answer. "Remember, you're also under contract for *Graves,* but unless we rescue *Pushkin* from the oblivion to which it's surely headed, *Graves*'ll go down the drain even faster — *if* TCFP even decides to go ahead with it." She sat back, small triumphs dancing in her eyes. "You remember I *did* tell you that things simply aren't the way they used to be."

"No," I said. "Not Paul." I looked out at the Park. Funny. He lived on one side of it and I lived on the other. *That* hadn't changed.

Her voice was carefully level. "No?"

"No."

"A quote from Paul might open the way for lots of others, not to mention the reviewers. TCFP couldn't afford to ignore a groundswell."

I sighed and said again, "No. I don't think so, Maxine." Certainly not. No more save me, white folks; it had to end, this sad, sad volleyball game. Who but white folks, on the other hand, had kept me afloat? Was it now really very cool to refuse the lifesaver?

"Sweetie," she said. Her voice carried a warning. "Pride goeth before the you know. Why do you have the hatchet out?"

"There's no hatchet."

"But you behave as though you'd be hurting *him* instead of him helping you." She curled her tongue over her lips after she swallowed the last of her pêche Melba.

Hurting him. Hurting *him*. But yes of course that was it. He'd love to do it. He'd do it for me (even though lately it was being said that he no longer gave quotes) because I was in his ball game, in his ball park, into which I'd strolled at the wrong time. But it was time to cut off the nose to etc., etc. It was time.

"Another friend of yours," Maxine said, seeming to hide her face behind the cup of coffee she was drinking, "Roye Yearing, remember him?"

It was true I had not heard from him since our panel of readings. I assumed that he was, as always, working on something that would soon be coming out to good reviews but would make him very little money. He was, after all, a "serious" writer and being serious was somehow equated with being retarded.

"Of course," I said. "What about him?"

"He's down in the Bowery."

"What's that supposed to mean?"

"Just what you think it's supposed to mean, and he's not doing research."

Ah, no, I thought. But she was threatening me with a similar fate, and I laughed. The more puzzled her expression became, the more I laughed.

"I'm sure *he* doesn't think it's so funny." She leaned toward me. "Look what happened to Ike, too — zzzzip!" She pointed her thumb toward the floor. "And Amos, he's not such a hotshot anymore, either, is he? And now Roye. What do — "

"No," I said again. "Let's go."

She touched my arm. "Right now I know that Jock and Maureen are contemplating a print order of no more than thirty-five hundred copies of your book. How's that strike you? Advertising budget? Hah! Unless everybody loves it, zilch, and how can they love it if it isn't available, and how can it be available if we don't hustle the goddamn thing?"

"Uh-uh."

She studied my face. "I have to tell you, Cate, that I'm in only until *Graves* is published."

"Dropping me?"

"I'm dropping all of you. I've got my other career now, and I'm going to make some bucks, big bucks, lotsa money, instead of dealing with you — artists — for a lousy ten percent."

" 'S'all right," I said. "It will have been a long time."

She was standing now, gathering things. "Yes," she said. "A long time. It's all changed, Cate."

"I suppose it always does."

We stopped outside. "What're you going to do this afternoon?" she asked.

"Sulk, I guess." Something made me ask. "You want to sulk with me or something?"

She took a deep breath. "Walk a little way."

We started walking. "I don't know," she said. "I don't think you really meant it. Bored, maybe? You don't really want to do it with a forty-eight-year-old sex object, do you?"

I laughed. "No, I guess I don't, though there's nothing wrong with the sex object."

She grinned. Instantly, an indefinably superfeminine motion was added to her stride. "You know," Maxine said, "Paul and I are friends. *Good* friends. Even before they broke up. He'd do it, give you the quote."

"No."

She had slipped on sunglasses. She stopped. "Okay, Cate. I'll call. You take care." And she disappeared through the crowds on slender, taut, black-stockinged legs.

Dear Dad and Allis and Mack:

How lucky a man you are to have *three* wonderful sons, *three!*

We have met Alejo. We adore Alejo. Forgive the delay in writing this, but we have been on a romp of getting to know each other. He looks like you. He cried when we met; he cried when he read your letter. He introduces me as his *hermano* and Maija as his *hermana*. Just like that. I can't tell you everything in this letter. There's just too much, too many emotions, all good.

We've been all over Spain with him and his girl, Dolores. She's a dancer. Fiery, as they say. The new democracy, Alejo says, is not very different from the last stages of the Franco times. We've been to Sitges and found the house where you lived with his mother. She's in Fernando Po.

We've also been to Paris.

Alejo is a good friend of Iris Joplin Stapleton. She's got a club in the Ramblas and sings a couple of sets a night. I know she's been around a while, but, boy, does she look good. Said she was thinking about packing it in and returning home, too. We just missed her niece, the daughter of Ralph Joplin, the playwright. Iris said the niece had studied with you. Do you remember her?

Listen. It's all all right. Alejo wants to see you and plans to come to New York as soon as he can. He's working on another collection now. He finds it astoundingly significant that we're all writers. He hopes Mack will be, too. Did I say "we're all writers"? I confess to having changed my mind. Had I ever changed it in the first place? But you knew, didn't

362

you? Oh! I got the galleys back in good time — air mail, too. Were you as restless with your first as I am? Impatient for the damn thing to come out even when you know the reception it's likely to get? Deep down don't you still feel that way, or am I just experiencing the first-book syndrome?

Hey, what happens if you get caught putting up those signs and cards? I mean, suppose one of the brothers isn't in on the plot?

More later. Listen, when you visit the prison, don't let them keep you there, okay? Lots of love from all of us. (We do wish you were here.)

Glenn

10

THE PRISON WALLS, buildings and fences pierced the snow, shining grayly in reflected light as if they were objects too big and too hot for any precipitation to stick upon. I parked in the space marked for visitors and looked up at the wall that had cast its shadow over me. I climbed out of the car and walked toward the floodlighted gate. A series of hums and clicks commenced. A small door within the gate itself opened, and a guard — corrections officer — a stocky black man with a weary air, let me in without question and pointed to still another door, another guard. To the second guard, also black, I gave my name because he asked for it. He looked it up on a battered clipboard, whistling softly a tune I did not recognize.

"Gonna talk about books and things, huh, Brother Douglass?" He smiled a sassy bright smile; his mustache flared out above his lips.

"Yeah, I guess so."

He cradled the clipboard on his hip like a quarterback on a bootleg play, and we moved into the prison, the guard opening this door and locking it and opening that door and locking it, until we were inside a long, gray hall that was stifling and hot. It reminded me of places I'd dreamed of racing through with nightmares at my heels.

"We got some heavy brothers in here. Don't let 'em eat you up, hear?"

He chortled deep down in his chest. "Warden Kelley's waiting for you. C'mon."

We continued through the halls, and guards, all black, now began to materialize at doors, unlocking and locking them without comment. It was like moving down into the belly of some vast, quite unconcerned being. I wasn't sorry that I had finally accepted the invitation of the librarian, Miss Dobbs, to spend a few hours with the inmates, but I wasn't sure either why I'd come. To preach down *these* walls? *These* bars and endless, thick doors? What could one do in a place like this? Was one to do anything? If not, why did one come?

Through film, people learned that the jails once were filled with white men in the images of James Cagney, Eduardo Cianelli, Edward G. Robinson, George Raft, Paul Muni. They made no films then or later of the Scottsboro Boys, the Dade County Four, the Wilmington Ten, the San Quentin Six, nor even of the Chitlin Three or the Porkchop Two, nor of Paul Crump. Forget the Genuine Bad Nigger.

Quite suddenly it seemed that all the prisons were filled with black and brown people, and so came the prison programs, the going into and the coming out of places like these, some of us seeking for a thing we could not know, others out of that do-gooding superguilt trip, some because it extended their knowledge and still others because they were paid.

The warden was a big man who walked on the balls of his feet as though he'd often worn high-heeled shoes. His manner was soft, his hands smooth. His face was pink and heart-shaped. He moved with a dainty grace for a man so large, and his hair was a mass of gray curls. He reminded me of the man old Harlem residents still spoke of, Legs Diamond's hit man, a huge faggot who wore lipstick and powder and danced closely with his lovers, his eyes closed, on speakeasy floors. No one laughed at him; they didn't even dare look in his direction.

"Good of you to come, Mr. Douglass. The men've wanted to talk to you for some time now, Miss Dobbs tells me. Coffee?"

"Yes, please."

"Purcell," he said to the guard who'd brought me, "get the men settled." As the guard left, the warden called, "Harvey." A young inmate, clean-shaven, his face prettier than a man's ought to be, his prison jeans and shirt tailored to his body, entered the room through a side door.

"Coffee, Harvey." To me the warden said, "Cream, sugar?"

"The works."

Harvey vanished.

Warden Kelley, bulging out of his chair, tapped his fingers on his desk.

Under the smell of paint, food, rust, sweat, shit and Harvey's cologne was the smell of urine; it was needle-sharp, as though men were pissing their pants with fear. The radiators hissed and banged softly, and in the halls outside there were voices, cautious, muted. I thought of my sons thousands of miles away and the one at home who could not understand why I would want to visit a prison. I wondered how many times in my life I had come close to being in a place like this.

"I haven't read any of your books," the warden said. I was always meeting people who hadn't read any of my books. "But I'm told that the men have, and like them. They'll be glad you've come."

Harvey returned with the coffee. Now I wondered if the warden too was thinking how come I hadn't wound up in his care.

"How long's the session?" I asked.

"A couple of hours. Play it by ear."

He swallowed his coffee and looked at the door through which Harvey had gone again. "And you teach at the university," he said.

"Yes."

"How nice." He swallowed again and glanced at his watch. He smiled at the knock at the door. He set down his cup. "That'll be Purcell." He extended his hand. "Good luck, Mr. Douglass." He took three great strides to the door and opened it. Purcell stood there. "Ready," he said.

I plodded beside Purcell, now sweating with the heat. The smells were stronger. When at last we entered the room they called the library, I was relieved. There were books on the shelves, maps on the walls, a catalogue stand, and here the solid, comfortable smell of aging paper and cloth.

The inmates were sitting, chairs drawn in a half-circle. A heavy, gray-haired woman introduced herself as Miss Dobbs. She took my hand and led me before the group. I felt that I was on trial and they were my jury.

"He's here," she said. "Cato Caldwell Douglass."

"Hear, hear!"

"Raht on!"

"Yeah!"

"Aw raht!"

Purcell eased into a corner, sat down and promptly started yawning. Miss Dobbs continued the introduction while I studied the group of about thirty, only three of whom were white. Five were Hispanics and the rest black. And they were studying me, in much the same way I'd observed students studying me in the classroom.

In another time the impulses that sent them on the ventures that had landed them here instead might have placed them in the midst of the exploration and colonization of Australia, of Sierra Leone, of Bermuda, Georgia. They might have sailed the seas, beating up on natives from one end of the globe to the other; they might have found Melendi, Goa, destroyed Montezuma. But those worlds were gone now.

I had had occasion, like all good marines, to have done a hitch in a USMC brig out in the islands. I'd disobeyed a white sergeant's order, and the penalty after the court-martial was five days piss and punk. There were two black Seabees there. They had killed a commanding officer who fled a Japanese counterattack somewhere in New Guinea. They were awaiting transport home — that is, to a naval jail in the States.

One of the Seabees was tall and the other short. They wore leg irons and they had learned to adjust, each to the other's stride. They walked as one misshapen being — a shuffle, slight hop and a stride, their chains clanking, clinking and clicking. You could hear them coming and going. They ate together, slept together, shit and pissed together. They were kids (and though, so was I, they remain fixed at a hard nineteen, clanking through my memory). How careful they were of each other, not to pull or jerk, so that the chains didn't scrape or hurt when they moved. Lovers, husbands and wives, it seemed to me, are never as considerate of each other. And now, looking at the inmates, I wondered if those two kids were still serving time. I'd not thought of them in years, had not even known their names. We'd called each other "Mate."

I began to talk. At first they listened, their faces expressionless, and then that choral mask slipped away and revealed that exaggerated politeness of people who possess both a wealth of time and experience, the range of which you could not begin to imagine. And this soon passed, meandered, actually, into the bullshit, fragile tenderness a veteran on the line might fleetingly feel for a replacement who has just come up.

They listen, other visitors had told me, but only until *they* can talk; it's important that they talk.

We all began to talk in that castle, the castle of our skins, of Wright, Huysmans, Ellison, Baldwin, Whittington, Hughes, Himes, Killens (they were not interested in the works by black women, though I told them they should be), but mostly we talked of the Man and his System, of those who'd "sold out," and, the politeness long since gone, we argued; they postured and played on my guilt, and they, perceiving that, insinuated about my being free while they were in jail, and cited Thoreau's statement to Emerson, and I, warming to the free-for-all, suggested that since they

367

knew so much about the System, they should've tried harder to keep their asses out of its way.

Like I did? someone asked.

There were chuckles and banks of laughter. Yes, like I did.

Of course they had to resent me. I hadn't thought about it before.

But a man had to stand up, *had* to, 'cause a man couldn't take but so much.

I agreed, but wondered why it was that we could never stand together, even though a basic function of the System was to keep us from doing so.

Someone drawled, "Nigguhs can't do nuthin' together. We're too individualistic. That's how come the Seventy-Sixers can't win no championship and keep it."

Keeyaw, keeyaw, keeyaw.

For over two hours, while Miss Dobbs sat enraptured by the exchange and Purcell dozed and yawned, I served as the safety valve through which they rammed their bitterness, into which they fanged their venom. Yes, that's what it was all about. Pissed on again. In this small, poorly lighted room, once a month, the System allowed the inmates to destroy it verbally, rip it to tatters, utterly to demolish it; the men became Joe Hills, Nat Turners, Bolivars, Sam Melvilles. Goddamn it! My function was to save Purcell's ass, the warden's, society's. Drain off the anger; bottle it up in libraries, saltpeter it to death with a stream of literary types.

I was tired now. Yes, I agreed, the situation was rotten, but then it had always been. No, I didn't know how a change could be effected without force, the judicious use of force. Why? Why not? Has the vote worked? Patience? Good will? World opinion? Prayers? Deals? I asked what had got them here.

Force.

How were they kept here?

Force.

How were they to get out?

In a box.

Parole.

Finish the sentence.

Breakout — force.

He hadn't said anything before. There was always a guy like him, anywhere in the world, all laid back, listening, marking every nuance, sifting the shit from the sugar, who would speak up when the curtain's about to ring down.

Purcell stirred in his chair; he was no longer yawning. Miss Dobbs's eyes gleamed.

I took a deep breath. It was all but over.

He said, this man in the back, muscled arms folded over a massive chest, "How does it feel to be able to walk into a place like this and walk out whenever you want to?"

"Great."

"Do you go to a lot of prisons?"

"No."

"Why not?"

"Why should I? Would you?"

Purcell was not the only one not yawning now; this scene had been played before, with other outside straight men.

"You're as much a prisoner as we are," the man said, his voice punching out of his body. "Aren't you, turkey, aren't you?"

"Yes, yes I am."

"So that don't make you much different from us, does it?" He looked around in triumph. "You can go home, sleep in a nice bed, eat good food, go out, travel, you and your wife — I read she's white — "

I said, "Yeah. And she's got kinda blond hair and kinda green eyes — was that some kind of point you were tryin' to make? I thought it was that I was a prisoner, too."

Miss Dobbs was flashing angry glances at the inmate. Others grumbled and cut their eyes at him.

"There's a difference, though," I said.

He was belligerent now; his remark had been considered foul. "Yeah? What's that?"

"I didn't have to go to jail to find out how much of a prisoner I was."

Hoot! Hoot!

Keeyaw! Keeyaw!

The inmates laughed at their man and slapped palms all around.

Miss Dobbs saw that I'd had it, and got to her feet and thanked me. I shook hands with the inmates, including the laid-back one. "Jus' jailhouse rap, bro," he said.

Purcell was quiet as he led me out through the halls and past other guards. At the gate he said, "All you folks come in here tryin' to find another Malcolm X." He shook his head as he hauled open the door and the cold air swept in, clean and blade-sharp.

"I suppose," I said. "Maybe we should stop trying?"

"Hey. That's up to you, man, now ain't it?"

Allis had beat me to the mail again. She gave me the green-bound galleys of *The Pushkin Papers,* slapped them into my hand as a baton is slapped in a relay race. I thumbed through them. Crane Duplicating, as usual. Who needed to read the book again? They were designed to make it easier for reviewers to read in advance of the actual book. For me this time out they seemed all gesture, like a coach whose team is behind 80–zip asking for one more for the Gipper.

"And," Allis said, "this." She placed the galleys of *Jumper* gently in my hand. They were bound in red.

"This I'll read for the changes," I said.

"But I wanna read it," Mack said.

I hesitated. How could you not let one son know his brother?

"It won't take long," he said. "Maybe about a month?"

Allis was nodding. "You might get an advance copy or bound galley of Paul's new book," she said.

There were lots of notices that Paul had a big, Hemingwayesque war novel coming out at the same time Glenn's and my novels would be out.

"Sure, okay," I said to Mack. He read while he watched television, that entity that sought to submerge all things in swamp and from which, day after day, we fought to save our son. Or we could of course read Glenn when Mack was out playing, or visiting, or just staring at walls, too exhausted with electronic living, whether watched, played or listened to, to move.

"They'll be home soon," I said, handing him Glenn's galleys.

"I know, I know, you already told me ten times," he said, bending back to a map I'd laid out for him. They didn't teach kids where things were anymore.

"Okay, fat mouth, I told you. But I'm telling you again!"

"Mom!" His voice echoed with indignation. "All I said was — "

"I know what you said and *how* you said it!"

Allis looked at me in that way she looked whenever Mack and I got into one of these stupid, idiotic, just-out-of-the-atmosphere things. For emphasis, I smashed an ash tray against the wall. I didn't need this shit today. Allis turned away. Mack stared at me with a mixture of disbelief and fear, and my stomach started leaking out my ass. Oh, crap. What was happening here?

We were motionless until Mack, the first to recover, said, "Sorry. Who's Al-ay-joe?"

"A relative," I said and then hurried to my corner of the bedroom. We'd not yet told Mack about his older brother. His sense of right and wrong was stronger than most kids', certainly far stronger than Glenn's at that age. Mack was for everybody's rights, black folks', white folks', cats', dogs' and sparrows' — even snakes' now. He hated kids who cheated at whatever game they were playing. He would wonder how Alejo had managed, how I could have been so cruel as to leave him, too. That Alejo had not been born when I left, that I had not been able to find him at first, wouldn't have mattered. In the fairy tales disguised as sitcoms everyone got found or married a prince or princess or at least resolved the problems at hand in only twenty-four minutes; he'd wonder how come I couldn't have done the same in twenty years. The relentless impingement of the world had not yet started to make an impact on his soul.

Yet, I thought, resting my head upon the cold metal of the typewriter, a man ought to be able to be some part of what his sons think he should be. Willie Loman believed that; believed it too much. You always had to keep something of yourself for yourself.

Mack, it wasn't just one of those things; it just turned out to be, for a while.

Ice rattling in a glass. I looked up as Allis set the drink down beside the machine. She leaned on the back of my chair and sighed.

Glenn was now moving through that great valley. For all our talking, he couldn't *know* and therefore our talks about book life always ended with me feeling the way I did at the end of some classes: *I had not made them understand.* In some twistingly subtle fashion he made me feel that I had not become a black Hemingway, say, because it was my own fault, the accumulation of my own blemishes, the root of which might have been my desertion of him.

¿Quien es mi padre?

Alejo no longer had to ask. He now knew. Yet what bitterness he must have felt all those years (I am still assuming), before Monica married into the security of political respectability. Nothing, they say, leaks that away like success, an abscess that has been drained clean.

"Thanks," I said, picking up the drink. It was weak.

"You found him, I guess," Allis said.

"Yep. I found the sucker."

She slipped off her shoes. "And?"

"We talked. Over drinks. Lots of drinks — "

"I could smell them — "

" — in a cruddy old bar. He's *really* drinking with another crowd now."

"Bad, huh?"

"Hopeless. I told him about the sales conference and, man, did he laugh his ass off. He fell out on the floor." I got up, put some muscle in my drink, surveyed the shattered clay I would have to clean up and came back. "Bad? It's almost hopeless. His head's together on his terms. Hope-less, if you mean he should be living like other people. And he's sick. Looks like hell, and I think he wants to ride that all the way out to the end. Hell, why not?"

"Is he doing any writing at all?"

"Naw," he had told me. "Thought about TV writing for a while. They asked me all the time and I said no. Naw, I won't even do that, now. That's lower than this."

His hair was long, dirty, swept to one side of his gaunt, gray face. His clothes were spotted and stained and he would have smelled worse had it been warmer.

"I don't believe you'd quit," I told him. "You're a chickenshit, lying honky."

He'd laughed and asked for another drink and after he led me to his room and gave me a box of typescripts. The name on the very top page surprised me. "This says Ike Plunkett. He's around here, too?"

"He was." Roye Yearing searched through one of the drawers in the splintered dresser and came up with a half-pint of wine. He knocked it back and exhaled deeply, coughed until phlegm the color of three-day-old death leaked out on his lips. He licked it down. "I heard he got wasted, but they can't find his body. He gave me this stuff to hold for him last summer when he was doing doorways and had no place to stash it. Poor guy. Hey, if you just happen to sell any of that stuff, my stuff, bring down a case of bourbon, willya? Or even if you sell some of Ike's stuff. He ain't drinkin' no more."

"Nobody wins any battles," Allis said, "let alone the wars. Maybe Mack."

"What?"

"He started taking Oreos to school again."

He'd stopped taking them because the kids called him Oreo. The meaning of the name had changed since the sixties. Now he could handle their laughter, their taunts. Mack was moving around and around ancient genetic fields. I'd explain it all to him later, when the laughter was a distant memory.

I came away from encounters like the one with Roye with the feeling that danger had passed close by me. Close, man. They used to say that a miss was as good as a mile, but they were using different shit these days; it was radioactive. If a direct hit didn't get you, radiation would, and God, I didn't want what was radiating around this town to get me.

372

11

AS THE LAST of the stiff March winds crashed and banged through the city, Glenn and Maija arrived home. They were aghast and disgusted by the dirt, the forever crescendoing noises. Allis and I smiled. It was always so: the place one left was superior for a time to the place arrived at.

They were filled with the cadences and airs of Europe — the frequent Spanish or French and sometimes Arabic or African phrase or word, the simulated belch of the North Europeans that served as punctuation, the feigned exuberance of South Europeans. For moments at a time they were insufferably arrogant with those who had been to the continent only on business or vacation, but not to live.

We smiled again.

Hours passed in our apartment or Maija's loft, to which Glenn had moved, talking about the old countries, ships' crews, Arabs, Africans, Europeans. We talked of the "kids," Alejo and Dolores, and how they seemed to be living their lives to the full, the crowds they drew wherever they went. We could not get over how much they'd done while still so young. We talked of restaurants, of legends and how they were catching up with us, the redemocratization of Spain almost fifty years since the last taste, and the rise of new class and regional antipathies. Blissfully, there was only passing mention of Iris Joplin and her niece who had studied with me, but with it a look in Allis' eyes, half-smile, half-something else, of scores settled, evened, *something* so perfectly conveyed that for the rest of that evening my interest, my attention, were forced to peek over the questions when? who? I didn't have to ask why, and I didn't need to know where.

Alejo had read my books there in both the English and the Spanish, the latter, Glenn conveyed to me, being extremely poor translations. Nuance had been missing or not understood, Maija said. For a while there *Clarissa* had been almost as popular as *La Choza de Tio Tomás.* "I think about a month, Alejo said," Glenn said, and we exploded with laughter, but I was looking at Allis and her eyes were calm with her yes, and we finished the evening with me barely on this side of sullen.

"Something the matter?" Allis said later at home when we were in bed and had just turned out the lights.

"Yes," I said.

"What?"

"You know."

"I don't. What?"

"Forget it," I said.

"All right. It'll pass." There seemed to be a smile in her voice.

She took my hand and placed it on her hip, where she liked to feel it, and within minutes was snoring softly.

It took several hours before I slept, consoling myself with the thought that Alejo would be in New York this summer.

My ten free copies of *The Pushkin Papers* arrived the next week. I went through a copy, noticing that the paper was cheap and would not last a year without yellowing or becoming brittle, and that the cover was paper, instead of cloth, over board and that the board was as tough as a wet sponge. The type, I had seen earlier in the galleys, was an ordinary Roman — nothing cute like Bodoni or Electra or Janson or Caledonia — and the jacket paper had the sheen of the high beams of a car bouncing off dense fog.

The package did not indicate great love for me. But it *was* coming out. It would be like scoring a touchdown in that 80–zip game to make the score 80–6, with seconds left in the last quarter.

Glenn's copies of *Jumper* came soon after, and his publisher, somehow, had managed to make them more cheap-looking than mine. I said nothing, watched my son elaborately signing a copy for us with multitudinous thanks for help, comfort, strength, etc., etc. I felt very good about him.

Then, as our pub date drew closer, he became like one who, under the stress of impending combat, forgets all the rules of survival. He'd made himself unavailable for assignments from Office Temporaries, to which he had returned. He fretted in our apartment or squatted behind Maija in the loft while she painted. A Kirlian photo, I was sure, would have revealed an extensive aura filled with unimaginable colors.

We got, as did Paul, the evenhanded good advance blurbs in *Publishers Weekly*. Paul's book also had a big ad, and the publicity about his new novel was coming like waves in a cycle, each one higher, each promising that this one would be the most masterful novel of the decade. It was called *Man on the Point*. His war novel. The only war novel written by a black ex-soldier that I could remember was *And Then We Heard the Thunder,* by John Killens, who did his dying in Paris. Even that, however, was about occupation, not combat. I had never had the slightest compulsion to write a novel about the war; shit, there was *always* war.

I thought more frequently about returning to my classes in the fall as I moved on toward the completion of *Graves*. Spring drifted in on soft, warming winds, but this time it barely stirred within me the sense of awakening from the winter cold for yet another season.

Maureen Gullian called, and in a hearty voice suggested mounting a book party for the publication of *The Pushkin Papers*. I had always been opposed to such functions on the part of *my* publisher, feeling that the money could be better spent on promotion. That TCFP would not be advertising was a foregone conclusion — quite well supported by word from Maxine. In any case, the cost for a page of advertising in any of the tabloid-sized book review sections was fast becoming equal to the purchase of a one-minute spot on prime-time television. (A fact some paperback book publishers were already putting to good use by advertising on the tube.) Jock Champion, Gullian said, was insisting. The party wouldn't be a bad thing and perhaps might help me in what I had to know was a sticky wicket. Gullian was adamant. Jock was adamant. There would be a book party. Where would I like to have it?

"The Plaza."

"No," she said. "Really."

It was upstairs at Sardi's and it drew the second- or third-rank reviewers, the folk who *might* write a review, but mostly would not. The top shelf didn't show, but then they never had, so I was not as unhappy as Jock pretended to be. If he'd wanted them there, they would have been there.

The free-loaders seemed to be younger these days. The older ones had learned to save themselves for the *big* bashes.

"The way they aren't throwing around copies of your book makes me think that the print order wasn't so great," Amos said. He and I seemed to be the only people drinking liquor; everybody else was into wine.

"It ain't," I said.

Maxine drifted by, smiling brightly, clutching one of those chicken wing "drumsticks" they were serving everywhere now, and whispered, "This is some turkey."

"But we knew it, right?"

"Rriiight," she said and moved on.

I glanced over at Glenn.

His publisher had arranged no party, had scheduled no ads and no promotion. Glenn concealed his shock well. I couldn't say to him, *I tried to tell you,* and I couldn't / wouldn't abandon him. I had to do whatever I could to save him from that sense of worthlessness all these calculated affronts were making him feel. (He would feel immensely better when *Jumper* was reviewed three weeks after pub date.) However, at the moment, he didn't understand what was going on. He didn't know that it was *just* a party, that nothing special was to happen, that no one special was to be there; he didn't know that the affair was designed to be written off, was designed to provide TCFP with the excuse that they had *done something* for my book. I knew that Glenn was remembering Alejo and all the exquisite Spanish courtesies that had been offered up to his younger brother, and thinking that *I* was having a party, and wondering: WHERE'S MINE? I'VE WRITTEN A NOVEL!

Aw, shit.

One talks to sons and it is perhaps this relationship, the talking, that makes them even tolerate fathers, for after all the sons have smelled the shit-stink in the bathroom after you've left it, or the odor of your cologne, or your breath, whiskey-laden or just plain bad; they have seen you draw on your pants one leg at a time and perhaps even caught you doing it to their mothers. No difference made here that you've tried to slice open the world for them, the way geodes are cut open to reveal color and form; sons must learn it all themselves, though fathering is about saving them that terrible trouble. Concreteness, practicality, were gone. If I was only to show him how to choose hardwood for arrows or ash wood for bows, or the cool spots in streams where trout lurk, the bends where bass bite best, or how the most innocent stone contains heat long past the setting of the sun and can therefore nurture seed. Nothing is that simple anymore.

Then I saw him hovering, he and Maija, close to Allis, like bodyguards, protecting her from those malevolent or nonseeing glances, and from the bumps that passed as accidental brushings, the general vibrations and vapors from the bitches' brew directed by the black women against her whiteness. He winked at me. The expression on his face had changed; he was digging in on the beach, for the ocean was lapping at his back and the tide was fast rising. He was remembering, then, all those talks, those throwaway lines, the words that should have been where none were spoken.

I say he was reviewed three weeks after his pub date, which was not bad, considering the number of books that came rushing down the belts from the mills every day, like butchered logs.

". . . *Jumper* reeks with the promise of great writing to come . . ."

". . . Glenn Douglass may well become another Wright, another Whittington, another Huysmans . . ."

He contained his ecstasy, not so much because I'd warned him of the comparison of such reviews to leaky old ships, but because of something else.

Paul Cummings made a considerable number of front pages in both book review sections and magazines. There were many ads, most of them full page. There were, the ads advised, one hundred thousand copies of *Man on the Point* in print. It was a Book-of-the-Month Club selection and was to be a major motion picture. (This had been said about some of his other books, but the pictures were never made, though I am sure Paul was well paid for them.)

Glenn absorbed all this and realized that *The Pushkin Papers* was not reviewed anywhere.

"Missed ole Poode and Selena," Amos was musing. "But I wouldn't have had too much to say to them, even if they had been at your party."

We were at one of those Columbus Avenue outdoor watering holes. Glenn sat with us.

"Did you notice," Amos said, turning to him, "that they didn't even mention your father when they wrote about you?"

"Yeah." Glenn flashed an apologetic look in my direction.

"Wasn't your fault," I said.

"I know," he said, "but — "

"Another drink," Amos said.

We drank and floated ourselves up to laughter between the abysses of bitterness.

"Let's hope they have a new bunch of salesmen by the time *Graves* is ready," I said. Then I told Amos about the note one of them had sent me: *I've always liked your writing, Cato. It's powerful and real and the things you say need to be said, but I wish you'd write white, use white characters instead of black ones. It's really true, you know. We can't sell black books.*

I had framed the letter and placed it above my desk.

"Somebody really *wrote* that?" Amos said.

The question possessed a remembered echo. "Hey, people are saying and writing things they were scared to say and write fifteen years ago. For them, it's back to the good old days."

Glenn looked morose.

"Cheer up. You'll get your turn at all this."

He laughed. "That's what I'm afraid of."

"What're you workin' on now, Glenn? Lemme see it, okay?"

"Sure. It's another novel. Not really into it yet. But I'm gonna hit the road again. I'll be workin' on it — "

"He figures," I said, "that if he keeps movin' they won't be able to hit him."

We laughed again.

"Keep this nigger running, huh?" Amos said.

Glenn put his arm around my shoulder. "No, no. That's only what it looks like. Sucker 'em into a rope-a-dope; let 'em swing away, and when they get tired, bam-a-lam!"

We laughed again and drank more and the spring night was warm, filled with traffic and people strolling by. We said little. Glenn left to go home to Maija. I recognized that itch that came with being at the right stage of high, when you truly believed you could make love all night long. "See ya, son."

We ordered some more drinks.

"Why do you and Allis stay here?" Amos asked.

"Why do you? Why does anybody?"

"Humph!" he said.

"Whatsat supposed to mean?"

"Dunno. Shoulda left a long time ago," he said.

"Aw, man, hush."

"You think I shouldn't have?"

"Shit. You didn't, did you?"

He was looking at a fine young thing, his eyelids drooping suggestively over eyes that were trying to widen like an old goat's. "Same thing anywhere else," he finally said.

378

I said, "C'mon, Amos. We've gone over this shit before. Let's just get drunk. What the fuck."

"You quittin'?"

"Quittin' what?"

"Writing."

I stared at him. "Me? No. Why should I? You crazy or somethin'? I'm gonna write, man. I'm a writer. Fuck these people — "

"Looks to me like they're doin' a good job of fuckin' *you.*"

"No they ain't. Premature ejaculation, that's all. You wanna another drink? I'm gonna have one. Why you ask me a dumb fuckin' question like that, Amos?"

He chuckled. "I guess 'cause I ain't too bright, Cate."

I closed my eyes and listened to the buzz that was growing in my head, and I thought about another spring night a long time ago, a night of dinner with Alex Samuels and drinking with Amos at the Showplace, a night filled with the sharp spikes of anger. I shook my head, remembering.

"What?" Amos said.

"I was just thinkin' how long we been cookin', man, on the front burner over high heat."

"Shit, now, Cate, I don't know about *front* burner." He abruptly lapsed into silence. Then he stirred and said, "Yeah, but I been burned, I mean *burned.* Bad."

I remembered. "Yeah," I said. "I wasn't burned that bad, but you know, man, for a while there I was playing eight ball with God, and Japanese soldiers were shooting all kinds of shit at me, and I was ready to hold conversations with Big Foot — you ever hear Big Foot when you had the place in the country? And man, I went to the University of the Wind — "

He had leaned close to me. "No shit?" He was almost whispering.

"Runnin' down hallways with death snappin' at my ass — "

"Why didn't you tell me?"

"What the fuck for? It was my party! And Allis split — "

"What!"

" — but came right back. Aw, man things were diddlin' inside her head, too. But it worked itself out."

"Gawdamn. Big Foot." He giggled. "You were way out there, huh?"

"Listen, man. If you ride *this* train, there're some trips you gotta take. I learned."

"What? That Big Foot got twelve toes?" He broke up, folded over the table with laughter.

I held up a finger and recited: *"Ecce signum — Cadit quaestio. Magna est veritas et praevalebit!"*

"What the fuck's that mean?"

"It's what I learned. Check it out when Tut gets here. Time for another drink!"

"Did you get to a shrink, Cate?"

"Shrink? Are you kiddin'! Ain't nuthin' a shrink can do about this shit out *here!* Not this diarrhea we're in! Hey, though, hey: Whaddya think of that Glenn, huh?"

"He's pickin' 'em up and layin' 'em down, ain't he, Cate? Ha-boy!"

Amos fell silent again and it took several seconds of meandering through my buzz before I realized that his kids would've been almost Glenn's age; closer to Alejo's. I squeezed his shoulder. "I got to go after this taste, champ."

He peered at me through unfocused eyes and groped around the table for his drink. "Yeah? I thought we was gonna hustle up some pussy out here. No, huh?"

"Naw. I ain't got the stamina for these chicks they puttin' out today! I don't want no heart attack."

"Whoooo!" Amos laughed. He fastened on his drink and guided it to his mouth with both hands. "Man, I am *drunk!*"

"Feels good in the spring, though, don't it, boy?"

Amos shook his head too vigorously, laughing in great spasms, and spilled some of his drink.

"You know anything about clickin'?" I was looking around for the waiter.

He said, "What?"

"Amos, can you click?"

"Whatsat you're sayin'?"

"Never mind." I reached for the bill that the waiter had flown down to our table. "Spring, yeah. But, you know, Amos, it's a lousy fuckin' spring."

"Yeah. Sure is, man."

He was moving backward and forward in his chair.

"You ain't got no brothers and sisters, huh, Cate?"

"No. You? You never talked about any. What the fuck. It's a lousy goddamn spring."

"I got — got — three sisters," he said. "They stopped s—— s—— speakin' to me when I married Jolene. We got married in the spring. She was darker than us. Jolene was too black for them. They stopped speakin' to us." He straightened and wiggled his head around on his neck. Defiantly. "*Good* black!"

"It's a lousy fuckin' spring," I said, peering at the bill.

"You right there, man. Spring stinks. No — spring sucks! Hawwwwwwwhaaa."

Laboriously we counted up our shares, haggled over the amount of tip to leave the sullen cocksucker who'd waited on us, decided to leave nothing, and then changed our minds because he was bigger than us and sober, which we, perhaps too loudly, laughingly admitted.

We thought we were strolling to the corner, in a cool manner, to get a cab, but we were staggering, each trying to hold the other up.

"Anyway," Amos said, doing a good Dean Martin trying to light a cigarette when drunk, "we're alive." The traffic had thinned out by now, and there were fewer strollers. "Plenty people," he went on, "*ain't.*"

"It's a lousy spring," I said. "Can't remember a lousier one."

A gypsy cab came and we climbed into the débris in back. I got out first, a few blocks away, rejecting Amos' plea for just one more, and he continued on home, his speech as I left him becoming, like the driver's, inflected with a West Indian accent.

The apartment was quiet. I checked for notes on the kitchen table. There were none. I poured myself a final drink and sat listening to the silence. Then I smelled something burning. I rushed to the stove. Nothing. I opened the oven. It was almost as cold as death. And as empty. I tiptoed through the apartment, the stench of *some*thing burning deep in my nose. I paused, wondering, and as I stood there, weaving, I realized just what it was, again.

12

I DIDN'T GO with Glenn and Maija to the airport to meet Alejo. There had been worked out elaborate, almost diplomatic, protocols:

He was coming to the United States for the first time. It would be overwhelming. Maybe.

It might be unsettling for me to be at the airport: crowds, customs, the long, hot ride into the city, and he would want to see things.

Therefore, like Glenn and Maija in Spain, a stake-out on neutral territory would perhaps be best.

Glenn reserved a room for him at a small Village hotel, one that had survived the demise of both the Albert and the Fifth Avenue. It was within walking distance of the loft. We thought Alejo might wish time to himself to reflect on things. We had also scheduled visits to Harlem for dinner at the Red Rooster (on a night when the band was not playing) and the Schomburg Collection, to Sugar Hill, where Guillén must have stopped. And there would be dinners at the Sevilla and the Spanish Pavillion and of course at our place and at Glenn's and Maija's. East Hampton would not *quite* resemble Cadaques, but might do for an overnight. I still spoke to enough poets to make a gathering, and there would of course be days in the country. And if we had not exhausted him, he could tour the eastern seaboard with Glenn and Maija.

In between these goings and comings there would be time for us to get to know each other. But first I had to tell Mack about the visit.

"Can we talk about Alejo?"

"Sure. When's he coming, next week?"

He was practicing a batting stance. One week it was Dave Parker, the next Mike Schmidt, the next Reggie Jackson or Pete Rose.

"Whuumph!" he said as he stroked, all pretty, as though there was a battery of photographers with two-hundred-millimeter lenses aimed at him. "Whuumph!"

"Yeah. Next week he'll be here."

Mack stopped swinging. "I saw all the pictures. He's a poet, huh?"

He planted his feet again and stuck his ass way out, swung, missed and twirled the imaginary bat. "Who was that, Dad?"

"Mickey Rivers."

"Right," he said. He sounded surprised. He lowered the bat that wasn't there.

"Yeah, he's a writer, a poet."

"A poet? Like Robert Louis Stevenson?"

"No, better."

Mack went back into a stance and then stopped and dropped his arms. "You said he was a relative. Is he my brother, too? Have you been married _three_ times?"

He sidled close to me, waving three fingers in my face. I pushed him off.

"I've only been married twice, but I've been with women I — loved — three times."

"So he's my brother?"

He went back into a stance, but I couldn't tell whose it was. He was swinging more slowly now.

"Yes."

"He looks like you? And a little like me?"

"Yeah, Mack, he does."

"He's been in Spain all this time?" He drew himself up and glared at me.

"Yeah, that's right."

"Well — did his mother like it that you weren't there?"

"I guess she didn't."

"Did Alejo?"

"I guess not."

"And you weren't married to his mother?"

"No, I wasn't."

He was pacing around now like a groundskeeper checking out a troublesome spot in the infield.

"Didn't you *worry* about him?"

"Yeah, I worried about him a lot."

"But — if you'd married his mother — then you wouldn't have married Mom and I wouldn't be here, right?"

"I think that's the way it would have worked. But, listen. I didn't know she was going to have him until it was time for me to leave Spain, and when I knew, I looked for her, but she'd gone away and I couldn't find her."

"But why?"

"Aw, Mack — "

"*Why* did she go away?"

I think I liked it better when he was batting. I said, "I guess she didn't want to be a burden. She knew I was just getting started with my writing." That sounded better than saying she understood that a deal was a deal but there had been a little accident. Sorry. Bye-bye.

Mack stared at the floor. He looked like an umpire about to make a late call.

"Are things like that a burden — if you're a writer?"

His voice was very level, as if balanced perfectly on home plate.

"They don't have to be. Some things are more important than writing, even to writers."

He was now too old and too wise to have to ask: *Like me?* He said instead, "Is Alejo mad at you?"

"Would you be?"

"I would. Is he?"

"I don't know. I hope not."

"Want me to talk to him for you?"

"Thanks, but — well, let's see how it works out, okay?"

"Is he nice, Dad?"

"Glenn and Maija say he is. We trust them, don't we?"

He came close to me again. "Does Mom know everything?"

I grabbed him. "Yes! And she forgives me!" He came softly into my arms, but I felt the lengthening and hardening muscles of his arms and legs and knew he soon would be gone.

"It was," I said, "something I'd never do on purpose."

"Glad you didn't do that with me," he said loosening himself. He picked up the bat, which had slipped out of his hands, and took up another stance. I didn't know whose it was. Munson? Mack began his stroke, sweeping his eyes across the plate and on up to the pitcher out there chewing tobacco. They eyed each other. Mack said, "Was his mother pretty?"

"Yes."

"Nice?"

"Yes."

He tightened his grip, dug into the box.

"Prettier than Mom?"

"Naw. You kiddin'?"

He stroked slowly again, sped up his swing, tensed for the pitch. Bases loaded. Bottom of the ninth. Two men out. Winning run at the plate.

"Is his mother married now? I mean, he's got a father since you're not — "

"She's married. He's got a father, and besides, Mack, Alejo's a big guy now. It's gonna be all right, okay? Okay?"

"Wait — wait — "

His swing was smooth and level. Pow!

"That sucker's gone!" he yelled.

We slapped palms down and palms up and trotted to the locker room. It was our ball game.

I am at the door at the same time the bell rings. I've heard the elevator stop, its doors open and Julio giving directions. I am both nervous and relieved. I am at last meeting Alejo. According to plan, Allis has taken Mack to the Park. Glenn and Maija have delivered Alejo to the building. By now they are picking up Mack to carry him to the Stadium, where the Yankees and Red Sox are playing. Allis will go downtown to have her hair done. The apartment is filled with the smells of food. Allis cooked all morning. It smells like some kind of feast day. It is a special day. I open the door. He looks like me, though I can see something of his Sierra Leonian grandfather in the cheekbones. He looks younger even than he is! His eyes remind me instantly of his mother. But, overall, he looks the way I do in those old boot camp photographs. "Alejo," I say. I embrace him. He sets his two shopping bags on the floor and embraces me in return. He smiles at me. His teeth are regular, strong and white. "Hello, Father," he says. We stand for another couple of seconds, and then he takes my hand, raises it to his lips and kisses it. When I lived in Spain, sons about to take leave of their fathers or returning home to them did that. I embrace him again, smelling his cologne, conscious of his exquisitely tailored Paseo de Gracia suit. I lead him into the apartment and have him deposit his bags in a corner. Gifts, I can see. He looks around the living room. His movements are tentative, respectful. He smiles again. I like his smile. I say, "I'm very happy you're here," and he then says, "It feels good to be here at last. How is your wife?" I reply, "Very well, thanks. And your friend, Dolores?" He smiles his gratitude. "She is fine, thank you. She drove me to the airport." His English is good, tinged with a Spanish accent. We are, I think, into the necessary ritual. However long it takes, it must be done. He says, "Glenn and Maija just left me, so I know they're all right, but Mack, my little brother?" I like the way he says it, boldly. What after all can be changed now? "He's okay. He should enjoy the ball game. We'll all be together later this afternoon. You'll see him." Alejo approaches me, places his hands on my shoulders. I notice the starched cuffs of his pima cotton shirt, the wisps of gold cuff links. "But how is my father? Are *you* well?" I place my hand gently against his face. "Yes, Alejo, my son. Your father is now quite happy. Your mother, is she all right?" "Ah, yes," he says. "She sends her warmest regards and congratulations." I say, "Thank you. That's kind of her. And Federico? Teresa?" He nods. "They're in good health, thank you. Federico is an anthropologist working with the Basques — a touchy business these days with bombs going off all over the place." "It's bad, then," I say. He nods again. "How is your er — father?" I ask, self-consciously. But he smiles his understanding. "Very busy and very well, thank you." Alejo takes off his jacket and we sit and talk of his work, my work, Glenn's work. We pause for wine and snacks. After, he goes into one of his shopping bags and hands me one of the gifts. It is a book, of course. "Please," he says. "Open it." I can already smell the old leather. No, it's lambskin. The pages are brown. The type is old Gothic, and then I see worn letters that had been stamped upon the cover: *Viaje al Parnaso*. But it cannot, simply cannot, be a first edition, three hundred sixty-three years old. Alejo sees the question on my face. "Yes!" he says, going to the bags again. "Glenn tells me that you like old maps. Well, you'll have to go some to find one as old and as accurate as this one!" He helps me to unroll it. We're on our knees on the floor. Cervantes' *Journey to Parnassus* now on a table. Alejo puts books along the sides of the map. "Do you know it?" I say, "The Dulcert Portolano?" He shakes his head. "Close. Nicòlo de Canerio, 1502." I cannot believe it. I finger the parchment. "The original?" I whisper. He's enjoying my astonishment. He smiles hugely. I think, *There is something wrong with all this.* But I thank him profusely while thinking that I should be showering him with gifts instead of just the

386

copy of *Pushkin* that I had had bound in leather and in which I wrote a careful inscription. He is gracious about my awkwardness. We settle back with more wine and he says, "When Glenn and Maija were in Spain, they took me with them to Sitges — how awful all those places along the shore have become. We looked up your friend Señor Yanez. He ran away with a nun; drove off in his old Seat. His wife is still at the hotel. A charity case, I suppose. She told us how you'd looked for my mother and how you'd come back. My grandmother told me too, years later. I just wanted you to know that I knew, and that if I ever thought badly of you, it was because I hadn't come to know yet. But she married Felipe and everything turned out all right." He shrugs. I wonder if Dickens could have arranged a better story. It feels so good that Alejo's here. I could weep. He is reading the inscription in *Pushkin* over and over again. Tears roll out of his eyes. We uncork another bottle of *vino blanco, muy seco.* We sit and smile at each other. It is good to have, finally, all present and accounted for.

I came out of the daydream when I heard Allis and Mack in the hallway. The door to the apartment banged open and they erupted into the foyer.

"Where *are* they?" Allis demanded. "I'm going to be late — "

The phone rang.

"What's goin' on?" Mack said. "We'll be late for the game."

The phone rang again.

"Lemme get the phone," I yelled. I rushed to the kitchen extension, my stomach plunging in foreboding. I could see Allis snapping glances at her watch. Mack was pouting.

"Dad!" Glenn was shouting. "The plane — "

"The plane?" I shouted back.

"What about the plane?" Allis was suddenly beside me and, changing her mind, then ran to the bedroom extension. Mack was suddenly quiet, suddenly very still.

"The plane's in, but Alejo's not on it."

I heard Allis groan.

"Maija's checking the passenger list now. He was on the red carpet list."

I knew Allis was thinking of all the food she'd cooked and the irresponsibility of young people. I groaned.

"What is it?" Mack asked. He was primed for a disaster. Tears were already welling up in his eyes.

"Maybe he just missed the goddamn plane," Glenn said, "but that's not like him. If anything, he's always early for his appointments — Here's Maija — "

We could hear them, then Glenn returned. "He wasn't on the flight, Dad."

"Would he have taken another, do you think?"

"He would've called. Five hours between here and Spain, Dad."

I was drawing blanks. I kept saying into the phone, "Hmmm. Hmmmm."

"Listen, Dad. I think we'll go back to the loft. He's got the number there. I know Allis has cooked — "

"Since you've got the car, we'll bring it down by cab," Allis said.

"Hi, Allis. I can't think of anything else to do, can you?"

"Honey?" she said to me.

"But there won't be another flight until tomorrow," I said, "unless he's taking another airline. Maybe we got the dates mixed up? Maybe it's tomorrow?"

"It's today, Dad, but maybe he'll come tomorrow. Leave the food and we'll get Chinese and just wait for a call or call him."

"Give me his number. I'll call before we start down."

"It might be better if Glenn calls, honey," Allis said.

"Oh, yeah. Okay. Depending on traffic — you oughta be at the loft in about an hour and a half?"

He thought so and hung up.

Allis returned to the living room with a scowl on her face. "To hell with the hairdresser," she said.

"No ball game?" Mack said.

"No."

"What could've happened?" she asked.

I didn't try to answer. To Mack I said, "Another time, okay?"

Glenn and Maija made good time. They'd already called Alejo; there'd been no answer. Maija, Allis and Mack went for the Chinese. Glenn and I drank and stared at the phone. It was smeared with Maija's paints. The heat was pressing into the place; the air conditioner worked in vain. Through the windows, the buildings seemed draped in a silver mist. *This,* I told myself, is the daymare. We ate with little talk and tried once again to call Alejo. Darkness settled over the city. Voices drifted up from the streets along with the sounds of traffic.

When the phone did ring, it startled us so much that none of us moved until it had rung the third time. Glenn, with a leap, snatched it off its hook, turning to wave us into silence.

"Yes, yes. This *is* Glenn Douglass." He listened. We moved closer to him. We watched his face, immediately cued into the slightest inflection in his voice. His eyes stayed locked with mine. "Monica Donoso — " He cupped his hand quickly over the mouthpiece. I was already shouldering my way to the phone when he said, "Alejo's *mother.*"

I held my hand out for the phone. "Monica? This is Cato. CAYto." My voice was shaking, my body, my hands. I tried to distill my complete being down to one monstrous ear through which I could hear and understand everything.

It was all over radio and television and in the papers. She had just flown in from Fernando Po, where the Spanish authorities had contacted her. Alejo and Dolores were missing, their car found empty on the *autopista* leading to the airport. There were bullet holes in it, but no blood.

My stomach settled uneasily down near the tops of my thighs.

The Falangists, she said, the dirt of the earth. They had not died with Franco. Dolores was very popular among the Andalusians, in her own way, more popular than El Córdobes had been, because she was political and had had some success bringing the Catalans, Andalusians and the Basques together. The people loved her. She was like La Pasionaria. People loved her concerts, too. She brought back the Republican spirit of the Civil War in the cause of a truly united Spain. The Falangists didn't want this. The ruling powers never want a united people unless they are fighting another country. They want the country filled with the powerless. Together, Monica said, Alejo and Dolores were very political. His second volume was even more political than the first. It was already being discussed. She snarled into the phone: "This redemocratization of Spain. A joke. This book will be even more for the people, not for King Juan Carlos and his group, or Suárez or González or even Carrillo. Carrillo didn't have to hide in a closet for forty years the way so many of them did." She paused. "They're missing, is the official report, but — "

"I'd like to come," I said.

"It would be awkward for Felipe," she said simply.

"I would have met him today," I said.

"Yes, I know."

"Let me give you my number, and address — after so many years." She took them down.

"Monica, what should we be prepared for?"

"We'll hope for the best, Cato."

"Are the police doing everything? Does Felipe have influence? Will it help if I call my publisher there?"

"By all means, call your publisher. Felipe has some influence. We will see how much. And the police? Well . . ." She stifled a sob. " 'Dios, Cato."

All the while I was telling my family what'd happened, I smelled something burning, and even on the way home, steam draped noxiously over the city, I smelled it, smelled it.

These forces, these people! How they attacked in silence, like worms, chewing holes in the fabric of things that should be. And they dared, *dared* come this close to *my clan,* reaching casually over language, culture, history and its accidents and propaganda, and oceans to do so! A poet! A poet just reaching twenty and a flamenca dancer with clicking heels and clicking castanets who threaten a portion of someone's world? Writing and dancing = dragon's teeth that might spring up armed and strong men and women? (And who else *but* a poet, *but* a dancer, *but* an artist — save those used like high-class whores who slip their fucks between the worlds?)

I called my publisher when we got home. Of course, all of Spain was talking about it. Like everyone else in artistic and intellectual circles, he was concerned, and would do as much as he could. After all, we had had many years together, and he knew my interest in Alejo was based on something more than mere admiration. He would keep me informed of every development.

We sat and stared at television without seeing it. Mack went to sleep. I carried him to bed, took off his sneakers. Allis slept, her head in my lap. The tube flickered on with its inanities and commercial messages. We could have gone to bed; a phone was near. It seemed inappropriate to sleep. Some messages of the mind might pierce the cosmos and be heeded; who knew?

The phone rang. Allis sat up, and I was at it with the second ring. It was not an overseas call and the caller seemed confused. I recognized the voice, I thought.

"Hu — hello? Is this Cato Douglass, please?"

Quite proper, approaching pompous, for seven-thirty A.M. "Yes, Jeremy?"

"Oh! You recognized my voice. Forgive me for calling so early, Cate. It's been a long time. How are you?"

"What's up, Jeremy? You're right. It is early."

"Sorry, but I wanted to get to you before Shelly Popper did. I understand that the young Spanish poet Alejo Donoso's in town and that he's a friend of yours — "

" — "

"Cate? Can you put me in touch with him for an interview?"

390

"He — Who told you he was a friend of mine?"

"Oh, apparently his publisher over there sent announcements to all the book people in New York. How do you know him, Cate?" The burn-smell grew stronger.

Allis was fixing coffee. She looked as though she hadn't slept in a week.

"He didn't come. There was some trouble. He's missing. I can't talk any more now. I want to keep the line open. Tell Shelly. Tell them all." I hung up.

I leaned against the wall. I felt like month-old shit.

"What do you think?" Allis said.

"I don't want to. I don't want to think about it," I said.

"I know. But you're gonna have to."

"He's all right," I said. "They're all right."

The spring had been bad and now the summer was worse. It was passing slowly, sullen with humid heat, and there was no word about Alejo and Dolores. Glenn and Maija had returned to Spain, being less of an embarrassment to Felipe than I would have been, but their letters were as empty of real news as the clippings they and Monica and my publisher sent. These were growing shorter, more perfunctory, crumbs to a still hungry, though diminishing, constituency. I was seriously wounded, but I didn't mind the wound half as much as my vulnerability, which had caused it in the first place. Inwardly I screamed and raged at my inability to do anything about anything.

I awoke mornings now feeling as though I had not slept even the few hours I usually did. I was surprised when Allis replied, to my complaint, that I had indeed been sleeping, and snoring like hell into the bargain. Anger became my shadow, and often tensed as if to take on life of its own. I was exhausted, made mean, by the constant struggle to contain it.

Yet around *Unmarked Graves,* in some desperately subconscious fashion, I had built an event-proof compartment. I escaped into it every moment I could, often to Mack's bewilderment and to Allis' alternating fury and despair. I felt nearly all right, almost whole, with things in balance when I was working on the book, and at a loss when away from it, perhaps like an actor who, playing Shakespeare one day, finds that he must play Simon the next.

Old dreams began to flash faraway lightning down the hours when I lay tensed between sleep and wakefulness. Almost, I thought; I'd almost found him. Then, enraged at myself for these thoughts that insisted on past tense presentation, I would try to switch off thinking. But, the thoughts kept coming, like Jupiter smashing right through Earth.

Old, dovetailed habits began to slip their positions, and I would look back at the end of each day, amazed that it had been so shitty. Fights with Mack. Arguments with Allis. Curses at my chairman, who was calling meetings in preparation for the school year. And when Glenn and Maija returned, empty-handed, newsless, I was short and gruff with them. What they wished to say I knew was not good. Therefore, I gave them no opportunity to say it. But they had brought back the typescript of Alejo's second collection, and Allis promptly dropped most of her clients to work on the English translation, since Alejo had not done so before he —

Well. I think Allis was doing it for me. And doing it for Alejo. Maybe she thought we'd get to know him through his raw work. And it was a challenge to her artistic instincts. More than anything else, I saw her work as an attempt to rewind the string about our lives that I was unraveling. What she was doing for my son, about my son, gave me great solace, as memorial services or monuments often do.

Nevertheless, I tolerated no serious talks about Alejo; rejected, almost even before uttered, any tenders of sympathy from those in my family. Of course, PEN, the Writers Guild and the Authors Guild had demanded earlier a full investigation by the Spanish authorities, but these demands had come to naught, and might just as well have been issued to South Africa on behalf of Steve Biko —

No. Biko was dead.

Classes began and so did my sojourn before the cynical innocents — for they were both. In such times how could they be otherwise? They could not, would not, understand my anger, my insistence on their learning about the world they believed to be real enough because they were in college. They slept. They wrote reams of bullshit on their examinations. They begged for higher grades. My colleagues smirked. And why not? *The Pushkin Papers* had slipped quickly down the tube and therefore they did not have to pretend to offer congratulations and certainly had no reason to be envious. Three weeks into the new semester, I decided to take another leave when the year was over.

Autumn fled before the harsh smacks of a winter pounding in from the North. I crept in and out of my compartment.

Glenn stopped calling. Maija ceased to suggest that this or that wall could use another of her paintings, which were, in fact, improving. But the burn-smell in my head continued. It made me think of Karloff in the first film of Mary Shelley's novel and her sense of the place of electricity not only in the body, but in creation itself.

God, don't short-circuit me yet, I thought.

13

THEN, the thirty-three-hundred-year-old boy-king came to town amid fabulous fanfare. We were ready, Allis and I, and that readiness, that opportunity to *do,* brought back a wider focus to my life.

Lines formed beneath the canopied entrance to the Metropolitan Museum. A small army of guards was posted throughout the exhibit. I shuffled along (Allis and Mack had already come and had provided me with the line of march) in a crowd that just as easily could have been headed for a fight in the Garden. Before each display I let slip half a handful of cards. I had pocketfuls. Most people walked on them, echoing each other in small ooos and ahhhs as if, on the ceiling above, a sign had flashed, reading: "Ooooooo" or "Ahhhhh."

Yet before the tour ended, a tour that, like so many these days, was, in addition to a fight crowd, like the disorderly surge of cattle to the culture, I heard a voice behind me — somewhere near the Treasury / Annex (a few feet and around the corner from the souvenir sales area, as it happened) — "What's all this stuff on the floor? These . . . cards?"

There was a falling-off of sound; people were listening to this loud, indignant voice that was reading: *"Ecce signum — Cadit quaestio. Magna est veritas et praevalebit."*

"Greek?"

"No. Latin. Hey, stop shoving."

"What's it mean?"

The voice grew louder. *It* knew Latin.

"Uh — look at the sign . . . See the — uh — proof . . . the argument collapses. The truth is . . . great! and will . . . come out? Prevail? Some nut! Look. They're all over the floor. It's a disgrace. Why don't the guards do something? They see them. Why're they smiling at *me?*"

There near Tutankhamen the Harpooner, I heard another voice, young and clear, rising above the respectful babbling of the crowd: "Hey, you know, King Tut looks just like Michael Jackson — "

Still another voice bellowed, as if in sudden fright, "Shut up! Keep movin'!"

So, once again, it did not pass as much as I had, on still another level, learned or was learning to live with yet one more wound, the way an amputee for a time feels itching in the missing limb. I was running once again in my sleep. Not explosively, as in the hundred-meter run, but, Allis said, with a puzzled look on her face, "as though you were loping along, going a great distance at a leisurely pace."

I lusted after her. I badgered, cajoled, seduced her into doing it at the most odd times, and with the most joyous lasciviousness. She pretended to be exhausted, often tried to beg off, but never meant it. It was a delicious time, during which I made my apologies to Glenn and Maija, read and made suggestions for his new book, a novel, and enticed Mack back to me.

"Hey," I said one night when he came out of the shower, "Couple more years and you'll have sprouts around your dong."

"Aw, c'mon, Dad." He was embarrassed, but he grinned.

"It's okay, Mack. I still love ya."

Banter and basketball games. Time with his homework. Talks.

In the classroom I smiled at the inanities of the students. I conducted myself with the utmost decorum at departmental and faculty meetings and even attended two or three meetings of committees I was on.

Then I asked Allis to give *Unmarked Graves* a read. She looked up from Alejo's poems. "It's done?"

That was it, the flood of light, the return (save for that sad itching) from the submerged caves of La Tortuga, the banter, jokes, apologies. I'd finished the fucking book. It *was* done.

I settled in for the rewrite as winter deepened and as Glenn grew restless to be off, somewhere, seeing things, people and places. If he was to be a target, he'd be a moving one, as he'd said. But all his plans were stored for the spring, the same time for which I'd been contracted for a couple of readings out of town, one in Denver, where I'd never been.

The day the invitation came from Denver (Allis was not home and so I wallowed leisurely in the mail) there came, too, a small, square package from Italy.

It has to do with Mr. Storto, I told myself. Mr. Storto. I opened it. His medal seemed larger, lying there in velvet, and for a second, the subtle sugars of good Italian ices caressed my taste buds. I pushed back the lid of the box so that it stood open. I took out the letter, feeling precisely the way I feel when I hear of disasters far from me, hear the bells tolling, absorb my own diminishment.

Era la voglia ultima di Signore Storto che lei ha questa medaglia, la Legione di Onore. E morto il venti settembre passato. Ha ricevuto la medaglia per eroismo e valore durante la battaglia per Vittorio Veneto, il ventiquattro ottobre, 1918.

Voglia gradire i miei cordiali saluti e migliori auguri.

Mario Mondadari,
Sindaco

"Morto" leaped out. He'd died then. On September 20. *"Medaglia"* okay. Medaglia d'Oro coffee. Medal of gold. Medal. *"Battaglia."* Battle — of? for? — Vittorio Veneto. Wasn't that a street? No. *Via* Veneto, *that* was a street in *La Dolce Vita.*

I looked up Veneto: "The region witnessed severe fighting in World War I but was largely spared in World War II. Bounded by Trentino– Alto Adige and Austria, the Adriatic Sea, Emilia-Romagna and Lombardy.

"In June 1918, the Austrians attempted an offensive on the Piave, crossed the river successfully and then were thrown back. [So, I thought, *that's* where it came from, *Il Piave Mormorava.*] This caused the Austrian war effort to collapse and made the general offensive by the Italians (Oct. 24, et seq.) a success that took Vittorio Veneto (Oct. 30), Trieste (Nov. 3) and Fiume (Nov. 5), by which time Austria was out of the war."

("Oh," Mr. Storto had said. "The rats; they were as big as dogs, eating what they ate.")

I looked at the medal again. I hoped Mr. Storto had not received it in one of those hurried ceremonies where the brass rushes in accompanied by aides-de-camp whose arms are filled with boxes containing medals that the generals pass out like samples of soap. I wanted the ceremony to have been special. You think of Caporetto and you think of Hemingway and Rinaldi and drinking *grappa;* you do not think of men like Mr. Storto, who lived his life at night because he remembered the rats.

I called Frances, down on the eighth floor. She was Italian. Her kid, Aldo, played with Mack. There was no answer. I wrote a note and went down to stick it under her door. I wanted her to come up and translate as soon as she came in. Please. I wanted it all to be there when Allis came home. No loose ends. She'd sometimes wondered if Mr. Storto was in pain, if the Italian doctors were as good as the Americans when it came to cancer.

Frances arrived a half-hour later.

"It was," she wrote out quickly, "Mr. Storto's last wish that you have this medal, the Legion of Honor. He died on the 20th past. He received the medal for heroism and valor during the battle for Vittorio Veneto, October 24, 1918. Please accept my cordial greetings and best wishes. Mario Mondadari, Mayor."

"Thanks," I said.

"He was a good friend?"

"Yeah, an old friend."

Frances looked at the medal. "I'm sorry." As she left, she said, "Tell Aldo no candy if he comes in."

I called Glenn to tell him about Mr. Storto, then returned to the desk for a while.

"What's up?" Allis was suspicious. I'd helped her off with her coat and fixed her a drink and some cheese and crackers. She looked around for the mail. "Huh?" she said with her mouth full. "What's up?"

"Mr. Storto died. He sent us his medal."

She reached for the box. She was chewing carefully and taking long swallows of her drink.

"I got Frances to translate the note," I said. She opened the box and looked at the medal. She sighed and reached for another cracker, more cheese. "You okay, honey?"

"Sure. Fine."

She got up and went to the record rack and put on the Brahms Concerto No. 1 in D minor. I fixed her another drink and had one for myself. We sat and did not talk until the record was over.

We heard Mack and Aldo whooping in the hall, and I folded away the letter and translation, closed the box with the medal and carried them into the bedroom.

14

MAXINE ACCEPTED the manuscript of *Unmarked Graves* somberly. The shelves in her office were mostly bare. She had already started cleaning out.

"You do remember what I said?"

"Yes, I remember," I said.

She drummed her fingers on the script. "What'd I say?"

"That you were out after *Graves.*"

"Right. I'll handle what there'll be of subsidiaries — "

"Okay, sure."

"Sorry, babes."

"Listen. Will they still do it?"

She half-turned in her chair toward the window and Madison Avenue. "Why wouldn't Jock do it?"

"You said times had changed."

"They have. How's Allis?"

"All right."

"These manuscripts from Roye and Ike — you can take them." She pushed them toward me.

"No good? I thought they were very good."

"C'mon, Cate. Ten years ago. Not today. Too serious. They make *demands* on people. Readers don't want that."

"Oh. Yeah. That's right. Shitbook time."

"Whatever. You want lunch?"

"No. Thanks."

"What's the next project, Cate?"

"Getting to shore."

"What?"

"Swimming through this shit to something solid."

"Uh-huh. I guess Maureen Gullian will be calling you after I send this over. Lunch with her."

"Do I have to?"

"You get the word from her, buddy-boy, remember?"

I stood. "Well — "

"Let's stay in touch, okay, Cate?"

"I didn't think we wouldn't, did you? It's not as if I'll be drinking with another crowd."

"I mean, don't let it get to you. Promise?"

"Okay." I paused. "I wonder what Queensbury would say about all the changes — "

"What?" Maxine looked puzzled that I had interrupted myself, but I knew what Sandra Queensbury would have told me.

"Nothing," I said to Maxine. I left.

Sandra would have told me: "Dear Cate. Be honest with yourself. Try to be. Try *hard* to be. You know as well as I do that for you and all like you nothing will ever *really* change. Do you understand, darling? Change comes from without, hardly ever from within." And she would have smiled and kissed me.

You are always saying goodbye to children; hello and goodbye; how ya been and where ya goin'; and you are always wondering why you don't hear from them. Summer was coming on fast, now. There had been nothing about Alejo and Dolores. An entire year had not passed, then, could not have passed. Yet it had, an aching, terrible year.

Mack was going off to camp this summer, his first time away, on his own, and he looked forward to it with an eagerness that surprised me. He could not understand my surprise and I could not understand why he didn't. And this one, too.

Glenn was chewing his piece of my chitlin with great distaste. They would not be serving them again in the Rooster until next fall. He grinned at me and shook his head: "And you *like* these things." He swallowed and gratefully returned to his crab cakes. Well, I thought, some of us have soul and some of us don't. I wondered if Alejo would have liked (would like!) the Red Rooster; it had something of the air of a Barcelona restaurant that had seen better days.

"I hope you're subletting your place to some dependable people," I said. "I don't want to be runnin' down there every other day."

"They're okay," he said. "And we're storing what good stuff we have. Don't worry."

"Good. I don't have any experience dealing with tenants. These days you can get killed behind that."

"Relax. It'll be cool."

I knocked back the martini that had gone mostly to water. I couldn't remember now when we'd had our first drink together. But I remembered waiting for that time to come. "When do you think you'll be finished with the book?"

"I dunno," he said. "It's going okay. Maybe by next spring."

"Good."

"Then there's another I want to start."

"Give yourself space, kid."

"Yeah. I will. There's plenty of that in this business, right?"

"Yeah, sure right about that."

"Don't worry. Hey, how do you like Maija's work these days?"

"She's improving. Really."

"You noticed. It was that first trip, Dad; some of the world got inside her head."

I guessed he meant Alejo and Dolores, too, for he suddenly stopped and flicked a look at me. He said, "We'll look for him, don't worry about that, either."

"I wasn't worried. I knew that. Say, that was nice, what you said to Allis, really, really nice, about the money she gave you."

"Well — "

"Okay." I laughed. "Anyway, it's nice not to have to worry quite so much about money, surviving. It was her father's."

"I gather you didn't get along for the usual reasons?"

"Yeah. Bad news."

"Sorry."

I could laugh now. "Why? Wasn't your fault. Naw. It's all right now, but it gave us some problems."

"Some soul, too, I guess. Especially Allis. She's a very good poet. Those translations are something else. Alejo'd be — he'll be crazy about them."

He'd been looking at me and must've seen my reaction; that must've caused him to change his own tenses.

"They're all strong, none weak."

"She worked on them, man."

Glenn pushed back. "Any wise words on publishing? When will we be published again? When is *any* good stuff going to be published again?"

"Just worry about the words," I said. "Like you did with *Jumper.* I love that book. First-born and all that. I'll worry about the publishing. The seasons are, well, seasons. A Phillis Wheatley this time, a Richard Wright the next. Hey, we're the last of the dreaming people here, like the blackfellows of Australia with their dreamtime. That's the affliction: believing that if we write well and truthfully, it will be read and, being read, it'll cause the imperfections to be corrected, the gaps filled in."

He sighed and gave me a sidelong glance. At that moment, he looked just like Mack giving me the same look. When Mack did it, he made me think of Glenn.

"You're right," I said. "I stopped dreaming, stopped believing. But that goes against the grain, against the impulse to harmony, rhythm, man, balance. Everywhere you look in nature there's some kind of harmony, maybe even truth, everywhere except in the affairs of men, us assholes — "

"Sounds like you're telling me to dream and to believe, while you've quit."

"Right, goddamn, don't do as I do; do as I *say* do."

"Is it supposed to be healthier or something?"

"Yeah. Anyway, you're doing it."

"Not quite," he said. "Let's have a cognac. On me." He waved to a waitress and gave the order. "I have a good teacher," he said, "so I'm not quite ready — "

"Yes, you are."

"No! I'm not!" he said.

"Then why did you decide to continue writing? To make money? To win fame? To win women? No, no, no. Hell, you haven't looked at anyone since you got together with Maija — "

"All right, then, why do you keep on writing?"

"Because I'm crazy, as you well know. I saw you cuttin' your eyes at me."

He bounced in the chair with his laughter. His eyes glistened for a moment. "I like having a crazy father. They aren't dull. No, man, never." He raised his cognac glass and we tapped them.

"I envy you all that great Spanish cognac you'll be drinking again. I think they're more serious than the French."

"I'll save lots for you," he said. "Lots."

"We'll be there, sooner or later. But for now, think about the words. Fly on your words. Fuck the wax on the wings. That's a Greek story. They were what we claim the Japanese are — good copiers. There wasn't shit in Greece; that's why they all went to Africa to study. They brought back Daedalus and Icarus, Phaëthon, Oedipus, all those cats and most of the gods, most of the knowledge. They copped everything that was coppable, and only Herodotus and a couple others dared to say so. Then the Greeks iced the stolen cake with their language. The wax on the wings is a hoax. Fly, son, fly, through a multiplicity of worlds."

I stopped, wondering what had got into me, why I so desperately wanted to tell him something. His smile seemed sad. I had a moment's panic. Had I been rapping out some senile, stupid line? I couldn't tell whether the sad smile was for him or for me.

The musicians came in. It was time to go before they broke our eardrums. We slowly climbed the stairs to the street, checked the newsstand.

In the car Glenn said, "So Phaëthon is not to drive his father's chariot tonight."

"Not swinging low for you tonight, man. You drive your chariot and I'll drive mine and we'll bury the sonofabitch from 'the Ganges to the golden sands of Tagus — ' "

" 'Deep to the underworld,' " he interrupted, " 'whose king and queen blink in terror of it.' "

"Hey!" I said. "I didn't know you knew Ovid."

I saw his grin in the streetlight as we pulled from the curb. "I borrowed your Miller translation."

We slapped palms, down and up, and I drove down Seventh Avenue — Adam Clayton Powell, Jr., Boulevard. The jump had gone out of it. As elsewhere this spring evening, there was an air of impending disaster. Changing the name had not been enough, would never be enough. It was, simply, too late.

Downtown we went in silence, through the everlastingly changing streets and buildings, all for offices, few for living, past frightened people scurrying along looking over their shoulders, clutching their bags tightly to their sides. ("Look at it," Glenn said. "Look.") This was now only one of the cities from which sedate flight had turned into a stampede; one of the cities inside whose walls the "barbarians" were marauding while the cops whined for publicly paid bulletproof vests and beat up on cadres of civilians who did their jobs better than they. Romes were falling everywhere.

"They're mugging in Barcelona now," Glenn said.

He'd told me before. I nodded. "It's all over."

I embraced him when I finally pulled up before his loft and let him out. I promised we'd visit as soon as we could. I checked the locks on the door and drove home. I could not drive them to the airport tomorrow. I was going to Denver for the reading.

Lemme hear from ya. Write, okay? Even if it's just a card. Hey, man, stay in touch, willya? But finally, it's always goodbye.

The Black Studies department, not the English department, had invited me to read. This was a normal exercise of academic racism. Nothing unusual. Most members of departments of English read assiduously the book review sections of the newspapers and magazines (lusting after invitations or even "nominations" to review for them), and, quite naturally, taking their leads therefrom whenever they even considered inviting writers to read their works or to lecture on writing or literature, found no suggestion that I deserved honoraria they'd accumulated by paying the part-time staffers peons' wages, and did not invite me. I say, this was normal and mine was not a singular case.

Thus, I found myself in the Mile-High City, home of Floyd Little, Number 44, of Sonny Liston, former heavyweight champ, nearby SAC headquarters, missile silos and nerve-gas factories, striding with very little pain indeed across the campus with a quartet of aging, fretful members of the Black Studies department to the reading. We had eaten well, if such can be said of anyone in Denver, and I had drunk my fill and the altitude had given me an additional blast. They had watched me throughout dinner, this quartet, with careful eyes, wondering, I was sure, if I would collapse on the podium. They seemed now reassured as I matched them stride for stride.

I had noticed about the campus the usual posters:

The Noted Author
CATO DOUGLASS
Reading from His Works
Jordan Hall
Eight P.M.
Sponsored by the Department of Black Studies

I thought that it might play well in Denver, but was certainly a bomb in New York.

The hallways of the building were quiet. The auditorium in Jordan held, I had been told, five hundred people, but when we entered, my

402

hosts gasped (or pretended to) and hurriedly conferred. They were really young men, younger than I, but the logrolling of academic politics must have aged them. While they talked in hisses and whispers (they were not clickers) I counted ten people, none white, spread about the auditorium in various stages of sleep. My hosts continued to confer with Negroid gravity. I understood. They didn't think I did. (They were, I knew, continually pressed for justification for the very existence of their department — but were given no rational budget to support that existence.) Now, I knew as well as they that Whittington and Huysmans or even Selena Merritt would not have got up to piss for the kind of honorarium they were paying me. But I *was* from New York; I *was* a writer; there *was* some fraying reputation. They'd hoped, obviously. How much hullabaloo they'd managed to raise was obvious. How many times, I wondered, had they called the department of English? And their own department? Surely there were more than ten students enrolled. I felt sorry for my hosts, but no silver clarions had sounded my coming, so their students slept the untroubled sleep of conservative revolutionaries who sought cause and solution with the same impossible breath.

My hosts decided to put the best face on the matter and guided me down into the well of the auditorium and introduced me. Then they sat down next to each other as though squeezed in by an overflow audience.

The applause was like the sound mice make when they have momentarily stepped off cotton onto linoleum.

I rose, voiced my thanks, mentioning each of my hosts by name and title, as is politic to do in these situations. I opened the folder containing *Unmarked Graves.*

"C'mon down front," I said, beckoning to the limp bodies tucked into vast, empty sections of the hall. "Come on. I won't bite you. Not too hard. Come on."

They moved reluctantly down toward the front rows and sat down. "Plenty of room," I said.

I shut out the emptiness before me and, sensing their embarrassment and pity for me, began to read. I imagined that the place was jammed; that people were pressed into each other; that everyone was hanging on to my every (yes, a side dish at dinner had been navy beans cooked with ham, a winner for the production of carbon dioxide) pppppt! My hosts, the closest people to me, held their breaths.

I read, glanced at my watch and read on. My voice came bounding back from that great emptiness, but I continued to read. The Chair glanced at his watch. It was like trying to do it to a mastodon. I heard a noise way back in the hall and saw an elderly white man in overalls shuffle to a seat. I thought, Eleven. For an hour and a half I read into emptiness and finally it broke me. I had intended to read more, but I quit. To hell with it.

The Chair leaped up. There had been no applause, or if there had been, I had not heard it. "I don't suppose," he said, "there are any questions for Mr. Douglass?"

A thin young woman rose. "I have a question."

I felt that she had come only to ask it.

"What are the responsibilities of the black writer?"

"To whom?"

"Well!" she said. "To black people!"

I closed my folder and glanced to the back, where the old white man was sitting. Was there a smile on his face? I wondered why each generation seemed to seize precisely on the questions asked by the previous one. I had been asked the question a hundred times over the years, but tonight was the first time I really heard it.

"They are," I said, "in exact proportion to the responsibilities the black community has to its writers, regardless of all obstacles, real or imagined. If the people feel they have none, then they cannot expect the writer to have them."

From the back came a measured clapping of a single pair of hands. The old white man in the blue overalls was standing. *Clap, clap, clap, clap, clap.* We turned to look up at him. I had the peculiar feeling that something in an old dream had been reversed.

"Are you through?" he asked. "Can I turn out the lights now?"

There seemed to be a mocking in his voice.

"Yes, yes," the Chair said. "We're quite finished. Turn them out."

As we left the auditorium a bank of lights went soundlessly out, and then another and another. One final bank over the well and podium remained, and then came an abrupt and total blackness.

"Guess, *guess,*" Allis said after we'd kissed, "who called while you were gone?"

"Easy. Gullian."

"Oh, she did call. Wants lunch. Call her back. But that's not who I meant."

"Who, honey? c'mon."

"Aha. A bad reading. Paul. It was Paul Cummings."

404

I groaned. Not after last night's kick in the ass.

"I told him it was good to hear from him after such a long time."

"Did he say what he wanted?"

"No."

"Leave a number?"

"No. Said he'd call back. Sounded like hell."

"Uh?"

"Sad, tired. So the reading wasn't a success. No young writers hanging on to every word, no women tempting you?"

"You got it, kid. Just like that. A bomberoo. Why do you suppose he called?"

"How should I know? Tired of the crowd he's drinking with, the people who buy all his books for movies and then never make a movie — don't know. Maybe he just wanted to, you know."

"Didn't he say anything, like *why* he was calling?"

"I told you. No. He'll call back. Maybe you'd better call Maureen, though."

I told myself that I ought to be pleased that he was calling *me,* but that didn't make me feel better. I wondered if he'd ever done Denver and what his reception had been like.

I got Nan Tyce, who sometimes hung out in Maureen's office.

"Glad I got you," I said. "I want to come and look at your machine."

"You're not supposed to," she said. "But. If you make it soon, like next Thursday night after seven — "

"Really? What's the rush?"

"I think I'm going to leave TCFP soon."

"Why?"

"I might tell you later, but don't tell anyone you're coming, okay? They don't want authors looking at their printouts. Here's Maureen now. See you then."

Gullian came on, her voice lilting and cheerful. "Sorry, Cate. Was in a publishing committee meeting."

"Yeah. What's up? You got the manuscript?"

"Got it. It's really, really marvelous. Just thought we could have lunch and chat about it."

"Sure. When?"

"Tomorrow all right?"

"Yeah, where?" Suspicion was already coiling, and I hung up feeling a slow twisting in my stomach. Lunch? And we weren't going to talk about anything except how marvelous *Graves* was? What did all that super-cheer in her voice conceal? What was that publishing committee meeting about? Me? Had they decided something? (But she'd called yesterday.) So? Maybe it took them two days to decide. Also, there was missing Jock's bullshit little note, that ego-stroking missive about the greatness of your book, the magnificence of your talent and the modest pride TCFP felt publishing you. It usually arrived special delivery. This time: zip.

"If it's only lunch, why are you looking like that?" Allis asked.

I didn't answer.

She said, "Oh. Oh."

I willed still the writhing. "I don't look like my usual, graying, debonair, self-confident self?" I circled behind her and gently grabbed, one in each hand.

Allis clasped her hands over mine and stilled my sexless graspings. She knew the movements for what they were — distractions — for me, not for her. I didn't seem to know what to do with myself.

"You mean your debonair egomaniacal self. No, you don't look at all your usual self, dear."

I released her.

"Maybe too many Denvers, too many Maureens, too many Jock Champions," I said. "And I'm tired. But listen, I'm not letting anyone tear up *my* notebook, kiddo."

She remembered and smiled. "I hate them all," she said simply. "I just hate them."

"Listen," I said, "let's call him. Let's call Paul."

"He's not listed," Allis said. "I looked him up, just in case. Had to get the operator. He's unlisted."

"Oh," I said. "Okay. Just a thought you thought I might have, huh? Guess I'd better unpack. The Mack's okay?"

"Sure. But tell me, honey, just how bad a reading was it?"

"Ten people showed up; eleven if you include the watchman. Altogether there were sixteen people, including me and the people from the department."

"Damn them. Leave any cards at the museum?"

"No. Figured it would be hopeless. If you can't get people in New York to wonder, you know what'd happen in Denver."

I thought about Paul for the rest of the afternoon and I looked at Mack, who was puttering over what he would carry to camp, and thought of Paul's kids; I looked at Allis, who was sewing labels on Mack's clothes, and thought of Betsy. I thought down all the years.

What could he have wanted; why hadn't he called back? And why, just why should I be wondering, even considering his call, after all this time? If, as they say, the matter was important, he'd call back; if it wasn't, he wouldn't. No big deal.

"It's going to be hot tomorrow," Allis said later, in bed. "Pity you have to get all suited up for that lunch. Eat fish, okay? And try to eat a lot. Cost them a bundle."

"I'll try, baby."

"Stuff yourself, if you have to."

"You don't want to cook dinner tomorrow, do you?"

She looked at me with hugely innocent eyes. "Good night."

I slept the sleep of the thoroughly spooked. Everything was either after me or stood between me and whatever it was I wanted. I had been born and was living in a great labyrinth; there was no series of passages that would lead me out. I would die in it, either from exhaustion from seeking exit, or attacking the walls that defined my boundaries. I lay amidst those layers of sleep and thought of my gun and told myself that I must not forget to look at it, oil it, go through the drill of slamming in the clip, cocking, aiming and firing. It had a bigger voice.

The labyrinth becomes jungle whose heavy, cloying stillness is pocked by gunfire. It is hot; it is smoky. There is war. Phantoms dash from sand ridge to sand ridge. The place reminds me of Tarawa, maybe Iwo. It feels familiar and right to be there. Snipers fire at me now from the upper floors of TCFP. Maude Tozer fires rockets. Sandra Queensbury scrambles through sand tossing me ammunition. Men cry out. Women cry out. Amos chews tobacco, prefers the Springfield '03 to the M-1 or M-16 to cover me. But where am I going? Someone screams, MEDIC! It's me. Crawling on elbows and knees, cradling her kit in her arms, Allis arrives. She binds my legs in gauze so that I cannot move and reopen the wound I did not realize I had. My father casts off death and swims strongly from the bottom of the sea near Murmansk and arrives where I am in three seconds flat; swimming faster than Shine, and changing into Paul Cummings, he comes up on the beach breathing hard. He pisses on me as I crouch in my foxhole and then trots off to catch a football thrown by Jeremy Poode, who avoids a tackle by Jock Champion and Bob Kass, and laterals to Selena Merritt. Walt Whitman shoots me in the head with a Japanese rifle from the Brooklyn Bridge, and Alejo (how can I know for sure — the face is only from photographs) runs up, leg-flips him and says, YOU MISSED MY FATHER. I glance behind me (exposing myself to a shower of hand grenades tossed by Maxine Culp) and see Glenn just about to enter the labyrinth. I call out a warning, but no sound comes. He keeps walking, but he is more wary than I was. A Samurai takes a swing at me with a roast Peking duck.* He misses. I shoot the duck in the ass with my .32 as it whizzes by, spilling cards upon the beach. On them is the legend: *Ecce signum,* etc., etc. The shot-up duck whacks Maureen Gullian in the snatch, out of which come bleeding books. Mack runs up, grabs one and turns on a dial. He squats down to watch *Moby Dick* starring Lionel Barrymore as Ahab. I shoot the great white whale with a mighty black toggle harpoon, which Lewis Temple quickly invents for me, which harpoon looks like a Maasi spear and keeps going and going and sticks Dick until he sounds clear through three over-lapping tectonic plates. A headless black marine trots up and we slap palms and he tells me that up ahead there is a machine-gun squad of southern Japanese who demand to know the extent of my responsibility to them. One of Maude Tozer's rockets takes out the marine. He looks like half a million red spiders on the beach. My mother turns away in disgust and raises her window shade over the sink to allow in a stream of pure, golden sunlight. She says, O GOD OUR GOD HOW EXCELLENT IS THY NAME IN ALL THE EARTH, and God bops down that sunlight carrying his cue stick in a golden cue-stick case, booming out, EIGHT BALL OR POINTS? The kunai grass in front of me parts in a sinister move-ment. I shit in fear. But it is only King Tut peering from around the La Venta Olmec head. Through the noise of gunfire he shouts, MICHAEL JACKSON REALLY LOOKS LIKE ME? Allis sits in the women's section of the synagogue in Toledo, throwing Spanish matzoh at her father, the cantor, who is singing "Swanee," while Dolores (how can I know for sure?) does a flamenco boogaloo across the floor. Every time Mr. Storto sets out an antipasto to sell from his organ grinder, big rats sneak up and eat it. I have moved no closer to any kind of exit. I begin firing the .32 in anger and frustration. It holds an unaccountably large number of bullets. The walls begin to shatter and crumble. I am elated, spurred on. Why have I hesitated? I fire again, a burst. More walls crumble and send up putrid clouds of white dust. Another wall. Bang bang bangity bang! Still another wall. Paul watches all this as he sits typing on his word processor. Then he saunters up a blue hill. At its crest he stops suddenly, cries out and runs back down. I burrow deeper in my foxhole. It stinks. I have shat, pissed and vomited in it. Night. Little old white men in blue cloaks float up and down the passageways of the labyrinth,

* A Samurai with a roast Peking duck?

conversing in a language I've never heard. RACK! God calls out, but I'm on the move again, to the left, left and left again; then back, straight ahead; now to the right, the right. *Faster!* Allis materializes, big as Randy Grossman, and pounds me to the ground.

"Honey!"

Strange voice for Randy Grossman.

"Cate!"

She was crying and screaming into the bed.

"Whuh!" I became motionless. Fragments were dissolving. *"Su caga la leche su madre!"* sprinted up from the street.

"Maricón!"

Allis was holding my legs.

"Was I — er — ah *running* again?"

Wordlessly she released me. It hurt where she had held me.

"Sorry. Was it bad?"

She turned over on her side, still breathing hard, her voice catching as if at snags in the air. *"Yes. Bad!* And Cate," she said, peering at me in the dim light, "they are coming more frequently. Almost every night now . . ."

"Aw, hell," I said. "I'm really sorry, honey. I'll take one of Hank's pills."

I rose, took the pill and came back to bed. I closed my eyes and thought of books bleeding from Gullian, books with dials on them. That made me think about the lunch and how much I feared having it with her. Bad things were going to come out of that lunch, very bad things.

I imagined Gullian's voice with its phony enthusiasms: *Yat, yat, yot.*

15

ON THAT Thursday evening then, the funeral over, Betsy straightening out things with Paul's estate, thus leaving us for the time being without her head on our shoulders, I went to keep my appointment with Nan Tyce. I felt like a sneak thief, since all was now ended with TCFP, but I also felt like a man intent on revenge, a man who had to know in order properly to shape that revenge. For there was nothing else left.

I took a cab partway downtown, then walked the rest of the distance toward the building where TCFP had its offices.

When I was a young man and had first come to New York, I loved, yes loved, walking around midtown, still emptying of people and slowly refilling with the dinner and theater crowds, gliding (I told myself) between those great architecturally insane structures all lighted for the silent armies of cleaning people who nightly just appeared, pails, mops and brooms in hand. Although fractured then as now by race and class, there was at that time an ambience that spoke of greater possibilities. Like so much else, that is now gone.

But I am no longer young, except perhaps in a wrath that, like my shadow in bright sun, keeps pace with my years. Why is that? They tell me that the wrath, the anger, goes with time, that it melts away before the compromises and the evasions of collisions that become patterns of behavior. I do not know why that has not happened to me.

I approach the building of my publisher, which is all glass and chrome-brightened steel even in darkness. The building is one of the newer insanities produced by modern architecture. I enter. The guards move slowly. They are gray-haired, insecure men who have made their bargains with the times. They could not guard a pile of week-old dogshit. Their ragged and shiny serge uniforms bespeak their forlorn stations. But now they are sharp-eyed, for they are in the early hours of their four-to-midnight shift. They pay me little attention. I do not look like a member of the FALN nor a Black Panther late to the fad; I look like a gracefully aging token editorial Negro, is what I look like.

I sign in: Porcius Greenberg — a phony name that, should they ever have reason to check it, would render havoc with their preconceived ideas. My destination — for it is on the same floor as my publisher — Uekusa Electronics Corporation, a subsidiary of Mitsubishi, which once made good planes. I walk down the long lobby into a corridor on whose walls is a listing of the building's tenants. The list is endless. The names remind me of the battle lists from the Somme or Stalingrad. The newsstands are closed and most of the elevator banks have been shut down. In all this polished, funereal emptiness only the guards shuffle about, speaking in soft, bored voices. I punch the indicator and wait, noticing the chrome finishing everywhere. We must have our chrome, our gleaming silver substitute, and South Africa must sell it and all the people and all the miles between the buying and the selling, all the laws of high and low morality, are as nothing. We must make nearly everything gleam.

The car comes and I step in and press the button for my publisher's floor. The doors close silently and there is an almost motionless moving. I stand wide-legged and think of a coffin, on end, speeding up to heaven, and I think of all the space growing under my feet, filled only by quietly moving steel cables.

Once I got off on the wrong floor and, deciding not to wait for another elevator, opened a door and walked up the flight to my publisher's office. The door was locked. I walked back down. That door was locked, too. I walked several flights down and up. At each landing the door was locked, and I concluded that the twenty doors above me and the fifty-six below me were all locked. I pressed my ear against the door to my publisher's office. I could hear voices, laughter, typewriters, people talking. I pounded at the door and shouted. My voice plummeted downstairs and back up the stairwell like a ghostly rubber ball. "Let me in! Open up! Help! I'm trapped!"

Inside, the voices fell in pitch. They were at least pondering the situation. Was I a trapped arsonist? A monster from the lower depths? A madman, who, on the way to the roof to fling himself off, had changed his mind?

I sat down on the cold steps. People would find my skeleton there years later. It would have mold on it from the dankness that seeped through the stairwell. They would find my out-of-style Bally shoes and Supp-Hose and the tatters of my modestly cut Pierre Cardin suit; they would find my PEN and Authors Guild membership cards, my driver's license and the third overdraft notice from the bank. My date book would have a notation in it for an appointment with Maureen Gullian.

I didn't even lift my head when someone finally opened the door and without a word held it until I'd risen and passed through it into my publisher's office.

The car stops with a slightly squeezing sensation. The doors slide open and I step out. Nan is there. She pushes the office door open and I slip inside. She can lose her job for this; she could be banned from publishing forever.

Hi, I say when we are in a tight, darkened hallway, moving fast.

Hello, Mr. Douglass. This way.

Through the art department. Editorial. Sales. Executive. Publicity. Advertising. Committee room. We slow.

Why are you doing this? I ask. There's always a price, it seems to me. A fuck, a favor, a fix of some kind. But I would have sensed that and I did not, so I am puzzled and must ask. I do not feel that time to work out all the answers is on my side anymore.

Why not? She stops and stands aside to guide me into a room. I brush against her breasts, a contact as meaningless as a dentist's nurse pressing her pudenda against you while helping to relieve you of your teeth.

Nan closes the door and pushes the light switch; the light seems to drift reverently down upon the machine. It is like being in a shrine. Why does a room with only a machine in it need such rich drapes? Why the vast print of *Guernica* on the open wall? Why such soft, rich carpeting? Nan locks the door and draws the drapes.

You can't see the light outside the room, she says, and, There it is, BOOK.

So this is it? I ask with a tremor in my voice which has become suddenly a whisper — just like hers. She does not answer. Her expression reminds me of the way some women look when they have suddenly come on a snake. Nan sidles to the machine. We stand together looking at it the way we might find ourselves before *La Pietà*.

Yet it is an innocuous-looking object, tastefully colored in shit-storm brown and rather futuristically molded. A display screen is centered on its top. It has gleaming racks and rubber rollers at the sides or near the bottom, and stainless steel slots. It feels comforting to the touch, giving the sense of being able to ward off all attacks, like the ridgeless turret of a tank.

Nan watches me study it, her hands folded just beneath the young swell of her stomach.

So, I say. This is the gadget that tells whether or not you're a writer.

No, Mr. Douglass, she answers. That's not what the gadget tells.

Her smile is exquisite. This gadget tells the business people, the company, only what they program it to tell, and no machine can tell about writing. They can't feel or be moved.

I say, I know. Yes.

What I mean, she says, is that what this machine seems to say about writing or writers is of no consequence to a lot of people. I'm quitting tomorrow because I'm one of those people. And for another reason, too.

She is so young. Whence came all this knowledge and what does such knowledge win?

I understand. Thanks. How does it work? Have you worked it before?

I can work it. I can work the hell out of it.

She steps directly in front of the machine and removes a key from her bag, then a plastic card. She inserts the key, and a low hum comes from the computer. She jams in the card and the display begins winking bright green blips, the kind of blips you see in kids' electronic football, basketball and soccer games these days. The machine begins to smell faintly of oil and chemicals.

Making sure it's cleared, she says. Clicking sounds inside. The blips blip silently on the display.

These — she starts punching — O eight five five zero: click click click click click (blip blip blip blip blip)

— O eight four four one: click click click click click click (blip blip blip blip blip blip)

O, she says, nine four five five two: click click click click click click (blip blip blip blip blip blip)

And o o six seven six: click click click click click click click (blip blip blip blip blip blip blip)

— these are the account numbers for the books you've done with the company. What they all add up to, really, is your name, Mr. Douglass.

Everywhere, I think, they'd rather you give them your number instead of your name.

Nan says, Now, if I switch to this bank of keys — daintily, she poises a finger over a triple row of buttons and presses — they give me your name.

And there it is, blipped in green, Douglass, Cato C.

Click clickety clickety click click clickety.

She points to the green-and-white-striped printout sheet just coming into view at the top of the computer. She says, This thing'll give you both a printout and a reading in the display. See? With your name your account numbers come up. It's a double-check.

Yes, I see.

Now, she says, let's see o eight five five zero. She presses a button marked *Advance,* another, *Print Order,* another, *Sales* and still another, *Subsidiary Rights.*

Nan glances at me and says, They've refined this gadget to include reviews. See? She presses a button marked *Reviews.*

They're rated from one bad to five rave.

She presses *Returns* and then *Items.* This, she says, gives the breakdown on subsidiary rights, paperback, movies, television, foreign sales, first and second serial rights —

Yes, yes, I say.

click click click click click click click click click (blip blip blip blip blip blip blip blip blip blip blip) click click click click click click click click click (blip blip blip blip blip blip blip blip blip blip blip)

The printout sheet edges tremblingly upward. The clicking stops; the blips quiver like Jell-O.

Okay, she says. Now, oh! She studies the figures. You didn't do too good with this one. She looks apologetic.

Well, let's try o eight four four one.

While she jabs the keys with a remarkably controlled viciousness, I walk around the machine, absorbing the softness of the carpeting through my shoes. I wonder if Nan ever made love on an office floor or if she would care to. The shrine is now filled with clicks; silvery-green blips devour each other, then overwhelm the neutrality of the display screen once again. BOOK smells more strongly of oil and chemicals and now, too, of heated wires. A kind of incense. Should we light candles and fall to our knees? Nan is reciting the correct litany for this place — endless arrangements of numbers that, translated, are but names, themselves translatable back into numbers, which possess as much meaning as the number of kilometers to Sirius A and B. What do all those numbers have to do with me, what I am, where I came from or where I'm going? Does an idea request numbering? A verb? How many numbers does onomatopoeia demand? Could I describe Paul's life with numbers?

414

The ages by which we tell ourselves are flooded with sweat and the dead reckoning of our generations. I return to BOOK again and stand beside Nan, watching.

Watching me. A sympathetic smile plays across her face. I think of the man she lives with. Gleason? I hoped he was nice. She says, Okay? Enough?

I nod.

She says, as she cuts off the switches, her mouth turned down in disdain, They pull the printouts, go into their offices and study them, and I think you know what happens after that.

Yes.

I didn't know you were a friend of Paul Cummings. Maureen told me. Sorry about his death.

I shrug. What can I say? I wasn't of his immediate family. Or was I?

And you don't want to do a book on him?

No, I say. It'd be a pretty boring book. He worked very hard. He had success, that's all. That's all there ever is, I guess, unless you have failure instead.

We go out. She checks the door while I punch the elevator.

Where'll you go now? Nan asks when we are riding down to the street. It's all so bad these days.

Don't know. I'll land somewhere.

Of course it was bad. We knew it first; we *always* know it first, and few people ever draw the relationship between what happens to us and what happens to them. Now it had caught up to them. It always has. As slavery was still catching up; as no one listening to Selassie at Geneva in 1936, that was still catching up; as George Washington Carver's peanuts and warehouseman Jimmy Carter were still catching up. Fuck them. They never want to learn, never wish to know about the connections.

We were out on the street. I checked the time.

I say, Nan, TCFP, every publisher, can use people who feel about writing the way you do. So you ought to stay. Maybe you can help to do something.

She laughs. That'll never happen. I can't go anywhere at TCFP. They never allow Jews past a certain inconsequential level.

Oh, I say.

Teichman, she says.

Yeh. Some things never change.

G'night, Mr. Douglass, she says.

She clicks prettily off into the night, unafraid. I like it that high heels have come back. Never liked those thick ugly things the fellas pushed into style.

Night. Thanks again.

It takes a long time before a cab stops for me. No, nothing's changed. In Barcelona the cab drivers would be fighting each other to get me, as, maybe, they were doing for Glenn and Maija.

A cab comes. Amos wanted to eat in the Village. Yes, I think, the ambience has gone, the possibilities dead. No more possibilities. The roster of dead and missing writers who informed those possibilities seems to wink from every neon light. No ceremonies for them. No marching bands. No flags. Better dead than read. Only machines like BOOK click and blip off the death tread of the marchers. Here today, gone tomorrow. Business. No hard feelings. America's excuse: business. We give the people what we want 'em to have. This year and last year and maybe the next, it's shit à la carte. Prefer the prix fixe? That's shit, too. Soup du jour? Ummm, that too, shit. Well done, of course.

I wonder how Amos likes *Unmarked Graves*. I want him to like it. Allis likes it, but she's my wife; she frames her judgment in other knowings. I don't expect him to publish it. I don't think he can. Anyway, we're survivors. But I do want him to maybe like it a little, maybe even love it. Twenty-odd years ago we were too young for each other. If we suspected ethnic conspiracies in high places, we believed in our own strengths more. We were too cocky. We had not really digested history. Life had not yet got around to shaping us completely. A time came and went. We never stopped knowing what we knew; would never stop. Nor would we ever be able to stop doing what we thought we did better than most. It was different now.

The restaurant looks familiar. Yes. That Spanish place we'd gone to when I came home from that first trip and Amos had found me newly installed in Mr. Storto's and had taken me for a drink.

Amos is sitting all sprawled back in his chair. A bottle of wine is already chilling. There is no manuscript on the table. Amos looks sly. I lift out the bottle. Champagne. I sit and order a martini up. Super-seco.

Bring him another, Amos says, and me too.

The Segovia is being chased by flamenco music. Clicking taps and castanets. I wonder where they are, where they can be.

Amos looks at me. I look at him.

Well, Cate. What's new?

Same ole, same ole.

Everybody okay?

Yep.

Betsy not bugging you again about *why?*

Nope. I look around the restaurant. It hasn't changed. That's comforting. Changes do not seem to be for the better.

I attack the second martini and say, So, how did you like *Graves?*

Watching me closely, he slides to the table, folding his hands, and says, How much you want for it?

I start to say something. He has surprised me.

He interrupts. Can't get you no white-boy money. Can't even get you what you been getting. But it'll sure beat TCFP.

We've always known that white-boy money was different money, just the way black-boy money would be different, which means better, or more, if we were in charge and pretending to be fair.

You can do it?

He is somber as he nods. Yeah, he says, and knocks back his drink, signals for another one.

Contract? I say.

He laughs and he snorts. Better get Maxine. They're printing up new contracts every other month these days, nibbling away, fucking you everywhere you're fuckable. Get Maxine.

What do they want me to give up?

Hey! What do they always want niggers to give up? It! All! Everything! Name it, they want you to give it up, like they know you supposed to eat, but don't really give a damn. You know how white boys are — in a two-dollar whorehouse they want it every whichaway and more than one time.

He looks down at the tablecloth. He seems to be debating something. He raises his head and smiles. Ready to eat, man? I'm starving.

Everything tastes delicious. It is as though my taste buds have been scraped clean and fresh and are now quiveringly alert to every microcosmic flavor of food. I am in love with *chorizo* again, the hard *chorizo.* The taste of it carries me back to Monica's kitchen. But, why do I have such proletarian tastes? Why do I possess no urge for pheasant under glass, nonvenomous snake chops, wildebeest wimples in wine sauce, bees' butts in butter?

We gorge ourselves, slobbering down this, sucking that, crunching the other, our watering eyes flashing at each other in admiration, gluttony, contentment. In between bites, sucks, slobbers and crunches, we talk.

The advance Amos finally offers is better than TCFP's, and he knows it. I can tell by his fleeting self-congratulatory smile. The publishing grapevine is like the gossip in a whorehouse. All the whores know about the Johns — if they are tremendous or tiny, if they are fuckers or suckers, if they are sprinters or long-distance humpers.

Amos rears back now like a preacher who's demolished three fried chickens at someone else's home. Good, he says, good.

Yeah, it was, I say, sighing, thinking of poor Allis at home with her yogurt and wheat germ.

Way I figure it, Amos says, I'm gonna see your book through and then quit. Fuck it. I had enough.

Why quit? There aren't any other black editors around. So, I think, this *is* to be a last hurrah.

I know, but hell, I'm tired.

Doing what, I wonder. Then I know what. Thinking. I don't say this, of course. I'm not supposed to know that he just plays with pencils on an empty desk. Besides, I am beginning to feel that there is something out of joint with all this. There is a smoothness that reminds me of a car skidding on ice.

Maybe I'll go into teaching too, Amos says. They're using editors in these writing programs now.

Yeah.

Cognac?

Yeah, why the hell not? The champagne's all gone.

I look around at the starched white tablecloths. They are startling in the semidark, dug in by elbows, blobbed by plates, pans and bottles, by glasses and silver. We are in the center of the room, and people have been noticing us. *Who are those niggers?*

The plates and pans go and the booze comes.

Listen, Amos says.

It's Miles's "Solea." Spanish blues. Moorish blues with muezzins praying out of minarets. Black blues. Tired blues. Amos said he was *tired.* Allis said Paul had sounded *tired. How* tired?

Amos is into the music. His head bobs. We listen as Miles finishes up the intro. The snare drums come in, militantly, aggressively, a thousand lithely marching cats on the move, the Peninsular War. The bass kicks in; the trombones pounce, threatening: doowawdooo, doodooda, doodooda; doowawdooo, doodood, doodooda, and then Miles climbs back on top of all this bad shit. I am moving now, head, feet, shoulders, hands. The cymbals come on shivering, silver, slight, suggesting delicate little clicks carried on the wind. Miles and Gil, I think, Paul and Cate. Do it, Miles. In your solitude. Hey, man, they never liked you. There was always something in your music, in you, that slipped the old image of Louie. They never like that. They won't name any tennis stadium after you, boy. They made what they did together work, Miles and Gil. Why not us, Paul?

Problem was we were both players, never arrangers.

Amos signals for more cognacs. I am feeling better than when I'm on Hank's pills.

Miles blowsblues down to the end, here feigning a whining, there leaping sprightly up, and then he starts tonguing on high, busts some notes — the risks you take when you go high without thinking high — and then, as though in a great ellipse around a hidden sun, slows, blows to a stop. On this piece he does not sign off with the old Da-da! (Fuck you!)

Amos hands over the plastic, signs with a flourish. We drain the last dregs of amber. It's time to go.

You going home, man?

Why does he ask? That's where I always go.

Yeah, I say, but I want to walk a bit.

Hmm, he says. And then he adds, maybe because I've hesitated (we give away so many things that we try to conceal through the flick of the eye, the click of the teeth or lips), I'll go with you, okay?

Sure, man.

Has he not just purchased — yes, bought — a book of mine? ACCEPTED. One of those Anglo-Saxon niceties that pretends, like tariff, like fee, like so many others, not to have to do with money. And hasn't he rescued me, for the present at least, from artistic (Haaaaaaa!) oblivion, into which so many forces, historical, racial, have worked so hard to closet me?

Yeah, Amos. And thanks for the dinner. Thanks for taking the book.

Hey look, it's good, he says. Too goddamn good for TCFP. You never shoulda gone there in the first place, Cate.

We're outside now, the Spanish smell closed off behind us. I ache with the thought of Alejo; I itch with the thought that we were almost together. The night is soft. The humidity has dropped. It is like old, childhood summer nights, filled with possibilities. I inhale this past, knowing it's gone, and then I look down the street, imagine Mr. Storto leaning against a light pole, biding his time until he will go to buy his Italian ice.

We walk. I smile. Amos has lost none of his elegance. Elegance is his truth. He has maintained it. I put an arm around his shoulder.

You have problems getting Phaeton to take the book? I say.

Naw, man.

In some way I cannot explain he acknowledges my touch, appreciates it. His tone is washed with disdain. That makes me suspicious.

What're they gonna do for me? I ask.

We walk several paces without speaking. I wait. It's a nice night. Allis is home. Mack is safe. My eldest son searches for his brother. I have finished another book, and still another is about to jell in my head. I wait until he speaks.

You know what it's like these days. When even the white boys start screaming, you know there's some bad shit goin' down. Like Gibson said, Wherever America's going, Newark'll get there first. They've been kicking black writers out of warehouses to make room for inventories for years. Black writers most don't get the good advances because some white writer has got hundreds of thousands —

You know I know all that, I say.

'Kay. Don't look a gift horse in the mouth. They don't wanna hear what you got to say. They really don't wanna hear what *any* of us have to say, and you ain't give up no ass, so they don't even have to pretend. Y'dig?

Yeah, man. I understand.

It's a good book, he mutters. White boy did a book like that —

He stops. I understand his floundering. It's all been said before, experienced before, to the point of cliché. The language surrounding it has been eroded, beaten down, and is now incapable of creating ancient angers or even indignation anymore. Repetition so effective in *selling* (advertising, politics), in this case sounds like, though it cannot ever be, really, bleating.

Fuck it! Amos shouts, reverting, as we always seem to, to the comfortable, well-used Anglo-Saxon terminology. His hands slash viciously through the night, destroying nothing but air.

I'm gonna go, he says and turns on his heel in a smart pivot and strides away.

Strange. When he decided to walk with me, I had the feeling that he thought I needed nursing. Now I feel that he needs it. But he is walking away hard, with long, long strides.

Thanks! I call out after him. Thanks!

He waves in response without turning, trailing after him the sound of clicking. The sound matches his stride. Hard heels. But I know he is a clicker. How can he not be?

I take the subway. I've not used it in a long time. Tonight I want to soak in the city. The graffiti are thicker, but less self-centered, like old Roman and Chinese wall posters. Everyone has something to say. But they are afraid to say it in public. Here in this rockbound belly there is anonymity which cushions the perception that signing one's name can be dangerous. So. Closet pamphleteers. The city must be filled with them. The legends are topical. In the bathrooms, in the stink of shit, piss and their accompanying corruptions, they are sexual and racial. No editor descends to put it all together.

I imagine an assignment for one of my classes: select a theme sprayed or written in the subway car you rode to class this morning and from it create a five-hundred-word story.

Subway riders seem older and more genteelly seedier than I remember. They sit stiffly, watchfully, like people being conveyed with the harshest grace possible to Devil's Island. There are cops everywhere. They talk to each other, shift about their slackly formed asses all the hardware of their trade. They seem to resent the population they are paid to protect. They cluster and vanish like fireworks thrown into the sky over Disneyland.

I think of *Dutchman* as we hurtle under the city. The heat has burrowed in down here. I see West and Hooks sweating. Lula and Clay, breathing this dirty, fart-fractured air. The air is overused. We will inhale it one hot summer day and drop absolutely dead. But Clay and Lula will survive. They always do.

The shattering, furious noise is suddenly increased a thousand decibels. We all peer from our isolations toward the door that has just been opened. Three huge youths (what *are* they feeding kids these days?) enter the car, padding like panthers in their Nikes, their Ponys, their Converses, and their eyes sweep the car as quickly and as silently as the most advanced radar.

Oh, shit, I say to myself. I knew I should've cabbed. Soak in the city indeed. This may just be too much soak.

They seem to be laughing, from the grimaces of their faces, but the sound is ground under the horrendous clatter of the train.

I curse myself. Dumb. Stupid, like, when playing pool, I always miss my second choice of shot, leaving the first, a pigeon, that I can always come back to. Maybe there is some superspade in me.

Like a sweeper without sound the kids fill the center of the car as they move along, slapping people, pulling up the dresses of the old cleaning ladies, exposing varicose veins and flabby thighs, tightening knots in the ties of aged elevator operators and doormen trying to pass as late-working executives.

They quickly punch out three or four single young men sitting in the car. One tries to battle back. He is demolished. The big kids work their way toward me, pocketing wallets, chains, watches.

I sit with a sinking, pounding feeling in my gut.

Now, bopping in their peer sneakers like nether gods, the frenzy of blood lust casting terrible auras about them, they approach me. I jump up, and just as quickly, as though they had read me, find myself back in my seat, the rear of my head ringing and clanging. I think I hit the back of the seat going down. One of them stands directly in front of me, the others on each side. They rock with the movement of the train. The one in front of me has a nice face. I would be attracted to him in a classroom. I would urge him on, convince him that I was really there during my office hours, take his phone calls to my home, grease his grades, because there is that something in his face. But now I want them all to go fuck with someone else. My head hurts. I am afraid. I feel a warming wetness slide down the back of my neck. I gather my feet to stand again and the boy in front, with a fearful swiftness, snares my chin in his hand and in the same motion forces my head farther upward. I look directly into his cold, black eyes. There is half a millenium, maybe all of history, resting as calmly, as plainly as a landmark that sailors know, right there. The war, I think, has indeed already begun.

I grab his wrist in one of those sudden, mad convulsions that is rooted in the action of hero movies, rooted, too, in my generational refusal to be raped of even material goods, and try to force him away. The others wait on him. I cannot move his hand. It is like steel welded to my chin. The expression on his face suggests a small smile, and I think, This kid's strong's a bitch!

People are slipping out of the car.

I grab the kid's wrist, this time with both hands, and carry him backward with his weight. His smile slips. He's coming. Motherfuck! He's coming! And I give him all the knee I can muster, exult in the feel of it smashing clear through his softness and gristles to the hardness of his pelvic bone, and a great satisfaction fills me, even as he yowls, even as lights and pain explode on both sides of my head, even as, holding back the darkness that's trying to wash over me in great surging waves, the lights of a station strobe into view, then slow and become focused. Cursing and moaning and running in soft thumps. The train stops.

I remain in my seat. This is not my stop. I couldn't move anyway. I breathe the dirty air, take my handkerchief and touch it to the places of pain. It comes away bloody. But there is more pain than blood. My left eye wants to close. Something big and round weighs it down.

New riders come on, looking curiously at me. A cop looks into the car; up and down he looks and takes a deep drag on the cigarette cupped in his hand. He has done his job. He withdraws, his radio squawking, and the doors close.

Helloooooo, Allis sings out when I get home.

Hi. I go directly to the bathroom and peel off my shirt and jacket.

You should call Maxine tomorrow for sure, Allis says.

Okay.

She has been working well. I can tell by the sound of her voice. I suppose I am the same way.

I draw cold water and splash it over my face and neck.

I raise to look at myself in the mirror. Allis is there, stunned.

What happened? Her voice rising to the next thing to a scream. It's true. I look as if I've gone fifty-five rounds with Jake La Motta.

But already she is rummaging for compresses, touching the bumps and lumps, running more cold water, digging out the ice bag.

Got beat on the train.

Mugged?

No. Just beat.

I can see she does not understand that. For most people, they're one and the same.

What *happened* to your eye?

I got punched in it.

Should I call Hank?

No.

She goes for ice cubes. I check myself again in the mirror. Jesus.

She's back with the ice. We dig out some aspirins, which I wash down with 80-proof vodka. With me in such a sad state, how could she have refused to get it for me? Allis keeps making that affricative click as she washes the cuts with hydrogen peroxide !tsk !tsk !tsk

Are you all right, honey? Sure you don't want me to call Hank? Should we go to the hospital?

I say, Only my ego's destroyed, honey. The eye will go down, the pain will stop, but my ego is in shreds.

I am ashamed for her to see me this way. I'm glad my sons aren't here to see how badly their old man's ass has been beat.

We are sitting now. Allis insists on holding the ice bag. There's nothing wrong with my hands, but she must do it. It's really time to get out the gun, I think. The place abounds with people attacking your body, your soul. Words slide like shit down a thousand-year-old latrine. Lord, deliver

Halley's comet in 1985–86. Right down the middle. Fast ball. Between the knees and the dick. Wipe it out. Destroy it. What right does it have to exist any longer?

A third vodka. It makes me feel better, I tell Allis.

It's later than hell and Allis will not go to bed. I know I can't sleep because I'm thinking of every movement on the train, every expression. Allis sits there, waiting, wanting to share what no woman can ever share with a man who has just got his ass kicked.

Amos is taking *Graves,* I say.

She nods. I thought he might.

Relief has replaced the commonplace celebration that accompanied other acceptances.

Who, I ask, was that guy who did a novel in which half the last page was filled with the word mercy?

Ah, she says, Bellow. No! Malamud. She looks at me. What a strange thing to remember, honey.

No it isn't. Listen, is it my turn to write Mack tomorrow?

Yes, but I'll do it.

No, no. I can do it.

We get up, walk arm in arm into the bedroom. I feel that I am somewhere near, watching us, overhearing our small, hushed talk, and I become frightened. My anchors seem to have slipped their ties. I had expected when I came home to have loved my wife with all the frenzy permissible when the kid is gone. Instead, she is my nurse. And where are my sons?

Groaning now, I make it to the bed, roll over and slip quickly down through several layers of sleep. I see Paul at a phone and I startle myself back to my living wife snoring softly beside me. Tomorrow, I think, will be better; it must be better.

16

IT ISN'T.

Maxine has never before sounded so incredulous, so very indignant.

So Phaeton's publishing *Unmarked Graves*.

I have a fresh ice bag and a cup of fresh coffee.

Did Amos tell you?

No.

She waits while I wonder. My eye is closed now. Burls have blown up out of my head. I phoned in response to her call. I don't need the theatrics, not this morning.

Well, who told you, Maxine?

One of my spies at Phaeton.

Anyway, you'll handle the contract for me?

That was the deal, if you still want me to.

Sure.

But there's another deal you ought to know about.

I hurt too much for all this heavy shit.

What, I say. I know Allis is on the extension. They'll pay and not print?

No, babes. They'll print. They'll even do a respectable run. The *deal* —

I flinch at her emphasis.

425

The *deal* is that your friend Amos resigns if they publish your book. They've wanted him gone, you know.

Cate?

My silence makes her nervous.

Shit, I say finally. He agreed to that?

Yes, he did. It was going to be sooner or later. He knew what he was doing. And he wanted to help. So . . .

I hang up and dial Amos at home. No answer. Silently, Allis takes and refills the ice bag. There are spaces in her movements, as though she's stopping to think or to cry. I make another pot of coffee.

I won't let them do it, I say.

They'll let him go anyway. You heard Maxine. Her voice catches. Amos would want to leave with — honor — the honor of publishing you.

Her eyes and voice are flat.

But the book, honey. They don't care about the book. They're just using it to get rid of him. I don't think anyone's seen it but Amos. It could be a roll of toilet paper.

Amos is neither home nor at work even by eleven. I leave messages. And I worry. I lie down with the ice pack, but my mind's racing. I get up and, with the eye closed now, write a letter to Mack, one of those peppy, somewhat gruff letters secretly clinging fathers write to their sons. I affix the stamp and curse. For as it rises endlessly in cost, postal service declines. The situation is everywhere.

I call Amos again, at his office. I'm told that he's out of town on business. That surprises me. He had not said anything last night.

I ask where.

California.

When did he leave?

This morning.

Do you have a number for him out there?

No.

When will he be back?

Next week.

By which time, I think, everything will have been processed and he will have ready all his answers to my questions. I could say no. I've signed no contract yet. (I can imagine Amos calling the office from his hotel room in Beverly Hills, telling Phaeton about the money we agreed on, and the people at Phaeton ripping off, perhaps this afternoon, a standard contract.) Hell, I could tell Maxine to send the contract back.

But I know I won't. I know it. I stretch out and lie down again.

426

Allis goes out to shop for food and to mail the letter to Mack. I do not think we need any food, but I say nothing. Motion, habit, are the weapons with which we guard the interiors of our sanity.

But I have to sleep.

It is late afternoon. The heat is oppressive. Street noises leap upward to fly into the apartment with the grit- and water-laden air through the windows.

Allis sits across from me, writing on a pad, her legs crossed. She smiles when I stir and look at her. She's gorgeous, I think. Look at those legs.

I must be feeling better.

She says, Feel better?

I think so, I say, but as I move, my head bursts with small bangs and clashes. I stop moving.

Want anything? Aspirin, water?

I lie still. Of course I *want*. I say, No thanks. I listen to the sound of her pen scribbling. How nice, how wonderful a sound it is. I listen to the noises of the street, to the sound of a plane making its final approach to La Guardia. It must be, I think, as hot as this in Barcelona. Hot, humid. At Mack's camp there are groves of cedars and white firs and maples and oaks; a great cooling lake . . .

We'll go to the country ourselves, I think, as soon's my eye opens and the bangs go out of my bumps. Get the fuck outa here . . .

There comes the rasp of the doorbell. Allis jumps. I jump, and pain runs an entire track meet through my head. We exchange a questioning look. The mail has already been delivered. Mack's friends are away at camp, too, and their parents have gone to the Hamptons, Woodstock, the Cape or to Europe. (The city now belongs to the Hispanics and the blacks.) We expect no one.

I get up, waving Allis back to her seat.

Three men stand in the open door. They are the same height. One is wearing a well-cut summer suit, gray with some more vague striping. The other two, stockier, could have got their suits off the rack at Klein's, if Klein's were still open. Their shirt collars are flared out upon their jackets. Thank you, Ben-Gurion, Allis would say.

Mr. Cato Douglass? the neat guy in the tie and expensive suit asks.

Yes.

He glances behind him down the hall. Can we please come in?

I move back, although the other two already are pushing inside the door. They have very steady eyes. I think I know the crowd they drink with.

I close the door behind them. Allis has joined us in the foyer, and there we stand, bunched and questioning. One of the stocky men looks startled to see her and then in clear, pungent disgust looks from her to me. We have seen the look before.

The other stocky one studies the bookshelves he can just see from where we stand. The books seem to be suspicious strangers to him.

The man in the gray suit says, I'm from the New York City Museum Association. These men with me are New York City policemen.

I feel a sudden dryness in my throat.

The neat dresser thrusts in front of my good eye one of our cards. *Ecce signum — Cadit quaestio,* etc., etc. He says, We traced these to Bergenbein Printers on West Seventy-second Street. They said you ordered them. Did you?

I am staring back at the cop who is staring at me. I hate him, too.

Are these yours?

Neat dresser doesn't wait for an answer. He digs inside another pocket and produces the order form with my signature.

We don't want to have you arrested, Mr. Douglass, he says. We just want you to sign a statement admitting that you *did* leave the cards and that you agree, *promise,* not to do it again, ever.

This, I have been told, is what they do with supermarket shoplifters. I clear my throat. It doesn't feel quite so dry. Allis is still and poised. But I know she's nervous, too.

What would be the charge, I ask.

Littering.

Lit-ter-ing? Allis lilts out the word. She is almost laughing.

The cop who stares is studying her. It is an insolent study, slow, suggestive, proprietary.

I'll sign, I say, reaching for the paper. I take his pen, a gold Cross pen, and write my name and return pen and paper.

Did it hurt? It's the insolent cop.

I ignore him and open the door.

Only the neat dresser moves, then stops, waiting for the others.

Don't he look suspicious? The insolent cop is all up in my face, looking at my eye, my lumps.

Yeah. Look at that face. The other cop. They sound alike. Tried to mug somebody, I bet, he says. Lotta muggings in this neighborhood.

Cops pronounce the g's properly when it comes to "mugging."

Please, let's go, the neat dresser says, one foot in the hall. He does not know that he never, in his most magnificent dream, had any control over those who he thought were available at his bidding.

We wanna talk to him about some muggings.

Neat dresser says, We'd better go. He's signed. We know who he is. Now, let's go.

The insolent cop comes closer to me. Our chests bump. He's staring at my closed eye with a smile that says, *We don't care* who *this nigger is.* He is a sudden blur before me; his thumb is pressed into my closed eye. It feels as if a million hot spears have been jammed into it at the same, precise time. I scream and push him off.

Striking an officer! he bellows, hardly able to conceal the glee in his voice.

Allis screams.

Neat dresser, frowning, understanding at last, cries, I won't be a party to *this!* (As if he had not been a party before.)

Insolent's partner, his legs suddenly spread, his back just as suddenly bent, his torso thrown forward, awaits my next move. I think, Something's wrong with all this.

My next move is a leap to the couch. Fuck it. Let's do it here. Now. Right now. From under the cushions I whip out the .32 and, whirling, holding the gun out from my body with both hands, aim right for Insolent's gut. I have no fear of hitting Allis. I hate this bastard too much to miss. I *feel* the gun to be precisely in the groove.

Allis' screaming rises in pitch. Neat dresser is frozen. Insolent's partner is incredulous. How, he seems to be thinking, did it get this far so fucking *fast?*

Only Insolent is in action, flipping back his jacket, his fingers together as though in salute, dipping toward his holster. I pull the trigger.

!CLICK !CLICK !CLICK!CLICK !CLICK !CLICK

Allis' expression swims into view. Her screaming ricochets through the apartment. She's removed the bullets! Removed them, I see in her sad, panic-stricken eyes, because she wanted to humor me by not hiding the gun, but, believing better days were here, removed the bullets to prevent the accidents she believed could happen.

Insolent has leveled his own, huge, illegal gun at me. Blinking in anticipation of its noise, he snaps his finger against the trigger.

CLACKGH!

His gun is jammed.

For one blindingly bright moment in the immense darkness of an ending about to be, I see him cocking the gun, anticipate the offending dumdums flying out across the room to thud against the books in the shelves, and hear Allis' voice echoing through a very long dark chamber:

> Wracked, soul in traction and
> sprawled, a wind-downed scarecrow
> among bound words heaped as though
> for burning, bound words blown of
> meaning, his sons absent, his love of
> them leaking redly in tiny tunnels
> crafted by an ancient, awful alchemy,
> is my husband, snared by their hate,
> my love. He speaks in clicks. I know
> his tongue. I !click back to him.
> I know the language. It is ours.

I pull up out of the dream guided by the scratchings of Allis' pen. Yes, wake, get out! I did not like it in there. Things burned without burning, and anyway, God, I didn't bring my cue stick. The sound of Allis' pen is louder, quicker. I take a long, deep breath of air. It is strangely sharp and wonderfully sweet.